BLINDSIGHT

A Novel

Tina Wainscott

Blindsight
Copyright© 2019 by Tina Wainscott
(originally published as Now You See Me from St. Martin's Press)
ISBN: 9781672505352
www.WrittenMusings.com
www.TinaWainscott.com
Cover Design www.AustinWalp.com
U.S.A.

This is a fictional work. All characters and events in this publication, other than those clearly in the public domain, are solely the concepts and products of the author's imagination or are used to create a fictitious story and should not be construed as real. Any resemblance to real persons, living or dead, is purely coincidental.

All rights reserved. No part of this book may be used or reproduced, stored in a retrieval system, or transmitted, in any form by any means, without the prior permission in writing, except in the case of brief quotations, reviews, and articles.

For any other permission, please visit www.WrittenMusings.com/contact for contact links.

DEDICATION

To Steve Ritter ... love you, Dad.

To Denise, Anastasia, and all of the Simonds family. Your courage and optimism are inspiring. Denise, you are one special lady.

BLINDSIGHT

CHAPTER 1

Wednesday, December 20

He watched her weaving in and around the stacks of Leggo sets. She had long brown hair and brown eyes. He figured her to be about seven. Yes, she was just right. He'd been waiting for her since the store opened, waiting for just the right girl to come through. Now he only had to wait for the right opportunity.

Her mother was engaged in a conversation with another woman, though she darted occasional glances toward her daughter. The toy store was in typical pre-Christmas madness. That always worked in his favor. Cheery music filled the air, kids were preoccupied with the toys, and their parents were preoccupied with their shopping lists.

"Mom, can I get one of those Leggo sets?" the girl asked her mother.

"We're not buying anything today. You're supposed

to be making a list for Santa."

The girl rolled her eyes. "Then stop talking to everyone and let's make a list," she said with exasperation.

"Don't be rude, young lady." The mother turned back to her friend. "So anyway ..."

Clearly bored, the girl quickly became entranced by a metallic pink VW Bug that zipped by her. It stopped, turned around, and bumped into her white sneaker. She looked for the source of the car's control, but was distracted when it turned and careened down the aisle. She followed, crouching down for a better look. The car headed into an adjacent room filled with tall stacks of boxes and kids playing with remote control cars, tanks, and trucks.

Her mother glanced her way. "Phaedra, stay close." She shifted back to her friend. "So, Marilyn tells me that I was supposed to drive the kids to ballet that week when she volunteered to do it. And you know what she has the nerve to tell me?"

"Mom, can I go into the room with all the remote-control cars?" Phaedra asked, glancing where the car had disappeared.

Her mother didn't even look at her. "No, stay here, honey. I'll only be a couple more minutes."

A couple of minutes. How well he knew how life could change just that quickly.

She went back to her conversation, peppered with dramatic gestures and sounds of annoyance. She should be more careful. There were all kinds of predators out there, sick men who got their thrills from molesting children. His gloved fingers tightened on the control box so hard, he heard the plastic start to crack. He eased up.

He wasn't like that.

Phaedra sighed in boredom. Her mother kept talking with no sign of ending the conversation. A minute later, Phaedra walked into the room to look for the Bug. It teased her, zipping past her and heading toward the "Employees Only" door. She tried to grab it, but it jumped out of her grasp.

The car bumped into his shiny black shoe just as she caught it. She looked up at him — and smiled.

"Would you like to meet Santa Claus?" he asked, putting his hand on the door.

"I already did."

"What did he give you?"

"A candy cane."

The Bug lifted up on its rear wheels at his command. "Would you like this car?"

She gave him an angelic grin, and her eyes sparkled as she took in the car. "Yeah."

He put his finger over his mouth and nodded toward the kids playing with the cars in the room. "Don't tell anyone." No one was paying attention to the guy in the gray maintenance uniform and cap pulled down low. "Santa's getting ready to leave, but he'll give you a car to take home."

He pushed open the door and glanced in the storage room. It was crammed with boxes of merchandise. The Santa suit was hanging on the edge of a shelf, the sleeve making it look like Santa was standing just behind the last shelving unit. "Follow me."

He walked in and waited for her to follow.

CHAPTER 2

Olivia Howe was having a hell of a time getting into the Christmas spirit even though she was surrounded by the music, crinkle of bags, and crowds doing their shopping. She refused to attribute her lack of Christmas mood to what had happened sixteen years ago. *Sixteen years ago today.*

She pushed away the thought and concentrated on her environment. The Waterfront area was crowded for midweek. No surprise since it was five days before Christmas and high season in the Florida coastal town. Palomera was trying to compete with nearby Sarasota to draw in both tourists and new residents. As it grew, so did the crime rate, something Olivia wasn't pleased to hear. Growth was a frequent topic of debate on the news. The increase of construction had brought an influx of transient workers. Olivia was glad she lived in the insular Waterfront area — except during season when everyone flocked to the upscale shopping area. People especially loved the Waterfront's mix of quaint shops, cafes, office buildings, and apartments all laid out along a slice of water that lead to the Gulf of Mexico.

She felt arms brush against her, everyone in a hurry. She knew this route well enough to manage it on her own, though Anastasia steered her around obstacles such as people not paying attention to where they were going or café tables in the foot traffic path. People commented on Stasia's gentle beauty, but her looks didn't matter. What did matter was her silky fur, her velvety tongue that gave Olivia loving kisses, and Stasia's devotion. Stasia wasn't only an Australian Shepherd, wasn't only her guide dog; she was her best friend.

Olivia sensed the alley between her building and the next by the hollow echo of her footsteps. The rich scent of coffee signaled she was at the end of that building. Another alley echoed to her left, and then the music store pumping the Beatles into the crisp afternoon signaled she was nearly at the Edgewater. The scent of popcorn drifted from the twenty-theater complex situated in the circular building with a courtyard in the middle. When she had moved back to Palomera last year from Columbus, Ohio, she had made a point to learn the layout of the stores near her apartment. Now she followed the map in her mind.

Stasia stopped at the intersection, though Olivia could tell by the sound of traffic that it wasn't safe to cross. When the light changed, Stasia weaved through the oncoming people. Once they were on the other side of the divided highway, she waited for an indication of direction. Olivia turned left.

The buildings here were mostly high-end stores and novelty boutiques. In December, Toyland turned their front entrance into a Christmas wonderland, or so she'd heard. It sure sounded like something special from the squeals of the children, the mechanical drone of animated characters, and the classic holiday music that flowed from speakers. It had been a long time since she'd seen the singular beauty of an ornament sparkling from the lush green of a tree. It had been a long time since she'd seen much of anything, but she could still imagine imitation snowmen and sparkling lights. She tried to remember when Christmas meant innocent fun in a safe world, before ...

She pushed the thought from her mind.

People continued to brush by her, some murmuring an apology. The cool breeze that blew her long hair into her face held hints of fresh perfume, coats permeated with stale cigarette smoke, and baking bread from the grocery store beyond.

The jaunty "Here Comes Santa Claus" punctuated the distance she felt from the world. Children laughed, people continued on to wherever they were going, others talked about their enormous gift lists as they wearily headed toward the melee inside the store. Olivia felt as though she were floating through the world in a bubble.

"Look, mommy, a doggie!" a child's voice called in delight.

"Don't go over, Kinsey. That's a Seeing Eye dog. The lady's blind."

Olivia knelt down and looked in the girl's direction. "You can pet Stasia. She loves children. Only pet a guide dog if you get permission first, though."

"She's beautiful," Kinsey said with awe in her voice. Her hand brushed Olivia's hand as she stroked Stasia.

"How old are you?" Olivia asked.

"Almost eight," Kinsey said with obvious pride. "Are you really blind?"

Olivia nodded. "Stasia is my sight."

Seven years old. When the world was grand and benign. What would be the defining event that would shatter Kinsey's belief? It had to happen. Hopefully not in the way it had happened to Olivia.

"Does she take you where you want to go? Like if you wanted to go to McDonald's, would you just tell her that and she'd take you there?"

Olivia laughed. "No, she's not my chauffeur. I have to know —"

"Kinsey, get away from the dog!" the mother said, and Olivia could hear the child being yanked away. Kinsey's whines followed her down the sidewalk.

Warmth flooded Olivia's face as she reassured Stasia with loving strokes. "It wasn't you," she whispered. "It was me."

Did her inability to make eye contact create that much of a wall around her? Was it her blindness that made people shy away or did they sense her difference went much deeper?

There were things about being blind she would never get used to. She didn't mind losing some of her independence, or even the devices that made living independently easier. She hated working so hard to remember what the world looked like and the fear that if she didn't, everything she'd ever known would disappear and leave her in a black void. She missed books and movies and sunsets. She hated the wall her blindness erected between her and the world. She hated that most of all.

Stasia licked her chin, bringing Olivia out of her thoughts. Olivia pushed to her feet and hoped the dull ache in her chest wouldn't linger as long as it sometimes did after she'd been snubbed. *Don't go over, Kinsey. That's a Seeing Eye dog. The lady's blind. There's something wrong with her. If you stand too close, it might rub off on you. Some of that tragedy or strangeness might taint you. Get away from her now.*

"Forward," she commanded Stasia.

They continued on to the bookshop two stores past Toyland. Books made great gifts, particularly for people she didn't know well. Unfortunately, the few people in her life fell into that category. The one person she was close to didn't always remember who she was. Alzheimer's was eating away her father's memory like acid, layer by layer.

As she headed toward the store's entrance, she heard her name. She jumped when a hand touched her shoulder. Her heart didn't stop racing when she recognized his Polo cologne.

Okay, she could scream if she needed help. Someone would help her ... right? "Terry, you're not supposed to be here."

His hand tightened on her shoulder. He kept his voice low enough so that only she could hear it. "You can't just push me away like this."

She shrugged out of his grip. "You have got to let this go. It's over."

"It's not over, Olivia. I'm trying to give you space, but it's hard." She heard his rushed inhalation. "It's damned near impossible. And now you've gone too far. A restraining order, for God's sake?"

Her throat tightened. "I didn't want to do it, but I didn't know what else to do. Please, Terry, leave me alone. Don't hang around in the hallway outside my door. Don't even come to my building. I'm ... I'm not who you think I am." She turned away from him so fast, she bumped right into someone. "I'm sorry," she said, to both that someone and to Terry. She had to take some of the blame. Probably she deserved every bit of agony he was now putting her through. That didn't make it any easier to handle.

"Hup up," she told Stasia, urging her to go faster.

She walked into the bookstore, relieved that he hadn't seemed to have followed her. The aroma of cinnamon-dusted cappuccino floated from the café on the right. Children *ahhd* and *oohd* over Stasia, and their mothers ushered them along in voices strained with impatience. "Can I help you, ma'am?" a young man asked. He'd recently had coffee and a cigarette.

"I'm looking for a book on Salvador Dali, something an admirer wouldn't already have." She'd heard Sebastian talk endlessly about melting clocks and warped women and thought he'd enjoy a book on the artist.

"Ah, I think we have exactly what you want. We just got a perspective on Dali's sexuality and possible psychoses. Some of the girls were giggling about it when it came in. Follow me." He faltered. "Do I ... should I ...?"

She reached for his arm and smiled, hearing his quick breath of relief "Lead the way."

He led her through the store, Stasia heeled close at Olivia's side. Olivia lifted her head and inhaled the comforting smell of paper, binding, and wood shelving. She pictured bookcases finished in rich, dark varnish and all those colorful book covers inviting her to peek inside. She missed going to bookstores and libraries and searching for literary treasures.

"It must be wonderful to work in a book store," she

said. "I can imagine the neat, obscure titles you come across while stocking and rearranging."

"Uh, actually, I don't read much. Other than my college textbooks."

Didn't read? But he could read! She wanted to shake him. *You can pick any book you want. You aren't limited to the titles available on Braille or tape.* She had escaped into books since she could read. Her father teased her about how much time she spent curled up in the window seat with a book. He forgot that there weren't many children in their gated neighborhood. Newgate Manor was populated with people who had already sent their children off into the world. Most of her parents' contemporaries had had grandchildren Olivia's age.

"What are you studying?"

"Forensic science. Kinda morbid, huh?" he said at the same time that she said, "Not really. Someone's got to do it, right?"

"How'd you know I was going to say it was morbid?"

She shrugged. "Just a lucky guess."

She'd had those kinds of guesses for as long as she could remember; guesses, hunches, feelings about things; blessing people before they'd sneezed and responding to questions before they'd been asked. Olivia's grandmother Dorothea had been delighted that she'd inherited her "gift." Olivia's mother had felt much differently about it. So had many others in her life. There was a time when a slip like the one she'd just had would have mortified her. Nowadays she just downplayed it and let it go.

They came to a stop somewhere in the rear of the store, she guessed. "We have two books that might suit you, actually. You can look …" He gave a nervous laugh as he pressed the book into her hands. "Uh..."

"Tell me what's in it." She gave him a reassuring smile. He obviously hadn't dealt with many blind people. She, on the other hand, had plenty of experience.

He described the number of pages and quality of color pictures inside and then gave her an overview of the second book.

"I'll take the first book." She suspected Sebastian would appreciate the sexual aspect.

"Great. Anything else?"

She'd already bought something for her friend Judy, and she'd made a painting for her father. The rest of her family was so distant, both geographically and relationship-wise, they didn't warrant shopping for. "That should do it."

This time he easily placed her hand on his arm and guided the way to the sound of beeping registers.

"Here's the line," he said, coming to a stop and releasing her. "Shouldn't be long."

"Thank you."

She expected him to leave, but he remained close by. "Line's moved up," he said a minute later, guiding her two steps forward.

Her mind searched for anything else she might need while she was in the bookstore. Not out of practicality, she realized, but a desire to continue this pleasant exchange with the young man. A connection, even though he was paid to be pleasant. There were people who would be surprised at her need to reach out. But this young man was safe to reach out to.

She pressed her watch. "11:03," the computer tone said. It would be getting even busier soon.

"How do you pay for stuff?" he asked, and then hastily added, "I'm sorry. I was just curious. Was that a rude question?"

"No, not at all. Most of the time I use a credit card."

"But with money ... how do you know what's a five-dollar bill versus a one-dollar bill? With change it's easy to tell the difference, but I always wondered how blind people managed with cash."

"I have a contact at the bank who folds my bills for me. Fives are folded in half; tens are in quarters; twenties in thirds and ones aren't folded at all. I never carry anything larger than a twenty. There are machines that read money and tell you what denomination it is, though this is way simpler."

"You're up, ma'am," he announced and guided her forward.

She grimaced at the word 'ma'am' even though she knew he was only being polite. Twenty-four was too young to be called ma'am. "Thanks for your help," she said as the cashier rang up the book.

Just as Olivia signed her credit card slip, a trill of alarm shot through her. She knew this feeling, yet it was stronger this time. So strong, it overwhelmed her. She gasped and drooped against the counter. The pen hit the floor with a clatter.

Alarm seized her again, this time accompanied by jarring images: a storage room, the flash of a man's face, a sign over a door. She heard someone say, "He's got her. Oh, God, he's got her," and only a few seconds later realized it was she who had said the words.

Fear, panic, and an awful smell rushed through her senses before everything went black. She struggled for breath as pain stabbed her temples. Stasia put her paws on Olivia's legs. The pain slowly receded, allowing voices through the fog.

Hands steadied her. "Are you all right, ma'am?" someone asked.

Her helper touched her shoulder and said, "Maybe you'd better sit down. Sometimes the holiday crowds get to people."

A cold sweat covered her skin as it always did when she was hit by a vision. But this was different. Why was it coming at her without her being involved in the child's story?

She reached out for his arm. "Tad, get me out of here. I have to get to the toy store!"

The sign over the door had read, "Toyland Emergency Exit. Alarm will sound if door is opened." The images were always so rapid, all she got were erratic flashes.

"Should I call someone?" he asked.

Her legs were rubbery, but she'd have to manage. "Just point us to the door."

The outside air chilled the perspiration on her skin. She rushed Stasia toward Toyland, where the upbeat "I Saw Mommy Kissing Santa Claus" was at odds with the residual panic flowing through her. The electronic doors slid open, letting out a wave of warm air and people carrying crinkling bags. Olivia pushed her way inside.

"Somebody help me! Is there a security guard here?" her shrill voice called out.

She felt a strong hand on her arm as a man said, "I'm security. What's the problem?"

"The missing girl, she's in a back room, maybe a storage room. There's an exit door. Please, find her before he gets her out of the store!"

The second of silence unnerved her as much as her own panic, and then he said, "What missing girl?"

"There isn't a girl missing?"

"We had a boy get lost yesterday, but no one today."

No missing girl? She couldn't be wrong, not when the feeling was this strong. Especially when it was so out of the blue. She clutched his arm. "Maybe the girl hasn't been reported missing yet. Go to your storage room! Please, you have to believe me. He's taking her right now!"

Another pair of hands took hold of her shoulders. "Ma'am, calm down. We don't know what you're talking about."

"I'm talking about a girl who's being kidnapped right now! You've got to get to the back of the store!"

Instead, the two men led her out the front door. "Is there someone we can call for you? A caretaker? Doctor?"

"I'm not crazy! I ... see things. I'm psychic. I saw somebody grabbing the girl, putting a rag over her mouth. Chloroform," she realized with dread. She could still taste it, even after all these years. "Go around to the back of the building, check out your storage rooms. If she's not there, you can call me crazy."

"Look, lady, we don't have time for this. We got two hundred people in that store, and half of 'em want to take something that don't belong to them. If you don't leave the premises immediately, we'll have to call the police."

"Yes, call the police!" She didn't need to be there when they came. She didn't want to deal with cops. They'd ask questions and think she was even crazier.

"Tell them to come right away!"

"Lady, go home and sleep it off."

She broke down into tears as she backed away from the store. "Somebody please ... anybody, look behind the store. Don't let him take her."

People's voices faded as they moved farther away from her. No one would believe her, no one would look.

Could she have the wrong store? "Forward, Stasia," she said. Maybe it was a Toyland in another city. She had to get home and listen to the news, see if she could pick up anything else.

It's already too late to save the girl from being taken. But not too late to help her get rescued.

Olivia hurried home.

Detective Max Callahan eyed the empty coffee pot. He was always the lucky stiff who got to make it. He maneuvered around in a break room so small, it had obviously once been a closet. While the coffee percolated, he grabbed a stale donut from the box and took a bite.

"Ah, you're back," he said as Detective Sam O'Reilly walked in. He dumped the remainder in the trash

Sam pulled out the pot and poured himself a cup. The coffee kept brewing, jumping and sizzling on the burner. He seemed oblivious, topping off Max's mug before returning it to the maker.

"You all right?" Max asked, wiping the dripping mess with a paper towel.

Sam dumped way too much sugar into his mug and drank it without stirring it. He came back from whatever faraway place he'd been in when he saw Max staring at him. "What?" Sam had been lost in his thoughts a lot lately.

"You all right?"

Sam blinked. "Yeah, sure. You forget to comb your hair again or something?"

Sam knew Max's brown hair was genetically predisposed to the mussed look, so Max figured he didn't want to talk about whatever had his attention. Max said, "Don't forget, poker game at my place tonight."

"I'll be there."

Max, Sam, Mathers and Graham tried to get together for a game once a week. Betting currency consisted of Budweiser, Miller Genuine Draft, and whatever exotic beer Nick Mathers had recently added to his collection. Max was the youngest of the group by over twenty years. Tom Graham was the most recent addition to the group, a bit of a hothead who hated to lose and accused someone of cheating at least once a night. The original three had a side pot going on when the guy would crack a smile. He didn't even groan at John Holland's bad jokes.

Sam said, "Ran into the director at Big Brothers/Big Sisters yesterday. She said they really miss you playing Santa Claus, that you were the best Santa they've ever had. Mathers didn't cut it last year. They got somebody else to do it this year."

"I didn't have time." Max had told himself that his mind was made up, that he'd never wear the costume again. But after the director had called him three weeks ago he'd found himself in the station's storage room looking for the suit. The empty box made it easy for Max to walk away. "You should have done it. You're the all-American guy here."

Sam should have been a screen star, with his silvery-blond good looks, bright blue eyes, and just the right amount of unshaven shadow. Sam had been a confirmed bachelor in his forties until meeting and marrying Annie, a woman fifteen years his junior. A year later, Annie had gotten pregnant.

"That'd make it too easy for you, me doing it. All right, forget Santa. Petey's party is this weekend. You're going to come this year, aren't you? You used to be like an uncle to him, you know."

Max tipped his head toward the door. "I've got something for him."

"Ah, hell."

Sam followed him into the large room crammed with desks, people, and noise. Max had learned long ago to tune it all out. Someone's radio was playing Christmas music. Red and silver tinsel decorated the walls in crooked waves, and the faded tree in the corner drooped under the weight of plastic ornaments. For a few years, while his daughter had been alive, he'd been able to enjoy Christmases again.

The box wrapped in silver paper blocked the walkway that separated his desk from the far wall. Max could hardly get his arms around it as he handed it to Sam, who stood holding his cup and not twitching a finger to take it. After an awkward minute, Max set it on the floor again. "It's one of those motorcycles for kids. You know, with a motor, battery, and all."

Sam eyed the box with contempt. "This don't mean squat if you're skipping out on his party again. I made excuses for you the last two years, man. I'm not doing it again. You tell him why you can't drag your sorry ass to his party this time."

Max settled against the edge of his desk. He wanted

to tell Sam to shove the box and his words into a really tight space. "Look, my days as Superman are over."

"No one said you have to be a damned superhero. He's too old for costumes anyway. Just come as yourself."

"Myself," he said in a low voice. He pushed the box closer to Sam with the toe of his shoe and muttered, "Whoever the hell that is."

"You're an ass, is what you are. You say you don't want to do the superhero thing, yet you always buy him the biggest, most expensive present."

"He's a good kid. I want him to have something special."

"Then how about you show up? That'd be real special."

"How about you shut up? That'd be real special, too."

Max imagined the party, the kids playing in the small yard, balloons tied to the chair at the end of a long table covered with bright paper. He could see Petey with his curly brown hair and blue eyes, a mirror image of his mother. Max's daughter Ashley was there, too, teasing Petey like she always did. The flirting kind of cat-and-mouse games kids play when they're too young to know what it really means. Hell, even in his early twenties Max had been too young to know what it meant.

He bowed his head and rubbed the back of his neck, trying to ignore the burning pain in his chest at the memory of his daughter. "Maybe I'll come by."

"Maybe, hell. Commit, yes or no."

Max started to say yes, but the thought of that party without Ashley tore at his gut. "No."

"I know you loved them, but it's been two years now and—"

Max shoved himself to his feet. Between gritted

teeth, he said, "I didn't love them enough."

"You're a coward, Callahan," Sam muttered. "You might as well climb in the grave with them and get it over with." When Sam looked at Huntington striding to his office, he gave Max a disappointed shake of his head and walked over.

Max had an insatiable urge to pound Sam for calling him a coward.

Do it! a harsh voice shouted. *Do it, you little coward!*

With a shudder, he closed the box those memories were packed in and cursed the man who, even in death, wouldn't let him go. He rubbed his hand down his face and then glanced around to see if anyone had been listening to their conversation. Everyone was busy with their own business, their own causes.

Every case had been a cause for him once. He'd been reprimanded many a time for what his superiors had called his pit bull tactics. But he'd had the highest case closure rate back then, and they sure hadn't complained about that. Maybe he was no longer that brave cop who had once traded himself for a hostage and put himself in the hands of a cop killer. But he wasn't a coward either. That left him somewhere in between, just short of nowhere, the way he figured it.

He dropped down into his squeaky chair and pulled the file for one of his current cases. Mundane crap was all they gave him now. Prostitute, transient and drug-related murders. Nothing too heavy. That was okay with him. After the Stevens kidnapping case, that was all he was up to anymore. He didn't want another case that would suck him in, chew him up, and spit him out in pieces. The Stevens case had done more than that — it had destroyed his life.

Max settled in with the murder conspiracy case he'd been trying to crack. Two business partners, a buttload of money, and just enough temptation to push one of them over the edge of murder.

A few minutes later, Huntington's voice boomed through the cacophony. "Callahan, in here!"

When the lieutenant called, there wasn't an officer in the place who'd linger a second before responding. It wasn't because Basil Huntington was tall or imposing. With his receding hairline and a nose so large, it dominated his face, he looked like he belonged behind the desk at a bank. He had a gap between his front teeth, and those rare times when he did smile, his cheeks nearly compressed his eyes shut. His iron command transmitted through his body language, his steely blue eyes, and his expectation that his men would jump. Though the man could be hard as hell, Max appreciated the slack he'd cut him since his life had crashed and burned.

Huntington had transferred to Palomera five years earlier when their lieutenant had retired. Mostly he kept to himself, rarely trading jibes or jokes with his men. That he had never spoken of family and had no pictures on his desk made some of the men wonder if some tragedy had befallen him. No one felt comfortable enough to ask.

Sam was standing in front of the desk, and Max took his place next to him and faced the lieutenant. "Yes, sir."

Huntington pulled a chewed-up pencil out of his mouth. "Seven-year-old girl went missing at Toyland. The store went into lockdown mode, but they haven't found her yet. I want you and O'Reilly over there."

For a moment, Max couldn't speak at all, and then, "Shouldn't Kilpatrick be working this case?" He'd had taken Max's place as the station's hotshot.

"He's eye-deep in the Hayward murders. This one's yours."

"Lieutenant, I don't think —"

The lieutenant eyed him. "Can't you handle it?"

Do it! his father's harsh voice shouted. *Do it, you little coward!*

"Yes, sir."

"That's what I wanted to hear." He went back to his paperwork, dismissing Max and any further protest he might have by humming a lethargic version of the usually cheery "Jingle Bells."

This wasn't going to be like the other case. The girl was hiding somewhere, that was all. And if she wasn't ...

"Let's find her," Max said to Sam as they headed out into the sunny, cool morning.

Two hours later, Toyland was in a state of what Max considered organized chaos--the same way his stomach felt. Uniformed policemen had cleared the store of customers and were now questioning employees. Other uniforms were scouting the area for witnesses. There was no getting around it: the girl had been abducted. The media was camped out front waiting for any nugget they could broadcast. They'd been given enough details to run a story in hopes that someone would recognize Phaedra.

Earlier, Sam had been in an upstairs office with Flora Burns, mother of the missing girl, and her husband, Pat. Her wails had scraped at the edges of Max's nerves. He knew that depth of agony too well. After getting a statement, Sam had walked them out and then returned to the upstairs office to help ready the security videotapes. Max worked with the crime scene investigators as they went over every square inch of the storage room until a uniform had called him out to talk to the security guards posted at the front door.

"Like I was telling that other officer, the only person out of the ordinary was a woman who came to the front doors acting kind of crazy," one of the guards said. He looked more like a bouncer at a bar with his buzz cut and brawny looks. "She was all upset, saying the missing girl was in the back room. Said she saw someone putting a chloroform rag over the girl's mouth."

Awareness prickled over him. "Had she been inside the store?"

"No. She came from over there somewhere," he said, gesturing vaguely to the right. "But here's the weird part: when she told us this, the kid hadn't been reported missing yet."

"Wait a minute," Max said. "Why didn't you say anything about this before?"

"We did. We told the first guy who was questioning the employees, and he told us to hang tight until you could talk to us."

Max tamped down his annoyance. "Did she say she'd seen the girl being taken? Like maybe she'd been by the back exit?"

The second guard was stringy; only his scarred face gave him any menace. "I don't think she could see anything. She looked ... blind. She had one of those guide dogs, and her eyes didn't focus on anything."

The first guard said, "But she said she saw things, like in a psychic way."

A cold chill snaked down Max's spine despite the fact that a blind woman wasn't a good lead. Unless she *wasn't* blind, or she *was* trying to create a diversion for someone else to get the girl out of the store. He wasn't even going to delve into the psychic claim.

"Callahan!" Sam was waving him upstairs. "They have the security video ready."

Max nodded to the two guards. "Come up." He headed up the stairs and met Sam at the top. Max gestured for the guards to stay put and walked into the manager's office with Sam. "You got anything?"

The grooves running from Sam's nose to his mouth deepened as he frowned. "Nothing yet. Mrs. Burns had been talking to a friend when Phaedra went into the remote-control room."

Max had interviewed the employees on the first floor while Sam had taken the customers who had been nearby. Max asked, "No one saw anything? None of the other kids in the room even?"

Sam leaned against the desk. "One boy said he saw a man who looked like a maintenance worker go into the room but didn't pay much attention to what he looked like other than he was about my age and wearing a gray uniform. He was too entranced by the Super Hot Rod Buggy, which he was able to describe in excruciating detail. Another kid thinks he saw Phaedra Burns chasing one of the cars but didn't see her leave the room. There were several kids, but they were all too busy playing to notice anything unusual."

The only other exit out of that room led to a storage area where the suspect apparently lured the girl and then took her outside from there. Exactly where the blind woman said the girl would be.

Sam said, "There isn't a camera at the back door. They figured with the door wired for the alarm, they didn't need it. The suspect knew what he was doing. He knew the layout of the store and how to cut the wiring on the door without tripping the alarm."

Max said, "Could be someone on the inside. An employee or former employee. The manager is pulling all employee records for us now. We'll start by running background checks, see if anyone has any priors. We're also pulling the records of all recently convicted child molesters in Palomera. We've got Sarasota doing the same, and they're putting out a bulletin on the girl over there, too. Fliers are being made now, and they'll be distributed all over the region."

"Hopefully we'll see something on the security video," Sam said as he led the way into a small conference room.

Max waved the guards in, and they gathered around the television with the Toyland's chief of security. Bob Thornton was a tall, thin man whose balding head reflected the overhead fluorescent glare. "We rewound the tape to when the store opened. This is the one facing the entrance. We have another camera pointed toward people leaving the store."

Max said, "Fast forward it to right before lockdown." He turned to Sam. "There's something I want you to see."

Everyone in the room leaned forward as the grainy black and white film sped ahead in fast motion.

"Who's that?" Sam asked when someone in a Santa costume walked in.

"That's our Santa, Claude Fernley."

Max nodded. "We've verified that he was upstairs

doing his Santa gig when the girl was taken." He glanced at Thornton. "Keep going."

The people coming and going seemed perfectly normal... until the woman ran into view. "Stop and rewind a little," Max said. "This is it."

The woman approached from the north and gestured crazily, but unerringly toward the rear of the store. The guards spoke with her, one putting his hand on her arm.

Max said, "This woman came in warning the guards about the missing girl. Get this, before anyone knew she was gone."

Sam leaned forward. "Whoa, that's something. What's she saying?"

As the guards relayed the woman's words, Max watched her movements. She had long, dark hair that swung with her frantic gestures. He couldn't see her face clearly, but she looked attractive and well dressed. Her dog, tethered on a leash by a harness, cowered. They watched the guards escort her outside.

The beefy guard said, "She tried to get someone outside to help her. You have to understand, we just thought she was crazy. Holidays bring that out sometimes. We didn't know a girl was missing yet. We watched, ready to subdue her if necessary. Then she left."

The thinner guard said, "A minute later, the girl was reported missing, and the store went into lockdown mode."

Max watched the woman walk away when no one would help her. "Where did she go?"

"I think she crossed the street," the other guard said.

"You ever see her before?" Max asked.

"Not that I remember, though I just moved here," one

guard said.

"I've never seen her."

Max ran his hand over his face. He turned to the officer who was in the room with them. "Okay, let's get both tapes down to the station and have our people analyze it. Have them look at everyone who came in and match them up with everyone who came out. The one who never came out is our man — or woman. Odds are, the suspect's a guy and went in alone. I want a print of the woman's face, as close as we can get. We've got to find out who she is."

One of the officers knocked on the open door. "Got someone you should talk to." He brought in a lanky young man wearing a green smock with the bookstore's logo on it. "Tell them what you just told me."

"When the officer asked if we'd seen anything unusual, well, this definitely fell into that category. It'd be kinda cool if she was involved, and I had the missing piece that got her."

"All right, let's hear it," Max said.

"I was helping this blind woman buy a book, and she kind of freaked out at the counter."

"A blind woman?" Max repeated, getting out of his chair at the same time Sam did. "What'd she look like?"

"Medium height, long dark-brown hair. Nice-looking, too, probably in her late twenties."

Sam was already instructing Thornton to put in the tape again. "Is this her?" he asked a moment later.

"Yeah, that's her all right."

Adrenaline shot through Max like intravenous caffeine.

The kid said, "When she was checking out, she got all weird and slumped against the counter."

"Did she say or do anything just prior to, er, freaking out?" Sam asked.

"We were talking about stuff, you know, just normal stuff. I was asking her how she knew what bills were what, that kind of thing. She seemed really nice about it. Then she checked her watch by pressing a button, and it said the time. It was right after eleven, I remember, because I was thinking, cool, it's only an hour before my lunch break."

Max and Sam traded looks. She was sounding exactly like a planned distraction, checking the time, getting ready for a rendezvous. Sam asked, "Then what happened?"

"That's one of the weird things." The kid made sure he had their attention. "She said, 'He's got her. Oh, God, he's got her.' Like she was in pain or something. Then she said she had to get to the toy store." He smiled triumphantly when the officer lifted the bag he'd been holding. "That's the book she bought. She left it."

Sam took it and pulled out a book — and a receipt. "Credit card. Smith, run a trace on it and take the security tapes back to the station with you."

The officer carefully took the bag and the tapes and left.

All right, maybe this case wasn't going to be so hard after all. Then Max remembered something the kid had said. "You said 'one of the weird things.' What was the other one?"

"Well, she's blind, right? Has the dog, had me lead her to the book section and describe what was in the book. When she was freaking out, wanting me to tell her how to get out of the store ... she called me by my name." He touched the nametag pinned to his apron. "And I'm sure

I never told her."

CHAPTER 3

"Olivia Howe has no criminal past, no driver's license," Sam told Max once they'd pulled out of the station a short while later. "She just moved here about a year ago. But here's something interesting: she recently filed a restraining order against Terry Carlton."

"*The* Terry Carlton?"

"Yep." Terry Carlton was a hometown boy who'd made it to the NFL. After a short career, he'd blown out a knee and come home the local hero. "I doubt it fits into the case, but it sure makes me wonder what the story is."

Max didn't care. All that mattered was the missing girl. His gaze shifted to her picture and information on the car seat between them. *Her name is Phaedra. Phaedra Burns. She's not just a victim!* Phaedra's father's voice resounded in his head, shrill and to the point. He'd overheard Sam referring to 'the victim' at the station. Bad move on his part. Families couldn't understand that cops had to keep their emotions out of it so they could concentrate on the facts. Something Max had had trouble with until two years ago. But this case …

Every passing minute wrenched his gut. He already felt close to the edge just looking at the girl's picture. Dammit, she looked like Ashley: long brown hair, brown eyes, with a touch of baby fat around her cheeks and chin.

Sam was clenching his fists. "We need this to be a lead. We got nothing else so far."

"We're going to play it cool, right? Finesse her a bit, see what she knows," Max said as he drove into the Waterfront section.

Five years earlier, the area had consisted of a few warehouses. Then someone with foresight and big bucks bought up the land, scraped it clean, and built six buildings, stacked two-deep in three rows, running along the waterway. They looked European, maybe Mediterranean, hell, he didn't know. He guessed they were supposed to look like a Venetian village. Soon other developers moved in and eventually created a whole new upscale area of town.

Sam said, "What would be really nice is we find the girl at Howe's place along with the guy who took her. One neat, tidy package, and everyone gets to enjoy the holidays."

"It never happens that way, and you know it."

"Ah, ever the pessimist."

They were pretty sure the guy wearing the maintenance clothing was the suspect. He wasn't on the tapes that they could tell and wasn't an employee. Max found the building Olivia lived in: the center one closer to the road, third floor. He lucked into a spot and killed the engine. Time to face the girl's picture.

It's not Ashley.

He knew that. Ashley was gone, in one quick instant

of heat and flames ... gone. Then why were his hands shaking when he held up the picture? Her features were the same, but she didn't have Ashley's fragility. Probably didn't have all of Ashley's other problems either.

The bag containing Olivia's book crinkled as he grabbed it and got out of the car. He squinted up at the building; he'd forgotten his sunglasses again.

The small lobby was simple, just one bland painting above a table laden with a silk flower arrangement opposite the elevators. They took the stairs to the third floor and followed the brass plaques to the last apartment on the left. A low, sultry voice asked, "Who is it?" a minute after Sam knocked.

"Detectives Max Callahan and Sam O'Reilly with the Palomera Police Department."

The door opened after she'd unlocked a deadbolt and chain. He felt a hitch in his chest at the sight of her, and the jolt of seeing someone he knew but hadn't seen in a long time. He was sure he'd never seen her before, other than on the surveillance video. She was nice looking, with long brown hair, pale skin, and eyes an unusual shade of hazel. She wore a yellow shirt and vivid blue pants, no makeup.

"You're not from the singing telegram company, are you, pretending to arrest me for stealing Terry Carlton's heart again?" she asked.

Sam raised an eyebrow. "No, ma'am. You left your bag at the bookstore. We're here to return it."

"You're really cops?"

"Yes, ma'am."

"Can I see your badge?" she asked.

See? Max's eyes narrowed, and he held it toward her. Her soft fingers touched his arm first and followed it down to his hand. The movement was graceful and reminded him of the ballet dancers his daughter had loved watching. He tried to ignore the sensual shiver that rippled through him. As she ran her fingertips over the grooves of the badge and worn edges of black leather, it felt as though she were still touching him.

She dropped her hand and seemed to look right at Max. "You're here about the missing girl, aren't you? I heard the special report on the news. I've been waiting for an update."

The television was tuned to one of the main stations, now showing a soap opera.

"Have you found her yet?" she asked.

"No, not yet." Max set the bag on a nearby table.

Sam closed the door behind them. "We'd like to ask you some questions."

The apartment was simply decorated, though the furniture was first class. Butter-soft leather covered the low, sleek couch and matching chair. The solid oak coffee and end tables were covered in a high sheen, as were the wood floors. No pictures or other decorations, just one lamp in the living room that wasn't turned on. Only the sun coming in through the closed blinds shed dim light into the front room. Max smelled vanilla and had to stop himself from leaning close to see if it was her perfume. Her dog was standing at her side giving Max a curious look with its light blue eyes. She had an interesting mix of colors, mottled brown and gray on her head and a mixture of gray, white and brown on the rest of her coat.

He knelt down to the dog's level. "Beautiful dog. What kind is it?"

"Anastasia's an Australian Shepherd."

"I thought guide dogs were usually German shepherds or golden retrievers," Sam said, not masking his suspicion.

"A woman in Deltona trained Aussies as seizure alert dogs and started training them for sight assistance, too. How can I help you?"

"Let's sit down." Max said.

The cushion nearly swallowed him in luxurious, velvety leather. Even Sam couldn't help running his hand over the surface. She perched on the stuffed arm of the chair. Her gaze was aimed just past Max without focusing on anything specific. She was fidgeting, her fingers twisting around each other. Despite that, she sat up straight, regally.

Anastasia sat at Olivia's side, glancing from her to him and back again. Even the dog looked nervous. A computer tone voice said, "Three-zero-one." Olivia had pressed a button on her watch, though he wasn't sure if it was on purpose or as a result of her fidgeting.

A wisp of smoke trailed from a candle on the end table. Ah, so the vanilla scent wasn't her.

"You keep asking about a missing girl," Max said. "What do you know about her?"

"You *saw* her get abducted?" Sam said.

She lowered her head and massaged her temples. "Yes."

Sam got up, jammed his hands into his pockets, and casually walked across the living room. "And yet you're blind. Isn't that interesting?"

Max raised an eyebrow: *Keep it cool.* To Olivia, he said, "How long have you been blind?"

She was tracking Sam's movements with her head. "Since I was eight."

"And yet," Sam said in a cynical voice, "you told those two security guards at the toy store that you see things."

"I'm telepathic," she said, facing Max. "Telepathy is direct mind-to-mind communication. You've probably heard at least one story where a mother gets a strong sense that her child is in danger. Some women have actually 'seen' their child even though they're miles away. One mother, for instance, saw her daughter get hit by a car even though she was nowhere nearby. In that same way, I *saw* her get taken in my mind, only I saw it happen through Phaedra's eyes. I was ... hoping the guards would check it out and stop the guy."

Sam leaned next to Olivia's face, making her jump. "You say 'the guy.' You're sure it's a man."

"Yes."

"What's he look like?"

"I didn't see his face clearly, just a quick succession of images."

"That's convenient," Sam muttered.

"That's how it works," she said through rigid lips. "I ... I think I saw a cap. He was wearing a cap."

"What color?"

"Gray, I think."

Max said, "When you said, 'He's got her. Oh, God, he's got her,' that was when the guy grabbed her?"

She nodded, lacing her fingers together so tight, her knuckles went white. "The connection comes suddenly." She seemed to be staring at her hands, but then she lifted her face to his. "Do you have any idea who took her? Where she is?"

Sam said, "You'd have a better idea than we would, being psychic and all."

She lowered her lashes as her face tightened in anger. Just as quickly, she regained her composure. "She's been knocked out with chloroform. I can't connect to her when she's unconscious. Hopefully I can find out more when she wakes up."

"Would you mind if we take a quick look around?" Max said, getting to his feet.

"Why?"

"You have to admit, it seems pretty odd, you warning the guards about a girl who hadn't even been reported missing yet." And knowing the guy was wearing a gray cap.

She let out an impatient breath and rose to her feet. "Go ahead, but please hurry. Don't give him time to hurt her."

This time her voice did betray an emotion, but it wasn't guilt. It was the same urgency that pulsed through him. His instincts were screaming that she was involved, but they also warned him to take her slowly. He wasn't going to tell her that she was their only lead so far.

The room where they'd talked was the living room. Nearly half of that large room was set up as an artist's studio. An easel held a partially finished abstract painting that looked vaguely like two fiery eyes. Eerie.

The wooden floor was covered with thick sheets of opaque plastic splattered with paint. Two other paintings leaned against the wall, swirls of colors that looked like eyes of all shapes and colors. He recognized the smell of acrylic paint.

Sam was going through her kitchen, quietly opening and closing cabinets. "Without turning to him, she asked, "What exactly are you looking for in there? Do you really think I stashed her in with my spices?" Sam looked a little chagrinned as he closed the cabinet.

"Who's the painter?" Max asked, wondering if there was a boyfriend in the picture. A boyfriend who had a reason for taking a young girl.

"I'm the *artist*."

"Really?" A blind artist? Oh, yeah, he'd gotten the hint: artist, not painter.

"Yeah, well, I wanted to be an airline pilot, but I didn't like all the travel." She'd delivered the line totally deadpan.

Sam waved to get Max's attention and pointed to a custom bookcase filled with collections of Shirley Temple movies and *I Love Lucy* shows. She also had another bookcase filled with books in Braille. Magazines, too. She had an impressive collection of music CDs, all labeled in Braille. Max's fingers ran over the raised dots, and he wondered how anyone could decipher them. He was tempted to test her, but he didn't want to put her on the defensive any more than Sam had already done.

Everything in the apartment was neat. The desk in the dining room was organized, with a stack of unopened mail in one corner, a computer in the center, and what looked like a copier beside it. A talking clock sat on the other corner. An open newspaper covered half of the dining table. To the left of the table was the kitchen, which was divided from the main room by a long counter. Late afternoon sun slanted in through French doors, where beyond was a stone balcony that held two wrought iron chairs and a small table. All the appliances sported worn blue Braille labels on the buttons. A Dymo labeler sat on the corner of the counter.

A computer tone voice said, "Three-fifteen."

He glanced at Olivia, who was facing them with her arms crossed in front of her. Ah, so pressing that button wasn't an accident. She was making a point. She wanted them out. Whether it was because she didn't want them to find anything or because she wanted them out looking for Phaedra, he didn't know. What he did know was the minutes were ticking away, every one leading to a less hopeful conclusion.

A wall separated the living room from the bedrooms, creating a long hallway. The first door led to the master bedroom. It was as neat as the rest of the house, done in rich colors that invited a man to come in and get comfortable. She had a king-sized bed that sat up high and was covered in pillows. The muted floral bedspread touched the floor on one side and showed the mattress on the other side. Another door off the hallway led to a second bedroom with a treadmill and exercise bike in the corner and a flowered futon tucked beneath the window. At the end of the hallway was another small bathroom. No sign of a child having been there or anyone else for that matter.

"Three-seventeen."

She had followed him down the hallway.

"Live here alone?" he asked.

"Yes."

He abruptly turned around to face her. "How'd you know the bookstore employee's name?"

She was taken off guard either by his movement or the question. "What?"

"You called the employee who helped you by his name. He never told you."

"Sometimes I just know things. I can't explain it."

Sam's sniff of disbelief sounded more like a snort.

"I've got a dead grandmother; find out where she hid her millions, would you?"

She lifted her chin in his direction. "In years past, those gifted with psychic abilities were murdered because others were afraid of them. Don't be afraid or threatened by something you can't understand."

Sam winced at her patronizing tone. "I'm not afraid or threatened. I'm suspicious. I've never met a psychic who wasn't a crook. If psychics were real, there'd be people consistently winning the lottery or solving crimes. We could prevent political assassinations and clear out villages before the volcano erupts."

"I don't care if you believe me or not. As long as you're willing to explore what I might be able to tell you." She surprised Max by grabbing his arm, finding it unerringly. "If those guards had checked out the storage room, they could have stopped him from taking her. Promise me you'll at least check out what I tell you." Her pleading voice tightened his insides, making it impossible to reply.

Sam obliged by saying, "Oh, sure, because psychics have been so helpful in the past. I don't think a psychic has solved one crime. And I'm not talking those vague clues that could be interpreted to be correct after the fact. I'm talking concrete evidence. There was an old woman who used to come into the station whenever we had a high-profile case. She dropped those mystical nuggets—'The girl is near a building. A square building with white on it. And there's a tree or maybe a bush or a blade of grass nearby.' Then she bragged to the press how she solved the case."

Olivia crossed her arms over her chest. "I knew the girl was missing."

"Proves you knew something about the crime. Doesn't prove how you knew it."

Max said, "Here's my card. If you think of anything else, give me a call." He pressed his card into her hand and folded her fingers around it. She took a surprised breath, and he forced himself to let go. Her hand clenched around the card, crunching it.

"Wait." She walked over to the desk near the kitchen and pulled out what looked like a large TV remote control without the numbers on it. "Give me your number, Detective Callahan."

As he gave her the numbers, she pressed the pads. She heard a male synthesized voice repeat each piece of information she inputted. "Max. Callahan." And his number.

Sam walked closer to her. He wore his skepticism like a mask. Very slowly, he moved his hand toward her face — and she flinched.

"What are you doing?"

"Watching what you were doing," he offered casually. "What is that thing?"

"This is Louis. Well, that's what I call him. It's a Braille computer and organizer. I named it after Louis Braille."

Max eyed it, wondering what secrets it held. Wondering if he could get a warrant for a full search and quickly figuring he couldn't. "Thank you, Miss Howe," Max said as they headed toward the door.

Just before he closed the door, she said, "Remember your promise." She was looking at him or at least it appeared she was. "At least listen to what I have to tell you. It ..." Her face shadowed. "It might help." She didn't sound as sure that time.

They said nothing until they exited the building into the cool, afternoon sun. "What a friggin' phony," Sam said. "We ought to haul her in for doing those creepy eyeball paintings alone."

Max got into the car. "We don't have enough evidence. Besides, if she's working with someone, and she knows we're onto her, she'll be more careful. Which is why we were supposed to be cool, as you'll recall."

Sam got in on the passenger side before saying, "Sorry, but I couldn't stand there and pretend to believe that crap. You're obviously better at that kind of thing. All those psychics, tarot card and crystal ball readers, they're a bunch of crooks. But in this case, she's lying to cover someone's ass along with her own. Pretending to be blind so as not to be a viable suspect, distracting security so her lover or whomever can get the girl out of the store, and then claiming to be psychic. We ought to put a tail on her."

"It's all circumstantial. Hearsay, actions that could be interpreted in different ways—"

"She knew about the gray cap."

"We don't know for sure that the suspect was wearing gray, or that he even exists."

"She saw my hand!"

"She could have felt the air." When Max saw Sam's surprised expression, he shrugged. "I'm playing devil's advocate."

At the red light, Sam repeated the motion. "Any air?"

Max had to admit, "No. But that's not going to get us a warrant. After the last faulty warrant Judge Garrett granted, and all the bad press we got out of it, we're going to need a smoking gun. For what it's worth, I think she really is blind. Maybe she knew about the abduction and a guilty conscious propelled her to try to stop it."

Sam sat back in his seat, a smug look on his face. "She's guilty. And I, for one, am going to enjoy nailing her. Nothing worse than a deceptive woman."

Max had a feeling it wasn't going to be that simple. She knew something, that was for certain. And he was damn well going to find out what it was.

CHAPTER 4

Max and Sam met Detective Nick Mathers at the Bruns's house, a large Spanish-style structure on the water. Mathers was helping on the case while he could. He was the oldest of their poker group, in his early fifties Max guessed. He had the start of a gut, probably due to his exotic beer collection. He kept one for the collection and drank the rest of the pack. He was married to a homely, quiet woman who served up cold beer and chips on poker nights with all the cheer of an underpaid waitress.

Cop cars, both marked and unmarked, littered the driveway and street. Barricades kept the usual clusters of neighbors and reporters at bay.

Mathers asked, "What'd you find out?"

Sam said, "Olivia Howe is a phony blind woman and a phony psychic, and I don't have a doubt that she's involved. If we can catch her on the blindness angle, we can crack her on the rest of it."

"She claims she's psychic," Max clarified. "That's how she knew about the girl being taken."

Sam snorted. "We need to find out who she's working with. We know she didn't take the girl; her role was to distract while the guy grabbed the girl."

Max said, "Why distract the people in the front of the store when the suspect was way in the back? To be effective, she should have had her fit just outside the remote-control room. And why direct security to where the suspect made his getaway?"

Sam's expression shuttered. "Max likes playing devil's advocate."

Max asked, "What do you have here?"

Mathers nodded a head of enviously neat, silver hair toward the house. "The mother's hysterical, the father's distraught." That didn't mean much, not when family members who acted hysterical and distraught committed the majority of child abductions. "My gut feeling is that they're not involved. Flora didn't kidnap the kid herself, of course, and Pat was in his office. I've got a squirrelly feeling about Pat's brother, Mike, though. He's a mechanic at the Ford dealership. We're trying to verify whether he was working this morning. He's got a prior. An ex-girlfriend claimed he exposed himself to her daughter, but she backed out of her story. Could be she was trying to burn him, or could be he intimidated her. For what it's worth, the Burnses don't believe he had anything to do with that incident or their daughter's abduction. Something else to throw into the pot: Phaedra was adopted. It was an open adoption when Phaedra was an infant. The Burnses apparently waited to have children until later in life and ended up adopting. The birth mother hasn't had any contact with the girl since."

Max could believe that Olivia was helping a distraught mother try to kidnap her child before believing she was helping some sicko. Yet, he wasn't hopeful on that score. "It would seem odd that she waited all these years before having second thoughts, but it happens. It's something to check out."

"No ransom demands?" Sam asked.

"Not a one, but we're wired and ready if we get a call."

"Good job. We'll take it from here."

Mathers's phone chirped, and he answered it. "Yeah, thanks for checking on that. He wasn't. How long? Okay, thanks. Detectives Callahan and O'Reilly will be by to pick up those timecards." He disconnected. "Mike Burns went out this morning, supposedly because it was slow. The timing's tight, him getting to the toy store, getting the girl, and then getting out. He clocked out fifteen minutes before it happened, and it's about ten minutes from the toy store to the dealership. He never returned to work; he came right here."

Sam clapped his hands. "I believe we've got Howe's partner."

Max felt that first hit of adrenaline. Just like last time, when the leads started jibing. The Brad Stevens kidnapping. He swallowed hard. His last big case. That time Saul Berney, the kidnapper, had called with a ransom demand: five hundred thousand dollars. The parents were willing to pay it, but Max didn't want the bastard to get a penny of it. The thought of anyone abducting a child made him crazy, and his own demons had driven him too far. He'd wanted to grind Berney up. He wanted all the other Berneys out there to get the message. He'd nabbed the kid and taunted Berney into taking the money. Then they'd nabbed Berney.

Max had been a real hero for the second time in his life. That time, though, he'd gotten to revel in it. It hadn't been tainted with shame and shoved under the carpet. The city of Palomera had honored him with a ceremony and everything. He'd hoped it would ease his drive to be the big hero — and finally erase the reason for that drive. He'd enjoyed knowing he'd saved that boy, and yeah, he'd enjoyed the accolades. At least until Berney got his revenge on Max.

"We'll time the drive," Sam said, tearing Max from his grim thoughts. "Where is Mike Burns now?"

Mathers nodded toward the Burns's house.

Sam said, "We'll need a picture of him to show the toy store employees and to check against the security tapes. If we can place him there, that'll make things easy. We'll take him in for questioning, see if we can shake him up a bit."

When they started walking toward the house, Mathers held Max back. "You all right being on this case?"

"Have to be."

"What was Huntington thinking?" He shook his head in answer. "Be careful, Max."

Max nodded, a lump forming in his throat at his comrade's concern. He headed toward the house where Sam was waiting for him. "Nice place."

The house had enormous ceilings adorned with fancy architectural touches like arched doorways, rounded corner beading, and crown molding. Sculptures and oil paintings depicted different aspects of Florida: seashells, sunsets, pelicans. In contrast, tinsel, snowmen, and Santas adorned every visible surface of the home. In reverence to the real reason for the season, an elaborate manger was set up on a table. The festivity mocked the fear, grief and frustration that permeated the house. Several officers were inside as well as friends of the family.

Flora Burns rushed into the living room, followed by her husband, Pat. "Is there any news?" Hope burned in their eyes. They thought he and Sam had come with new information. Max shook his head, unable to look away from their disappointment.

Pat's expression stiffened. "Don't tell me you're here to question us, too."

Mike Burns was sitting on the couch. He was in his late thirties, Max figured, with thick, dark hair parted on the side. His eyes kept shifting to the left, listening to them while pretending to study a map he'd unfolded on the coffee table.

In his low, calming voice, Max said, "We have to look at all the angles. Unfortunately, a family member is often involved in these types of cases." He glanced at Mike to get a reaction. Not even a flinch.

Pat said, "No one in this house would hurt Phaedra."

Sam straightened a crooked wreath on the wall. "What about Phaedra's birth parents?"

Flora's mouth tightened as she shook her head and looked at Pat, who said, "We already told that other officer, I'm not dragging the mother into this. She moved to Arizona after Phaedra's birth, and we haven't heard from her since. She never told anybody who the father was, but it was clear she had no intention of letting him know he even had a child."

"We still need to look into it. It's always possible she had second thoughts, even after all this time."

After a hesitation, Pat nodded. "Fine, we'll give you her information. For all we know, she doesn't even live at the address we have anymore." Pat went to a computer in a nearby office. He returned and handed Sam the piece of paper he'd printed out.

Flora said, "I don't want her to know about ... about what's happened." There was a different fear in her eyes now. "If she thinks we're bad parents, that we let someone take her daughter ..."

"*Our* daughter." Pat held her close. "She couldn't take Phaedra from us now." He looked at Max and Sam, who said, "We'll do it quietly."

"Stop wasting time investigating us," Flora cried out, gripping her husband's arm with white fingers. "And start looking for the maniac who has our daughter!"

The Stevenses had also been upset at the investigation into their life when their boy went missing.

"We're doing everything we can to find her," Max said. "We're making fliers to be distributed within the tri-county area. Between those and the news reports, everyone in this whole area will have seen Phaedra's face. A grid search is underway —"

"Grid search?" Pat asked.

"Yeah, it's where we break up the town into grid sections. Teams of officers take each section and question people, looking for witnesses or suspicious behavior. Any vacant spaces are investigated. They're particularly focused on the area around the toy store, looking for anyone who might have seen a vehicle parked out back." Officers were beginning to track down previously convicted child molesters, too, but he wasn't going to mention that.

"And you're looking into us," Pat said, straining to keep his voice level.

Max didn't answer, since it hadn't been posed as a question.

"We can help, too." Pat turned to his wife. "We'll

hire Joanna. She's done a great job getting the word out about the restaurants. A publicist has all the right connections."

"We'll need to clear whatever you release to the public. There are some details we don't want leaked."

"But why?" Flora asked. "The more information that's out there, the better the chance of someone remembering something."

Max said, "Some details, like the gold shamrock necklace Phaedra was wearing and her pink socks, are important to keep under wraps. It's our way of weeding out the crazies who call claiming they have the girl when they don't."

Flora grabbed his arm. "Why would anyone do that? Why?"

He awkwardly placed his hand over hers, as though that would somehow comfort her. "I wish I knew."

She narrowed eyes smudged in black and tightened her grip on his arm. "You found that boy. You're the one, aren't you?"

He didn't want to talk about the Stevens case, but he nodded. Maybe it would put them at ease. He'd been capable once.

"But this isn't the same man, is it?" Pat asked. "He's still in jail."

"Yes, he is."

Two uniforms were escorting Mike Burns out of the house. He went willingly, but grudgingly. Flora started crying. "Don't worry," Mike said to her. "Nicholson will get this all straightened out, and I'll be back to help find her."

Max uttered a few words meant to reassure the Burnses and headed to the front door. Sam paused and watched Mike get into the car. "He's one cool customer. Too cool."

When one of the officers called Sam over, Max glanced back into the house one last time. He hated thinking of that little girl, cold, alone, and scared. Every hour that passed diminished the chance that she would survive. And while she was alive, she could be suffering unmentionable atrocities. Another girl flashed into his mind, scared and crying. His fists clenched. No child should be touched by violence.

As he turned back to the door, a painting in the formal dining room caught his eye. A blood-red sun dipped into a black ocean. No, not just any painting. The sun looked like an eyeball. He walked into the formal dining room, flipped on a light switch, and tried to read the signature.

"Who painted this?" he asked the Burnses, who were watching him.

Flora said, "A local artist. I don't remember her name. I got it at the LaForge Gallery over at the Waterfront. I like to support local artists."

"Do you have any more of her paintings?"

"No, that's the only one. Why?"

"Does anyone else in your family own her artwork?"

She shook her head. "Not that I know of."

"What does this have to do with our daughter?" Pat asked, pulling his wife closer.

Max glanced once more at the painting. "I don't know, but I'm going to find out." He met Sam at the front door.

Sam said, "We have to find a connection between them."

"I may have found it." He nodded toward the paint-

55

ing. "Flora Burns said she supports local artists but acted like she didn't know Olivia personally. It's just a loose connection. Could mean nothing."

Sam's eyes glittered. "Or it could be the start of a beautiful conviction."

"You work on Mike Burns; I'll work on Olivia."

"Why do you get Olivia?"

"I don't think your bonehead techniques are going to get us anywhere with her." Before Sam could refute that, Max said, "Let's get Mike's photo from the DMV and show it to Toyland's employees, see if anyone recognizes him. I'll call the manager."

Olivia was washing dishes when the phone rang. Without thinking about it, she grabbed up the receiver.

"It's Terry. Don't hang up on me. I'm calling about the girl, the one who was taken from the toy store today."

Her fingers tightened on the handset. "What about her?"

"You told me about that connection you have with kidnapped kids."

She had told him about that, hadn't she? When he'd swept her away, or maybe when he'd simply swept away her good sense. She'd been too honest about some things; not honest enough about others.

He said, "You're connected to her, aren't you? I can feel your anxiety. That's how close we are. That's how connected I am to you, the same way you're connected to these kids. Olivia, I'm coming over. I don't want you alone through this."

"Terry, no, you can't do that. Don't make me call the police."

"Olivia, dammit, you need me! How can I prove that

to you?"

She hung up and returned to the sink to finish rinsing the dishes, trying to ignore her shaking hands and the ringing of the phone. Would he ever give up? And now, using that poor girl as an excuse to call her...

She stopped her movements. Using that girl. "No. That's crazy. He wouldn't..."

She couldn't even finish the sentence. For a month Terry had continued to pursue her. He'd used singing telegrams, false emergencies, lies about leaving town and wanting to see her one last time for closure, any excuse to contact her. She had gone from wondering when he'd give up to wondering how far he'd go to get her attention.

How far *would* he go?

The panic struck her again. The bowl dropped into the sink and shattered against the porcelain. She clutched the counter, but her legs wouldn't hold her up. She sank to the floor as Phaedra's fear rocked her.

The images came like gunshots.

Fear!

Panic!

Near-darkness.

Where am I?

I want my mommy!

Stasia nuzzled her, and Olivia opened her eyes and sucked in a deep breath. When she caught her breath, she used the counter to push herself to her feet. Her head was pounding. She laid her cheek on the cool surface of the counter and tried to recall what she'd seen. She replayed the barrage of images, but her mind stopped on one in particular.

"She's in a cage. Oh, God, a cage."

She'd seen bars like that before.

"No, no, don't think about that."

This was about Phaedra's kidnapping, not hers. Two totally different events, sixteen years apart.

Then why were they melding in her mind?

Because she'd been abducted on December twentieth from a toy store in Palomera. That coincidence was why the connection was so strong this time, had to be.

She'd been eight years old. A fun day of shopping had been spoiled by her mother's announcement: she'd entered Olivia in a New York City beauty pageant to be held in January. She'd promised — *promised* — that Olivia wouldn't have to endure another beauty pageant until the following spring. When her mother had run into another pageant regular, Olivia decided to punish her mother by hiding.

The man had lured her out a side door, shoved a chloroform cloth over her mouth, and the world had gone dark. She'd come to in the trailer of a semi. At the sight of the cage, panic gave her courage to fight him. In their struggle, she was knocked out. When she woke, she was blind. Though he'd never sexually molested her, he'd done other, terrible things to her. Her hand automatically went to her collarbone. Four days later she'd been rescued, and her abductor had killed himself.

She didn't know what the man had done to her eyes; no one could figure that out. Nor could they figure out exactly why he kidnapped her. Something else happened, triggered by the trauma of the kidnapping: she lost her eyesight, but gained another type of sight. The psychic tendency she inherited from her grandmother had been intensified. Because heightened emotions wrought the change, they also triggered the strange connection to abducted children. She connected to the child not only emotionally, but psychically. Once she realized the gift — and the curse — that it was, she used it to help find missing children.

She found her cell phone. She must call Detective Callahan, the one who wasn't so suspicious. The one who had filled her senses with his low, patient voice, the smell of his woodsy cologne, and the feel of the muscles in his arm. Somehow, she knew she could trust him. She had to tell him what she knew. The panic in her stomach migrated through her body as she called up his information on Louis and had the computer dial the number. This wouldn't be like the last time she'd tried to help.

Her throat tightened with every ring. When he answered, she said, "Detective Callahan, it's Olivia Howe. Phaedra woke up. He's got her in a dark place. And ... she's in a cage."

Max hung up with Olivia just as he walked to his desk at the station. A cage. The thought shivered through him. Why a cage? Anything but a cage.

If Olivia was involved, she was playing with them, leading them on. If she wasn't involved? an inner voice asked. Could she be for real?

No, that was crazy thinking.

On the way back to the station, he and Sam had timed the route from the car dealership to the toy store. They arrived at the interrogation room at the same time as Mike Burns's lawyer. They'd known that Burns would be a fool to give anything away with his lawyer hot-footing it over. Mike Burns didn't look like a fool. He in fact looked like a clean-cut guy, except for the dark grease in the creases of his trimmed nails. The scent of cologne filled the air around him.

Paul Nicholson set his briefcase on the table and greeted Burns with a nod. Then he faced off with the detectives. The man would have towered threateningly if he'd had any meat on his 6'2" frame. "Are you charging my client with a crime?"

Sam said, "No, we're just trying to get some information out of him. If he'd answer, he could save himself a lot of trouble."

"Information about what?" Nicholson asked.

"Burns's niece was abducted from a toy store this morning. At roughly the same time, Burns here took off from his job. He won't account for his whereabouts. His prior exposure arrest slots him into the offender category."

Burns pounded his fist on the table. "That was a setup! She was pissed because I owed her some money and couldn't pay it back when she demanded it."

The lawyer put his hand on Burns's shoulder. "Those charges were dropped. It has no bearing on this case whatsoever."

"We just want to know where he went," Sam said.

Burns flattened his hands on the table. "I told you, I was driving around Last I knew there wasn't a law against that."

"Can anyone verify your little tour?" Sam asked.

"I'm sure someone saw me, but no one I could point out to you. I mean, I was right out in the open, driving around."

Paul Nicholson said, "What can we do to allay your suspicions?"

"Let us take a look at his place, inside and out."

Burns bristled, but before he could respond, Nicholson whispered to him. Burns leaned back, crossing his arms in front of him. "It's the principal…" He waved his hand. "Fine, take a look."

"You can search his house and premises," Nicholson said.

"And vehicle?"

Another whispered discussion. "And his vehicle. He's got nothing to hide."

"Now?"

"Yes." Burns pushed up from the table. "I'll take you. I don't want my place trashed."

It was small consolation. If Burns was willing to let them look, he was either innocent or knew the place was clean. There was always a chance he'd forgotten something, though. A small chance, but one worth taking.

"One more question," Sam asked as though it were an afterthought. "Does the name Olivia Howe ring a bell?"

Mike gave away no sign of recognition. "Nope."

"Your sister-in-law has one of her paintings on the dining room wall."

"She's got lots of paintings around the house."

"Have you ever been to a showing or a gallery and met any of the artists?"

"Nope."

Sam shrugged. "Just wondered. Shall we go?"

After checking out Burns's house, Max and Sam returned to the car. They watched Mike and his lawyer exchange a few words at the front door. Burns shot them a smug look before getting into his truck and leaving. All they'd discovered was that Burns had a heavy affection for porn movies. Dog-eared catalogues were scattered everywhere, and Burns had obviously ordered many movies from those catalogues. Every movie in his collection sported a yellow Post-It scribbled with a critique. None of them included children and none were hard-core.

Sam leaned back in the seat. "I want to nail that bastard."

"*If* it's him. The timing's pretty tight."

"But doable. It's him. He's got slime bag written all over him. And that woman at the store — Olivia Howe — she's involved in this, too. All that panic was a distraction so Burns could get away."

Max's gut rebelled at the thought of Olivia being involved, and he tried to figure out why. His phone rang, and he spoke with someone at the Flagstaff station where Phaedra's birth mother lived. "Okay, great. Thanks." He disconnected and said, "Birth mother is still in town and has been since she left Florida. She's a secretary at a hotel there and hasn't missed work in the last five days. She's been married for five years and has three kids. They're going to keep an eye on the house just in case, but it doesn't look like she had anything to do with the abduction."

He looked at his watch. They were closing in on six hours. No ransom call meant that whoever took Phaedra probably had other plans for her. He didn't want to think what those other plans would be.

He pushed away the memory before it had a chance to edge into his mind.

"Hey, Max, you okay?"

He blinked, realizing he'd zoned out. "Just thinking."

He called the station and talked to one of the officers going over the surveillance tapes. "What do you have for us?"

The woman let out an exasperated sound. "Do you realize how many people went in and out of that store that morning? It's a mess. Some people walked in with one group and walked out with a different crowd. We assume they weren't with either group, but it's still making it hard to single people out. So far, nobody stands out, but we'll find our suspect."

"Thanks." He hung up and let out his own sound of exasperation. "Nothing from the tapes yet. The manager claims that no one is able to use the entrance the girl was taken out of, even the employees. It's strictly for emergencies. That left the loading dock as a potential place for the suspect to have come in, but they've already looked over that tape. No way did the suspect come in that way."

"Then he or she will have to be on the tapes at the front entrance."

As soon as they returned, he started the ball in motion to obtain the DMV picture and assemble the employees. He looked at Phaedra's picture on his desk. Every police station in the state had been given one. Everyone wanted to find this girl. Max could feel the hunger to be that person rising inside him, just like when finding the Stevens boy had taken over his life. The drive to be a hero came from a dark, deep place inside him.

As a boy, Max had not only looked up to Superman, Spiderman, and Batman, he'd become them. He could see himself with his brown mop of cowlick-ridden hair and fringe of eyelashes the girls teased him about, wearing a cape made from an old red sheet and scouting the neighborhood in search of someone to rescue and dragons to slay. He was the one who found lost dogs posted on street signs and saved the skinny kid from the bullies.

His fierce need to slay dragons and drive villains into the ground started as a defense mechanism for a boy who was bullied and taunted by a villain he could never defeat. The greatest evil he would ever face — his father.

CHAPTER 5

Thursday, December 21

A jolt of fear woke Olivia. She bolted upright in bed with a sharp intake of breath.

"Good morning," *a male voice said.*

The murky silhouette of a man's face.

The cage door opening.

A McDonald's bag tossed inside. The scent of sausage and hash browns.

The alarm clock went off and Adam Sandler's Hanukkah song broke the connection. She slapped her hand down on the snooze button to silence it, then laid her head back on the pillow and massaged the spear of pain in her temples. Her heart was slamming inside her chest, and she took deep breaths to bring it back to normal. Her skin was drenched. She wasn't sure which side effect was worse, the headache or the wash of sweat.

He was there with Phaedra now, bringing her breakfast. At least he showed her that kindness. If only Olivia could hold onto the connection and find a useful clue she could pass onto the detective. She'd never been able to call up the visions or return to them once the connection had been severed.

Stasia always slept at the foot of her bed; now she was pressed against Olivia's thigh, her nose buried beneath her leg.

"It's okay, sweetie. It's been a while since you've had to go through this with me. You're not used to it anymore." As hard as it was, Olivia had had to bury her head in the sand for a while. Normally she had to get emotionally involved in the kidnapping story before the connection would start. That's what was so strange about this one. It had sucked her right in.

At her touch and soothing words, Stasia lifted her head and positioned it in Olivia's hands. "But we have to help her, you know that. I can't turn away, even if..."

She'd come so close to going over the edge last time.

When the alarm went off again, the radio deejay was talking about the kidnapping. She listened, hoping to hear good news, but knowing there would be none yet. The police were working on some leads, but no suspects could be named, he said.

She used to listen to national radio all the time, waiting to hear about a missing child, hoping to connect and see something that might help. For a long time, she phoned in the clues anonymously so she wouldn't have to face the kind of skepticism and rudeness Detective O'Reilly had displayed. Sometimes the child was found, and the police would say that a hunch had played out to help solve the case. Other times... well, sometimes the child wasn't found in time.

She pushed herself out of bed. "Time to get up and

going."

She fed Stasia, showered, and got dressed. Although what she really wanted was a candy bar, she chose a more sensible Pop-Tart and cup of coffee. "We're visiting your grandpa today," she said as she grabbed the harness.

Visiting her father was bittersweet. Besides her grandmother, her father was the one person who had accepted and understood her, psychic quirks and all. Back then, though, he'd worked all the time.

After letting Stasia run in the park, they walked the remaining ten minutes to her father's assisted living facility. Across the street she could hear the rush of water from the water treatment facility. She used to imagine it was a waterfall until she'd heard a recent news story about some kids breaking in. One of them drowned, and his family was demanding better security.

Her father had chosen the Livingston when he'd finally accepted his diagnosis of Alzheimer's. It fit the Howe criteria: overpriced, ostentatious and luxurious. When the fifth doctor confirmed the diagnosis, he took the news with dignity. He liquidated all his assets and went on Medicare to spare his family the financial burden. He set up Olivia with a trust and put himself on the Livingston's waiting list. A year ago, when he'd been accepted as a resident, she had decided to move back to Palomera with him. She wished she could take care of him properly, but at least he lived within walking distance.

Her soft-soled shoes squeaked on the marble floor of the lobby. The place always reeked of disinfectant, making her wonder what odors they were trying to cover. This time of the year, the cinnamon, holly, and fir smells overpowered even the strong pine scent.

"Good morning, Miss Howe," one of the nurses said. "He's in his room."

"Thank you."

The door to her father's room was usually open during the day. She touched the frame of the doorway and paused. "Daddy?"

She wanted to run into his arms and lose herself, to smell him and remember the times he'd held her after a nightmare. She hated even admitting she still wanted someone to hold her for that or any reason. It seemed like, in any important relationship, it was all or nothing — she was either over-protected or alone. Being alone was preferable.

"Hello?" His once authoritative voice was now soft and uncertain. "Who are you?"

She hoped she masked her disappointment. "It's your daughter, Olivia." She walked closer. "And this is Stasia."

"They said I had a daughter." A bad day. The doctor had started him on a new medication, but she'd warned it could take weeks to see any improvement.

She perched on the side of the bed. "Yes, you do."

She remembered him in his elegant three-piece suits. He was the tallest, strongest, most handsome man she'd ever seen. That's how she pictured him now, with his chin held high and his thick graying hair slightly mussed from a long day wrangling the stock market.

"You're very pretty," he said, making her wonder if he meant her or the dog. Once a man had complimented her looks and she'd thanked him. To her utter embarrassment, he'd meant Stasia. "You must take after your mother," he added with a soft laugh, clarifying the compliment.

"I take after you. Mom had blond hair and a round face. She was very petite. Do you remember her at all?"

"I remember ... a woman ..." After a pause, he said, "No, I don't."

"There are pictures on your dresser." He'd told her about them. Now she heard him pick up one of the frames.

"What was she like?" he asked.

For years, he'd worked with her on remembering what things looked like. Now she helped him to remember. "Mom was very refined. She knew all the right things to do, what not to do." Even now, she sometimes heard her voice: *Knees together. Sit up straight. Lower your voice; young ladies don't shout.*

Even now, she sometimes did the opposite out of spite.

Every time he asked about Elaine, she chose her words carefully. Their marriage hadn't been bad, but only because they hardly saw each other. Olivia wondered if Elaine had grown bored with being a corporate wife and that's why she'd decided to have a baby so late in life. Olivia had felt like her special project.

"Where is she? She doesn't come to visit."

"She passed away two years ago." To change to a cheerier subject, she said, "You and her mom, Lily, got on grandly. She'd give you stock tips and tell you what colors would bring you luck. I think you even believed her. She was psychic." She had died in her sleep ten years earlier. Olivia missed her more than her own mother.

"Here's a picture of a little girl wearing a crown. She looks like a princess."

Those awful beauty pageant days. "That's me." From before Olivia could remember, Elaine prettied her up and entered her in one pageant after another, just for the glory of it. After the tedious makeup process, she didn't even recognize herself. That other girl had to sing and dance while everyone judged her. Her competitors whispered about her, trying to distract her and crumble her confidence. When she was that other Olivia, that's when Elaine warmed to her the most. *Livvy, you're so beautiful. You did so well today, you made your mother proud.* That's when Olivia learned she had to be someone else to be loved by her mother. Later, she learned that men were the same way.

"Tell me about yourself," he asked.

"Well, let's see." Every time he asked, she picked different aspects of her life to talk about. "I love all kinds of music, though I have a particular affinity for rock and roll. You and mother wanted me to be cultured, and it helped me to appreciate all the art forms. I'm an artist now. I paint pictures for a living." Sometimes she didn't tell him she was blind. If he asked about Stasia's special harness, she'd tell him. She always lied, though, about how she'd become blind. No point in dredging up those memories. If only *she* could forget.

"Was I a good father?" James asked.

"You were the best, daddy." She leaned forward and hugged him harder than she'd intended to. "It's okay if you don't remember me." Emotion clogged her voice. "Because I remember you. I love you."

"I love you, too." After a moment, he asked, "What did you say your name was again?"

Hold in the tears. "Olivia. I'm Olivia."

Olivia was still fighting tears as she made her way on the sidewalk. She steered her thoughts to her surroundings. She couldn't afford to get lost in her thoughts. Even with Stasia guiding her, Olivia had to be in tune with everything going on around her.

The grocery store was straight ahead. Usually she called ahead to arrange for someone to help her shop, but she only needed a couple of items. She heard snippets of conversations all around her. Someone to her right brushed her arm, and she moved away from the contact. Traffic rushed past on her left.

A few moments later, she was sure, absolutely sure, that someone had touched her hair. Her muscles contracted. Terry? She didn't dare call out his name. If he were there, he'd take that as an invitation to respond. She didn't detect his Polo, though, only an overdose of a drug store brand of cologne. With her lips pressed together, she forged onward. She suspected that Terry sprayed Polo outside her apartment door sometimes in a pitiful attempt to remind her of him. She'd think Terry himself pitiful if she didn't know how strong and determined he was.

As she walked, the sound and wind from the cars driving past grew louder. When her shoe touched the edge of the sidewalk, she realized the crowd had slowly nudged her to the left, close to the street. Or maybe one person had.

"Olivia."

The word was so faint she couldn't identify the voice. As she turned in response, she felt a shove at her ankle. Someone bumped into her other side, spinning her around. She wasn't sure how it happened, but suddenly she was off-balance ... pitching forward. Everything was a mental blur. She heard the sound of a large truck approaching as she tumbled to the ground. Where was she? In the road?

A horn blared to her left, and she realized with horror that it was coming right at her. Brakes howled, tires squealed, gears ground. She was all turned around and too paralyzed with fear to even scream. Stasia's claws scrabbled against the asphalt next to her.

Someone grabbed her arm and yanked her backward. She smelled burning rubber and heard the truck come to a hard stop in front of her. Behind it, another car screeched to a halt, and beyond that, a horn blared.

"Are you all right?" the man who had hauled her backward asked. She thought he was the one wearing the heavy cologne, but wasn't sure. Her nostrils were full of the scent now.

"My dog, where's my dog?" Stasia immediately put her paws on Olivia's legs. Olivia knelt down to make sure she wasn't injured. "Someone pushed me." She came to her feet, her shaky hands tight on the leash. Her heart was pounding. "Did anyone see what happened?"

She could hear several people around her. "I didn't see anyone push you, dear," an older man said.

The man who had pulled her back said, "You tripped, that's all. The sidewalk is buckled over there. You couldn't see it."

"No, I felt someone push me. They said my name and pushed me. I think it was a man."

A woman said, "Who would do such a terrible to you?"

"Why would someone push you?" the man asked. "You got turned around and tripped, that's all."

"You're all right?" the older man asked.

"I'm ... fine." She said "Thank you" to those around her and directed Stasia to lead them home. Only when her heartbeat had resumed a somewhat normal pace did she feel the sting of the scrapes on her hands. Her body was still shaking, and her skin was clammy.

Had someone tried to kill her? It seemed paranoid. Outrageous. But she knew one thing: she hadn't just lost her balance.

More than twenty-four hours after Phaedra's abduction, Max wasn't a bit closer to solving the case. Or making any sense out of it. He sat back in his chair and massaged his forehead. There was no ransom demand, and not one person at the toy store could place Mike Burns in the store either prior to or at the time of the abduction. He wasn't on the tape either. Several previous sex offenders had checked out or moved away. Some couldn't be found, but there was no reason to think they had recently been in the area. The phones were ringing with the usual false leads and crank calls.

Despite the lack of hard evidence, Sam was on Burns like a bloodhound. He'd followed Burns from the mansion-turned-headquarters to his house after midnight. If Burns was keeping the kid somewhere, he hadn't checked on her lately.

They needed a break, and they needed it now. Max's gaze kept going to the clock. Every second mocked his failure, and every passing minute tortured him with thoughts of what she was enduring.

Detective Nick Mathers tried to look casual as he walked over. He set a hand on Max's shoulder. "How you holding up, Max?"

"Not too good by the look of his pen," Detective Tom Graham said from his desk next to Max's. He gestured with one of his scarred hands to Max's pen, which he'd chewed flat. "You're picking up Huntington's habit."

Tom spent all of his free time working on motorcycles. He always had gashes and burns on his hands and arms as a result. His dyed hair looked blue in the overhead lights. "This case must be getting to you."

Of course, it's getting to me, you idiot! Max wanted to yell, but that would ignite Tom's tendency toward hotheadedness. He held his tongue and was rewarded with more bullshit.

"I look at each case like it's a game," Tom continued, as though he were baiting Max. "So far the kidnapper's winning."

Max could understand why Tom's wife of fourteen years had decided to leave him a few years back. He couldn't imagine living with someone who viewed life as a game and one not worth playing unless he thought he would win.

Before Max could respond, one of the other detectives gestured for Max to join him in the break room. "Callahan, you might want to hear this."

The television mounted on the wall was tuned to the noon news. Several men were crammed into the room watching an interview with Pat and Flora Burns.

The reporter asked, "So you don't think the police are doing all they can to find your daughter?"

"No," Mr. Burns said. "I understand procedure is to investigate the family, but they seem to be fixated on us instead of looking at the whole picture. No one in our family would harm our daughter."

The reporter asked, "But isn't Max Callahan working

on your case? Surely the fact that he found Brad Stevens must put you at ease?"

Flora said, "Not until he finds our little girl." She held up a picture of Phaedra with shaking hands. "Someone must have seen our girl being taken from that store yesterday. The police seem to have no leads, so we're appealing to you out there." Her voice was filled with tears. "Please, everyone, look at this picture carefully. Whoever ... has her is someone you know. Maybe the guy next door. You can help bring her back to us."

The reporter kept her voice neutral, though her expression was sympathetic. "And you're offering a reward?"

Mr. Burns wiped his eyes with a handkerchief. "Fifty thousand dollars for the safe return of our daughter."

Max ducked out of the room, but as he passed the lieutenant's office, he heard, "Callahan, in here."

"Yes, sir."

Huntington pointed to a seat with a pencil so gnawed, it hardly looked like it could write anymore. His lips were dotted with flecks of yellow paint. His feet were propped on the edge of his desk, and Max noticed that one of his Argyle socks was blue and one was dark red. "Give me an update."

"There isn't much to report right now, sir. O'Reilly and I have split up to cover more ground. The grid search of the area has turned up nothing. The only viable suspect we have so far is the uncle, though we don't have anything concrete to pin on him."

"What about Olivia Howe? Everyone's been talking about her, saying she's some kind of psychic nut."

"She claims she's psychically connected to the girl. She supposedly felt — and saw — when the girl was taken. She called me last night to tell me she saw the girl in a cage. We believe Howe may be an accomplice, a decoy to sidetrack us. We're not even sure if she's really blind. We're working on a connection between her and Mike Burns. So far all I've got is a painting." He explained about Olivia's painting being at the Burns's house. "It's loose, but it's a start." What bothered him was his inclination to say that she probably wasn't a perpetrator when he had no evidence to support his feeling.

Huntington nodded. "Keep working on it." He went back to his paperwork, humming that lethargic version of "Jingle Bells."

"Sir, may I ask why you assigned me to this case?"

The lieutenant studied him, a perusal that always unnerved Max. "You heard what the family's been saying?"

"Have you?" The broadcast had only been minutes ago.

"They've been doing interviews throughout the day. The airtime and exposure are good for the case, but they're casting doubt on our ability to do our job. Do they have reason to doubt, Callahan?"

"I give my all to every assignment, sir."

"But what about this one?"

"I'll do my best to find Ashley."

"Ashley?"

Max's chest caved as he replayed his words. "Phaedra, I mean."

Huntington leaned back in his chair. "You asked why I assigned this case to you. Because I want to either shake you or break you. It was a horrible thing, what happened to your wife and daughter. We all feel for you.

But two years later you're still floating around here like a ghost. Yes, you do your job, but your heart isn't in it. Your biggest asset was your driving hunger to bring in the bad guy, even though you went over the edge at times. Now you have nothing."

Max swallowed hard on those words. "I appreciate your leniency, sir." Appreciated it? He would have dropped to his knees in gratitude for his not pushing Max — or sticking him in a desk job.

Huntington's gaze softened. "I care about you, Callahan. I care about all my men. Part of my job is to keep an eye on your mental welfare. I've been a cop for a long time. I know the crap you go through. *You* went through hell. It's time to join the living, if that's possible. I know you'll do your best on this case. I wouldn't have put you on it otherwise. And while you're on it, you're either going to pull your act together or fall apart. I'd rather have that than have you hovering around here like the undead."

Max wanted to live up to his lieutenant's expectations. "I want a warrant for phone and credit card records for Mike Burns and Olivia Howe. Our first step is to tie them together."

"Do you have enough to back it up? I've already caught hell for getting warrants when we didn't have enough evidence. Marco Gencarelli is trying to sue us for the search we did on his businesses."

"Our guys thought they had enough on him."

"That was the problem. We thought we did; turned out we didn't."

"That's all I have. Howe and Burns."

He considered it. "Give it a try. See if Judge Garrett goes for it."

Max headed back to his cluttered desk. Huntington was watching him through the glass window and didn't even look away when Max caught him. Max turned his attention back to Phaedra's file. Phaedra, not Ashley.

Maybe he wasn't doing all that he could. He'd worked hard not to be the coward his father had called him. When his wife and daughter were killed, he'd lost his drive to be a hero. He lost his drive for just about everything. Could it be time to find another way to make a living? He liked using his hands. At home he was always working on some kit. He'd started with cars and moved into resin model kits featuring characters from horror movies. Creating Frankenstein and Nosferatu kept his mind occupied. As soon as he finished one project, he shoved it onto an overloaded shelf and dove into another. He would hardly consider himself an *artist*, though.

Right now, he had a girl to find. He took a copy of Phaedra's picture and his notes and went to see Judge Garrett. He outlined the case thus far and held up the picture.

Garrett shook his head. "It's not enough. Burns has cooperated."

"But he's hiding something."

"Can you prove that?"

"No, Your Honor."

"I want to find this girl as badly as you do, but we can't go off half-cocked. You guys have been doing that too much lately. Give me something more, and I'll let you have the phone records."

"Keep this picture, your honor. I'll be in touch soon."

Olivia washed up, treated the scrapes on her hands, and had just enough energy left to drop down on the couch. The doorbell jarred her from a deep, dreamless sleep sometime later.

"Who is it?" she asked, her voice still slurred.

"Delivery from Palomera Flowers, ma'am."

"Who from?"

"I don't know. You'll have to read the card."

She sagged against the door. They had to be from Terry, probably the hundredth bouquet he'd sent her. "I don't want them. Send them back."

The young man's voice grew whiny. "But ma'am, I have to deliver them. It's my job. Besides, they're our most expensive 'I'm Sorry' arrangement. Can't you at least take them? You can throw them away, or burn them, or do the hoochie-koo dance around them for all I care."

She opened the door, and the fragrance of roses assailed her senses. "They're an 'I'm Sorry' arrangement?"

"Yes, ma'am," he said.

"Read the card."

"Uh ... all right. Let's see. 'I'm sorry. Love, Terry.'"

Well, that was a big help. What was he sorry for? "Take them back. Tell Mr. Carlton I refused delivery. Hold on." She returned with a five-dollar bill. "Thank you."

"If you say so."

She heard his footsteps down the hallway. Just as she was about to close her door, a cellular phone rang in the apartment across from hers. The ring was loud enough to make her suspect the door was open. It closed with a rapid snick. That was odd. The owner supposedly used the apartment as a stopover on business trips, but no one had been there in the year she'd lived there.

Now that she was awake, she decided to get some housework done. It was better than moping around worrying about the girl. She was in her closet hanging up clothing, feeling for the little Braille tags that identified what color the item was. Judy helped her pin the small metal tag onto any new item that she bought. She was feeling for the tag on the last item to be hung up when she felt the flash of panic and sank to the carpeted floor. She needed to hold onto the connection this time, to see where Phaedra was being held.

She heard his voice first, eerily like the man who had abducted her years ago.

"Hello, Rose."

The girl scooted to the back of the cage, the bars pressing into her back. He walked closer, his shoes clicking on the concrete floor. Just a scary shadow. A cap on his head shaded his face. A light was behind him.

He knelt down in front of her.

Scissors flashed in his hand!

"Why do you make me punish you all the time, Rose? Why can't you be a good girl and make your mother happy?"

She cringed at the back of the cage, but it didn't matter. He could reach her anyway.

"Please," she whispered. "Please don't hurt me."

"I'm your father, Rose. Call me Father. Say it."

"Father ... please."

"Don't move, and I won't hurt you."

His hand gripped her arm and pulled her closer. His other hand slid around her neck, holding her head against the bars. He grabbed a hank of hair and chopped it off. He showed her the gum lodged in the long brown strands, gum he had put there. He kept cutting. Long hair rained down on her scuffed-up knees. Tears fell on those knees, too. Fear clogged her throat. She heard the last swish of the scissors.

"Now, maybe you'll learn." His voice grew bitter. "But you'll never learn, will you? You never do, Rose."

And in the silence, a sound like a clock ticking.

He watched the girl feel the chopped ends of her hair. Her whimpers crawled across his skin, leaving gooseflesh behind. She looked more like Rose now. That was phase one. In four days, the transformation would be complete, and this tormenting rage inside him would be assuaged.

For a while.

No! This time it would stop. It had to stop.

With gloved hands, he stuffed the strands of long brown hair into a plastic grocery bag. The battery-powered lantern behind him left his face in shadow. Not that he was worried about her identifying him. No one would find her here. He doubted she could escape, but he wasn't going to take the chance. He even wore a cap to further obscure his face. Certainly no one would hear her screams, or at the moment, her soft whimpers. It was ingenious, finding this place. The whole city was looking for her, and she was right under their noses. Sure, they'd checked the building during the grid search. They just hadn't checked carefully enough.

Water dripped into the old porcelain tub in the nearby bathroom. Because this place had long ago been abandoned, the corroded pipes only allowed a small amount of water to trickle through. By the time he'd need it, the tub would be full enough for his purposes.

"I ... want to go home," she said, catching her breath between words. She was staring at her clenched hands. "I want my mommy."

His voice thundered when he said, "Don't you dare talk about your mother, not after what you've put her through. You've been a bad girl, Rose."

As he walked toward the door, he could hear her desperate pleas. "I'm not Rose. I'm not Rose!"

CHAPTER 6

Despite the expensive waterfront location, the LaForge Gallery was approachable, and the artwork wasn't exorbitant. Not Max's type of art, but interesting, nonetheless. One whole section of the gallery was devoted to local talent. He found Olivia's pieces right away. They stood out with their rich hues and abstract eye shapes. For a blind woman, she sure did like vivid colors.

A plaque gave a little background information on her. Very little. *Olivia Howe is a native of Palomera.*

"She's blind," a man said, coming up behind Max. "She won't let me put that on the plaque even though I think it's a great selling point. Amazing, isn't she?" His hair was bleached almost white and set off vivid blue eyes. He was a nice-looking guy, in his mid to late forties. He held out his hand. "I'm Sebastian LaForge."

"Detective Callahan, Palomera Police." Max accepted the handshake, but he was looking at the four paintings. "They're very ..."

"Deep," Sebastian finished when Max couldn't find the right word. "You almost *feel* the emotion."

By the way the guy was looking at Olivia's paintings,

Max could swear he had a thing for her. "Is she like that? Deep and emotional?"

"Oh, yeah." Sebastian's eyes sparkled. "And beautiful."

Max cleared his throat and looked at the paintings again. "Is she really blind? Or is it a gimmick?"

"She's blind. Otherwise, she'd have gone for me years ago." At Max's raised eyebrow, he shrugged. "Two beautiful people should make beautiful love together, don't you think? I'm shallow, what can I say? Besides, I find a sensual relationship helps me to" — he slid his hand down a bronze sculpture of a naked man holding an obscenely long penis out like an offering — "relate better to the artwork. Which means I can sell it better."

"I thought she was seeing Terry Carlton."

"*Was* seeing him is right. They were hot and heavy for about six months. He even moved in with her. Then she broke it off. Wouldn't say why, but she's pretty private."

"You the only gallery in town that sells her work?"

"Sure am. I gave her a break, and she stays loyal to me."

"Does she do any showings?"

"I've talked her into doing one. She hates being in the spotlight. Can't imagine why. She won't do interviews with the press. With her looks and that sexy voice of hers, she'd be a star."

Max rested his gaze on her paintings again. She managed smooth lines and color transitions for someone who couldn't see her work. Which made him wonder, "Must be frustrating when you can't see your end product."

"She gets her joy out of creating it. I've watched her paint. She's *really* into it." He stroked the statue again.

"You know Mike Burns? He may have come in with someone who bought one her paintings, the one that's like watching the sun set from beneath the water, only the sun looks like an eye."

"I *love* those! She's supposed to be working on one for me right now." He tapped his lower lip. "Mike Burns, Mike Burns ... doesn't ring a bell."

"How about Flora Burns?"

Sebastian narrowed his eyes. "Wait a minute. They're the people whose girl was kidnapped, right?"

"We're trying to find that girl, Sebastian." He pulled out Mike Burns's DMV picture. "I need to know if this man was ever in your gallery."

Sebastian gave the picture a thorough look. "Not that I can remember. But I have a couple of people who help out." He nodded toward some strange metal sculptures that Max suspected were nude women. "Then I can create a little art myself." His gaze slid down Max's body.

The guy was interested in Olivia. Right? "Maybe he came in during Olivia's showing."

"Could have. We had a bit of a distraction, so I lost track of who was coming and going."

"A distraction?"

"Terry Carlton showed up. This was after they'd broken things off. People were all excited to meet him, have him sign autographs. Olivia was not happy about his being there, but what could I do? People loved it."

It was hard to picture Carlton as the lovesick spurned suitor. He seemed like the kind of guy who'd be doing the spurning. "I assume you keep records of your customers."

"Sure. We add them to our mailing list. I guess you

want me to look up this guy, huh?"

"Right on."

He sat down at the computer and slipped on some colorful reading glasses. "B-U-R-N-S?"

"Right."

Max watched him type in the wildcard symbol in front of Burns. Four came up, including Flora eight months ago. None were Mike. But that didn't mean he hadn't been in the gallery.

"How far back does this go?"

"Since we opened, two years ago."

"How many of her paintings have you sold?"

He punched the keys. "Twenty-two."

Max tapped his palm on the counter. "Thanks for your help. I'll be stopping by later to show the picture to your employees."

The mid-afternoon sun was bright but tempered by a moderate breeze. The Waterfront was crowded with people lucky enough to have their shopping list as their biggest worry. Christmas music wafted over the breeze from Poppy's Café on the corner. A little girl was in danger, and life just went on.

He glanced in the direction of Olivia's building and felt a pull. Instinct, he guessed; he never ignored his instinct. He cut between the rows of buildings and passed a coffee shop. Unable to resist, he doubled back and bought a cappuccino, hoping no one he knew saw him. He liked what the other guys called "Wussy" coffee. He dug the foam. Besides, he could use the jolt of caffeine. He removed the plastic lid and took a sip. His cell phone chirped as he opened the door to Olivia's building. He stepped aside and answered.

Sam said, "What'd you find at the gallery?"

"Nada. Zip. Zilch. Burns could have been there, and then again, maybe he wasn't. I'm going to check back with the other employees later. What about you?" He could already tell Sam had found something by the tone of his voice.

"The good news is Mike Burns is seeing someone. I just talked to the folks at the Ford dealership. When the shop is slow, he takes off now and then. He usually makes a call before he leaves. One of the mechanics said when he returns, he looks like a guy who just got laid, though Burns denied being with a woman."

Max leaned against the building and thought of Sebastian. "Maybe it was a man."

Sam nearly choked at that possibility. "No, I mean Burns smelled, well, womanly. Perfume, fruit flavors—"

"Fruit flavors?"

"Yeah, you know, those flavored gels."

"Oh, right."

"The edible ones."

"Yeah, I got it."

"That you can lick off—"

"Can it, Sam." Max didn't want those thoughts floating around in his mind when he went to see Olivia.

"We're one step closer to tying those two together. The bad news is, I've gotta back off from him. His lawyer just talked to the lieutenant, crying harassment. I swear that guy couldn't have made me, but he says he's being followed. He's paranoid, which is good. Maybe he'll start getting nervous and make a mistake."

Heat emanated from the building and soaked into Max's tense muscles. He flattened his back against the salmon-colored stucco and closed his eyes for a moment. "I'll ask Olivia if she knows Mike, see what her reaction is."

Sam said, "In seasonal traffic, he would have had about five minutes to get from his truck into the toy store and take the girl. Maybe Olivia was tracking the girl for him and alerted him to the fact that Phaedra went in the store. Or he could have known they'd be at the store that morning. She would have gone willingly with him. Maybe she thought they were playing a trick on Flora Burns."

"We'll figure it out. I'll meet you back at the station in a bit."

Max reluctantly pushed away from the warm wall and headed inside. A tall man with brown, greasy hair flecked with dust was patching a hole where the picture had been hanging. It had fallen down and pulled a chunk of drywall with it. The man's gut rubbed against the wall with his movements. He didn't even glance up at Max.

"Excuse me," Max said. "You the building manager?"

"Yeah."

Play dumb. "Can you tell me where Olivia Howe's apartment is?"

The guy didn't even look up. "Third floor, last apartment on the left."

"Ever see this guy with her?" Max showed his identification and then Mike Burns's picture.

Finally, the guy gave the picture a cursory glance. "Nope."

Max took the stairs and headed to the end of the hall. He knocked, waited a minute, and knocked again. Canned laughter drifted from inside. Another sound caught his ear and shot the hairs on the back of his neck straight up. A droning voice came from deep within the apartment.

He pounded on the door. "Olivia! It's Detective Max Callahan. Let me in!" After another few seconds, "Dammit, open up!"

That protective feeling reared inside him again, bringing to mind the image of that little boy in the cape rushing to save the damsel in distress. He set his coffee cup down and raced downstairs to find the manager. His tools were there, but he was nowhere in sight. Max ran back upstairs and pounded on the door again. There were procedures for this kind of situation, but all he could think about was making sure she was all right. Reacting on instinct and adrenaline, he backed up and rushed the door. Pain radiated from his shoulder, but he'd felt the frame give. He tried twice more before the doorframe splintered. Another try, this time on his other shoulder, and the door broke open.

One of her *I Love Lucy* tapes was playing. Over the laughter, he heard Olivia droning on in a voice that sent goosebumps across his skin. He followed the sound to the walk-in closet. She was huddled in the far corner, rocking back and forth saying, "I'm not Rose, I'm not Rose, I'm not Rose."

Her dog was sitting beside her, looking worried. The dog glanced up at him, at her mistress, then back to him. *Help her.*

Olivia didn't seem aware of his presence. Maybe she was having a seizure.

He knelt beside her. "Olivia. It's Detective Callahan. Max. Olivia, can you hear me?"

She didn't respond at all. Her arms were wound around her bent legs, muscles tensed. He tucked her long hair behind her ear so he could see her face. Her legs were wet with her tears, but he could only see a small portion of the side of her cheek. She was soaked with sweat.

"I'm not Rose, I'm not Rose." Her words sent a chill like a trail of ants down his spine.

"Olivia!" Even his louder voice didn't faze her. What was happening to her? He'd seen something like this in an autistic child once, but Olivia hadn't struck him as autistic.

Acting on instinct again, he sat down beside her and pulled her into his arms. His mouth was next to her ear, and he kept repeating her name in a soothing voice. Heat radiated off her, and she was soaked with sweat.

"Olivia, come back. Come on, you're safe. You're okay. Come back to me." If she didn't respond in another minute, he'd call an ambulance.

She clamped her mouth shut and lifted her head. Now was the time to back off, but he only said, "Are you all right?"

Abruptly, she jerked out of his embrace and scrambled to her feet.

"It's okay. It's me, Detective Callahan." Max rose slowly to his feet so he didn't startle her.

It took her a moment to catch her breath. Stasia climbed all over her in obvious relief, and Olivia smoothed her hands over the dog. "Detective ... Callahan?" She rubbed away the beads of sweat across her forehead. "What are you doing in here?"

"I didn't mean to startle you. You were in some kind of trance. I could hear you from outside the door. You wouldn't answer, and I didn't know what else to do."

Wait until she saw that door. Or at least discovered

what had happened to it.

She made her wobbly way to the bedroom and sat on the edge of the bed. He stayed close by, his hands at the ready in case she lost her balance. Stasia jumped up beside her and rested her chin on Olivia's leg.

"What was happening to you?" he asked, kneeling in front of her.

Her hair was mussed and damp from tears; he stopped himself from reaching to smooth it down. She was obviously still shaken, probably by both the seizure and his presence.

"Is there someone I should call?"

She shook her head.

"You should see a doctor." Again, he felt that odd protectiveness and an urge to pull her back into his arms.

As though she sensed his feelings, she straightened and lifted her chin. "No, I ... I'm fine."

"You kept saying you weren't Rose."

She shivered at that, and Stasia shifted closer. In a faint, hoarse voice, she said, "I know." She squeezed her eyes shut and rubbed her temples. "This is all wrong. It's all mixed up."

"What do you mean?"

She took another steadying breath. "I was connected to Phaedra, seeing through her eyes."

"That's what you were doing?"

She was fidgeting again, her face lowered toward her hands. "I could see the man who has her, but his face was in shadow. There was a light behind him, and he was still wearing the gray cap. I saw the cage again, but ..."

"But?"

"I think my connection to Phaedra is getting mixed up with another kidnapping."

"Has this ever happened before, this mixing up of images?"

She lifted her face to him. "You ask that as though you believe me."

"I'm a cop. I have to explore every possibility." And because he didn't feel much like a cop kneeling in front of her, he rose to his feet.

"No, it hasn't happened before. But this time, it's different. Stronger. And there are other factors." Before he could ask about that, she said, "I know how your partner feels about what I told you — about my being connected to Phaedra. Do you believe in psychic powers?"

"I believe in hunches that pan out. I believe in strong feelings about things. I attribute them to instincts, and I believe that instincts, hunches, all of that could push beyond the five senses. But what you told us, that goes way beyond the boundaries of believability."

She nodded. "Most cops feel the same. My ... hunches, feelings, whatever you want to call them, I've had them since I was a child. I inherited them from my grandmother, who used to host séances and tarot reading parties. If my mother had any abilities, she was too embarrassed by my grandmother to admit it. Then I came along and, well, you can imagine how that went over with my mother. She ..." She paused for a moment before saying, "Sorry, I'm babbling." She paused again. "There's something you should know. The reason I connect to kidnapped children — and only kidnapped children." Her body tensed. "Maybe if I tell you, you'll understand. Maybe you'll believe."

"What's the reason?" he asked after a moment.

She was gripping one hand with the other, crushing

her own fingers in a tight grip. "I was kidnapped when I was eight."

He couldn't help his quick intake of breath in surprise. "You were kidnapped?"

She nodded. "A stranger abduction. He held me captive for five days before I was able to escape. Because of the heightened state of my senses — fear, anxiety — my sixth sense was also heightened. It wasn't until years later, when I got out into the world, that I realized what had changed. The first time I heard about a child being kidnapped, I was drawn into the story. Not just in the way that a once-victim would be drawn into a story of another victim. If you were a victim of a dog attack, say, and you heard a story about another dog attack victim, your emotions would be heightened to the story, right?"

Max caught himself nodding. "Yeah, I understand that." Too well. He leaned against the wall across from her, putting some comfortable distance between them.

Olivia stroked Stasia's fur in a quick, rhythmic motion. "That's how it is for me, only my senses take me a step farther. Once I'm emotionally connected to the child, I see through their eyes. It comes in brief flashes, like images from a movie screen. I have no control over the images or when I connect. The child's emotions trigger the connection. When they're suddenly in a heightened state, I'm pulled to them. It overcomes me. That's what happened at the bookstore, and that's what was happening when you came in."

"So, what you were doing... that's normal?"

She gave him a Mona Lisa smile. "If you can consider any of it normal."

"Well, yeah." He wanted to ask more about her kidnapping, but she continued.

"Whenever I got something useful, I would call it into the police anonymously."

"Why anonymously?"

"First of all, I didn't have to explain where the information came from. They may have thought I was involved in the crime, but at least they couldn't question me as a suspect." She raised an eyebrow in his direction. "I could understand why they would suspect me, but I didn't want to go through all of that. Secondly, well, I was used to hiding my abilities. But the important part was they investigated my leads. And sometimes... I think they helped. Two years ago, back in Columbus, Ohio, I came out of the closet, so to speak. I gave the police information that didn't help find the child but turned out to be right. The next time a child went missing, they called on me."

"Why didn't you tell us this yesterday?"

Her face tensed, and she massaged her temples again. "Because that case didn't go very well."

He could hear the pain of her admission. He didn't know what to make of her. Something inside him wanted to believe her. Maybe he was that desperate for a lead. And maybe, he had to admit, he simply wanted to believe her.

"Why tell me now?" he asked.

"I didn't want to say anything with that other detective around." Max could tell just what she thought of him by the hard tone in her voice. "But if it might help find Phaedra, it was worth telling you."

You. As though she trusted only him.

"Who did you deal with in Columbus?" he asked.

"Captain Jack Richards."

A captain had believed her. "The man who kidnapped you," he couldn't help asking. "Is he alive?"

"No. He can't hurt me or anyone else. I wish I could help more. Now I'm not sure how much of what I see to trust." She pushed herself to her feet. "I'm fine now. You don't have to hang around."

He wanted to ask her more about her own abduction, but she obviously didn't want to talk about it. Besides, it couldn't have any bearing on this case if the man was dead. "There's, ah, a small matter I need to rectify. I broke your door in when you wouldn't answer."

"You *what*?"

"I'll take care of it. Lie down for a bit. You look frazzled. I know a guy who'll come right out."

She followed him to the living room where Lucille Ball was trying to swing her leg up onto a ballet bar — and failing comically. "I don't want to lie down. And I don't want you hanging around. I'm perfectly capable of handling the situation."

He followed her as she made her way to the door. She had clear pathways delineated throughout the apartment. All of her furnishings had rounded edges. If she was faking it, she'd been perfecting the technique a long time. And yet, she sometimes slipped and made contact with an object as though she could see it.

"Be careful," he said, joining her at the door. "Splinters."

He took hold of her hand just as she was about to run it across the splintered wood. She turned toward him, and he was overcome with a rush of something he couldn't explain. Whatever it was filled his chest and made his fingers tighten on hers. He abruptly let go, and she pulled her hand against her stomach as though he'd singed her.

"I'll call my friend," he said.

In the hallway, he wrangled a promise that Rob would be right over. Then he grabbed his cup of cappuccino and walked back inside. She was bracing herself against the wall and trying hard not to look like she was.

"Sit down and let me fix you something to drink," he said.

She walked toward the couch. "I don't want anything." Her voice still sounded shaky, and he had to stop himself from helping her. Her legs gave way just as she dropped down onto the cushion. In a resigned voice, she said, "Some tea would be nice. It's in the last upper cabinet on the right."

He filled the teapot and set it on the stove. His gaze went back to her. She was murmuring words of comfort to Stasia, who followed her like a shadow. He didn't like the protective feeling Olivia engendered. He couldn't afford to be this drawn to someone ... especially when she was a suspect.

CHAPTER 7

Olivia wanted to crawl into the crack between the cushions and die, but she couldn't damn well do that with Detective Max Callahan rummaging around in her kitchen. Even more disconcerting was coming out of the trance and finding a man holding her, his hard, warm body pressed close to hers, coaxing her back with his sultry voice. It was comforting and disturbing at once.

Was she crazy?

Very probably.

What she hadn't told Max was that the connection was stronger if the case was similar to her own — a stranger abduction. Phaedra had been taken from a toy store on the same date that she had; that had to be why it was so strong, and why the connection was getting mixed up with her memories.

"Here you go." He set the cup on the coffee table in front of her. "Do you need sugar or milk?"

"I can get —"

He squeezed her shoulder. "I'm sure you can. But right now, relax and let me get what you need."

She tightened her mouth. In another situation, with

someone who didn't put her on edge, this would be nice. "Sugar, please."

He returned a few moments later. "How many spoons?"

"I can handle this part, thank you." She knew she didn't sound very appreciative, but she wanted to be alone. She poured sugar through the cracks between her fingers, monitoring the amount. "So, break-the-door-down heroics one minute, serving tea the next. I suppose I should be amazed. And grateful."

"And yet, it doesn't sound like you're either." She could hear the sardonic smile in his words. He sat down on the sofa beside her.

"That's because I don't need a hero or a waiter."

Or a sexy cop hanging around. Oh, yeah, she didn't need to see the man to tell he had sex appeal. He had strong hands; she learned that the first time they'd met. His voice was soft in a masculine way. His scent of man and cologne evoked memories of family trips to the Michigan cottage on the lake: fresh breezes, earth, and pines. The way he'd felt with his arms wrapped around her, and the way he'd cared about her, appealing in a man, but not what she needed just then.

She cleared her throat. "Look, you don't need to stay around. Your friend will be here anytime now, and I can deal with him."

"I'd rather stick around while he's here."

"Don't you trust him?" She could feel him lean back and get more comfortable.

"I don't trust anyone. You shouldn't either."

"Why, because I'm blind?" she said sharply. What she couldn't get across with subtle eye contact she could manage pretty well with her voice.

"You sound like you're feeling better," he said, obviously catching the tone. "And I'm not trying to be a hero. Yours or anybody's."

She could also detect those same subtleties in others' voices. The subject of being a hero was tender. "Good, because I don't need one." She'd already said that. Why was he unnerving her so? He wasn't touching her, wasn't sitting too close. But he was close enough for her to know he'd recently had cappuccino with a hint of cinnamon. Close enough to reach out and touch.

She even got as far as wondering what he looked like before she squelched that thought. Bad idea. She picked up the cup and blew across the surface. He'd chosen the mango tea, her favorite. Lucky guess.

"So, you just happened to be in the neighborhood," she prompted.

"Something like that. I wondered how you knew Mike Burns." The question didn't come off as casual as he probably wanted it to. "Isn't that the missing girl's last name?"

"Mike's her uncle," he said.

"Is he a suspect?"

"The Burnses have one of your paintings at their house. I thought maybe you knew Mike, that maybe he was the reason his brother has your painting."

"The name doesn't ring a bell. I'm bad with putting faces with names." After a moment of silence, she added, "That was a joke. If I did meet him, he made no impression on me at all." Mike was obviously a suspect of some kind or Max wouldn't be asking about him. Now he was trying to connect her to him. "Wait a minute. You think Mike took his niece, and I had something to do with it. That I was, what, in cahoots with him?"

"Like I said, I can't afford to discount any possibility. Or to discount the coincidence that you were the one warning the guards about the missing girl who just happens to be his niece."

She laughed, letting sarcasm shine through. Tea sloshed up over the edge of the cup, and she set it down again. She licked the drops of tea from her fingertips. "But you just said it. If I was involved with Mike and the girl's abduction, why would I warn the guards about it?" Her mouth drooped into a frown as she remembered how desperate she'd been and how the guards had ignored her.

Footsteps sounded in the hallway, and she hoped it was his friend. She wanted her door fixed and both of them on their way. But it was her friend Judy's voice saying, "Wow, Olivia, what happened to your door? Oh, hi."

Judy tended to over-pronounce her words, substantiating everyone's opinion that she was slow. "Just a misunderstanding. This is Max Callahan. He's a cop."

"Detective," he corrected, coming to his feet.

"This is Judy Ford. She's the building manager's daughter."

Olivia thought they shook hands, and then Judy dropped down onto the chair to their left. Only then did Max resume his seated position.

"I help him," she announced with pride.

Even though she was thirty-four years old, she acted more like a child. Olivia was pretty sure Judy was smarter than anyone gave her credit for, even Judy herself. Her IQ was just on the low side. Unfortunately, her father kept her from growing into an independent woman by keeping her under his supervision.

"I help Olivia, too," Judy said with that same pride.

"How do you do that?" Max asked.

"I mix paints for her. And read the newspaper. She pays me."

"That's nice of you," he said in a genuine voice. Most people tended to dismiss Judy, or condescend to her. Olivia hated that. "What do you spend your money on?"

"Sometimes I buy a brownie at The Beanery. I save most of it because Olivia says I should. I keep it hidden in my bedroom. My dad doesn't pay me anything to help him. Olivia says thank you *and* she pays me. Like double bonus points!"

A few awkward minutes of silence followed, filled only by the *I Love Lucy* tape she'd put in earlier. Olivia didn't know what to say, and she wasn't good at small talk. Besides, she really wanted some time alone to sort out what was going on in her mind. She'd hoped that once Max had the information he'd come for, his dutiful charade would be over.

Judy asked, "Do you need any paints mixed?"

"No thanks, hon. If you can come up tomorrow, though, that'd be great. The usual time. I need to finish that one on the easel for Sebastian. He's been bugging me about it."

"Max Callahan, you made a face. Don't you like Olivia's paintings?"

"My nose itched," Max said, but Olivia picked up on the lie that threaded through his voice. If people only knew how much their voices gave away. Since most people relied on their visual senses, they didn't pay as much attention to their other senses. "I think her paintings are dramatic. Vivid." His low voice was aimed at her. "Alluring."

Olivia picked up her tea again, needing something to do besides listen to his voice. "Thank you. I think."

"I'm not much of an art critic," he said by way of apology.

"Me either," Olivia said.

"This time he smiled," Judy informed Olivia.

Olivia caught herself nearly asking what kind of smile. Half a minute passed. She pressed the button on her watch. "Two-zero-one."

Judy sighed and pushed out of her chair. "Okey-dokey, I'm going now." Her footsteps were heavy across the floor, something Olivia had been working with her on along with her pronunciation. She wasn't about to call her on it now, though.

"Judy, don't tell your dad about the door, okay? No need to bother him with it. It'll be fixed by tonight."

"It'll be our secret," she whispered. "I'm good at keeping secrets. Bye cop detective Max Callahan. Bye, Olivia."

Her footsteps pounded down the carpeted hallway and faded away, and another set of footsteps sounded soon after. Most people who ventured down this way were visiting her. Except for whoever was staying across the way.

"Good job, Max," a man's voice said, followed by a whistle. "They ought to put you on the S.W.A.T. team."

"Yeah, yeah. Thanks for coming. This is Olivia Howe, the owner. Olivia, Rob Miller."

They exchanged pleasantries, and Rob went to work on the door. She wondered if Max knew for certain that she did own this place, and how much, for that matter, he did know about her.

She listened to Max's voice; not the words, per se, but the cadence and pitch. It was smooth, soft-spoken, yet strong at the same time. She was trying to figure out what exactly made it sound so contradictory when both men's voices were drowned out by sound of wood cracking. She drank her tea and checked the time again. She wanted him to leave and find that girl, not stay and watch over her.

"Who is Rose?" Max asked, startling her because she hadn't heard him approach.

"What?"

"You kept saying, 'I'm not Rose' over and over in your trance."

"I don't know who Rose is."

He was wandering around again. What was he looking for? Between the bursts of noise Rob made, she heard Max pick up her phone, press a button, and hang up a moment later.

She was about to tell him that really, he didn't have to stay with her, when a chirping sound filled the air.

"Callahan. Hey, Sam. Yeah, I'm near one. What channel? All right."

She could faintly hear a man's voice on the other end. "You're not going to like it."

Max didn't say a word as he walked into the dining area, turned off the videotape, and changed the channel. Was there news about Phaedra? She found herself getting to her feet and walking closer to the television.

A man who sounded like a reporter asked, "Mr. Burns, could you tell us why you suddenly lost faith in Detective Max Callahan? He did find that other missing boy, after all."

"I have it on good authority that his family's deaths have affected his job performance."

A woman said, "We understand that he hasn't been assigned to a case like this since then. There must be a reason why, and I know what it is. He might have been one of the best cops on the force once, but he isn't anymore."

Mr. Burns said, "We've asked for the case to be reassigned, but they've ignored us. They think it's because we're angry that they're looking at us as suspects. It's not." His voice cracked. "We just want our little girl back."

The reporter said, "We have a phone statement from Detective Callahan's superior, Lieutenant Huntington. Lieutenant, the family is accusing Detective Callahan of letting the past slow him down on this case. Is he up to handling another abduction?"

"Callahan's one of my best detectives. I wouldn't have put him on the case if I didn't believe that. Remember, he found that boy and brought him back to his family safe and sound."

"But then the kidnapper retaliated," the reporter said.

"That has no bearing on this case."

"Saul Berney killed Detective Callahan's wife and daughter. How can that not impact his abilities?"

As Olivia sucked in a breath at those words, she heard Max do the same.

"Berney *allegedly* committed the crime," Huntington clarified. "We were never able to prove that. Callahan's dealt with that. He's giving his all to this case. We have all the manpower we can spare doing what we can to bring this girl home. Unfortunately, we don't have a lot to go on right now. Something's going to turn up sooner or later, and when it does, we'll break the case wide open."

"We understand you have a suspect?"

"We're questioning a couple of people, and that's all I can tell you at this time. We'll keep you informed. Thank you for the opportunity to comment."

Max turned the sound down. She could sense him looking at her and wished she could see the expression on his face. She knew she looked shocked.

"My God," she said when he said nothing. "How did he ... do it?"

When he finally answered, she could tell he wasn't looking in her direction. "He put a pipe bomb in my wife's car." He was working at keeping his voice neutral, but the emotion lurked just under the surface.

"How terrible."

"It was two years ago."

"You don't get over something like that in two years. Maybe never."

"It's not a matter of getting over it. You just go on because you have to. Do you want some more tea?"

An obvious deflection.

"I'm fine." She knew she should let the subject drop. He didn't want to talk about it, and it was none of her business. But it touched her in a way she couldn't ignore. "How old was your daughter?"

"Ashley was six."

Did he see her flinch? So young and innocent. "I'm sorry." She couldn't tell if he was wearing a wedding ring, and there was no telling whether it was his dead wife's or a new wife's ring if he was. Or why she was even pondering it. Detective Max Callahan was the last man she'd be interested in romantically. They both had way too much baggage between them.

And still, when she'd convinced herself of that, she asked, "Have you remarried?"

His "No" was fast and final. He turned *I Love Lucy* back on, discussion closed.

So, he still loved his wife very much. Maybe he was one of those men who never got over their lost loves. Some people never got past the tragedies of their lives. Because she was one of those, she felt an odd affinity toward Max.

That had to stop here and now.

"Your lieutenant said he was questioning some people. Am I one of those people?" She settled back against the desk that served as the command center to her life: phone, notepad, clock, mail.

"I can't discuss the case with you."

"Because I'm a suspect." She pushed away from the desk and crashed right into him. She hadn't realized he was that close.

His hands automatically went to her shoulders to steady her. "I'm still trying to figure out how you fit into this investigation."

She couldn't help but think of her earlier suspicion. "I'm not sure if I should even mention this."

His fingers tightened almost imperceptibly when he asked, "If you know something..."

"It's going to sound crazy."

He released her shoulders. "Like your being psychically connected to a kidnapped girl."

"Not that crazy. I was dating Terry Carlton up until a month ago. He's been having a hard time letting go of the relationship since we broke up. For the most part, he's been harmless. He's never out-and-out threatened me or assaulted me. It's his persistence that worries me. Phone calls, flowers—"

"Singing telegrams?"

"How did you ... oh, when you came by yesterday. Well, yes, he's been crazy in that way. But now I'm not so sure it's harmless. I think someone tried to push me into traffic this morning."

When she lifted her scraped palms, he took her hands in his and traced his thumb around the raspberries. His touch was soothing and sensual at the same time, and she gently tugged her hands free.

He asked, "Did you report this to the police?"

"No, because no one saw anything suspicious. And maybe someone just accidentally bumped into me. I'd rather think that's what it was. Then later, Terry sent an 'I'm Sorry' bouquet. It made me wonder what he was sorry about exactly, and how far he'd go to keep me from being with anyone else. Or get me back. You know, scare me into thinking I need him. He knows about my connection with kidnapped children. In fact, he even called to see if I'd connected with Phaedra Burns." She shook her head. "I doubt he had anything to do with it. I mean, to kidnap a child to get a woman's attention? That's beyond crazy. Forget I mentioned it."

Of course, Max wouldn't forget it. He was a cop, trained to investigate anything that might lead to a solution to a case. "Has he given you any indication of being that desperate?"

"Not in a concrete way."

"Hey, Max!" Rob called from the front door. "You're all set, man."

In a low voice, Max asked her, "You going to be all

right by yourself?"

"I always am." She heard weariness in her voice and hoped he hadn't. "But thanks for asking." He cared, and that touched her. Maybe because there weren't many people who did care about her.

And that's the way she liked it. Life was easier that way.

"Goodbye, Olivia." As the door closed behind him, she heard him thanking Rob for coming out so fast. Max's voice was the last to fade. Maybe she was still hearing it in her mind.

She touched her shoulder, still feeling the imprint of his hand. Like the residual humidity left over from a mid-day shower, he clung to her senses. Even his voice echoed in her ears long after he'd left. She was drawn to him for some reason. She wanted to think it was his tragic loss, but she really couldn't attribute it to that. She'd felt this before she knew about that.

Hopefully they'd find Phaedra soon, and she wouldn't have to deal with him again.

"You Terry Carlton?" Max asked the man who answered the door, though he recognized him.

"Yeah." He took in Max's badge. "Don't tell me you're going to arrest me for sending her flowers. Besides, it doesn't count when she didn't even accept them."

"Can I come in for a minute? I just want to ask you a few questions."

Terry stepped back as he ran his hand through his curly, shoulder-length hair. "Sure, man." He gestured to a white sofa and dropped down into a matching recliner.

The sofa, it turned out, was covered in fake fur. Max

held back his grimace and surveyed the rest of the house. It was large, but sparsely furnished. A few contemporary pieces here and there and lots of room for more. Nothing suspicious about the house or Carlton's behavior.

"What were you sorry for?"

Carlton reached for a picture frame on the end table. "I think I startled her yesterday. I just happened to see her out walking, and I went up and talked to her." He ran his finger over a picture of Olivia. "No crime in that."

"It is a crime when she's placed a no-contact order against you. What about today?"

"I haven't seen her today."

Max casually stood and meandered toward the dining area. "Nice place." He took the opportunity to scan the back rooms and listen for anything out of the ordinary. He wasn't sure what to make of Olivia's story about being pushed, or her thought that Terry might have taken the girl to get her attention. For all he knew, they could be working together, but he doubted that. "Why Olivia?" he asked, walking back to the living room.

"I know what you're thinking. Why does a guy who can have any woman he wants go after a woman who doesn't want him around?" He shook his head, looking at the picture. "There's something about her. She's soft, delicate. I just want to protect her from the world."

"Are we talking about the same Olivia Howe?" But they were. The woman in the photograph was definitely Olivia.

Carlton's mouth lifted in a half-smile. "I was her first lover. And I intend to be her last. Her only. She'll come around."

Max headed toward the front door. Nothing that would help him find Phaedra there. "Let her come around in her own time."

Carlton's smile turned smug. "I was taught that persistence pays off. That's how I got to the NFL." He rubbed his knee. "That's how I'm going to get back. And that's how I'm going to win that woman back. Without breaking the law, of course."

"Be sure that you don't. Thanks for your time."

The sun glinted off Max's windshield as he approached his car. His sunglasses were sitting on the seat. When he picked them up, they were hotter than a barbeque briquette. He flung them back on the seat with a curse and called Sam. "How did you know I wasn't going to like the news broadcast?"

"Sorry, buddy. That's the last thing you need, all that dredged up again. When the Burnses' publicist arranged for a last-minute spot, the television station called Huntington so they could run his comment afterward."

It meant a lot that Huntington believed in him.

"Did you get anything out of the blind woman?" Sam asked.

"Her name is Olivia, and no, I got nothing." Nothing he'd tell Sam, anyway. He'd never give credence to her vision, and she hadn't given them anything concrete anyway. "She says she worked with a Captain Jack Richards on the Columbus, Ohio police force, helped him with some cases. I'm going to put in a call and see if her story pans out."

"Well, so far she hasn't been a great deal of help. Half the guys at the station think she's nuts. The other half thinks she's involved. I vote for both. Did you ask her about Burns?"

"She says she doesn't know him." He relayed her suspicion about Carlton and his subsequent conversation. "The guy might be an obsessed jerk, but he doesn't strike me as deranged." Max tried to pick up the sunglasses again and discovered the metal frame was bent.

"What about her blindness? She given herself away yet?"

He tried to unbend the frame and broke off the arm. "If she's faking it, she's damn good."

"Women are the best actresses in the world," Sam said in an uncharacteristically bitter voice. He cleared his throat. "All I'm saying is, don't buy into her act."

Max tossed the broken glasses in the back seat. "I'm not buying into anything. What do you have?"

"We just got a break in the case. We know who took the kid."

"And you waited this long to tell me? Who is it, already?"

"Santa Claus."

Max let loose with an expletive. "Funny."

"No, seriously. Remember we saw Santa walking in on the videotape. Well, guess what? That wasn't the guy the store hired to play the great giver of gifts. Our people matched up everyone on the tape. They didn't catch it the first time, because Claude Fernley walked in with a group of people and kind of blended in. If you'll remember, he's a little spit of a guy. Probably needs plenty of padding for his costume."

"Claude Fernley. Isn't he the guy who played Santa?"

"Yeah, but he's not our guy. See, our folks saw Santa walking in and then we had cleared Claude and had him on the list of those who left the store. At first, they didn't come up with any extra people. They went through the tapes again and that's when they saw Claude. It turns out that the guy walking in wearing the suit never left. Not out the front door, anyway."

"Son of a bitch."

"What?"

"There's just something sick about Santa abducting a kid."

CHAPTER 8

He knocked on her apartment door. There was only a slight wariness to her voice when she asked, "Who is it?"

"Officer Bill Williams, Palomera Police Department. I'd like to have a word with you about the Burns case." His southern accent wrapped around his words as snug as a rubber glove.

She opened the door. "Yes?" Her dog pushed its nose through the opening.

"Miss Howe?" he asked, though he knew it was Olivia. When she nodded, he said, "I work with Detectives Callahan and O'Reilly. I heard about your, uh, special skills and wanted to talk to you."

Her eyebrows furrowed at the words *special skills*. "Can I feel your badge?"

He held it out for her tactile inspection.

"I'm not sure what you mean by special skills."

"Your psychic connection to the girl."

Her shoulders sagged a little at that. "I suppose everyone at the police station knows about me."

He tempered his words with soft laughter. "Well, when you have a woman trying to warn security about a missing girl who isn't missing yet, it does get our attention."

Her mouth quirked. "I suppose."

"Can we talk inside?"

After a slight hesitation, she said, "Come in."

She gestured toward the leather couch and sank into the nearby chair.

He stepped around the dog that was still looking at him and sat on the couch. "There's something you should know about me. I have special skills, too."

"You're psychic?"

"I know exactly why you don't want everyone knowing about your involvement, because I've been there. I try to hide it when I know things I shouldn't, try to explain away slips of the tongue." Empathy softened her expression, so he forged on. "It's even harder when you're a cop. You can only explain so many things as hunches. How can you explain knowing what a killer is thinking?"

She leaned forward. "You connect to the killer's mind?"

He made his words come out thick, as though each was painful. "It's the hardest thing I've ever had to deal with." He let a suitable pause go by. "I understand you're connected to the kidnapped girl."

"Yes. I always connect to the victims. Probably because I was a victim once. I relate to them on more than one level."

"Well, I certainly don't relate to a murderer or a child molester."

"I'm sorry, I didn't mean—"

He touched her hand, establishing physical contact. "I know you didn't. Sorry, I can be a little touchy. I shouldn't feel that way with you, of all people. We're on the same side." He gave her hand a squeeze before releasing it. He'd put himself on the defensive and hopefully had drawn her in a little closer. "We understand each other."

She settled more comfortably into the chair, but still leaned toward him. "Are you saying that you've connected to the man who took Phaedra Burns?"

"I ... I think so. Since her kidnapping, I've been getting these images. A large room with concrete floors and green walls. I see the girl, too. She's ... well, I hate to even say it. But I think she's in a cage."

He watched Olivia's face light up. "Yes, that's what I've seen, too. So maybe that part is real."

"Real?"

She waved that away. "I saw the cage. And ..." She ran her fingers down the length of her hair. "Well, it's mostly been flashes. Quick glimpses, rushes of her panic and fear. That's what triggers the connection, when her emotions spike."

"Interesting. What I get seems to be random. Maybe there's a trigger I haven't figured out yet. Can you see the guy?"

She shook her head. "A light behind him casts him in shadow. And he wears a cap."

She had that much right. Then again, she had a lot right.

He said, "I feel a lot of rage coming from him. It's aimed at the girl."

"Does he know her?" Olivia asked.

"I don't think so. She represents something he despises." The dog was sitting at her feet, and it still looked at him suspiciously. Its ears were even tilted back.

115

Olivia said, "And yet, he brings her food. Fast food, orange juice."

"He wants to keep her alive."

"But for what purpose?"

"A sacrifice," he said in a low voice. "She's going to be sacrificed."

She shivered. "Oh, God. But why?"

"Maybe he's a religious fanatic. I haven't gotten enough from him to figure him out. I was hoping we could work together, pull our skills and find her. I want you to be our mouthpiece, Olivia. May I call you Olivia? I feel like we've got a bond, you and I." He touched her hand briefly to punctuate those words. To his relief, she squeezed back.

Her expression was open, trusting. "Yes, you can call me Olivia."

"Call me Bill."

"What do you mean, you want me to be the mouthpiece?"

"If I come in knowing things ... well, I could hurt my career. I've already been passed over for several promotions because the guys in the department think I'm strange. They wouldn't want one of their own to be known as one of those *weirdo psychics*. You know how cops can be."

Olivia nodded. "O'Reilly made it more than clear he didn't believe me."

"O'Reilly doesn't believe in anything out of the ordinary. He's a real hard-ass. What about Callahan?"

"He's at least willing to listen."

"Unfortunately, O'Reilly's attitude is the prevailing one at the station. Psychic clues are disregarded, and if they were to come from a cop, well, I'd lose the respect of the guys and my superiors." He leaned forward, close to her. "You can't imagine how glad I was to hear about you. I knew you'd understand. That you'd help me."

"I'll do whatever it takes to find Phaedra."

"I thought you would. And if you're thinking that I want to be the one to crack the case and get the glory, you're wrong. In fact, if anyone finds out I'm talking to you, it could be my job. Some of the officers and detectives are still working on the Burns case, but I'm not. Maybe if I'm careful about revealing my special skills, I'll move up someday. I need your word that you won't say anything about my talking to you."

"If you're sure ..."

"I'm sure. Maybe if we can find the girl using your-slash-our skills, they won't be so closed-minded about psychic power." He pushed to his feet, paused, and let out a sigh. "There's another reason they might not believe me. I have to be honest with you." He sank back down again. "The one time I laid myself out there and admitted I had a 'feeling' ... I was wrong." Again, he'd let his voice become thick with emotion. "Have you ever been wrong, Olivia?" He had read profiles on a couple of well-known psychics; the cases where they were wrong haunted them.

At least one case haunted Olivia by the shadow that crossed her face. "Yes," was all she offered.

He continued, "I was so sure the missing woman was in the suspect's workshop. I went there instead of checking out another lead. Turns out the lead would have probably led us to the woman in time. If I'd only gone there first ..." He put a hitch in his breath. "How do you know when you've got it right?"

She was twisting her hands in the hem of her shirt.

"You have to go by instinct. There is no way to tell for sure."

He stood again. "Thank you, Olivia. For listening. For helping."

She stood, too. "I'm glad you came. Is there a number where I can get hold of you?"

"I'll be in touch with you, don't worry about that." One more squeeze to her hand, just to seal the bond. "We can find her, Olivia, and prove we're for real."

She had proven to him that she was real. He hoped he'd proven the same to her. That was essential to the plan.

A child-abducting Santa Claus. It was a start. Max and Sam met at the LaForge Gallery and showed Mike Burns's picture to Kristine Banks, the employee working that afternoon. Several people wandered around the gallery pretending to look at the art, but surreptitiously listening to them.

Kristine's country-fresh looks with the sprinkling of freckles across her cheeks contrasted with the slick atmosphere of the gallery. She pursed her mouth as she studied the picture. "He may have been here during her showing."

"May?" Sam asked.

She shrugged. "I'm not sure. We have a lot of people at our showings, coming and going." Her smile turned positively glowing. "And Terry Carlton came in, and he is just *so* hot."

"Look at the picture again," Sam urged.

"He looks kind of familiar, but ..." She shrugged again, handing the picture back.

"You're not sure," Sam finished, his disappointment obvious.

"Sorry. What's this about, anyway?"

"Ongoing investigation. Look, here's my card. Call me if you remember anything more definite."

As soon as they stepped outside, Max pulled out his cell phone. "Judge Garrett asked for a little more when I tried to get a warrant for phone records this morning. He's gun-shy because of the Monterra and Gencarelli cases. Maybe that Santa suit will give us an early Christmas present."

They stepped to the wrought iron railing away from the overhead speaker spilling festive music. Max waited until Garrett came on the line and outlined what he had.

"You said a little more, Your Honor. I admit it's only a little. But look at that picture I left with you. Are you looking at it?" Max didn't have to picture Phaedra's face. She was smiling from several fliers tacked to posts and taped inside store windows.

"You're pushing me, Callahan."

"I want that girl home by Christmas. Help me." That only gave him four more days.

Garrett paused, and Max held his breath.

"All right, I'll give you phone records for both of them and credit card records for Burns. Give me an hour."

"Cell phone, too?"

The judge paused. "And cell phone."

Max exhaled in relief. "Thank you, Your Honor."

"Show your gratitude by finding that girl and not making me look bad."

Sam had been following the conversation as best he

could, and he made a triumphant gesture when Max thanked the judge. "That's the most spunk I've seen out of you in a couple of years."

Max ignored that. "We've got phones for both and credit cards for Burns in an hour."

"Great. That gives us enough time to eat."

The aroma of steak made Max's stomach growl. Poppy's Café was in the corner of the adjacent building. Tables spilled out from beneath the awning so diners could enjoy a view of the water and the people strolling by. Poppy's was pumping out their own Christmas music; their hip-hop version clashed with the traditional tunes coming from the overhead speakers.

Max nodded toward the café. "Let's grab something here."

Sam eyed the place. "This is one of those overpriced joints, probably charges twelve bucks for a burger and fifty cents for cheese besides."

"I'm buying."

Sam followed Max to the hostess stand. "Can't hardly argue with that."

They were seated at one of the outside tables. Bright rays spilled out from behind the cloudbank that covered the lowering sun, reminding Max of a religious painting. He stretched out his legs and leaned back in the small ornamental chair. More ornamental than comfortable, to be sure.

Sam was staring across the way, lost in his thoughts. Not good thoughts, if the lines etched across his forehead were any indicator. He had been Max's mentor and friend over the last several years. Max always had older men as friends. It had something to do with the father figure thing, but he'd never given it much more thought than that. After all, he was too old to need a father. Sam was his closest friend. Their families had done things together, boating, picnics, birthday parties. All that seemed so long ago.

The surprising remark about women being great actresses echoed in his mind. "How's Annie?"

Sam blinked. "Annie? She's fine. Great."

The waitress brought two sodas and took their order: two twelve-dollar cheeseburgers.

"See, the cheese is included," Max remarked as he handed his menu to the waitress.

"Such a deal."

To the untrained eye, the setting sun was a fitting end to a peaceful day. Max knew that somewhere in town, it wasn't peaceful. Somewhere, a little girl was waiting to be rescued.

He saw that movie in his mind again, the boy in the cape, candlelight flickering against the walls, and the moment that haunted him still. *Coward!* But he hadn't been a coward, not that time.

"Maybe this Santa thing will be our big break," Sam said, busting into Max's thoughts.

"I sure hope so. We could use one. It's a hell of a case so far." He felt guilty sitting there eating while Phaedra endured God-knew-what. He reminded himself that people all over were looking for her, either physically or by way of digging up records and backgrounds. Prayer vigils were going on all over town. He glanced at his watch.

Sam drummed his fingers on the glass tabletop. "We haven't had a stranger abduction in a couple of years. Does that make it more or less likely that's what this is? We know it isn't Berney anyway, since he's in jail." Realizing that was a sore subject, he said, "Nick Mathers said the lieutenant called you into his office this morning. Said you looked a little shook when you walked out."

Max shrugged. "He thinks I'm a ghost."

"Huh?"

"He says I've been walking around like the undead." He weighed how much to tell him, and then decided to dump it all and get a second opinion. "I know he's cut me slack these past two years, not putting me on cases that involve children or anything tough. Maybe it's softened me. Maybe I'm not cut out to be a cop anymore."

"That's bull. You told me you wanted to be a cop since you were a kid. And you're one of the best cops in our station."

Max hadn't told him *why* he'd wanted to become a cop. He hadn't told anyone about his past. His wife Diana used to tease him about being hatched, though beneath that teasing tone was hurt that he wouldn't share his past with her. Just one more thing wedged between them. All he would say was both his parents were dead. To say more would mean telling her everything. That was something he couldn't do.

"*Was* one of the best. I'm honest enough to admit I'm not anymore. I don't even know if I can be that guy again." There, he'd said it. He felt a weight in his chest lift.

"I think you're ready to come back. Oh, you've been fighting it, but you're ready."

"That's just it. I'm not ready. I don't have the drive anymore. Not for the job, not for anything. Maybe a change would do me good. Change of job, even a change of scenery."

Sam narrowed his eyes. "Sounds like you're running away."

"Getting away. There's a difference."

"Yeah, right."

A change of friend was looking good, too.

"What you need," Sam continued after a moment of silence, "is to sell that house. Too many memories. There's your change of scenery. You haven't changed a thing about that house since ... since then. You just sit there doing those creepy monster kits. Morbid, if you ask me."

Hell, he wished he hadn't opened this conversation. But Sam was right. Their memories were there. Diana's memories lurked in the closet, the bottom drawer in the dresser, and all the other places she stashed her bottles of vodka. Sometimes, out of long-engrained habit, he still checked. The drawers were empty now, but his anger was still there. He held onto it the same way she'd held onto her addiction.

When he'd helped her off the booze the first time, she'd promised to come to him if she felt herself slipping. As far as he knew, she'd been clean for two years before she got pregnant. There was no reason to suspect she'd taken it up again. Then again, he wasn't home much. He'd been too busy chasing the bad guys.

All she'd wanted was his forgiveness. Sometimes he wished he'd given her that, or at least pretended to, before she'd died. His anger never went away, not when he was constantly reminded of what she'd done.

Ashley had finally started growing out of the physical effects of Fetal Alcohol Syndrome: the flat bridge of her nose, the lack of a ridge on her upper lip. When the doctor had informed them that the deformities were a result of Diana drinking during her pregnancy, she had been in denial. It had taken her a year to admit she'd been drinking heavily for a good part of her pregnancy, and that the problems Ashley faced were her fault. Then she'd gone through a phase of blaming everyone else for her drinking, including Max.

There wasn't time for a lot of blame, though. Ashley had several problems through her first years that required attention, including two surgeries to repair her damaged heart. She was smaller than average, too, which had made Max feel even more protective of her. She'd been so damned brave through all those doctor's visits and the surgeries, he'd wanted to cry.

Then the behavioral problems had started: hyperactivity, poor judgment, trouble learning from consequences. By then, Diana had taken responsibility for her daughter's health and started dedicating herself to doing whatever she could to make Ashley "normal." She'd also rededicated herself to their marriage. Max had stuck it out because they owed Ashley a family. He'd do anything for her, including staying with a woman he no longer loved, but he couldn't make himself love Diana again. That hadn't made him any less shattered over her death. In some ways, it had made it worse.

The waitress brought their food, and Max pulled himself out of his grim thoughts. He realized that Sam had also been deep in thought, staring blankly at a blonde walking by. They ate, and Max paid the bill so they could collect their warrants. They would compile a list of area costume shops while they waited for the phone records to come through, and then start hitting them in the morning. If they could tie Burns to a Santa suit, they'd be on their way.

As they both pushed to their feet, Max's pulse jumped. He saw Stasia first, and then Olivia walking behind her. She wore a dark blue shirt and a long orange skirt.

Sam followed his stare. "Why, if it isn't the enigmatic Miss Howe."

Max only nodded, unable to stop looking at her. Her long hair swung gracefully as she walked, and her shoulders were high and straight.

Sam snapped his fingers in front of his face. "Let's go."

That they'd follow her was assumed. If she met up with Burns ... that's why Max's heart was racing. Maybe this would be their break in connecting the two of them. He couldn't pinpoint why the thought turned his stomach.

Surely the woman wasn't derailing Max, though he couldn't forget the image of her licking drops of tea off her fingers, the mango scent wafting from the cup. Or the way she measured out sugar.

The walkway was wide and covered with light and dark red bricks in alternating patterns. The railing was ornate black wrought iron accented by an old-fashioned streetlamp every few yards. It was a perfect backdrop for a beautiful woman walking with her dog.

Sam said, "You like causes, Max. Underprivileged kids, Fetal Alcohol Syndrome ..." He paused. "Blind women with that fragile look."

Max forced a laugh. "That woman is nowhere near fragile. She's not even in the same country as fragile." He tried not to think about her huddled in the closet or the way she felt in his arms.

They stayed several yards behind her. She passed the

round Edgewater building and the crowds of people waiting for their movie to start. When she led Stasia to the dog section of the park, Max and Sam casually leaned against one of the large oak trees. Even if she couldn't see them, Mike Burns could. Max scanned the area, but his gaze kept returning to Olivia.

"Max, why don't you head on back to the station and pick up those phone records? I'll hang around here and keep an eye on her. It looks like she's going to be here a while and there's no use both of us standing around."

Max reluctantly pushed away from the tree. "All right. I'll meet you back at the station."

For some reason, he wanted to tell Sam that he should be the one watching her. He kept the words inside and headed to his car.

Olivia had the strongest feeling that she was being watched as she made her way back to her apartment. She had never considered herself paranoid, but now she was beginning to wonder. She remembered a girl she'd gone to school with. Lisa Morris had been rendered blind in a car accident two years earlier. Her biggest fear was not being able to see if someone intended to do her harm. "You can't tell if someone is coming at you or following you," she'd told Olivia. "They could be right there, and you wouldn't see them. By the time you'd know you were in danger, it'd be too late."

Lisa's words echoed as Olivia opened the door to her building. She knew there were certain vulnerabilities to being blind, but she didn't want to dwell on them. Now, though, they were hard to ignore. She breathed out in relief as she reached her door. Just as she inserted the key into her door lock, someone grabbed her arm.

She spun around, her heart going into overdrive.

"I'm sorry, I didn't mean to frighten you," a woman's voice said. "My name is Flora, Flora Burns. I'm Phaedra's mother."

Olivia was even more startled by the woman's identity than by the sudden touch. Before she could gather rational thought, Flora said, "I understand that you're involved in my daughter's case. That you're a psychic. Please, I need to speak with you."

Olivia took a deep, calming breath. "Come inside. I'll fix some coffee." She flicked on the light switch for Flora and hung up her coat. After releasing Stasia, she went about the task of brewing coffee. "How did you hear that I was involved in the case?"

"My husband said he didn't know who told him. Apparently, someone called and told him, but didn't identify himself."

"Was it the same person who made him doubt Max Callahan's capabilities?"

"I think so. He doesn't tell me much, to be honest. I only overheard him telling Joanna, our publicist, about you. He was concerned that if word got out about your involvement, all manner of unstable people would come forward and clutter the case. Oh, I'm sorry. I didn't mean to imply —"

"I know." That's just how people were, and why cops like Bill had to keep their talents hidden.

"I'm a Christian woman. I just hope He doesn't punish me for coming here to see you. You being psychic and all," she added.

Olivia tried to hold back her annoyance at people who thought the devil must bestow such powers. "I believe God gives people the ability to go beyond their five senses. How they use it is another matter altogether. How do you like your coffee?"

"I'm glad to hear that. Oh, here, let me." She spooned in sugar and stirred noisily. "I understand you're ... well, they said you were blind."

"I am." Olivia measured in sugar and milk and stirred. "Let's sit down in the living room." She led the way, settling into her favorite chair while offering Flora Burns the couch. "You want to know about your daughter?"

"Wow, you are psychic. I didn't know ... well, I'm impressed."

Olivia smiled. "It doesn't take a psychic to understand why you're here, Mrs. Burns."

"Please call me Flora. You've seen my daughter. That's what they said, that you can see her. That she's alive."

The raw hope in her voice made Olivia wish she could offer more. "She is alive. The man who took her hasn't hurt her, and hasn't touched her in any sexual way." She wouldn't tell her about the cage, or about Bill's feelings that the girl was to be sacrificed. "That's all I know, I'm afraid." Olivia wondered just who had told Pat Burns all this.

"Can you go to her now? Give her a message from me?"

"It doesn't work that way. I can't summon her up or speak to her. I see through her eyes when she's at a heightened state of emotion. I see flashes and get emotional impressions. I've been trying to see where she is. All I know is that it's a room, and it's fairly dark."

Flora smothered the sound of a sob with her hand. "She's so afraid of the dark."

"He leaves a light on for her."

"Oh, thank you, God, thank you, God."

Such small consolation. "Mrs. Burns — Flora, I'm not working with the police. I'm a suspect, actually. You should know that."

"Why? What could you have possibly had to do with her disappearance?"

"I knew she was abducted before anyone else did. Before you even knew."

Another sob erupted, though Flora regained control again. "I told her to stay close, but I kept talking. I didn't make sure she stayed nearby."

Olivia reached out and touched her arm. "Please don't blame yourself. It only takes a few seconds. They wait for the slightest opportunity."

Flora wrapped her fingers around Olivia's hand. "We're suspects, too, Pat and I. The police said it's usually a family member who's involved. And ... well, Pat took out an insurance policy on Phaedra. Five hundred thousand dollars. The police think that's a large amount to take out on a child. I don't know why he even did it. It's like he was investing ... betting on her death." She stifled another sob. "Our restaurants are on shaky ground financially. The police will eventually find out, and they'll think he arranged this horrible act for the money. But I know he couldn't hurt our daughter. I know that."

Olivia thought she might be trying to convince herself. Unfortunately, she couldn't say anything to quell the woman's doubts.

Flora loosened her grip on Olivia's arm. "You'll keep trying to see where she is, won't you?"

Olivia's voice was thick with conviction. "I'll never

give up."

"I'm sorry I barged in on you. I just had to speak with you."

"Please don't give up. Detective Callahan is doing the best that he can. He'll do anything within his power to bring your little girl home." Somehow, she knew that was true.

Flora stood. "May I come to see you again? I feel closer to Phaedra when I'm with you."

Olivia touched her hand. "Come anytime."

A few minutes after she locked the door behind Flora Burns, Stasia growled. The hairs on Olivia's neck sprang to attention, and she tuned in with all of the senses she had.

Breathing. She could hear someone breathing. Her chest felt tight, making it hard to draw a breath. She could smell cologne--the same cheap stuff she'd smelled before someone pushed her into traffic!

"Terry?" she whispered.

She'd changed her locks after he'd moved out, but she supposed he could find a way to break in. Taking deep breaths to calm her heart, she unlocked the door and stepped into the hallway. "Flora? Hello? Is anyone out here?" Only one of the apartments was occupied full time, and she rarely ran into her neighbors.

Stasia growled again as she pressed close to Olivia. Soft footsteps came closer. A scream froze in her throat. Someone was standing in front of her. She had never felt so vulnerable since ... since her own abduction.

Then he walked past her and down the hallway. She sagged against the wall. The door to the stairwell opened and closed. He made no attempt to rush or to mask the sound of his departure. That arrogance sent a shiver through her.

She pushed away from the wall and was about to slam the door shut when she heard faint music coming from the apartment across from hers. She knocked on the door. "Hello? Is anyone there?"

She wiped a shaky hand across her damp forehead and knocked again. No answer. She wobbled back to her apartment and locked the door behind her. With the adrenaline draining from her body, she dropped into the chair in the living room. Stasia jumped up into her lap. She held her dog close and fought the nausea rumbling through her stomach. Someone had been in here waiting for her. Listening to her conversation with Flora Burns.

Should she call the police? And tell them what, that she thought someone was in her apartment but couldn't prove it? And that that someone could be Terry Carlton? They'd probably still think his persistence was a romantic gesture and wonder why he was wasting it on a cold fish like her.

The phone rang, jarring her. She made her way on shaky legs to the nearest phone.

"Olivia, it's Terry. I'm just checking on you, making sure you're all right." He was on a cell phone.

"Why?"

"It's our connection, sweetheart. I felt distress just now."

He was full of it. She wrapped her fingers around her throat. "I'm fine. Goodbye, Terry."

How far would he go to prove that she needed him?

CHAPTER 9

Friday, December 22

Ah, there was his Rose, huddled in the corner of the cage. He came by in the pre-dawn hour before most of the world got started. In the dim light, he saw her wide eyes watching him as he approached the cage. She was trembling, and her small hands were wrapped around the bars. There were no windows down here, no natural light at all. The air was thick, only what came in through sophisticated ventilation systems.

"I'm a good father, leaving that light on for you, aren't I?"

She wasn't looking at him.

"That's all I ever wanted, you know, to be a good father. To make you into a good person and keep you in line. You can't blame me for that, can you? Can you, Rose?"

She wouldn't answer. That's how she'd always been.

Wouldn't listen to him, wouldn't answer. They had been adversaries since the beginning.

He walked around to the other side of the cage. "You don't care what I do for you. It's never enough. You think you're entitled, don't you, Rose?"

He set a large cola next to the cage and collected the wrappers from the sandwich he'd left the night before. Not a thank you or a please to be found. "Drink the soda. All of it, right now." He also set a gallon jug of spring water within her reach.

She picked up the cup and finished the soda through the straw. "I'm hungry," her raspy voice said. She sounded breathless when she looked up at him and said, "I'm hungry, please."

That was better. He held up the bag of food. "What have you done to deserve food? Did you scream after I left?"

She vigorously shook her head. No one would hear her anyway, not through four feet of concrete. He should have brought a tape recorder to see if she had. She was always lying to him. Just last month she'd looked him right in the eye and told him she hadn't left her bike out by the road. Two months before that she'd lied about leaving the carton of Rocky Road ice cream on the counter to melt.

"You're lying, Rose."

"I'm not."

He shook the cage, and the little bit of bravado she'd mustered shrank away. She huddled into a ball again. He couldn't move the cage much. It was made of heavy steel. He'd fashioned it from a storage bin, working with a blowtorch. The bars went around three of the sides; it was solid in the back.

"You're always lying to me, Rose, from the moment you could talk. You learned 'mama,' 'milk,' 'hi,' and 'bye,' before you learned to say 'father.' That hurt me, Rose. You never loved me, did you?"

"I'm not Rose." Her voice was stronger this time, even though she was saying it into the crack between her knees.

He let out a long sigh. "And still you deny me. I want you to call me 'father' again."

She shook her head, her face still pressed to her knees.

"Say it!"

She didn't move this time, didn't respond at all.

"Your mother and I don't know what to do with you anymore, Rose."

She let out a gasping sob at the word *mother*

"You've made her very upset. You know that, don't you, Rose? She cries in frustration. Do you know what that does to me to see her crying?" He slammed his fist to his chest and his voice cracked when he said, "It kills me. You won't be a bad girl ever again. After Christmas night, you won't ever make your mother cry again."

Max and Sam spent the morning checking out local costume stores, all the while dogging the phone companies and credit card company for their records.

"That was a waste of time," Max said as they headed to their car after the last shop.

"He could have bought it out of town."

"Or at a garage sale, for that matter."

"Or ordered it from out of state." Sam settled into the driver's seat and expelled a long breath. "Maybe Pat ran into financial trouble and hired Mike to get rid of the kid for the money. Olivia could be involved with Pat or Mike, though no one seems to think Pat is having an affair. Kinda strange when a father puts a big life insurance on his own kid. Unless..."

"He's planning to cash in," Max finished for him. "We've seen it before. But Pat took out the policy three years ago."

"That's what insurance policies are for, in case you need them in the future."

Mike was their prime suspect, with Pat Burns as a secondary, but Max's gut feeling told him neither was involved. Sam, on the other hand, would not let go of the only leads they had: Olivia and the Burns men.

"We're going to nail them," Sam said, determination burning in his voice. "One way or another. Don't get too interested in Olivia Howe, Max. She's going to go down with them. I wonder who'll squeal on who first."

"I'm not interested in her." But his stomach rebelled every time he thought of her as a suspect.

"Because the way you looked at her last night when she walked by —"

"She's nice-looking, and that's the end of it. If I wanted sex, I could probably scare up someone to oblige."

It was more than sex appeal that drew him to Olivia, though she certainly had appeal. It didn't take much to conjure an image of running his fingers through her hair — he loved long hair — or opening that cynical mouth of hers with his tongue ... no effort at all. He couldn't afford to explore what the draw might be exactly.

"What about that blonde who was after you?" Max asked, steering both their thoughts away from Olivia. "The neighbor who was always needing a man to help her fix or move something. Didn't she have a boyfriend who was stalking her?"

"Helene?" Sam shrugged. "Not a thing. The boyfriend's out of the picture now. I told her to stop bothering me."

Max's phone chirped, and he took the call. "Great, thanks." He disconnected and turned to Sam. "Credit card records are on their way. Let's grab some lunch and take it back to the station."

They both looked up when a Cadillac sped past them.

"Isn't that Pat Burns's car?" Sam asked.

"Yeah. He's in a big hurry. Let's see where he goes."

"Whoa, take a look at this," Sam said as Burns's car pulled into the Waterfront apartment parking lot a few minutes later. He jumped out of his car and barreled toward the buildings.

Max said, "He's checking out the numbers like he doesn't know where he's going exactly."

"Maybe Olivia usually met him somewhere else. Now that we're moving in on them, they're getting panicked."

They followed Pat Burns at a distance as he walked into Olivia's building. Raised voices filled the third-floor hallway.

"I had a feeling you were coming here. Dammit, Flora, she's a fraud! How much money did you give her?"

"Nothing!" Flora said. "I just wanted to talk to her. She didn't ask for a dime."

Olivia said, "I don't want your money."

Max and Sam rounded the corner to find the three of them at Olivia's doorway. Pat stalked over when he spotted them.

"I hear that you're employing psychics to find my

daughter. Is that the best you can do? People aren't going to take this case seriously when they hear about this."

"She's not working the case, Mr. Burns. She came to us with some crazy story, that's all. The woman's a suspect." Sam looked at Flora. "I'll bet she didn't tell you that."

"Yes, she did, right up front."

"Oh."

"How'd you know she was involved in the case?" Max asked Pat, thinking that was the obvious question here.

"I don't want her anywhere near my daughter's case." Pat turned on his wife. "And you, stay away from her! She might not be asking for money now, but she will be. That's how they all work. She doesn't know anything. If she did, we'd have our girl home by now."

"Amen to that," Sam muttered.

"Flora, go home. I'll meet you there." Pat started to leave, but paused and looked at Max. "If you botch this, I'll have your badge, your home, and your car."

"Where are you getting your information?" Max asked again.

"I don't know. Someone's been leaving messages at my office."

Pat left, followed quickly by his wife after she'd whispered an apology to Olivia.

"I want to know where the hell he's getting his information," Max said to Sam before walking toward Olivia. "You all right?"

She gave a noncommittal shrug. "A little yelling and deriding never hurt anyone."

"You didn't contact Mrs. Burns?" Sam asked.

"No. I never contact the family, only the police."

Sam put his cynicism into full gear. "Oh, that's right, all those cases you've solved over the years."

She faced Sam. "I did help once. I described the man who had taken the boy. If they'd used the sketch publicly, they would have caught him much sooner. Over the years I've given the police a bit here and there."

"And was it enough to catch the perps?"

She shored up her shoulders. "No." And she hated herself for it. Max knew that feeling too well. "And sometimes the connection ... stops before I can get any clues."

"Why?" Sam jumped in.

Her mouth tightened. "Why else?"

"Your so-called psychic power peters out? Runs out of juice? Needs another quarter?"

Her fists clenched tighter with each word. She didn't want to say it. Max could see the reluctance and pain on her face. He was about to say *Lay off*, but she answered before he could.

"They die, dammit! I can't see through their eyes when they're dead!" She sank against the closed door, her voice and anger draining. "They die, and I couldn't help them."

Max was clenching his own hands now. "That's enough, Sam."

"Let's get out of here," Sam said, heading toward the stairs. Once they were outside, he said, "If Pat and Olivia are working together — maybe even involved — the last thing he wants to hear is that his wife is visiting his cohort. So, he calls her a fraud and orders his wife to stay away from her. Convenient. I want Pat's phone records, too. I'm getting closer — we're getting closer. I hope you're with me on this."

"Sure." But Max wasn't sure at all.

A couple of hours later, Max and Sam had gone through the credit card listings and were finishing up with the phone records. So far, they had zip to connect Mike and Olivia.

Sam surveyed the mess on the conference table. "It doesn't prove anything. Maybe they use payphones. Maybe Pat Burns made all the calls." He wasn't able to persuade the judge to give him warrants for Pat's phones.

"It was a waste of time." *And warrants*, Max didn't say. "Maybe the answer isn't here."

He slumped in his chair, feeling a mixture of relief and frustration: relief that it wasn't looking like Olivia and Mike were working together; frustration because he should be hoping for a connection.

Sam studied Max from across the table. "You're glad we can't pin it on Olivia, aren't you? I know she's a pretty blind girl and kinda tugs at your heartstrings. Add the dog, and it's sap city."

"No one's tugging at my heartstrings."

"A woman can have a way of appearing all soft and sweet and innocent and be the devil inside. Don't lose sight of that."

Max narrowed his eyes. "Are things all right between you and Annie? That's the third time you've said something like that."

Sam's expression shuttered. "Annie and I are fine." He pushed to his feet and grabbed Max's mug. "I'll get us some coffee."

When Max's cell phone rang, Sam paused.

"Callahan. Oh, yes, thanks for calling. Can I call you

right back? My partner will want to hear you, too." He hung up and redialed on the speakerphone. "Captain Jack Richards, from Columbus, Ohio," he told Sam as it rang. "I appreciate your calling me, Captain. I'm here with Detective Sam O'Reilly. We're working on a child abduction case, and Olivia Howe has become ... well, involved. She says she's psychically connected to the girl we're looking for and claims that she's worked with you in the past."

"Yes, she has," said the voice on the other end of the phone. "To tell you the truth, I didn't believe in that psychic stuff."

"Didn't?" Sam asked.

"Let me put it this way: I don't scoff at anything anymore. She was pretty right on with some things. We received a couple of anonymous tips in years past, giving us information that, along with our own leads, led us to our man. Then, two years ago, she walked in claiming to know what the guy who had just abducted a young girl looked like. She wanted to work with a sketch artist. We had no leads at the time, so we indulged her. Unfortunately, we didn't circulate the sketch. I didn't want it to get out that we'd used a psychic."

"You caught the guy?"

"Eventually. The thing was, he looked almost exactly like the sketch. It was enough to convince me to at least explore the possibility that she was real. A few months later a boy was abducted by his abusive, non-custodial father, so I called her in. It was a tough case. She did connect to the kid, told us she saw a barn. We tracked down the barn, but they were already gone. They had been there, though; hair samples proved that. Then she saw an isolated house, which was harder to track down. The problem was, by the time we could make use of what she was telling us, they were gone. It was rough on her, though she held up as best as she could. But afterward ... when we found the boy beaten to death ... she took it hard. Real hard. I know she blamed herself for not finding him in time. Soon after that, she told us she was moving down to Florida. Said her father had finally moved into a health care facility down there. That's the last I heard from her."

Max had seen a haunted look on her face. She had lost the connection with the boy, and it tore her up. "Did she want recognition? Money?" he asked, anticipating the questions from Sam.

"Just the opposite. From the beginning, she absolutely didn't want her name released or associated with the case. I wouldn't discount what she says, that's for sure."

"Thanks for your time, Captain."

"Doesn't prove anything," Sam said when Max disconnected. "Maybe she knew where the boy was because she was in on that, too. Maybe this is what she does, if not for fame or money, then for sick kicks. It takes all types, you know that."

"I don't buy it."

"I didn't figure you would." Sam grabbed his mug again, looked at the dregs in the bottom and set it down. "I'm going out for some real coffee."

Max watched him leave. Sam's body was tense, his movements stiff. What was going on with him? Sure, they usually zeroed in on a suspect early on and dug until they found something concrete one way or the other. But Sam's case against Olivia seemed personal. If he didn't know Sam better, he'd think it was because she was a woman first, and because she claimed to be psychic second. How well did he know Sam? Max had to wonder now.

Lieutenant Huntington stepped into the conference room and scanned the table. "Anything? Don't make me look bad in front of Garrett. I'm already on shaky ground with him."

Max shook his head. "If there's a link between Olivia Howe and Mike Burns, we haven't unearthed it yet. We're working on a link between her and Pat Burns. With the insurance policy he took out, we can't discount him as a suspect."

"Wasn't he at his office when the girl was taken?"

"That's what the office manager said. He could have slipped out a window or had Mike or someone else do the deed."

"What about the woman?"

"Either she's psychically connected to this kid or she's involved. I just talked to Captain Jack Richards up in Columbus, Ohio, where she lived for fifteen years prior to moving here over a year ago. He seems to think she's the real thing."

"What do you think?"

"I'm open to just about anything if it means a lead. Beyond what she said at the store, there's nothing to indicate she's involved in Phaedra's abduction." Max picked up her phone records. "I'll track down who she's been calling frequently and see if that leads us to anything interesting."

"And if that doesn't pan out?"

"We got nothing." He was staring at all the papers on the table, stacked and categorized. "It's like the girl disappeared into thin air." He ran his hand over his face and rubbed away the fatigue. He thought Huntington had gone, but he was watching Max from the doorway.

"You want off the case, Callahan?"

The words struck Max like a fist. He remembered the man's faith in him during the press conference. "Am I not doing a good job, sir?"

"You haven't found her."

"I will," he heard himself promise.

"Tom Graham has wrapped up his case and wants to work this one. He's just getting started on another homicide case. I'm giving you the chance to swap cases and step away with your dignity intact if it's getting too much. If you're sinking."

Coward! he heard his father say. Max slowly blinked, clearing away the harsh voice from the past. His father was dead. And Max wasn't a coward. No way was he handing Tom this case. Tom didn't have what it took, didn't have the patience. "I appreciate what you're doing, but I've got it under control."

He couldn't walk away. It was already too late.

All Olivia wanted to do was forget about that scene outside her door. She locked the door and intended to absorb herself in music to soothe her frayed nerves. When she turned on the stereo, the volume was so loud, it knocked her back a step. "All right, I know I like my music loud, but not that loud."

Wait a minute. The same thing had happened with the television that morning. She rubbed a fresh onslaught of goosebumps from her arms. Who would break into an apartment just to turn up the volume knobs? Unless that's not all he did.

Another crop of goosebumps blistered her skin.

Maybe she should report the intruder to the police after all.

"Yeah, I can't identify him, prove he was here, or tell whether he took anything, but oh, I know he turned up the volume on my stereo. They'd jump right on that."

Her sarcastic laughter rang hollow in her ears. Someone had come into her apartment. Who? Why? "Don't think about it. There's nothing you can do. Nothing." Frustration swamped her. She was pacing, hoping her movements would keep the fear at bay. "Not afraid," she whispered on a shaky breath. "I am not afraid," she said in a stronger voice.

The knock on her door nearly sent her through the ceiling.

"Who is it?"

"Bill Williams. I need to talk to you."

She recognized his honeyed southern voice and unlocked the door. Good. She'd ask him to take a look around. "Come in."

"Hi, there, girl," he said to Stasia. He remained near the door after he'd closed it. "I had another vision. I think I know where she is."

Her hand went to her throat where her heart had lodged. "She's all right? I haven't gotten much from her today. Just some unease, not enough to allow me to connect to her."

"She's fine. Well, as fine as she can be."

"You saw where she's being held?"

"She's on a boat. There were some numbers on the bow, but I couldn't see them clearly. There were letters, too, the name of the boat probably. I saw a T and an R. It was so quick, I couldn't see enough of it." His frustration at that was clear. "It's a serious fishing boat, probably more than fifty feet long. I think it has rigging on the sides and the chair in the back. It's painted dark gray, kind of old looking. It's docked in the harbor."

"Did you tell anyone?"

"Remember when I said you'd be my mouthpiece? This is the time. If you even hint that you got this from a cop, they'll know it was me, and my career will be sunk."

"But there are so many officers on the force. How would they know it was you?"

He touched her arm. "I'm the only cop they know who has special skills. Sam O'Reilly will be on me like a swarm of bees."

She remembered how cutting Max's partner was.

Before she could say anything more, he gave her arm a slight squeeze. "We can find her, Olivia. *You* can find her. You can be the one to prove that what we see, what we feel, is real. Then maybe I'll be able to use my skills openly someday."

She felt an odd apprehension at that. It was probably because of the difficulty in passing off someone else's vision as her own. "Can you get to the harbor and take a look around? Maybe you'll see the boat. Then I can send Max Callahan right to it."

"I can't. I'm on my way to relieve some officers on a stakeout. My partner's in the car right now, and it was hard enough to get him to stop here for a few minutes. You can do this, Olivia. Do it for Phaedra. Do it for every kid who didn't get found in time."

She swallowed hard and nodded. "Let me get the details straight." She recited what he'd told her, rewarded each time by an enthusiastic affirmation. He surprised her by touching her cheek. "This is an important thing you're doing. I'll be listening to the radio, hoping for good news."

With that he was gone. She found herself rubbing her cheek and wasn't sure why. She walked to her desk and picked up Louis, her personal organizer. Her finger traced over the buttons as she searched for Max's number. She held it up to the telephone and it dialed for her.

She was bothered by the catch in her breath at the sound of his soft, low voice when he answered. "Detective Callahan, it's Olivia. I think I know where Phaedra is."

"Max, I can't believe you're here because of that strange broad," Sam said as they traversed the boardwalk. "Hell, I can't believe *I'm* here."

"Because if she's right, I'll need your help. And because we don't have any better leads to follow. And because time is running out, in case you didn't notice."

"Yeah, and I also noticed you didn't exactly tell a lot of people we were coming out here."

"Just enough so that if we disappear, they'll know where to find us."

Sam snorted. "Comforting thought."

Max scanned the boats at the harbor. Most of them were luxury or sporting boats. He focused on boats spiked with fishing poles and radar antennae. Serious fishing boats.

"Keeping her on a boat makes sense," Max added. "Especially if they're moored far from the other boats."

The late afternoon air was filled with sound, possibly enough to cover any sounds the girl might make. His gaze went to one in particular that was moored farther from the rest. He could see no activity on-board, though a dinghy was tied to its side. It sported a dozen fishing poles and several antennae that speared the air. A high platform allowed the captain to scout for schools of fish. Sun and saltwater had dulled the gray paint. In scrappy letters on the bow was the word *Trawlblazer*. His heart rate doubled.

"That's it. She saw a T and an R."

"Yeah, and over there is the *True Blue*. And over there, the *Rutting Bull*."

"But they're not gray. Come on, let's find a way out to it."

Fifteen minutes later, they'd hired a guy with a small boat to come up beside the boat. Max glanced at Sam. "What is it you're supposed to say?"

Sam raised his badge and called, "Permission to come aboard! Palomera police."

A guy appeared on deck and scowled. "What's this about?"

"We'd like to take a look around your vessel. There's been a report that a young girl is on this boat, and we need to check it out."

Two other men appeared from inside. "I wish we had a girl on board," one of them said with a lascivious snort. "But we don't."

"Then you won't mind us taking a look around for ourselves."

The first man shrugged. "Come on aboard."

Max and Sam climbed aboard. Sam remained on deck with his gun prominently in view. Max took the search detail. His body was tensed, ready for anything. He could feel his heartbeat in his throat, pulsing in a combination of anticipation and fear. He kept his gun at his side as he went into the upper-level cabin. This had been a luxury yacht at one time, but age now tarnished the finishes. A couch wrapped around two sides of the cabin in the living room. The kitchen sported a full-sized refrigerator and even a dishwasher. He went below.

The cabins were cluttered, the beds unmade. He checked beneath the beds and in all the various closets and cubbyholes but found nothing more than the living habits of three unkempt men. It wasn't until then that his heart rate returned to almost normal. He kept his gun at the ready as he checked for any doorway or hatch he'd missed.

"How do you maintain the engine?" he asked the men when he stepped onto the back deck.

"Down here." The man lifted a small lid and gestured down some steps. Max climbed down them and looked around. He climbed back up and then checked out the captain's platform. He hated giving Sam a subtle shake of his head when he returned. "Thanks for your time," he said to the men and climbed down to the boat.

"I'm not even going to say, 'I told you so,'" Sam said as he followed.

"Good, because we're going to check out that boat over there, too. And if that one doesn't pan out, you cannot say it again."

"Don't tell me you believe that woman is psychic."

Max met his skeptical gaze. "Right now, I'd believe in the tooth fairy if I thought it would help us find that girl."

Olivia hadn't felt Phaedra all day other than a ripple of unease. As evening approached, she grew more worried. What was happening? Was she--?

"No, don't think like that. She's still alive."

She finished off her Snickers bar and realized all those calories were wasted. She'd been too busy worrying to enjoy them. It was just that Phaedra's fear had leveled off. She had been a captive for three days now, and the man's appearance alone wouldn't trigger her fear. In a sad way, she'd become used to the fear. Olivia remembered reaching that plateau. She couldn't handle being afraid all the time. As day passed into day, she had also started giving up hope of getting home again.

Hopefully Phaedra hadn't given up yet.

Max had kept his voice neutral when he'd called to tell her he had found nothing. He didn't have to tell her that she'd brought him disappointment and embarrassment ... and given his partner more fuel for his skeptical fire.

Bill had seemed so sure. Sometimes it happened that way. Like her seeing Phaedra's captor cut her hair, for instance, her mind inserting parts of her own trauma into the girl's experience. She knew other psychics got things wrong, too. Once she'd realized that she was connecting to these children, she'd done some research on psychic phenomena. Even the most renowned psychics made mistakes. It still didn't offer much comfort.

When the phone rang, she grabbed for it. Bill's southern voice filled the line. "I heard the bad news. I'm sorry, Olivia. I must have misinterpreted what I saw. Or maybe it's in another harbor."

"Well, I don't think Detective Callahan is going to check out any more harbors on my word."

"Probably not. What about you? Anything?"

"Nothing yet. I'm worried about her."

"Me, too. We'll find her. Don't give up on me, Olivia.

I'll be in touch."

Since the Snickers bar made no impact, she decided to open a bag of chocolate chip cookies. When she couldn't rip the bag's seam, she opened the cutlery drawer and grabbed a knife. She jerked back with a scream. Her first thought, as the blade bit into her finger, was that a snake was coiled in the drawer. "What the ..." She stuck her bleeding finger in her mouth and felt around the edge of the wooden tray with her other hand. The steak knives were always in the left slot with the edges pointed down.

Only the sharp edges were pointed up now. Every knife had been turned the wrong way. *On purpose.*

Terry's voice echoed in her head. *Dammit, you need me! What do I have to do to prove that to you?*

She slammed the drawer shut. "Okay, this isn't funny. The volume was one thing. This was meant to hurt me." It was time to report this to the police, whether they believed her or not. She wanted someone to take a look around and make sure there weren't any other booby traps. Dammit, if she could see — "Don't even go there."

She was trying to decide whether to call the main number at the police station or Max Callahan when intense discomfort flashed through her. She slid to the floor and let the connection take her to that dark room again.

Phaedra's voice, "Please, I have to pee. You made me drink all that water."

"I don't hear you unless you call me Father."

"Father ... I have to pee."

He lifted an empty gallon jug of water and then checked the floor to make sure she hadn't spilled it. "You'll have to hold it in. I only have time to bring you food, not long enough to take you to the bathroom."

"But—"

"Don't talk back to me, Rose. And don't wet yourself. You're a big girl; you can hold it. I'll be back later."

He couldn't leave her. He'd made her drink all that water. He couldn't make her hold it any longer.

But he was. He closed the door behind him. For a moment, silence. And then the sound again. Dripping water.

She crossed her legs as tight as possible and stared at the door. Please come back. Please. It was painful now. Her jaw was sore from grimacing.

A gold shamrock rested on her knees, dangling from a chain. She grabbed hold of it and ran her fingers over the edges. "Mommy, please come get me. Daddy ... that man, he's not my father." Her voice was raspy from non-use. "I'm Phaedra, not Rose, not Rose."

Olivia jerked out of the flashback, catching her breath. Stasia's cold nose was pressing against her arm, and she was pawing at Olivia's hand.

"You can't bring me back, sweetie," she said, stroking Stasia's head. "I know you're frightened for me, but I have to do this. I have to stay with her long enough to see where she is. I wish you could understand me."

She went over what she'd seen, confused again by the similarity with her own experience. The cap and the shadows obscured the man's face. She did see a splash of light against the wall — the wall was green, just as Bill had said. But the part about him insisting she call him Father, the haircut, him calling her Rose, and now the water ... why was she getting the two abductions confused? Why —

She slapped her hand over her mouth. What she'd *seen.* Why hadn't she realized it before? She had never seen the jug of water or the bars from inside the cage. As soon as she'd seen the cage as he'd been about to put her in it, she'd fought him. They'd struggled, he'd knocked her out, and when she woke, she was blind. She'd never seen any of that.

Yet she was seeing it now. Because it was real. All of it.

She rubbed her temples. "No, it can't be. He's dead." The authorities had been sure; there had even been a witness.

It had been logical to assume she'd gotten the real images and her memories confused ... but she had no visual memories to confuse. "It's him. He's alive."

There couldn't possibly be two insane men with the same agenda. That would mean the man who kidnapped her hadn't died. That he was still taking girls for a reason that had never become clear. What had been plainly clear to her was that he'd intended to harm her. He'd talked about punishing her on Christmas night, but he'd never said what he was punishing her for or how he was going to do it.

She walked on weak legs to Louis and had her personal organizer dial Max Callahan's phone number.

CHAPTER 10

The clock on the conference room wall read 9:30. They'd each taken half of Olivia and Mike's phone records to start tracking down who they had talked to prior to the kidnapping. Sam watched Max staring at the lines he'd drawn through several numbers. His brown hair was messier than usual, the random cowlicks sticking straight up in places.

Max absently tapped the tip of his pen on the stack of papers in front of him. "Something's not right about Olivia's boat vision."

"No kidding," Sam said. "I think she's trying to distract us from the real clues the same way she distracted the guards at the store."

"What real clues? We've got nothing." He continued the tapping motion. "No, it's something else. Something —" His cell phone rang. He dropped the pen on the table and picked up the phone. "Detective Callahan." His face transformed from interested to puzzled. "Okay." He hung up and pushed all of his papers into a file. "I'm going to head home and get a couple of hours of shuteye before I fall over dead. I'll have these figured out by morning. See you at seven."

Sam watched Max head out. They'd been working for hours. He could use some shuteye himself; tomorrow they'd be back at it. He shoved his papers into a file and walked out.

Max got into his car and drove out of the parking lot. Sam followed from a safe distance. Just as he suspected, Max led him right to Olivia's apartment. Sam wanted to follow him right up those stairs and call him on it. He glanced at the clock in his car. He had his own trouble to see to.

"Max, be careful," he said, pulling out of the parking lot. "Trouble can sneak up on a man just like that."

How well he knew that.

Olivia had sounded shaken when she'd called. Not that it mattered. Max would have rushed over anyway. That she wanted to talk meant she had something new. They needed a lead so bad he'd take anything, even from a psychic who'd been wrong. He wasn't sure why he hadn't told Sam about the call. Probably because he would have come along and blown it.

The moment he knocked and identified himself, she opened it. Again, he felt that upheaval whenever he first saw her.

"Thanks for coming so soon," she said on a breath of relief.

"You all right?"

"That depends on you." She backed up and let him in. Her hair was tied in a loose ponytail; shorter strands trailed around her neck. She wore baggy blue jeans and a white blouse. Her bare feet thumped softly across the wood floor as she walked to the kitchen. She said over her shoulder, "Coffee?"

"Definitely. Thanks." The aroma of coffee mixed with the vanilla and something feminine tantalized his senses.

The lights on her stereo danced in rhythm to Peter Gabriel's "Games Without Frontiers." He followed her into the kitchen and leaned against the end of the counter. "Need any help?"

"I've got it, thanks."

And she did, taking down two mugs and setting them on the countertop. She put her finger in the mug and measured out milk to the first knuckle. Then she sifted sugar through her fingers. Even as he doubted her, he found her blind idiosyncrasies intriguing.

"You've got quite an impressive music selection," he said.

"I love music. An ex-boyfriend took my collection and burned mixes for me so I could sort them by type of music or mood."

She pulled the carafe out of the coffeemaker and felt the mug's placement before pouring the coffee. She didn't look down at what she was doing. Her chin remained lifted, and she seemed to stare at the bank of cabinets in front of her. Both cups were under-poured, no doubt a safety precaution to keep from getting burned. He noticed her hands were trembling.

She handed him a large, blue mug. "Black, right?"

"Yeah. How'd you know?"

She shrugged and gave him what he'd call a Mona Lisa smile. "Sorry I don't have a cappuccino machine. Working with hot steam would probably be dicey."

"How'd you know I drink ... your sense of smell, right?"

"It's one of my major senses now. I rely on it the way

you rely on your sight. It tells me things that I can't see, and sometimes it tells me things that *you* can't see either." She took a quick breath. "Please, have a seat."

She tucked herself into the large chair in the living room; Stasia sat at her feet. Olivia rubbed the dog's back with her bare foot. He sat at the end of the sofa closest to her and took a sip of the richest coffee he'd ever had.

She cradled her mug in her hands. "I've been sitting here trying to think of how to say this. No matter how I put it, it sounds like crazy, so I'm just going to lay it out there." She took another quick breath. "I know who took Phaedra."

This reminded him of his conversation with Sam earlier. "You waited this long to tell me? Wait a minute. You're not going to tell me it's Santa Claus, are you?"

"I didn't know he was on the suspect list."

"Never mind. Go on."

Her fingers tightened on her mug, making her knuckles stand out. "I told you I was kidnapped when I was eight years old. I was taken from a toy store that used to be in downtown Palomera, December twenty, sixteen years ago."

"December twenty? That's—"

"The same day Phaedra was taken, I know. I thought it was just an eerie coincidence. He also lured me into a back room. When I woke up from the chloroform, I saw the cage he'd intended to put me in. I panicked and tried to escape. In our struggle, I got knocked out. When I woke, I couldn't see."

As she spoke, her foot movements became more rapid. "The man who took me tried to make me into someone named Rose. That's what he called me, drilling the name into my head. He also insisted I call him Father. He held me prisoner for five days, and almost every day he set me up so he could punish me afterward. I was lucky ... no, blessed would be a better word; I was able to escape thanks to a guardian angel. I pushed most of the details out of my mind. I don't even remember my captor's name; maybe my parents never told me what it was. But it didn't matter, because he killed himself before the police could apprehend him. We moved out of town soon afterward and started a new life in Ohio."

Max said, "Wait a minute. You were kidnapped down here? I thought ... well, I got the impression it had happened in Ohio."

"The kidnapping was why we moved to Ohio. Otherwise we would never have moved away. My father loved this area; that's why he wanted to come back."

Max's throat had gone dry and prickly. He was paralyzed, waiting for her next words.

Her fingers were so damp, they slid over the handle of her mug. She set it down on the coffee table and faced him. "But he didn't die. He's the man who took Phaedra. He's doing the same things to her, making her call him 'Father,' calling her Rose ... and the punishments. Some of the things I saw when I connected to Phaedra made me think that, because of the similarities of our kidnappings, I was getting my memories mixed up with what was happening to her. I didn't tell you everything I'd seen for that reason."

She nervously smoothed her hair back from her face. "I connected with her a little while ago. That's when I realized I wasn't seeing my memories." She shook her head. "When I saw her this time, she was rubbing a gold shamrock on a chain, and he ..." She took another breath. "I realized that I couldn't be inserting my own memories, because I couldn't see anything. What I'm seeing has to be through Phaedra's eyes. He's alive. Detective Callahan, are you listening to me? I know I gave you wrong information before, about the boat, but I swear to you that this is real. You've got to believe me."

"I'm listening." She knew about the shamrock necklace. It still didn't prove she was psychic. In fact, it was yet another reason to think she was involved somehow. The rest of what she'd said, that's what had made him feel as though his insides were being pressed between two blocks of ice. His voice nearly cracked when he said, "I'll look up your case and see what I can find."

"I wish I could help more. But I can only help if you believe me."

He pushed himself to his feet, and she mirrored his action. He was surprised when she reached out and grabbed his arm with her uncanny precision. "Find her, Detective Callahan, before he can punish her again."

"Tell me about these punishments."

"He played the same sick game with me that he's playing with her." Her face tensed with worry, and her fingers tightened on his arm. "He made her drink water all day today, but when he brought her dinner, he wouldn't let her go to the bathroom. He told her not to wet herself. But she's not going to be able to hold it." Her voice was breaking. "And when he comes back, he's going to wash her clothes and blankets and make her spend the night damp and naked."

Her eyes glistened with unshed tears. He didn't like this, her showing emotion. It was easier to think of her as cool or just plain crazy.

"She's going to be all alone in there, cold and alone." She released him and wrapped her arms around herself. "Yesterday he put gum in her hair and accused her of doing it herself. He chopped it all off, all those long brown locks. Tomorrow he's going to starve her all day, then leave a plate of fried chicken within her reach — and order her not to eat it. She will, of course. Just like I did." Her voice dropped to a scared whisper. "And when she eats it, he'll make her eat hot sauce, enough to get her sick."

She blinked, and two teardrops rolled down her cheek. In those few seconds of silence, he heard Peter Gabriel's haunting song, "In Your Eyes." It was all he could do not to pull her hard against him. The lieutenant was right. This case was sucking him in, but in a way he could never have imagined. So was Olivia Howe. He just hoped he could grab enough breath to last until he surfaced again.

"I have to go." He wondered if the desperation in his voice was as clear to her as it was to him. It seemed to take all of his effort to open the door and push himself through. *One foot in front of the other, just like always.*

He hoped she was crazy — or at least wrong. He couldn't afford to believe anything else.

Olivia pressed herself against the door after Max left. The coolness of the steel soaked through her skin to mingle with the chill in her heart. She looked up. "God, you led that boy to save me. Lead us — or someone — to save her. Please."

She had believed it was an angel that had taken her hand and led her to safety. His soft, cherub-like voice had said, "Come with me," as though he often saved lost girls. She would have gone anywhere with him. His small hand was tight on hers, pulling her away from the hell she'd endured for five days. Once they'd started running, all she could hear was the hammering of her heartbeat and the buzz of fear. And his erratic breathing. He'd been as afraid as she'd been, but even when she'd fallen, he'd been in control, pulling her to her feet and urging her on.

She turned off the light and wondered if she were tired enough to sleep for a while. Tired, yes; but way too wound up to even think about it. She felt the rush of panic at the same time that the sound of an opening door took over her consciousness. Her legs went to jelly as she slid to the floor.

"Rose, were you a good girl while I was gone?"

A cry escaped her mouth. The pee was strong enough for him to smell. No way to hide it. The wetness soaked both her underwear and pants and felt clammy against her bottom. "I ... couldn't hold it anymore. I'm sorry." She tried to bite back the sob. She wanted to tell him it was his fault. He couldn't punish her for wetting her pants. But she was afraid to make him madder. For good measure, she even pushed out the word, "Father."

She saw his mouth grimace. "All I asked is that you hold it in a little longer. Was that too much to ask?"

She didn't answer. It wouldn't matter what she said.

He thrust his hand through the bars. She flinched at both that and his harsh voice as he said, "Give me your clothes. Now!"

As she pushed out of her pants, he said, "What kind of father would I be to leave you in soiled clothes? I'll wash them for you."

Trying to keep her lip from quivering, she handed him

her pants with the cotton panties wadded up inside them.

"The shirt, too."

She pulled it off and handed it to him, even though it wasn't wet.

"And the blanket. I'm sure you got that wet, too."

"I didn't."

He held his hand out, and she pulled the blanket from the corner and gave it to him.

"I can't believe my daughter still wets herself. It's shameful, that's what it is. Your mother thinks you're doing it on purpose, maybe to punish me for being so strict."

He walked into the bathroom at the end of the hallway, rinsed out her clothes, and hung them over a shower rod to the right. He shut out the light and walked past her. Without another word, he left, locking the door behind him.

She curled up on the floor of the metal cage, cold and damp and naked. Only then did she let herself cry.

And in the background, the dripping noise. Coming from the bathroom. Water dripping from the clothing into the tub. *No, can't be the clothing, because I heard it before. Water dripping into a partially filled tub.*

With a searing flash of pain in her head, Olivia came out of the vision. Stasia whined and set her chin on Olivia's leg. She scratched the dog's head, pulling her thoughts back to the connection. She'd been able to stay longer this time. Perhaps Stasia hadn't realized her mistress was having one of her strange visions until just then.

He wasn't keeping her in a truck trailer. This was a building of some kind with a regular bathroom. And a tub that was filling with water. What was he planning to do with it?

She wished she could help, wished she could somehow comfort the girl. She kneaded her aching temples, huddled the same way Phaedra had been in her cage.

It took a few minutes to gather the strength to get to her feet. She used furniture to help her get to a phone.

"Hallo," Judy answered in her usual way.

"It's me, Olivia. Do you have time to mix some paints for me?"

"You're painting now? It's kinda late."

"I know, but it's important. Can you get away for a few minutes?"

"Sure. Dad's not here. I'll be right up."

Olivia had to do something to help Phaedra. She had just enough time to change into her painting clothes before Judy knocked on the door.

Olivia let her in. "Thanks for coming up."

"What colors do you need?"

Olivia conjured the colors in her memory. "Gray-white, black, and a medium green with a gray tint added."

"Okey-dokey."

Olivia could have used primary colors that didn't require Judy's help in mixing, but she wanted to get the shades just right.

"That Detective Max Callahan was really cute." Judy liked using people's full names, a habit Olivia had dissuaded her of where her own name was concerned. Judy was good at remembering names, though, a skill she could take to the workplace someday. If her father ever let her get a real job.

"He was, was he?" Olivia said, trying not to sound too interested.

"Yepper. Brown hair, kinda messy, like he'd been riding a motorcycle. Dark green eyes, like Emerald Green."

She was obviously thinking of colors she had mixed in the past. "No, more like Moss Green. Do you remember what Moss Green looks like?"

"I think so." She tried to conjure up a memory of moss growing on a tree trunk.

"And he has girly eyelashes."

Olivia couldn't help but laugh at that. "Girly, huh?"

"Black comes before Green, and W for White is last. Yeah, thick and curled up. Do you want to go out with him? 'Cause you were smiling when I described him. I think you should be with Terry Carlton."

Olivia frowned. "Why is that?"

"Because he said so."

"He did, did he? Recently?"

"Yesterday."

Olivia tried to hide her annoyance at Terry enlisting Judy's help. "I don't want to go out with either of them."

"Good, then I can go out with Terry Carlton. He's nice. Oops." One of the jars hit the floor, and Judy swiped it up. She recited the formula for the color she was mixing. "But I remember you said to be careful around men."

"That's right, hon. You're a special woman, and a man could take advantage of that."

"I'm retarded," she said so matter-of-factly, Olivia flinched.

"You're not retarded. Who called you that?"

"Dad calls me that all the time. And other people sometimes, too, uh-huh."

"You're not retarded. You're just a bit slower than some people. Don't let anyone call you that. And remember what I said about the *uh-huh*."

Olivia wasn't expecting the hug, and it nearly took

her off-balance.

"You're so nice to me," Judy said, sounding choked up. "I love you, Olivia."

"I love you too, hon." Olivia's throat felt tight as she hugged Judy back.

Judy pulled away. "Okey-dokey, I gotta go before dad comes back. He doesn't like when I leave the apartment at night."

As Judy turned the doorknob, Olivia asked, "Who owns the apartment across the way from me?"

After a pause, Judy said, "I have to go. Night, Olivia."

She said, "Wait!" The door had already slammed shut.

She locked the door and inserted the magazine of women rocker CDs into the stereo. The Bangles filled the room with their sassy music. She related to the simple messages of rock and roll, good old-fashioned sex, and plain attitude. It was the music she wasn't allowed to listen to growing up and the attitude she wasn't allowed to have. Her parents were right; the music wasn't appropriate for a sophisticated young lady. Which made it all the more appealing when her friends at the Barfield School for the Blind had played it.

She set the painting in progress to the side and put a fresh canvas on the easel. Could she capture where Phaedra was? She pulled the chair in front of the easel and oriented herself. She dipped her finger into the gray paint and swirled it across the canvas. It was easy to imagine that much of it, but hard to imagine a more final product. If only she could see amber again, or ochre ... or Moss Green.

Don't think about what he looks like. What does it matter anyway?

She'd long ago given up trying to imagine what people looked like. She'd never get it right anyway. So why did she want to "see" Max?

She pushed Max from her thoughts and concentrated on the painting. Working with concrete ideas was harder than creating abstract art. She had no idea if she was keeping the lines straight or connecting them. The more she worked, the more she was convinced she was doing nothing more than messing up a canvas. She'd been working for an hour when she rubbed the paint off her fingers and stretched. "Time for a break. Let's go for a walk, Stasia."

Stasia whined happily at the prospect, though Olivia was less overjoyed at leaving the apartment. On the way out, she paused by the door of the apartment across from hers and listened for any sound. It was silent tonight. Maybe it was nothing, and maybe Judy didn't know anything about who owned the place. But she couldn't ignore the feeling she had about that apartment.

CHAPTER 11

Two hours later, the notes on Olivia's case were coming across the fax, pulled up by a clerk in archives. Max tried to ignore the crushing sensation in his chest while he waited. Once all the pages had come through, he headed to one of the conference rooms and shut himself in. His shaking hands made the papers unreadable. He set them on the table and tried not to let his gaze skip ahead. He read every word, just to make sure; but he didn't need to make sure. Something deep inside him had known from that first meeting. That's why he'd felt drawn to her.

Olivia had been kidnapped sixteen years ago, December twentieth. Taken from Boyd's Toys. Without a trace. By Bobby Callahan — Max's father.

Max had tried hard to push that part of his life into the farthest corner of his soul. Now it reared up in his face. Only brief notations alluded to Max's childhood: *mother deceased, moved around with father a lot*. Cold facts that said nothing of his life and what he'd gone through.

For as long as he could remember, it had been only him and his father. They moved to wherever Bobby could get work, usually living way out in the boonies where he could fiddle with truck engines.

His father was a disciplinarian. Whatever he said, whether it made sense or not, was the law. If Max disobeyed, he paid for it. Not that Bobby hit him. His punishments didn't leave marks. Max shivered, feeling colder by the minute. They were like Olivia had described: psychological in nature. Being locked in his closet all night for talking back; going without food for a day if he didn't finish every crumb on his plate. And then there were the tests.

Sometimes Bobby wanted to use Max to get revenge. He forced Max to release the neighbor's goats because they had asked him to keep the noise down as he tinkered with his truck. When one of the neighbor girls had snubbed Bobby, he tried to get Max to cut off her long braid. Other times, Max didn't know the reasoning — if there was any. Eating live worms from the backyard, for instance. Letting a roach crawl on him.

Do it! Come on, you little coward!

Sometimes he passed the test, and sometimes he failed, refusing altogether. Either way, he felt like a coward. Even pretending he was Superman didn't help. His father was his kryptonite.

Bobby found a job as a truck driver when Max was eight. For two years that job was a godsend, both financially and emotionally. It meant his father was away for two to three days at a time. Though Max always had a list of chores to accomplish before his father's return, he treasured those days of peace. If Bobby was going to be gone over a weekend, he either took Max with him or left him with his sister, Odette. Though Max liked riding in the rig, he preferred the timid Aunt Odette, who let him do what he wanted.

Leading up to the day that changed his life, Bobby had started acting more agitated than usual. Moodier. Darker. Max hid his flu symptoms, not wanting to do anything to incite his father. They usually spent Christmas Eve and day with Odette at her farm. Max was doubly glad to hear his father announce a five-day run that would take him until Christmas night. The plan was to leave Max with Odette. She was visiting with a friend the three days before Christmas, and her friend had four children. She couldn't take Max with her when she realized he had the flu, so Max had gone with his father.

Bobby hadn't been happy about that, but he'd simply thrown Max's suitcase back into the cab and headed out. He'd given Max only one order, and he'd repeated it every day: do not go into the trailer of the truck. If he'd listened, he wondered what would have happened to Olivia.

He hadn't listened. They'd pulled into the back section of a rest stop for the night. They were the only truck in the lot. As usual, Bobby ordered Max to stay put and went into the trailer. He went back there several times during the day and spent hours there every night. Max was feeling dehydrated from the stomach flu he'd had for five days. Bobby had been giving him prescription cough syrup to help him sleep, but it had upset his stomach that night. He didn't want to face the wrath of his father if he got sick in the cab. As it was, Bobby was also starting to come down with the flu, complaining of queasiness and fatigue. Max knew he would catch hell for giving it to him.

Max climbed down and inhaled the fresh, cool air.

A car pulled into the rest stop. A small strip of trees separated the truck lot and the building. Even through the trees, he could see a family stumble out of the car, stretch, and head toward the building.

He felt a stab of longing. Two young boys, a mother and father. Laughter crossing the distance. A family, heading somewhere for Christmas. Max had his comic books, his superheroes. That's all he needed.

Except for a 7-UP. He didn't want to get sick again. Odette sometimes gave him a can to settle his stomach, but he didn't have any change. He searched the ashtray and other crevices and came up with twenty-four cents.

That when he'd heard the sound. It was faint, like a mouse being captured by a hawk, only it sounded like it was coming from inside the trailer. Was his father okay? He walked around to the back of the trailer. Bobby's warning rang in his head. He heard the sound again, but it was abruptly cut off.

Maybe he'd just peek through the small door in the back and make sure his father was all right. He opened the door and found a box partially blocking his view. He pushed his head into the opening so he could see around it. Two flickering candles provided the only light inside. A tub sat near the back corner with several jugs of water around it. An empty cage sat in the other back corner. Had he captured an animal?

His father was wearing a military uniform, an old one. He was kneeling over something, talking in low, ominous tones.

A shiver trilled down his spine when he heard the sound again. Whimpering. *Human* whimpering. Bobby was looking down at something — no, someone ... and he was holding a knife. Max closed the door and sank to the pavement.

The family was returning to their car. The boys were both eating Popsicles from the vending machine. Should he get them to help? He didn't even know what was going on.

A scraping sound sent him to his feet. The door swung open. He rounded the corner of the trailer a second before his father rushed into the woods and started throwing up. Max didn't have to think about what he should do. He'd played Superman and Batman long enough to know. He climbed into the back of the trailer — and froze.

A girl was lying on the floor, her hands tied to the bars of the cage. She was dirty and smelled like urine. Her hair was cut in ragged lengths. She was only wearing a pair of pants, and a fine cut stretched diagonally across her small, bare chest. She was awkwardly curled up on her side choking back sobs.

"Don't cry, Livvy," she told herself over and over, as though giving herself orders.

He didn't give himself time to feel the horror that churned his gut and threatened to overwhelm him. He grabbed the knife Bobby had left on the floor.

She gasped when he'd placed his hand over her mouth and whispered, "Shh, be quiet, Livvy," as he cut the ropes. "Come with me."

He helped her to her feet and led her toward the door. Would his father come back before they could make it out? His heart was thudding in his chest, and he wondered if Superman's heart did the same when he rescued Lois Lane. Their feet pounded across the floor. She wasn't moving very fast, but she clung to his hand.

He pushed the door open and breathed in relief when he didn't see his father. In fact, he heard him dry heaving in the bushes. She stumbled on the bumper of the truck, and he caught her around the waist. She was probably a couple years younger than he was. Her light brown eyes were wide with terror, and her cheeks were shiny from tears. The cut was oozing a thin line of blood. He grabbed hold of her hand again and yanked her across the parking lot. He'd just reached the small strip of trees when he heard his father's voice.

"What the ..." A moment later, "*Max!*"

He ran even harder through the woods and out to the pavement again, but she stumbled and skidded. Bloody dots covered her knees.

"*Max! Come back here!*" It was a bellow that carried the threat of death.

Out of instinct — or maybe he was a coward after all — he stopped.

His father kept advancing. "Max, do what I tell you. Bring her back."

Kryptonite, he thought. He couldn't move, couldn't speak. The girl was breathing hard, nearly gasping. He looked at the car. The two boys were throwing away their wrappers; their parents were already in the car. She tightened her grip on his hand as Bobby neared them. *Coward!* Not his father's voice, but his own. Max made a decision. He jerked the girl to her feet and headed across the immense lot.

He could hardly breathe, but he called out, "Hey! Don't leave!"

The older boy got into the car and slammed the door shut. The younger boy reached for the handle.

"Help!" Max shouted.

He didn't dare look behind him. He imagined not his father but one of the many all-powerful villains in his comic books. Tentacles reached out to pull them back. Death rays shot past them.

"Help!" he shouted again as the boy started to get into the car.

He paused, catching sight of them tearing across the lot toward them. His eyes widened in alarm, then focused somewhere behind them. Apparently, he said something, because everyone else got out of the car. The father rushed toward them, followed by the mother.

Chills of relief crossed his skin as they neared each other. He stopped and in heaving breaths said, "You'll be okay now. Stay right here." He had to go back to his father.

His father had retreated to the shadows of the woods. Max's fear was overridden by his shock and disgust at what he'd been doing to that girl. Oh, he knew he'd be punished. Badly.

"Max, get over here now!"

He barely had the energy to push himself faster, but that voice spurred him on. He only spared one backward glance. The family was surrounding the girl now. She was safe. That's all that mattered.

Bobby grabbed his arm and pulled him through the woods. He didn't say another word as he grabbed the knife, slammed the doors shut on the trailer and hauled him into the cab. Max didn't put up a fight. He'd disobeyed and he'd be punished. That was how it worked. He'd take it like a man.

They were on the highway within minutes. His father's breathing was heavy, too, and his arms were tensed as he gripped the wheel. The knife sat on his thigh. Max knew he should wait until his father spoke, but he couldn't.

"What were you doing to that girl, father?" Bobby insisted Max call him *father* "Why were you hurting her?"

"You think you were being a big *hero*, don't you?" He said hero as though it were a dirty word.

"No." Max had hesitated at the sound of his father's voice. That sure wasn't being a hero.

Bobby pulled the rig onto the side of the highway and shoved the knife at Max. "Kill me!" He pointed to his chest. "Right here, just shove it in hard."

Max had taken the knife; otherwise it would have fallen. He looked at the place where his father jabbed and shook his head.

"You might as well finish me off. Oh, sure, now you're the little coward again." He grabbed the knife from Max's flaccid grip, tossed it aside, and started forward again.

A half-hour later, they pulled into their small town outside Tampa. Max kept his gaze glued out the window, even envying the ragged hitchhiker thumbing for a ride. The road became two lanes, and then turned to gravel. The houses were spread out here, surrounded by scrubland and oak trees. Bobby came to a stop on the road that led to their neighborhood.

"Get out."

Max didn't question that command. He opened the door and jumped down. Was his punishment going to be walking the rest of the way? That wasn't much. He walked this distance and more to get to the bus stop every day.

Dread knotted his stomach. No, this was only the

beginning.

The truck continued on. The passenger door was still open, and it flapped back and forth. Max watched the truck disappear before starting to walk home. Twenty minutes later, he'd made it to the long gravel road their house was on when he heard the familiar engine. His heart started thudding hard as he turned around.

The truck rounded the corner with its tires squealing and took out the stop sign. Still Bobby didn't slow down. A cloud of dust rose up behind the truck as it, in fact, gained speed. Max was fairly certain his father wouldn't run him down, but he wasn't taking any chances. He ducked into Lynn Wells' yard and hid behind a bush. The door was closed now as the truck barreled past him and veered to the right — *aimed toward their house.*

It was like a movie, not real at all. The impact sent him to his knees, and the ensuing fireball took his breath away. Flames tore up into the night air like fiery fingers from hell. When the gas tank exploded, windows everywhere rattled. People were already running out of their homes. It was Bill Wells who found Max on the ground with his watery gaze pinned to the flames and billows of smoke.

Lynn said, "Oh my God, I hope Max wasn't home! Or in that truck!"

"Max is here!" he hollered to Lynn and their kids. "He's all right."

Max wouldn't be all right for a long time.

The remains they'd found in the cab of the truck had been identified as Bobby's, and Max had been sent to live with Odette. Though he'd been grateful that she'd taken him in, she wouldn't answer his questions about his father and why he'd done such a terrible thing. Max wasn't allowed to talk about it to anyone. All she would tell him was that the girl was all right.

Livvy. Her face had haunted him for years.

According to the police report, Olivia claimed Bobby had done something to her eyes, though there wasn't any physical evidence to support that. Max made note of the doctor who examined her.

Had she been blind then? That explained her stumbling. He'd figured it was due to her fear; his own legs had barely held him up. Had his father done something to her eyes? The thought made his stomach lurch. Thank God he hadn't molested her. Max wasn't sure he could have handled that.

He rubbed his forehead, hoping to get rid of the tension that was building into a headache. Obviously, and understandably, Olivia's experience had marred her life. She was delusional, reliving her kidnapping because of Phaedra's. That had to be the explanation, because his father was dead, had been for sixteen years. He couldn't begin to contemplate his father being alive. The thought paralyzed him, just as his father's voice had paralyzed him all those years ago.

He couldn't tell Sam or the lieutenant about his past connection with Olivia. He'd be yanked off the case. As much as he hadn't wanted this case, no way could he let that happen now. He'd limit what he told Sam until he had a better handle on Olivia.

His gaze went to the word *angel* on the report. She had thought an angel had rescued her.

He glanced at his watch. It was after midnight. He wasn't going to get to sleep anytime soon. He doubted Olivia would either. He grabbed up the notes and headed out.

CHAPTER 12

Fatigue wore Max down as he approached Olivia's building. The past tangled with the present, tearing him in two. He was that boy again, wearing the cape and believing that good always triumphed over evil. He was that cynical adult, too, who didn't believe in much anymore. He thought he'd buried the boy long ago, but like a ghost, he kept haunting the adult Max.

He spotted Olivia and Stasia walking toward the building. *Livvy.* Now he knew why he'd been struck by that odd sense of *deja vu* every time he saw her.

Her hair was still tied back, but even more wavy tendrils had escaped.

As he neared her, he said, "Olivia, it's me, Max Callahan."

For an instant her body tensed, but she smiled with relief. "Hello, detective."

"Call me Max. This is an unofficial visit."

He knelt down to pet Stasia, who licked his hands in greeting, her whole rear end wagging.

"Sounds like she likes you," Olivia said. "She doesn't greet many people like that."

"Guess I'm special." He was looking at Olivia as he straightened. "Can we talk?"

"Sure."

They walked in silence to her apartment. He had to keep the words from jumping out of his mouth as she unlocked the door and walked inside. Joan Jett and the Blackhearts greeted them with a song about their bad reputation. The apartment was dark but for the dancing lights on her stereo equalizer. The colored lights played off her face and gave her an otherworldly look.

Standing there in the dark was doing strange things to his senses. "Is it okay if I turn on the light?"

"Like I'd even know you'd done it," she said, unleashing Stasia.

Her white shirt was covered in splotches of color, and he picked up the scent of fresh paint as he passed the corner of her living room where she had her easel set up. Her painting outfit, then. Odd she'd chosen white for it. Maybe she didn't know. Her white cotton pants had a drawstring waist that rode low on her hips. They were covered in several years' worth of spills and missed brush strokes. He guessed years because the fabric was so worn, he could see the peach hue of her behind as she walked into the kitchen. He wondered if she had any idea how tantalizing she looked, and then doubted it.

Olivia came to a halt. "Are the French doors open?"

His body automatically responded to the alarm in her voice, and he made his way to her. "Yeah."

"I didn't leave them open."

"You're sure?"

"Very." She turned around to face him. "Yesterday, when I returned to my apartment, someone was in here. I could hear him, smell him ... and feel his presence."

"Why didn't you call the police?"

"My best guess is that it was Terry. Do you want me to tell you how seriously I was taken when I went to the police to file a restraining order against the great Terry Carlton?"

Max could only grunt in understanding. "No one likes to believe their hero is a creep. You could have made a report at least." He jiggled her front doorknob. "Lock hasn't been messed with. Nothing looks disturbed or out of place."

Her expression was troubled. "I didn't think so either, at least as far as I could tell. Terry seems to think that I need him. I think he's trying to prove it."

"By doing what?"

"Turning my knives upside down, knowing I'd grab for the handle and cut myself. He also turned the volume knobs up on my television and stereo. I'm worried about what else he's done."

His gaze went to the bandage on her finger. Anger bubbled through him that someone would take advantage of Livvy's blindness, that someone would try to hurt her. "Stay right there. Let me take a look around." He touched her shoulders as he passed by.

Olivia, not Livvy.

He checked the patio first, closed the doors, and then the back rooms. "I didn't see any sign of tampering."

She had her arms wrapped around herself, and he wondered if it was the cool night air or fear.

"I'm going to make some coffee," she said. "Would you like some?"

"Sure." He leaned against the long counter dividing

the kitchen from the rest of the living area and watched her prepare the coffee. "I could talk to Terry again—"

"You've already talked to him?"

"Yeah, but without proof, that's all I can do."

A sigh filtered through her words. "Yeah, I know. And honestly, I can't see him doing something that would hurt me. But who else could it be?"

"You thought he may have pushed you into traffic."

She let out a long breath. "I just don't know, for the same reason. Unless he's getting desperate." She poured coffee and handed him the blue mug. Paint was embedded in the creases of her fingernails. Each finger was a different color. She painted with her fingers. Intriguing.

"What's the story with Terry Carlton?" Max asked as he blew on his coffee.

She poured her own coffee after measuring out cream and sugar with her fingers, then leaned against the counter facing him. "We dated for six months, right after he officially retired from the NFL. He swept me off my feet. At first, it was great. What girl wouldn't like a man wanting to spend all of his time with her, buying her flowers, taking her out for fancy dinners? He even took me to Paris for the weekend. He was charming and fun and passionate, everything I wanted.

"He started talking about marriage on the third date. A month later, he asked me to move in with him. I should have told him I wasn't ready for that kind of commitment, but I made up an excuse that I was used to my apartment and the proximity to everything. The next night, he showed up with his belongings and moved in. It never occurred to me that he'd give up his big house. I didn't want to hurt his feelings, so I didn't object."

His fingers tightened against the edge of the counter. "Sometimes being nice can get a woman into trouble,"

She rubbed her temples. "I know, but I thought I was in love with the guy. Then he started taking over my life, doing everything for me. That's when it got to be too much. It wasn't fun or charming anymore. I asked him to move out, told him I needed my own space. He even suggested we buy two apartments that had come available in another building. Because they were at the end of the building, they shared a wall. He thought we could put a connecting door between them. That's when I realized he wouldn't be happy with anything less than my total submission. So, I broke it off. Since then, he's been calling, sending flowers, telegrams, you name it. He even came to my showing. Everyone thinks he's cute, pursuing me like he does."

"Has he ever threatened you?"

"Not in so many words. He asked me how far he had to go to prove I needed him. I'm not even sure it qualifies as a threat."

"But it made you uncomfortable."

"Because I really don't know how far he'd go to prove that. He's passionate, impulsive. He's used to getting what he wants and being in control."

"I'm sure, being a football star and all. You're probably the first thing he's ever wanted that he couldn't have."

"Don't I feel special?" The corner of her mouth lifted in a wry smile, but her expression shadowed again. "I can't help thinking I'm somewhat responsible. If I hadn't lied—"

A knock on the door interrupted her. "Olivia, it's Terry. I need to talk to you. It's important."

She walked to the door. "Terry, you're not supposed to be here."

"I can arrest him," Max said. "In fact, I'm supposed to arrest him."

She pinched the bridge of her nose, clearly not amenable to that option. "Terry, go away. There's a police detective here."

"Good, he should hear what I have to tell you, too."

This was going to be interesting.

She opened the door. When Terry saw Max, he blinked in surprise. "You're not here because of me, are you?"

"Tell us what you're here about," Max said.

Terry took in Olivia and Max with a palpable possessiveness in his expression. He even stepped between them. "I came by earlier. I know I'm not supposed to be here, but I just wanted to leave this" — he pressed a Santana CD at her — "wedged above your doorknob. To remind you of us."

"Like she could forget." Yeah, Max's voice sounded terse. He pushed the CD back at Terry. "Go on."

"I saw some guy walking away from your apartment. I asked what he wanted, but he didn't answer. Worried me, so I knocked on your door. Apparently, you weren't home. I tried to find you, then came back to make sure you were all right."

"How long ago was this?" Olivia asked.

"About forty minutes."

"Did you go inside her apartment?" Max asked.

Terry kept his gaze on Olivia. "I don't have a key since she changed the lock. Something happened, didn't it? Olivia, are you all right?"

"Can you describe the man you saw?" Max asked.

"He was about your height, maybe a little bigger, but he was wearing a bulky overcoat and a hat, so it was hard to see much. He kept his head down. I'd say he was older, maybe forties or fifties."

Conveniently vague, Max thought. "If that's all —"

"If that's all?" Terry said. "I'm not leaving Olivia alone. She needs protection."

Maybe from you. Max wasn't sure what was going on here. Was Olivia imagining things? Forgetting she'd left the doors open? Or was Terry playing games with her?

Olivia pointed to the door. "Terry, you have to go now. Max isn't here because something happened in my apartment. He's here because of the kidnapped girl. If you don't leave, he's going to have to arrest you."

Terry looked as though he were going to plant himself there, all two hundred and eighty pounds of him. Max wasn't looking forward to tangling with him. Luckily, Terry relented and moved toward the door. "Olivia, I care about you. If you need help, or you're afraid, call me. No strings attached."

After he left, she said, "Did he look like he was lying? about seeing the man? I couldn't tell from his voice."

"He seemed earnest, but I've seen a lot of earnest liars. Like you, I don't know what to make of him."

"And you think that maybe I'm just imagining all this stuff. Being forgetful, maybe."

"You do have a lot on your mind." Except for the knives, none of the incidents were harmful. "Is there some reason why, after filing a 'no contact' order against him, you're reluctant to have him arrested when he violates it? You said something about lying."

She blinked and waved it away. "Forget about Terry, and forget about me. It's Phaedra I'm worried about.

Did you read about my case?"

His throat tightened. "Oh, yeah."

"Can you track down the monster who kidnapped me?" She closed her eyes and leaned her head back. "I can't believe I'm even talking about it. Nobody knows, not Terry or even Captain Richards. I never told him why my emotions only heightened enough to connect with kidnapped children. It happened so long ago, and most of the people I know now didn't live here then. It's like my dirty little secret." She looked in his direction again, waiting for his answer.

He took a fortifying sip of coffee and wished to hell it was beer. "Like you said, the man who took you died when he rammed his truck into his house."

"That's what they told us. But he didn't die."

"Yes, he did."

Her expression hardened. "How do you know? All you did was read some old case file. Maybe he jumped out of the truck before it went up in flames."

"He was in the truck."

She clenched her fists. "How can you be so sure?"

"Because I saw it happen."

He watched her face as she tried to understand — and obviously gave up. "What?"

"The man who took you was my father. I was the boy who rescued you, the one you thought was an angel."

The disbelief was instantaneous, as was that smart-assed tone in her voice. "You're playing with me. I don't need this from anyone, especially you."

"You think this is easy for me? Do you think I'm *enjoying* this?"

She crossed her arms in front of her. "I don't know. Are you?"

"Livvy..."

That word stopped her cold. "Don't call me that."

"Why not?"

"I was Livvy when I was young and needed someone to protect me. I'm not Livvy anymore."

"All I knew was that you were okay, and your first name was Livvy. I didn't even know you were blind." He took hold of her hand. "Come with me."

She stiffened.

"Come with me," he said again, trying to say it the same desperate way he had then.

Her skepticism melted, and her mouth went slack. "It was *your father*?"

He was glad she couldn't see his cheeks flaming hot with anger and shame. "Yes."

Her fingers were pressed so hard against the edge of the counter they were almost white. "You saw him drive into your house?"

"Yes. He made me get out of the truck, then he drove off. He returned about twenty minutes later, passed me, and rammed into the house."

Her eyebrows knitted together. "How old were you?"

"Ten."

She gently pulled her hand from his and pressed it to her mouth. "I don't know whether to believe you or not. Please don't play games with me, not about this."

He walked around the counter. His eyes drifted shut as he sank back to that time. "I put my hand over your mouth and whispered, 'Shh. Be quiet.' I cut the ropes around your wrists and pulled you to your feet. My father had gone outside; he was puking his guts out thanks to the stomach flu I gave him. I didn't know what he was doing to you or why. I never found out. But

I knew I had to get you out of there, and that there was a family at the rest stop."

He hated reliving the details, too, but he'd do it to convince her. "They had two boys, one was about fifteen, the other twelve. We ran across the parking lot. You fell." And for a second he'd frozen. "I yelled for them to help us. My father was ordering me to come back. I told you to stay there and went back to him."

She swayed. He put his hands on her shoulders, and he might have given in to the urge to pull her against him if she hadn't turned around just then. "Oh, God. Is it really you?"

"Yeah, it's me."

"Say those words again. The ones you said to me."

"Come with me." They came out thicker than he'd intended, and he wondered if it was that leak of emotion that made her shiver.

"Do you realize how many times I heard those words over the years? How often you said them in my nightmares just before you led me out of them?" She opened her eyes and whispered, "Thank you." Her laugh was throaty. "That hardly seems adequate for saving my life."

"I don't know what he was going to do you. I've hoped, all these years, that his intentions weren't murderous. That he was just crazy."

"I think they were, and he was. He kept talking about my final punishment being on Christmas night. That he could never forgive me for what I'd done, whatever that was. What happened to you? I didn't want you to go back to him. I was scared for you." She paused for a moment, her expression troubled. "Did he punish you?"

"Only by destroying our house." He cleared his

throat. "He died in that wreck. I could see him in the driver's seat when he drove by. The police found his remains."

"They were wrong."

"I'll put a call into the station that handled the investigation just to make sure, but we have to believe he's dead."

"What are the odds that two men are saying and doing the same things to the girls they kidnapped? But you don't think my connection with Phaedra is real, do you?"

"I don't know what to think. Nobody knows that she's wearing a shamrock charm but the family, the police ... and you."

She leaned against the counter. "Which either proves what I'm saying or makes me look guilty."

"Exactly. My job is to keep an open mind while I explore every angle. That's what I'm trying to do."

"Keeping an open mind means looking into your father's death, and accepting the possibility, no matter how crazy, that he's still alive."

His knees went weak at the prospect. "Do you know the ramifications of that?"

"Oh, yes, I've been going over them since I realized it was the same man. You think I want to believe that monster is alive? It means he's been out there all this time, doing God knows what."

That thought left Max cold. He hadn't seen his father in sixteen years. Would he recognize him? Max looked nothing like his father; he had taken after his mother. Add the years, take away some hair and the beard ... he could be nearly anyone in the age range of forty-eight.

Olivia had to be wrong.

He rubbed his hand over his mouth. "I need to know something. When you told me about seeing the boat, the T and the R ... it's been bugging me, and I just realized why. From what you said, you only see through the child's eyes in real-time." He watched her tense as she nodded. "How could you see the boat then? You're a telepath. You connect to Phaedra's mind, so seeing that ship is outside of your abilities."

"You remembered." She walked over to her painting and sat on the stool, facing the canvas. She dipped a finger into one of the wells of paint and traced a line across the bottom of the canvas. "The boat wasn't my vision."

He walked over and stood behind her. "Then whose was it?"

"I can't say."

The canvas was a mess, streaks of black against an ugly green background. No eyes, though. He took hold of her wrist as she was about to add another streak. "That's not good enough."

Her shoulders slumped. "I promised I wouldn't tell. He's psychic, too. He saw the boat and the letters. He also saw the green walls and the cage, just as I saw. He asked me to relay the information to you as my own."

"Why couldn't he come to us?"

She pulled her arm free of his grip. "Because he's one of you. He said his job was at risk, that his career had already been stalled because of his so-called hunches. He wanted to work with me to find Phaedra."

Max didn't like this. "And you believed him?"

She shrugged. "He believed me."

He held in a curse and ran his hand through his hair. "I've never heard of a cop in our station with unusual hunches or high case solves. Give up his name, Olivia."

She jabbed her finger into the paint well again and slid it across the canvas. "I gave him my word."

Her loyalty bothered him, though he wasn't sure why. "I understand where you're coming from. The guy believes you when we don't, and he's supposedly psychic like you. Why don't you let me check him out? He gave you false information."

"Sometimes it's hard to interpret what we see. That's what he thought he saw. And he did have some things right, like the walls and the cage."

"Maybe because he's been there. You can't afford to trust him." He knelt down beside her. "Let me quietly check into the guy, make sure he's on the up and up. I won't give him away."

She let out a soft breath. "Bill Williams."

Max repeated the name. "I haven't heard of him."

"He said he worked with you."

She wiped her finger on a cloth and turned toward him. "After you left, I connected with Phaedra again. Just like with me, the man came back and punished her for wetting herself. She watched him walk to a bathroom at the end of a hallway and wash out her clothes. I saw more of the room. It's a bigger place than I thought. The bathroom looked regular, not one you'd see on a boat, I would think. Or in a truck. I tried to capture it." She nodded toward her canvas. "Does it make any sense?"

He studied the painting. "Not really."

She slid her fingers over the canvas, smearing the paint even more. "I'm not good with details, only abstract ideas."

"And eyes. You put eyes in all your paintings."

She dipped her finger into the black paint and drew a

large eye in the middle of the canvas. "That's what I see in my mind when I slip into a creative trance."

"I'd say it's your theme."

She gave him one of her Mona Lisa smiles. "I guess I do incorporate eyes into my work a lot, now that I think about it." Her fingers worked methodically, finishing the eye. She then started working on a white eye against the green background.

He watched her paint for a few minutes, feeling a sense of peace steal over him at her graceful movements. She seemed immersed in her painting, so he turned the large chair in the living room group around and settled into its cushy confines. Stasia curled up between him and Olivia with a rope chew toy. The CD changed to Pat Benatar, who sang about love being a battlefield.

He watched Olivia's finger swirl across the canvas. She reached down to a rack of jars and ran her finger across the Braille labels. She grabbed the fourth jar and poured some of the paint into one of the empty wells. The murkier green color complemented the background green. She had a different color on each of her three fingers; sometimes she used another finger to blend the colors together.

"What's it like to not see your final product?"

"Frustrating. I can imagine what it looks like, but I'm sure it's nothing like that in reality." She glanced over her shoulder. "Just like I could try to imagine what you look like, but I'd be off by a mile." The thought of her trying to imagine what he looked like seemed intimate somehow.

"Do you remember what colors look like?"

"I do, but only because I work at it. Otherwise my

visual memory would fade away. It's like a muscle I have to exercise or lose forever."

Her words had grown soft on the last part, but she gave no other indication of how that prospect made her feel. She continued to paint with her back straight and her chin up.

"I paint, too," he said, though he hadn't meant to admit it.

"Really?" She turned around.

"Something I started doing a couple of years ago, to keep my mind busy. I did model cars for a while. Now I do resin kits. You paint them and glue the pieces together."

"Are the kits cars, too?"

"They're figurines. I've done a lot of horror film classics, like The *Phantom of the Opera* and *Frankenstein*."

"Movie monsters," she said, seeming to give it a lot of thought. "Who was your favorite?"

"*The Man Who Laughs*," came out of his mouth. That surprised him; he hadn't thought about that piece in a long time. It was crammed on the shelf with the others.

"I haven't heard of that monster."

"He wasn't a monster, just a hapless victim in a silent film from the twenties."

She was facing him now. "Tell me about him."

"His name is Gwynplaine, the son of a Scottish nobleman that King James II executes. The king disfigures the boy's face and gives him to a band of gypsies who abandon him during a blizzard. As the boy trudges through the snow, he discovers a baby. He rescues it and is then rescued by a troupe of actors who take him in. He becomes a famous clown ... and falls in love with a beautiful blind woman." He paused at the profundity of it. "Anyway, go on and paint. Forget I'm here." He settled into the chair.

After a moment, she turned back to her canvas. It took her another few minutes to get back into her groove. Her brown, wavy hair hung to just beneath her shoulder blades. It was bound loosely with a blue ribbon. He had an urge to lean forward and untie the ribbon. If he could move, that was. He had melted into the chair, and for the first time in years, peace flowed through him. Watching her did that. Her whole body moved with each stroke of her fingers. She feathered streaks of yellow over the dark red and, with a flourish, added a light line of pale yellow. Her pinky remained aloft the entire time.

He sank into a hypnotic state. No thinking, no suspicions, no doubts. Just watching her and floating along with the words to "Promises in the Dark." He lost himself in her fluid movements; she was moving in rhythm to the music.

"Max?"

He blinked, coming out of the trance. "Hmm?"

She turned around. "You were breathing ... differently. Louder. Faster. Why?"

He ran his hand down his face, feeling heat on his skin. He thought about telling her he'd fallen asleep, but he wasn't in the mood for a lie.

"Because watching you paint is a turn on."

Her mouth opened slightly, but nothing came out. Those words, spoken bluntly and honestly, took her completely off guard.

His voice was low. "There's something about the way you move. It's sensual, almost spiritual."

Her mouth tightened. "You're not coming onto me,

are you?"

He chuckled. "I'm too tired to come onto you."

Her cheeks warmed. Had she made one of those embarrassing *faux pas* again? She slowly dipped a finger into the paint.

"I'll leave if you want me to," he said. "I didn't mean to make you uncomfortable. You asked, and I told you the truth."

She was turning him on. The knowledge of that flowed through her like a glass of wine, warm and tantalizing. "You don't have to leave." Had she just invited him to stay longer? Sounded like it to her.

"I'll just close my eyes and listen to you paint."

What she needed was some time alone to sort this out. Max the suspicious, sexy detective, her savior? Her first reaction to that revelation was disbelief. As he'd recounted the events of that terrible night, her disbelief melted away.

He'd been an adversary of sorts these past few days. He'd once been her rescuer. Now his blunt honesty was making her see him as something else: a man.

Which was such a bad idea. She resumed her painting after realizing she'd come to a standstill. Max Callahan was a likely candidate for a rescuer personality, the kind of man who would want to keep her safe and protected. Add in that he'd once done just that, and it became a recipe for romantic disaster. There'd be the question of whether their feelings were a result of that long-ago connection that many rescuers/rescuees had. She'd already built him up to be a hero. Surely, she'd carry that into a relationship with him, should she choose to pursue one.

Reason enough to keep that particular door closed.

She didn't need to spend herself in an emotional relationship with a knock-the-door-down rescue type. Especially one who had lost his wife and daughter and still couldn't come to terms with it.

Then why did you ask him to stay?

Why, indeed.

He'd called her Livvy, and the *way* he'd said it...

She squeezed her eyes shut and listened to his breathing. Not the deep, heavy rhythm, but a slow, even one.

"Max," she whispered.

No change in his breathing. He'd fallen asleep. She had heard the exhaustion in his voice. Once he'd closed his eyes, his body gave into it. He'd said he was too tired to come onto her, but he hadn't said the prospect was out of the question.

The Man Who Laughs. Laughing on the outside, crying on the inside. And the beautiful blind woman he'd fallen in love with, did she love him back? Did they have a happy ending?

"Once there was a man," Pat Benatar sang in her song "One Love." Olivia tried to assemble the description Judy had given her into a face, but it was impossible. She whispered his name again as she wiped her fingers on the cloth and came to her feet. Her chest felt tight as she walked closer. Her fingers traced along the back edge of the chair until she felt his hair. She stopped, taking a soft breath. *You shouldn't be doing this. It's crazy.*

His hair brushed against the back of her fingers. His breathing was doing strange things to her, compounding the intimacy of the moment ... making her want to curl up in his lap and feel safe.

Not that she was afraid. She'd stopped being afraid a

long time ago.

The need pulled at her, the need ... to feel loved, cherished. It hit her in the stomach, stealing away her breath. Where had it come from so suddenly, so powerfully? What she really wanted was to be accepted and understood—psychic oddities and all.

She needed to "see" what he looked like. She leaned over him. Her hands skimmed over his hair. It was short and soft and followed no particular style. She followed his thick, arched eyebrows with the pads of her fingers. Both fingers ran down the very straight ridge of his nose and fanned out over wide cheekbones. He had an intriguing dip at the bottom of his chin. His mouth was lush, soft. She traced the ridge of his upper lip and felt the cool air of his exhalation. Fine stubble scraped across her pads. She could make out a face in her mind: Max's face.

Without warning, he grabbed her hands. "What are you doing?" His voice was throaty.

"I ... I wanted to see what you looked like. I didn't mean to startle you."

"You did startle me. I was out."

"Can I have my hands back now?" She tugged, and he let them go. "Maybe you'd better go. It's late." She pressed her watch. "One-thirty-two."

After a moment, he got to his feet. "Let me turn the chair back around."

"There's masking tape on the floor to indicate where it goes. Everything has to be in a certain place, or I'll walk into it."

She heard him shuffling the chair into place. He grabbed his keys off the small table and walked to the door. "Lock your door."

Then he was gone. She sank against the arm of the chair for a moment before forcing herself to the door to lock it. It had been easier when they'd been in opposing corners. She was great at fighting, at keeping people at a distance.

It was different with Max. And that was dangerous.

CHAPTER 13

Saturday, December 23

Max arrived at the station early. He glanced at the clock and calculated how many hours Phaedra had been missing. Too many. He couldn't imagine how her family would face Christmas if their little girl were still missing.

He ran his father's name through the system and found a surprise: Bobby Callahan had been a cop once. He'd joined the Orlando police force when he was eighteen and quit two years later. Max had been a toddler then; he didn't even remember living in Castaway, the small town near Orlando. There was nothing about him in the system after that, no surprise there.

He called the Castaway sheriff's station and asked the clerk to dig into the archives for details of Bobby's death. She didn't sound eager to jump on the task but promised to get someone on it as soon as possible.

His father couldn't be alive. Olivia had to be inserting her own experience, just as she'd suspected in the beginning. That made more sense. That possibility didn't make his stomach twist and turn.

If Sam discovered she knew about the shamrock, he'd haul her right in. Maybe that's what Max should do, too. He didn't know if he believed her, and he didn't know if he disbelieved her. Next, he put in a call to human resources and asked the clerk to check on Bill Williams.

He pulled out the notes he'd made on Olivia's abduction and called the doctor who had examined her eyes after the kidnapping. He left his request with Dr. Gambel's answering service and hung up just as Sam walked in. He didn't look happy, but then Max realized why: Petey's birthday party was that afternoon.

Max leaned back in his chair. "Annie mad about you working today?"

"She's used to my schedule, but Petey isn't. I told him I'd swing by at least." He dropped into his chair at a desk caddy-corner to Max's. His eyes looked bloodshot and for the first time he looked every one of his forty-nine years. "Where are we going on this case, Max? Nowhere, that's where. We've got nothing new, nothing concrete. The girl's parents were out front when I came in. Huntington's with them now, so be ready to catch some hell when he gets here."

Max didn't want to mention that investigating all of the area's convicted past offenders hadn't turned up anything yet either. "You all right, man?"

"We're supposed to be working this case together, right?"

"Yeah," Max answered carefully. "But we agreed to spread out and cover more ground."

"Yeah, I remember. I'm just feeling left out of the loop."

Max ran his fingers through his hair. It was still damp from his shower. "I'm working on a few things I'm not ready to let loose yet. They're probably dead ends, but I've got to check them out first. Give me some line, and I'll fill you in on everything soon enough."

Sam's eyes narrowed. "This has something to do with Olivia Howe, doesn't it? She's trouble, Max."

"I've got a handle on it. Have I ever screwed you over?"

Something Max couldn't identify crossed Sam's face.

"Callahan! O'Reilly! In my office!" Huntington's voice bellowed as he walked into the detective's area.

Max pushed himself to his feet. "There are only five guys in here, and he still has to yell."

Huntington's face was red as he tapped his ragged pencil on his desk. "I'm taking heat from the parents, the media, and the Commissioner. Their publicist is running us into the ground. Why haven't you found that girl yet? Did I make a mistake putting you on this case?"

Max was startled to find that icy stare pinning him with that question. "We're doing the best we can with what we've got."

"Which isn't a lot at this point," Sam said.

The lieutenant asked, "What about Mike Burns?"

Sam said, "He's still a possibility, but he's slippery. I'm working on finding out who he's been seeing, but he's apparently cut off the affair since the abduction. Through his credit card bills, I nailed down a restaurant that he frequents. I'm going to talk to the waiter tonight and see if we can ID a girlfriend."

So, Sam was holding back information, too. That was the first Max had heard about that.

"And Pat Burns?"

Sam said, "I've been doing some quiet inquiries at his chain of restaurants. There are whispers of financial trouble, but rumors aren't going to get us a search warrant. If he did his kid for the money, he'll have to make sure she's found soon."

"What about the Howe woman?"

Sam turned to Max. "Callahan's been working that angle. He'll have to give you that update."

"I'm tracking down some loose threads now."

"How come you didn't tell me about checking out the harbor? Heard that from one of the guys. Did this happen to be one of Howe's leads?"

Sam shot Max a smug look. Max said, "Yes, sir. We didn't have any other leads. I figured it was worth checking into."

"Well, it's not worth it. Either she's a suspect, or she's not. Is she?"

Sam said "Yes" at the same time that Max said, "No."

Impatience tightened Huntington's features. "If she's a suspect, treat her like one. But we're not working with her, understand? I don't want to give Pat Burns's publicist a reason to think we are. And how the hell is Burns hearing about her, anyway?"

Max said, "I'd like to find that out myself. Someone's been leaking information to him."

The lieutenant took them both in with his steely eyes, but they remained on Max longer. "You still on the surface, Callahan?"

"Yes, sir." He wasn't going to admit how close to going under he was. That girl, every passing hour, and

Olivia, they were all dragging him under.

"Don't screw up this case." He looked over at Sam. "Lucky for us, even the Burnses' P.I. hasn't found anything yet. That means that either we're all incompetent, or the guy who took her has his bases covered. Either way, it doesn't look good. Any leads on the Santa suit?"

Max said, "We had officers check every Dumpster in the area, but nothing turned up. We're widening our search for out-of-town costume stores."

The lieutenant tapped his fingers on his desk. "I don't want to have to tell these parents that we couldn't find their girl. She's their only kid. We haven't had a stranger abduction here in two years. Since your last big case," he said to Max. "You came through for us that time. Come through again."

Max could only nod as he backed out the door. Sam paused. Was he going to mention his suspicions that Max was getting involved with Olivia? He didn't need a facedown with the lieutenant just then, and he wasn't ready to divulge what he knew.

Sam said something brief to the lieutenant and walked out of the office. He headed to the break room instead of returning to his desk. Max's phone rang; it was Dr. Gambel.

"Sorry to bother you on a Saturday, doctor, but I'm working on a case and I need information as soon as you can get it for me. It concerns a girl who was kidnapped and lost her sight: Olivia Howe." Max gave him dates and other details.

"I vaguely remember that. I'd have to have someone pull the records from storage."

"I'd appreciate that. We've got some facts that need

clearing up as soon as possible?"

"I'll have my office manager pull the file. That was before we computerized everything. She can meet me at the bridge club, and I'll call you from there."

Sam returned with a mug of coffee. Normally they would both go, or one would ask the other if he needed a refill. Sam was probably the only real friend Max had, but this case was tearing them apart. They'd never worked at odds like this. Sure, they'd had different opinions, but they always kept an open mind. Because of Sam's dogged suspicion of Olivia, and because of what she'd told him, that door had to be closed.

As other detectives filtered into the main area, the noise level rose.

Graham said, "Hey, Callahan, any new psychic leads to chase down today?" He burst out in his loud, raucous laugh, and some of the other guys tittered along with him like little girls.

"Lay off," Mathers said. "Don't you have better things to do than act like a bunch of kids?"

Graham's expression darkened as he turned back to his paperwork.

Max didn't need anyone to protect him. "I'd go to every psychic in town if I thought something would lead me to that girl. It would be a lot more productive than sitting around talking out of my ass."

Some of the guys laughed at that, too. Graham slammed his drawer shut and stalked out of the room. He didn't like being the brunt of a joke, but he sure enjoyed grinding up a guy now and then. Just like he teased Max about his resin kits, and Holland about the gory police novels he was trying to get published, but he bristled at any comment about the motorcycle graveyard around his double-wide.

Just to prove Max could be objective about Olivia's innocence, he ran a check on Sebastian LaForge, the only person she called with any frequency. His real name was Bob. He had a number of speeding tickets, but nothing else on file. Sebastian/Bob had shown him a metal art sculpture he'd done. Where did he work on his art? Had to be a warehouse, somewhere he could use a blowtorch. Someplace a kid could be stashed, a place without windows, with a bathroom. A blowtorch could create a cage.

Max blew out a long breath. He was basing his suspicions on what Olivia had "seen" in her vision. Everything was getting all twisted inside him. He got up and stretched, then grabbed his coffee cup and went to the break room. He splashed cold water on his face and caught his reflection on the metal towel dispenser. He looked as bad as Sam did.

When he returned to his desk, Sam had Max's cell phone. "Dr. Gambel called," he said with a smirk in his voice to match the one on his face. "Olivia Howe's not technically blind. There was nothing wrong with her eyes, not a scratch, no chemical damage, nothing. Her pupils even dilated. He thinks she convinced herself she was blind to fool her abductor." He tossed the phone to Max. "Her *abductor*?"

Nick Mathers looked their way, obviously picking up the confrontational tone in Sam's voice.

Max grabbed up his phone and jacket. "Let's take a walk, Sam."

They headed out the back way where the throng of reporters wouldn't pelt them with questions about the investigation. Max was glad that it was Huntington's job to deal with them.

Twenty minutes later, Max had told Sam what he could. He left out the part about Olivia "seeing" the shamrock and that she thought his father had taken Phaedra.

"So why couldn't you tell me she was a kidnap victim?" Sam asked.

"Because there are a few other details I have to check out."

"Are you looking at her as a suspect, Max? I don't understand all the secrecy."

"That's all I can tell you right now. After what she went through, I don't see her being involved with another abduction."

"Let me see her case file."

"Give me some time on this, Sam. For the sake of our friendship." When Sam hesitated to commit, Max said, "You keep dogging Burns. Find out who he was having dinner with. If it's Olivia, I'll turn over everything I have."

Sam whipped out a Polaroid photo of Olivia walking Stasia. "I got it this morning. I'm going to show it to the waiter. If she's the one he was seeing, I'm bringing her in." He tilted his head. "Do you believe that's she's somehow connected to the missing girl?"

"I don't know what I believe anymore. I don't disbelieve her the way you do." He ran his hand over his face, squeezing his burning eyes shut for a moment.

"You can't think she's telling the truth. She's lying about being blind, no doubt about that. She 'sees' way too much. Even you doubted it, obviously."

"I just want to clear it up."

"Well, now we know." Sam started to walk away.

"Hey, Sam. Do you know a cop named Bill Williams?"

"Never heard of him. You mean someone named their kid William Williams?"

"Maybe." He was going to have to dig further on Williams.

Max called Dr. Gambel back to verify what he'd told Sam. He also got the name of the neurologist Gambel had referred Olivia to: Dr. Bhatti. Why did these things have to come together on Saturdays? He headed inside to get the number. He had to put the question of Olivia's blindness to rest.

"Good morning, Olivia. It's officer Williams. I just wanted to check in with you." He leaned into the phone booth near her building. "Have you connected to Phaedra Burns lately? I haven't gotten anything, and it's driving me mad. If something happens to her ..." His voice broke perfectly.

"She's all right, at least so far. I saw the green walls you mentioned. You had that right. And ... I think I know who her kidnapper is."

He had to catch his breath. "What?"

"Detective Callahan is checking into it. It's too long to get into now. I can let you know when he verifies it. Give me a number where I can reach you."

If Max was checking into it, he must believe her. "Meet me for lunch. Tell me what you know. Maybe I can help on my end." He didn't want to risk going to her apartment again in case someone identified him. He needed to lure her out this time.

"Give me your number, Bill. I'll get back with you on that."

Was she getting suspicious? "You didn't tell Max

about me, did you? You didn't mention my name."

A brief hesitation. "No, of course not."

He couldn't be sure. He'd had her, right up until when he wouldn't give her his number. So, he would. "Okay, ready? My number is 464 —"

He severed the connection.

CHAPTER 14

Olivia waited for Bill to call her back, but he never did. That was strange. Maybe his cell phone had lost its signal, or his partner had walked up. Or maybe... she thought of Max's suspicions and shivered. She couldn't believe she'd been duped, especially if Williams turned out to be Phaedra's kidnapper — and hers.

"Guess we'll go for our morning walk," she said, sending Stasia into a frantic happy dance. Or at least it sounded like it, her claws tapping and scraping on the floor, excited whines and yips.

She could hardly enjoy the crisp air and sunshine washing over her as they made their way back from the park thirty minutes later. All she could think about was Phaedra. She had once again felt a ripple of unease. "Father" hadn't scared Phaedra when he'd come early that morning. He'd probably given her back her clothes and then left without feeding her. She was confused and hungry, and there wasn't a damn thing Olivia could do to help her.

She wasn't sure what made the hair on the back of her neck stand up. She continued walking, but all of her senses were focused on her surroundings. People chatted and laughed, and Christmas music filled in the background. All normal, cheerful happenings. Maybe it was just her worry over Phaedra that was skewing everything.

Someone brushed up behind her. She came to an abrupt halt, causing a couple of people to skirt around her. She turned and inhaled. No particular scent stood out in the cool breeze.

"Terry?" she asked.

No answer, just bits and pieces of conversation as people passed by. He always answered if he were around. She quickly headed home, her unease sucking away the warmth of the sun. Terry had claimed to see someone lurking around her apartment. Was he sneaking in and then making up the guy to scare her? Who else could it be?

The faint scent of Polo lingered in the upstairs hallway when she exited the elevator. Footsteps sounded on the carpet, and then a door opened and closed. She knocked on the door across from hers, sure that was the one she'd just heard. "Hello? It's Olivia Howe, your neighbor."

She could hear nothing inside, and no one answered. She sure hadn't imagined hearing a cell phone ring in that apartment. Mr. Ford, the building manager, had told her that a corporation had recently bought the apartment when she'd asked him about it. He'd been vague about the corporation's name. Judy had brushed her off when Olivia had asked her about the apartment's owner. Maybe her paranoia was just stretching to encompass something as innocent as a CEO's love nest.

She stepped into her apartment a few minutes later and stood perfectly still. Nothing felt out of the ordinary. No smells, no sounds, no feeling of someone being there. Stasia didn't growl. Olivia locked the door, released Stasia, and started a pot of coffee. What she needed was a few minutes to think through recent events. She fixed a cup of coffee and carried it out to the balcony.

Her foot caught on something, and she pitched forward. Hot coffee spilled across her arm and the mug shattered on the floor. She tried to grab something on the way down and ended up taking one of the heavy iron chairs with her. Her shoulder took the brunt of the fall.

For a crazy second, she thought someone was there, ready to take advantage of her fallen state to finish the job. She reached around for something to help push up with and found that her small glass and iron table was only inches from where she'd landed ... inches from her head. With a pounding heart, she scrambled to her feet and felt for the masking tape. The table had been moved more than a foot from its original location.

She traced her steps and found what had tripped her — a broom handle. The woman who cleaned for her wouldn't have left it outside. It was propped up on the doorstep, positioned to trip her. Max had checked out here the night before, but he probably wouldn't have noticed it. He wouldn't have realized the furniture had been moved, but she knew exactly where everything belonged. A knot tightened in her chest.

When she heard the doorbell, she hoped it was Max.

She held her sore shoulder as she walked to the door. "Who is it?"

"Detective Sam O'Reilly with the Palomera Police Department."

Not only disappointment, but dread. She opened the door. "Yes?"

"I need you to come down to the station and answer some questions."

This she didn't need. Why wasn't Max here? "Let me feel your badge."

He hesitated, and his voice held a patronizing note when he said, "Sure thing." A few seconds later, he said, "Amazing how your hand goes right to the badge, isn't it?"

She returned his sarcastic tone with her own. "Yes, it is. What's this about, anyway? Don't tell me you've become a believer."

"After making asses of ourselves at the harbor looking for the gray boat with green walls? Not likely."

"Why can't I answer your questions here?"

"I'll explain when we get to the station."

"All right, but would you please do me a favor? Take a look at my balcony and tell me if anything looks awry. I think someone came into my apartment last night and rearranged my furniture in order to trip me. This way."

She heard him following her. "Was anything taken?"

"I don't think so, but I can't be sure."

"Stereo and television are still here, as well as the appliances and your computer."

She opened the French doors and stepped aside. "When I returned home last night, these doors were open. Detective Callahan was with me. He saw it."

He stepped onto the balcony. "Was the front door unlocked? Had it been jimmied?"

"No."

"There's what tripped you. The broom fell over." She heard him set it in the corner. "Otherwise, everything looks normal." He stepped back inside and shut the door. "You think someone broke in, rearranged your furniture, and planted a broom to trip you?" His disbelief was obvious. "You couldn't have fallen over the balcony railing from tripping. So, someone did all this because ..." When she didn't answer immediately, he said, "Surely you have a theory. Or maybe a psychic feeling?"

She wanted to smack that sarcasm right out of his voice, but that was probably a felony. "Someone's either trying to hurt me or scare me. Possibly Terry Carlton, my ex-boyfriend."

He laughed — *laughed!* "Yeah, right. Because the guy has so much money and can't get any woman besides one who can't even see all those rippling muscles of his, he's stalking you. Look, I don't see anything suspicious here other than a woman whose imagination has run amuck. I've got more important things to do than check out the arrangement of your patio furniture."

She clenched her hands at her side. *Felony, felony.* "Like take me in for questioning?"

"Exactly. Let's go."

Damn. She let out a huff of breath. "I need to harness my dog—"

"You won't need her. I'll guide you."

"I always keep my dog with me." She donned her coat again and got Stasia ready. With one last sigh, she turned off the coffee pot and headed to the door.

O'Reilly didn't say much as he drove to the station. She wanted to ask why Max wasn't there, but that smacked of a need for him that didn't exist. She wondered how much this guy knew about what she'd told

Max.

After he led her into the noisy station and down several hallways, they ended up in a quiet room. He settled her into a smooth, plastic chair and asked, "Can I get you anything? Coffee? Water?"

"No." She hoped this wasn't going to take long. Then, out of long-engrained habit, she said, "Thank you."

He was doing something near her face. She felt air move across her skin and involuntarily backed away. Someone else walked into the room.

"This is Detective Tom Graham. He'll be sitting in on our conversation."

The man only grunted in greeting and took a seat some distance from her. She smelled cheap cologne and tried to recall if it was the same scent she'd smelled before.

O'Reilly's voice lost its former polite, reserved tone. "There are a few things I need answers to, and it will be easier on you if you give us the truth now."

"Don't I have a right to a lawyer?"

"Sure, you do. Do you need one, Miss Howe?"

"No. I haven't done anything wrong." Sending for a lawyer would make her look guilty, that's what he implied. "Go ahead and ask whatever it is you have to ask so I can get home."

"Oh, we have a few issues to deal with. Let's start with you knowing about the shamrock."

On the way to Dr. Bhatti's office, Max detoured to Sam and Annie's place. The side street gave him a skewed view of their backyard, where balloons caught the sunlight in blinding flashes. About twenty kids were in attendance, some playing on the swing set Max had bought Petey last year.

He spotted Petey racing around the yard wearing a gaudy gold crown. The kid started to glance his way, maybe hoping to catch a glimpse of his father's car. Sam wasn't there either. Annie followed her son's gaze, but Max had already hit the gas pedal.

He arrived at the doctor's office early and waited outside the carved mahogany doors until Dr. Bhatti pulled into the spot next to Max's.

He shook the doctor's hand. "Thanks for meeting me on a Saturday."

"You're welcome." Dr. Bhatti returned the handshake, then opened the door and flicked on the lights. "But as I said on the phone, I'm not sure how much I can tell you. Olivia Howe's case was a long time ago." He led Max into an office lined with cherry wood bookshelves and picked up the file sitting on his desk. "I had my secretary pull the file for me. Please, sit down." His high-backed leather chair squeaked when he sat in it. "And there's doctor-patient confidentiality."

"I understand. Here's the bottom line: this girl is missing." He set Phaedra's picture on the desk.

"Yes, I saw that on the news. Very sad. But how is Olivia involved with this?" The surprise was evident in his voice.

To help loosen the doctor's tongue, Max decided to be honest. "My partner thinks she's a suspect, but I don't. I'm trying to clear her."

"Give me a minute to look over her file and reorient myself. I'll tell you what I am comfortable divulging."

"You can tell me in general terms, if that makes you feel better."

They exchanged a knowing look, and the doctor scanned the file. Max left Phaedra's picture on the desk in case the doctor had second thoughts about helping.

After a few minutes, Dr. Bhatti closed the file. "You know about her kidnapping, I presume? She was referred to me when they couldn't find anything wrong with her eyes, yet she claimed she couldn't see."

Claimed. The word stuck in Max's throat. "Right. I need to know if she's really blind."

"Blind? She's still blind?"

Max nodded. "She has a seeing-eye dog, Braille labels, the works."

Dr. Bhatti did not look pleased. He removed his glasses and rubbed the bridge of his nose. "First of all, my job was to confirm that there wasn't any physical reason for her blindness. I can tell you that much, that she had no physical indications. There was evidence of a head injury, a mild one, but no evidence of permanent injury to the brain. Whoever kidnapped her hadn't done anything to her eyes."

"So, she *is* faking her blindness." He hated that conclusion, and he hated that he hated it. He shouldn't care either way, other than as a lead in the case.

"Malingering."

"Pardon?"

"It's called malingering when a patient pretends to be blind. I can tell you that she wasn't malingering either."

And he shouldn't feel relief at that, but he did. Relief and confusion. "If she's not malingering, and she's not blind..."

Dr. Bhatti steepled his fingers and rested his chin on the tips of them. "Have you ever heard of conversion disorder?"

"No."

"How about hysterical neurosis or hysterical blindness? Those are other terms for it, though we don't use them anymore. Unfortunately, back then, I did call it hysterical blindness, and that may have been the problem. I'm speaking in general terms now, you understand." He gave Max a pointed look. "I have seen several cases, so I can speak of what I have seen.

"Conversion disorder is not a new problem. In the nineteenth century, doctors used sexual instruments on women to treat it. You see, many more women suffer from this than do men. Sometimes the instruments worked, though I believe they did so by removing cortical suppression that is often the cause of hysterical symptoms. But I see I'm losing you."

"A little." Max was leaning forward in his chair, his elbows on his thighs, trying to absorb what the doctor was saying. He was still lost, and obviously showing it.

"Conversion disorder is the conversion of internal conflict and/or stress into a physical symptom. That symptom is a loss of a bodily function — for example, blindness, paralysis, or loss of speech."

Max snapped his fingers. "I worked with a boy who wouldn't speak for a year after watching his father murder his mother."

"Wouldn't? Or couldn't? That is the key to conversion disorder. Because the sufferer of this condition does not realize he or she is suppressing the function. It's all on a subconscious level. It is triggered by a traumatic event, such as that boy witnessing his mother's murder. However, there is always another ongoing stress factor that keeps the person from regaining their function. That stress is relieved by the loss of the function."

"Do you mean that Olivia — I mean, that a person could subconsciously suppress their vision? That's incredible."

Dr. Bhatti gestured to a model of the brain that was sitting on a shelf. "The mind is a powerful organ. We don't know what it can do, but I have seen some amazing things. Even Freud had a theory about hysterical blindness. He thought it was due to the sexual pleasure in looking at forbidden sights. That the repressed sexual instinct shut down the eyes that were allowing those sights into the mind. Not that I subscribe to that theory myself."

Max ran his hand through his hair, taking it all in. He glanced at her file. "How sure are you when you make this kind of diagnosis?"

"Very. We run every test available. Then I urge the patient to seek psychotherapy. The underlying stressor must be identified, and the sufferer taught to deal with that stressor in an effective manner. If this is done soon after the onset of conversion disorder, the symptoms literally disappear." He gave the file a chagrinned glance. "I assume, given the facts and high chance for recovery, that the person will be taken for the necessary therapy."

Max felt his chest tighten. "Her parents never took her for that therapy."

"Sometimes it's hard for the patient — and their family — to accept a diagnosis such as hysterical blindness. They argue that the person is not hysterical at all. That is one of the symptoms, however. It is called la belle indifference, which means that the sufferer seems to take the loss of function in stride. And if that family member is perhaps the cause of the stress factor, that could be another reason to avoid therapy. If, say, the mother was oppressive and overbearing. If she chose to see things only as she wanted to see them."

"Her mother is dead. If she were the cause of the stress, wouldn't Olivia's sight return after her death?"

"After that many years, the eyes and the brain aren't used to communicating."

"Wait a minute, though. She flinched when my partner moved his hand in her direction. She seems to know where things are. She'll reach for a bag, for instance, and go right to it."

"Ah, that is why you think she is malingering."

"Partly. Mostly."

"She could have felt the air from the motion, or it could be blindsight."

"What's blindsight?"

Dr. Bhatti gestured with his hands. "It's a feeling or impression of something not seen. To put it in layman's terms, what we see with our eyes goes through two pathways to our brain. One is a 'where' pathway that determines that something is there, where it is, and how it relates to us spatially. It's a primitive pathway. The second is the 'what' pathway, which then tells us what the object is and how we should react to it. That first, primitive pathway sometimes still works in blind people. She may sense something is there, even if she can't see it. Do you understand?"

"Yeah, I think I do." He sat up in the chair. "What can I do to help her see?" There he went again, wanting to save her.

"Confronting the patient is the worst thing you can do. They believe their condition is physical, and as such, it must be treated that way, along with psychotherapy."

"Will she be able to see again?"

Dr. Bhatti shook his head. "After this much time has passed, the prospect of recovery is very low, I'm afraid. I once operated on a patient with a longstanding squint. The part of their vision that was blocked by their eyelid is still blocked. The brain was so used to not seeing that area, it still couldn't. I believe that our minds can influence neuronal plasticity and thus alter the neuronal processing of information indefinitely."

Max didn't even bother to ask him to clarify that jumble of words. "There has to be something..."

"Charcot introduced hypnosis to treat conversion disorder. I have heard of case studies where this has supposedly healed a patient, though it is controversial. There's a doctor in Miami who has had success using this method. I can give you his name." After flipping through his Rolodex, Dr. Bhatti scribbled down the information on the back of his business card and handed it to Max. "Does this help clear Olivia?"

"I hope so. Thank you, doctor. I appreciate your time." He started to head out but paused. "One more question. If someone had ... psychic tendencies, could a head injury enhance it?"

The doctor raised an eyebrow, though he didn't give Max the crazy look he'd expected. "I have heard of head injuries giving people enhanced extrasensory skills, but I've never seen it myself."

Max smiled. "Thanks."

He grabbed a sandwich on the way back to the station. First, he'd tell Sam to back off from Olivia and explain about her blindness. *When* he'd broach it with her was another matter.

He hadn't even made it to his desk when Detective Holland set down the gory book he'd been reading while he ate and said, "O'Reilly's got your suspect in the interrogation room. Mathers just came out for coffee and told us what she's been saying."

"My suspect?"

That's when he spotted Stasia peering around the corner of John's desk. "Yeah, the one who's ..." He made a crazy gesture with his hand. "The blind one."

CHAPTER 15

Max dropped his sandwich on the nearest desk and shot out of there. What the hell was Sam doing? Had he connected Olivia to Mike Burns? Something inside him rebelled at that thought. Not when Max had finally proven, at least to his satisfaction, that she wasn't malingering.

He jerked open the door in time to hear Sam say, "I'm going to ask you again: why are you lying about being blind?"

"O'Reilly, can I see you for a moment?" Max asked in a strained voice. Amazing, since he was ready to yank him out of there by his collar.

Olivia lifted her head at the sound of his voice but didn't say anything. A mixture of anger and confusion lit her face. Tom Graham settled into his chair, his dark eyes glittering as he readied himself to enjoy a fight.

Max said.

Max pulled Sam out into the hallway, and leaned in to Tom. "We won't need you anymore, Tom."

Tom slid by them and made slow progress back to his desk.

Max waited until he was out of earshot. "What is

going on? Did you tie her to Mike Burns?"

"No, but I've got plenty of reason to bring her in."

"Then why didn't you call me? I told you to let me handle her."

Sam's laugh was bitter. "Yeah, you're handling her, all right. And falling for her, too."

The door made a clicking sound and popped open an inch. Tom hadn't latched it. Max shoved it closed and walked into the adjacent room.

"I'm not falling for her. I'm trying to get her to trust me so if she does know something, she'll open up."

"I think you're hoping she'll open up something else."

"Don't be a jerk."

"You lied to me when you left last night. You went to her place. I saw you." The disappointment in his voice made Max feel like a kid caught in a lie.

"That's why I lied, so you wouldn't get the wrong idea."

"And you're withholding information."

"I told you I had things to check out."

"Like that she knew about the shamrock charm? That's a biggie. I don't know if I can trust you anymore, and dammit, I hate that."

Max swung one of the orange chairs around and sat down backward. "What did she tell you?"

"Stood by her supposed connection with Phaedra Burns. She thinks it's the same guy who abducted her sixteen years ago."

"It isn't. He killed himself right after she got away. I don't know what to make of her story. It's one of the things I'm checking out." So, she hadn't mentioned that the man who'd taken her was Max's father. He wasn't ready for Sam to find that out yet.

Sam perched on the table. "You can't believe this crazy psychic stuff. It's ... it's ... well, it's crazy, that's what it is."

"I'm not discounting it."

"What about the false clues? A boat, for Pete's sake."

"She said she got that information from a psychic cop. Someone here. That was the Bill Williams I asked you about." Interesting that she was still trying to protect the guy. That both annoyed and worried him. "So far, I haven't been able to verify that a Bill Williams works for us."

"Big surprise. She made him up as a scapegoat."

Max narrowed his eyes. "How'd you know about the shamrock?"

Sam at least bothered to look chagrinned. "I looked at your file when I came back after our talk outside. You left it right out on your desk. I'm not the only one who's wondering what's going on inside your head. Mathers was looking at it too. I didn't read all of it, but I got a glimpse of your notes about the shamrock. Look, I know what's going on. She's getting to you. It happens. She's probably using her suspicions that someone is breaking into her apartment as a ruse, just like Helene, my neighbor did. It put her in that victim role, and it's all too easy for guys like us to respond to that." He cleared his throat.

"That's not what it's about."

"You think her being a kidnap victim makes it unlikely that she's helping someone else do the same thing, right? Ever hear of Stockholm Syndrome?"

Max rested his chin on the back of the chair. "That's when a victim becomes emotionally involved with their kidnapper while they're still being held captive."

"It's not always during the abduction. I've been doing some checking. Sometimes it's after the victim is no longer with the kidnapper. A twelve-year-old boy was abducted in Idaho. He was tortured for two weeks before he escaped. Five years later, guess what? He takes a young boy and does the same thing to him. Olivia didn't take the girl herself, but maybe she met up with some sick bastard who pulled her into his game. If she confided her own experience, he could have used it against her. We've seen some twisted stuff."

Sam ran his fingers through his short, blond hair, making the ends stand up. "Look, Max, she knows about the shamrock because she's been with the girl. She's probably *seen* the girl. I was this close to getting her to crack."

"She's blind, Sam. I talked to the neurologist her eye doctor referred her to. Ever heard of conversion disorder?"

Even after Max explained what he'd just learned, Sam was clearly skeptical. "But she reacted to my hand when I waved it in front of her face. You saw it. She grabbed the bag right out of your hand. She's done a lot of things like that."

"That's what bothered me, too." Max explained the concept of blindsight as best as he could remember. "If she's involved in the kidnapping, I want her as badly as you do. But my gut says she's not."

"There's more, isn't there? Max, I want it all. And if you're involved with her—"

"There is more, and it's complicated. But you've got to trust me." His butt would be yanked off the case if anyone knew how close this was to him. Thank goodness he hadn't included his father in his notes. "I'm not sure how it relates, *if* it relates. I'm asking you to keep her connection and the shamrock under your hat for a little longer. I'm not endangering the case. If anything, I'm getting closer to finding Phaedra Burns." Max crossed his arms on the back of the chair and pressed his forehead against them.

"If Huntington finds out you're still talking to Olivia ..." Sam shook his head. "Remember when he locked Samson in the bathroom stall for an hour because he was always reading magazines in there? Or what about Detective Johnson? He'd had some real problems shooting a guy in self-defense, but he wouldn't see a shrink. Remember Huntington making him sit in his office and write five pages of how he felt about the shooting? He wouldn't let the guy leave before he was done filling the very last line. I can only imagine what he'll do to you. I'm giving you another day, but that's it. I can't keep working at cross-purposes with you. One of us is going to have to walk away from this case."

"Let's agree on this: there are two ways she could know about the shamrock: either she's involved with the kidnapper or she's psychic. Give me a chance to find out which it is. If you haven't blown it for me."

Sam hesitated, an unhappy expression on his face. "Just be careful that you're not thinking with the wrong part of your anatomy. A little girl's life is on the line."

Max didn't even dignify that with a response other than pushing out of the chair. He knocked on the interrogation room door before opening it.

She turned toward the doorway. "Who is it?"

Oh, yeah, she was pissed. Anger saturated her voice.

"It's Max Callahan."

She was the only bright spot in the otherwise generic room. Her blue-green shirt set off her yellow pants. Both clashed with the red and orange paint staining her fingernails. He glanced at the slim window in the door and saw Sam watching, probably looking for some sign of their involvement. The problem was, there was involvement, more than Max wanted to admit.

"Why did that other detective accuse you of falling for me?" she asked as soon as he sat down across from her.

Damn, why hadn't he made sure the door was closed? "He's misinterpreting my actions and intentions."

"And those would be?" A direct challenge.

He lowered his voice. "I admit to feeling a certain ... protectiveness about you."

She crossed her arms in front of her. "I don't want your protection, Detective Callahan. Or anything else you have to offer. I'm tired of men pigeonholing me into the innocent, fragile category. I'm neither, and I haven't been for a long time."

She'd opened up an intriguing avenue of question. One he didn't need to explore because it had nothing to do with the case.

Her mouth tightened. "Why was your buddy accusing me of faking my blindness?"

He wasn't sure how much to tell her, because of Dr. Bhatti's warning about confronting her. But she'd already been confronted and now she needed to hear all of it. "Because your eye doctor said there was nothing wrong with your eyes after the kidnapping."

He saw her blanch at that. "*You've* been checking into my medical history?"

Had he imagined the slight emphasis on the word *you*? "We needed to verify that you are, in fact, blind. It's been a point of doubt from the beginning. If you were lying about that--"

"Then I was lying about everything," she finished in a flat voice. "So even *you* thought I was pretending to be blind?" This time there was no doubt about the emphasis.

"As a cop, I can't discount any possibility. Especially with a girl's life hanging in the balance. I just spoke with Dr. Bhatti."

"I thought doctors weren't supposed to talk about their patients."

"He only gave me some general information — that just happened to apply to you. He was doing it to clear up the matter of your blindness--to help me clear you as a suspect."

Her laugh was bitter as she shook her head. "Well, you *handled* me well."

This time he blanched. Why had he used that phrase? He didn't have a chance to comment, because she said, "I trust you got your answer, which brings me back to my question: why was he accusing me of faking it?"

"You're not blind, Olivia."

A moment passed as she absorbed his words. "You have got to be kidding." She waved her hand in front of her eyes in a jerky motion. "I can't see. Doesn't that qualify me as blind?"

"It's called conversion disorder. Your mind isn't letting you see."

She sat back in her chair. "That sounds like crazy."

He touched her hand, but she jerked away from him. "I don't need you to hold my hand to soften the news, to *protect* me."

"You're not crazy." He wasn't going to use the word hysterical. "It was a way for your mind to protect you from the terror of the abduction."

"Then why didn't my sight return after I was rescued?"

"There was some other element in your life that being blind let you avoid."

"This is ridiculous. Is this another way of *handling* me, Detective Callahan?"

"Talk to Dr. Bhatti. He thought your mother was going to take you for therapy. Did she?"

"I saw a psychologist for a while, but that was for the nightmares and residual fear. She enrolled me in a special school for blind children and collected pity the way other people collect donations."

He found himself wanting to explore that further, but now wasn't the time to ask. "If there is a possibility that you could see again, would you want to?"

"No." She pushed back her chair and stood. "I lost one sight and gained another. If I lose my connection with those children, who will help them?"

"I asked Dr. Bhatti about the way your psychic ability changed. He's heard of cases where someone has gained extrasensory abilities after a head injury."

Her shoulders relaxed somewhat. "Do you believe me?"

"Do I believe you have a connection with Phaedra Burns? Maybe. Do I believe your theory of who has her? No." The cost of believing her was too high.

"But you're checking into it, right? Because you have to explore every possibility."

His mouth quirked at her use of his earlier words.

"Exactly."

"I want to go home. Where's Stasia?"

"I'll take you to her."

She had to let him slide his arm beneath hers to guide her back through the station. She wasn't happy about it by the stiff way she walked and the way she avoided any but necessary contact.

As soon as Stasia saw Olivia, she barked, probably letting her know where she was. Detective Holland had volunteered to watch the dog. He kept pictures of his two Rottweiler beasts on his desk like other cops kept pictures of their children. As far as they knew, that was all the family he had. He untied the leash, but Stasia didn't wait to be led to Olivia. She ran and put her paws against Olivia's legs. Olivia knelt down and pressed her cheek against Stasia's cheek. Max watched them for a moment, then looked up to catch Sam watching him.

Sam said, "I asked John to take Miss Howe home so we can get back to work."

Max only nodded. Protesting would be a bad thing, even though he wanted to do just that. He wanted some time alone with her, to explain the handling comment and to make sure she was all right. Of course, she would interpret that as a protective gesture, and he was fairly certain that's not what it was at all.

John Holland introduced himself and led Olivia from the area. Max turned back to Sam. "I just found out where Sebastian LaForge works on his sculptures. It's a storage area about thirty minutes from here. Let's check it out."

"Don't tell me you think Olivia and Sebastian are working together?"

"No, but LaForge is a link to the Burnses, and he has a

facility" — he held back from saying *like the one you've been seeing* — "that could house an abducted child. I think it's something to check out, and it's better than sitting here pulling our hair out." He looked at the clock. Where was the time going? He grabbed up his keys and a new pair of sunglasses. "I've got the records being pulled on every missing child case in both Palomera and Sarasota."

Sam followed him to the door. "You think this guy has taken other kids?"

"The more I think about how good he was at getting that girl out of the store without anyone seeing him, the more I think he's *too* good. Since we're hitting dead ends with the family and Olivia, we need to start broadening the search."

Lieutenant Huntington was watching him through the open blinds in his office window. Had Sam told him about the withheld information yet? A few of the detectives were watching him, too. Everyone seemed to know about the case. Was he just imagining that they were all waiting for him to go under?

Detective Holland's low, soft voice had an almost eerie quality to it, though he'd said little beyond what was necessary. Otherwise, he murmured to himself as he drove through traffic. When he stopped at her building, he leaned past her and opened the door. "Be careful, Ms. Howe."

"Careful?" That was an odd parting phrase.

"It's a dangerous world out there, especially for a blind woman."

"Thanks for the warning." She guided Stasia out and quickly followed. "And the ride." It was only after she heard him drive away that she realized he hadn't asked her where she lived.

Once again, she took stock of her apartment, Holland's warning still echoing in her head. She released Stasia from her harness and went directly to the phone. What Max had told her ... it was impossible, of course. Information gave her Dr. Bhatti's number, and his answering service took her message.

He called ten minutes later. "I thought I might be hearing from you soon. I hope I wasn't overstepping my bounds by talking to the detective. He said he wanted to clear you of suspicion."

Max was a cop, first and foremost. His priority was finding Phaedra and so was hers. That he had betrayed her by doubting her sight shouldn't bother her so much. But it did.

Dr. Bhatti confirmed what Max had said. He chose his words carefully, as Max had done. "He wasn't supposed to just tell you."

"The other detective accused me of faking my blindness. Max — Detective Callahan walked in and told me about conversion disorder. If this is true ... am I crazy?"

"No, you're not crazy. It is a survival instinct. We all do it to some extent. For instance, say there is a dinner party you absolutely don't want to attend but feel obligated to. To avoid the party, you get a stomachache, and darn, you cannot go. The difference between that and conversion disorder is that the former person is aware that the impending situation is the cause of the sickness."

"Detective Callahan said the kidnapping triggered the blindness, but another factor caused it to stay."

"This is the question I ask my patients: by being blind, what did you get out of that you hated doing or having done to you? Labor? Physical or emotional abuse?"

"Beauty pageants."

"Pardon?"

"My mother made me enter beauty pageants. I hated them." If she had stopped doing them on her own, she was as sure as a child can be that her mother wouldn't love her anymore.

Dr. Bhatti said, "She did not want to accept what I told her. Her question was the same as yours: was her child crazy? I assured her this was not the case, but that psychotherapy was essential. She did not like that, but she promised to think about it. Now that I am looking at the case notes, I see that I followed up with her a week later. She told me she was taking you for therapy."

"I was seeing a psychiatrist to help me deal with the trauma of the kidnapping. But we didn't talk about the blindness or anything else relating to it, other than coping with it. I don't remember having trouble with that, though."

"No, you would have easily accepted it. That's what conversion disorder sufferers do."

"Are you sure? About the diagnosis, I mean."

"Yes. I ran a full battery of tests on your eyes; there was nothing physically wrong with them. All the factors indicated conversion disorder."

"It's" — she wanted to say *crazy* again — "incredible. I can't get my mind around it."

"You'll likely need to talk to a mental health specialist familiar with this diagnosis. I can give you a couple of names." As she typed the information into Louis with shaky fingers, she remembered Max's final question: Did she want to see again? The darkness had been a comfortable place for so long, she wasn't sure she did.

"Could I see again if I got psychotherapy?"

A pause. "If you didn't use your arm for sixteen years, and one day you decided to use your arm, I doubt that you could. Your muscles aren't conditioned to move, and your mind is no longer conditioned to receive signals. Is it possible? Yes, anything is possible in the realm of medicine. Is it probable? I'm afraid not."

She swallowed hard. "I need some time to digest this."

"Yes, of course. Please see someone to help you, as you said, get your mind around it. This is a traumatic revelation, especially when presented the way it was. If you want to meet with me, make an appointment with my office. I'll make sure you get in right away."

"Thank you for calling me back so soon, Dr. Bhatti. And for being honest."

She took a deep breath after she'd hung up the phone. Elaine had blamed her for the kidnapping. After all, she'd been hiding, giving that madman the opportunity to take her. Olivia had accepted that blame, and neither had ever really talked about it. Even when Elaine was dying, she wouldn't discuss it. She only wanted to talk about the good things, like the beauty pageants, the glory days. Olivia had gone along with her because — well, because she was dying.

When the phone rang a few minutes later, she knew it was Max. Her fingers went around the handset, but she didn't press the button. Her answering machine kicked in, and she heard his voice. "Olivia, it's Max. I know I dumped a lot on you. I wanted to make sure you were all right. I'm sorry it came out the way it did."

She remained there, holding the handset and letting

his voice echo in her head after he'd hung up.

"Snap out of it." She turned to where she sensed Stasia was. "What should we have for dinner, girl? A package of Oreos is sounding pretty good about now." She scooped canned dog food into Stasia's bowl and placed a vanilla Oreo on top. Then she poured a glass of milk and sat down to an unhealthy dinner she totally deserved.

As it turned out, Sebastian was happy to show Max and Sam around his "genesis of art" workshop. It was a clean, immense warehouse. He and a few of his friends were working that evening when Max and Sam just "happened" by. Olivia wasn't among those friends, though her one attempt at sculpture was: a warped clay person. Max didn't like the image of her and Sebastian working on that together, but he didn't delve into exactly why.

Afterward, he and Sam walked around the rest of the warehouses and found nothing out of the ordinary. They'd returned to the station to pick up the case files that had been dug up so far and went their separate ways. Max was on his way to the Chinese restaurant for some to-go food when he passed the library. He found himself pulling into the parking lot and walking inside. He took the newspaper film from a long-ago December and inserted it into the reading machine.

Olivia's face flashed by, and he backed up. He printed out the pages that covered her disappearance and recovery. After returning the film to the drawer, he paid for the copies and headed out. At the restaurant, he decided on the spicy version of General Tsao's chicken. It was going to be a long night.

It would be a longer night for Phaedra.

After dinner, Olivia harnessed Stasia and they walked out into the hallway. As soon as she locked her door, she got a strong whiff of Polo. Had Terry dumped more cologne on the carpet?

Someone pushed her against the door. Before she could even react or scream, a mouth covered hers. She shoved him back and kicked him in the shin. "Terry, stop it! God, you scared me!"

"Ouch, dammit. Olivia, I'm going crazy here. Let me move back in. I *know* something's going on. I can't sleep, I can't eat, all I do is think about you. Why was a cop here yesterday? Does it have to do with the missing girl? Of course, it does." He moved closer and cradled her face in his big hands. "Let me take care of you, baby. You don't have to face this alone."

Tears pricked the back of her eyes. After facing her connection alone for so long, after being shunned by the few men she'd dated because of it, the thought of having someone to face it with would be a treasure. But not Terry. He didn't want to understand it; he just wanted to use it as a way to get closer to her.

A door down the hall opened, and voices filled the air. "Do you have everything?" a man asked.

"I think so," a woman said, though she didn't sound sure at all. "Are you sure your mother will have a curling iron?"

"She's got every hair implement known to man. Or woman, I should say." Luggage wheels squeaked as they rolled across the carpet. "You have the tickets, right?"

"Of course," she said as they rounded the corner to the elevator. A minute later, the car dinged as it arrived, and then it was quiet again.

"If you really didn't love me," Terry said, "you'd have screamed your head off. You'd have me arrested. But you don't. You've probably never even reported that I've come over or called you."

He was right. She said, "I was hoping the no-contact order would make a point. I thought you'd get the hint and leave me alone. I never actually wanted you to be arrested."

"Because you love me."

"I don't love you. I don't even like you anymore. And you wouldn't like me if you knew the kind of woman I really am."

"And what kind is that? Look, if you were a man before, I'm okay with that. I mean, all your parts work now."

She slapped her hand over her face in disbelief. "It's over, Terry. You have to accept that. No more coming around here, no more calling me."

"Dammit, Olivia, you're messing up my timetable."

"What timetable?"

"By this time next year, I'm going to be playing football again, and you're going to be my wife and at least a couple months pregnant. Well, unless you were a guy. I don't think medical science can do that yet."

Hysterical laughter bubbled in her throat, but her anger pushed it down. "What about what *I* want?"

"You don't know what you want."

"I don't want to be your wife, I know that. I don't want to see you again. I *do* know what you want: whatever it is you can't have. But that's not going to change the outcome. Save yourself a lot of hassle and let me go. Use the energy for football."

His voice was low when he said, "You'd save me a lot

of hassle by coming back to me now. But if this is how you want to play it, then I'll play your game." He was walking backward as he spoke. "And I'm good at playing games, Olivia. Remember that."

She waited until the stairwell door closed behind him. The echo of his footsteps and the door opening on the first floor finally allowed her to release her breath. She didn't need this, not now.

When she walked out the front door of her building a couple of minutes later, she wondered if he was waiting there for her, intending to follow her. She thought of the person who had touched her earlier, of the things that had been changed in her apartment. She didn't need someone to protect her, dammit. Not Terry, and not Max.

Max. Her mouth tightened, and anger flushed her cheeks. She hoped he never came around again. She had started to see him as an ally of sorts.

And more.

He probably did think she was crazy. He would never believe anything more she said, and Phaedra would...

Don't think it!

Max would find her with or without her help.

Once at the park, she let Stasia loose and sank onto the bench. O'Reilly had accused Max of falling for her. She didn't like the way that accusation tickled through her body, not when getting involved with him was the last thing she wanted. Certainly the last thing she needed. Their relationship was already too complicated, and they weren't even technically in a relationship!

An ominous feeling coursed through her. It wasn't fear that pulled Olivia to Phaedra this time. It was hunger and the agony of decision.

He'd starved her all day, giving her only a glass of juice in the morning. Then he'd returned bearing a plate of yummy, fried chicken. He'd set that plate in front of her and told her not to eat it. Why had he been so mean?

So hungry. Dizzy from it. He'd left her there to wrestle over feeding her hunger and disobeying him. She kept looking at the door, waiting for him to return. Her stomach ached with hunger, making her curl in on herself.

Have to eat.

She reached through the bars and grabbed a drumstick. Just one little drumstick. She'd hide the evidence. Oh, it was good, cold or not. But it was gone so fast, and she was still so hungry. Two more pieces sat there on the plate, and she couldn't resist them any longer. He'd know anyway. It was already too late. He knew how many pieces he'd left. She'd take the punishment. At least she'd have food in her tummy.

When she licked the crumbs from her fingers, she heard the door opening.

Too late. And now the price for disobeying seemed larger than her hunger had been.

"Hello, Rose."

The light was behind him, as usual, though she could see the shadows of his face. "You disobeyed me." A disappointed voice. An angry voice. "You disobeyed me, Rose."

"I was starving."

"That doesn't matter. I told you not to eat. What matters is that you disobeyed me." His voice grew louder with every word, echoing like thunder. "And now you're going to pay for it."

He unlocked the cage and grabbed her arm. As much as she hated being in that cage, being torn out of it was even worse. At least she knew what was in the cage, and she was *safe from him.*

"Don't fight me, Rose. You'll never win."

Helplessness overcame her fight, and she let him drag her the rest of the way out of the cage. "Do you know what happens to bad girls who don't listen? Who eat things they're not supposed to eat?" He pulled out a small, thin bottle. Tabasco sauce, like her daddy put on his eggs. "Open your mouth, Rose."

"I'm not Rose," she said in a squeaky voice.

"Open your mouth!"

When she still didn't open up, he stuck his fingers in and forced it open. "I'll pour it down your nose if you don't leave your mouth open."

Be brave, she told herself. Like when the boys in the neighborhood try to scare you.

The pungent odor of the sauce burned her nostrils. Then the sauce squirted inside her mouth. She closed her eyes and swallowed when she had to. It burned down her throat and made her eyes and nose water. He tossed the bottle aside but still had a hold on her arm.

"Don't ever disobey me again, Rose. It's a war between us, isn't it? You against me, ever since you were a baby. I'm tired of being the bad guy. I'm a good father. But how can I be good when you're so bad?"

She didn't know how to answer that.

"You haven't called me Father yet today. I want to hear you say it, Rose."

She shook her head, knowing she would have to give in. He squeezed her arm even harder.

"Father," she said on a raspy breath. And then her stomach heaved.

He let her run to the bathroom and throw up into the toilet. She barely made it in time. She was crying and vomiting at the same time. His chest heaved with anger. Why did she disobey him? His word was the law. He made his wishes very clear.

"No one disobeys me without being punished."

Her crying got louder, though she didn't stop retching. She was kneeling in front of the toilet in the small bathroom. After several more minutes, she got to her feet. She turned on the water, splashing her face and rinsing out her mouth. When she turned around, her face was wet and her mouth red.

"Come here, Rose."

She hesitated but forced herself to step toward him. He opened his arms. "Give your father a hug."

Her lower lip pouted, but she stepped into his arms. She smelled like the hot sauce, which had spilled on her shirt, and vomit. He hugged her close. "Don't make me mad, Rose. I can't be responsible for my actions if you keep making me mad. If only you were good ..." But she wouldn't be. He knew how it must play out. "Get into the cage."

She quickly obeyed him, just as it should be. He clamped the lock into place.

He wasn't like his father. He'd never touch Rose in inappropriate places. He'd never do those terrible things his father had done to his sister. Things he couldn't stop. The bastard had never been punished for what he'd done. He'd died a hero.

But *he* was a good father who only wanted to keep his daughter in line. That's all he'd ever wanted, and she'd made him go too far. He flushed the toilet and walked to the steps. "I'll bring you food tomorrow. You won't scream when I leave, will you?"

The only time someone might hear her was the moment he opened the door, but even that was a remote possibility. Still, he couldn't take any chances.

He liked that Max was on the case, felt closer to him because of it. Max had been a bad boy a long, long time ago. He'd been punished when that car bomb went off and killed his wife and daughter, but it had backfired. Ashley wasn't supposed to have been with Diana that day. Maybe that's why his anger with Max never completely went away, because it had gone terribly wrong.

He'd killed his own granddaughter.

CHAPTER 16

Max spent the evening poring over the case files in the living room — and finding nothing. It occurred to him that this was another dead end, but it didn't occur to him to stop looking. He had every missing child case in the last ten years in the area. Sam had the previous ten years' worth. Luckily, there weren't all that many, and most had been solved. On the closed cases, he jotted down the names of the men convicted with the intent of seeing if they were still in prison. The outstanding cases looked nothing like either Olivia's or Phaedra's cases. Those two were connected by the date of abduction, almost down to the hour. It was a hard coincidence to ignore.

He stretched his legs and propped his feet on the coffee table. His latest project, The Wolf Man, sat untouched among a jumble of paint tubes and mixing dishes. He glanced up to the shelf where his small masterpieces were all crammed together. Back in the shadows, Gwynplaine's macabre grimace managed to catch the light. He shifted his gaze away. The television was on low, some news program. Just enough to make it sound like maybe there was someone else in the house.

Like maybe it was a home.

It hadn't been a real home since he found the near-empty bottles of vodka in Diana's drawer, hidden under her maternity bras. She'd even hid a bottle in a box of baby things that Annie had given them.

The living room and kitchen were lit up, but the rest of the rooms were dark. He glanced up at Ashley's pictures on the mantel. It hurt to see her smiling face, but he knew it would hurt more to put away those pictures.

The phone rang, and the human resources clerk gave him some disturbing news. No Bill Williams worked for any department of the Palomera Police Department. Was it his gut feeling that made him worry about Olivia? *Or maybe the gut feeling is something more than cop instinct. Maybe you just don't like that she trusts this guy. That she shares enough affinity with him to protect him.*

Sometimes he hated that censuring voice.

Bill Williams could have given her a false name to protect his job. Maybe it was nothing more than that. Still, he called Olivia and left a message on her machine about Williams.

At ten-thirty, he called Sam to see how he was coming along.

"I thought he was with you," Annie said, suspicion threading through her voice.

"We both took our case files home. Or at least I thought he was taking his home. Maybe he went back to the station to check something. I'll try him on his cell phone."

"His cell phone is turned off. What's going on, Max? Please tell me."

"It's this case, Annie, that's all. It's making us crazy.

He and I aren't agreeing on suspects, which is making things harder. But you probably already know about that."

"He hasn't been talking to me lately. Says he has his head in this case, which I can understand. But I think it's more than that. Even Petey's noticed it. He managed to stop by the party, but his heart wasn't in it."

"I wish I could help you, but I don't think anything's going on other than this case. I'll try to talk to him, though."

"I'd appreciate that. Hey, was that you driving by earlier today?"

"Wasn't me." *Coward,* his father's voice accused.

"He loved the little motorcycle. All the kids were jealous."

"Tell Petey I'm sorry I couldn't make it. Look, I gotta go. Don't worry, Annie. I'm sure it's this case, and God willing, we'll have it solved before long."

"Are you close to finding her? I've been watching it on the news, and there doesn't seem to be much to go on."

"That's what's so hard about it. We'll find her, and things will be back to normal."

That call bothered him. Sam was the most dedicated family man he'd ever known, and Annie was a good woman. He would never screw that up. Unfortunately, Max was hardly in the position to talk with him friend to friend. They were barely that right now.

He dumped out the rest of the coffee in the pot and rinsed it out. He was glad to plunge the kitchen into darkness with the flick of a switch. It was a mess. He just didn't have the energy or time to keep the place up. The cleaning lady was due tomorrow. She made it feel like someone lived there, too, when he came home to find the place clean and a frosty mug in the freezer.

He sat down on the couch again, the place he too often fell asleep. He stacked the folders in a pile and found the copies of the newspaper article about Olivia's kidnapping. Her picture was arresting for an eight-year-old. He understood why when he read the article. She was a little beauty queen, winner of numerous pageants both regional and national. In fact, she looked a lot like she did now, with long hair and those incredible eyes. But she could see then, and she was innocent. Fragile.

Her mother was a striking woman, too, though in a different way. She was classy, with white-blonde hair and a face that had seen a lift or two. Olivia's parents were quite a bit older than he'd expected. He could see the effect of that in her reserved, formal manner.

Over time, the story got smaller and farther back in the newspaper section, as it usually did. He got to the headline story where Olivia had been found. Max had never read anything about her rescue. Now he read about the brave young man who was hailed as a hero. The writer had used dramatic phrases, like "took his life in his hands" and "rescued the girl from certain death."

The police had found a tub in the burned-out trailer of the truck but couldn't say for sure what Bobby had intended to do with it. As far as they could ascertain, this was the first time he'd ever done something like this. No one knew why. There was a mention of Max going to live with his aunt now that he was orphaned. Olivia had suffered from one long cut across her chest, some bruising, and a slight concussion. That his father had not molested her made the motive that much murkier.

Livvy with her Mona Lisa smile looked up at him from his lap where the rest of the papers lay. He picked up the phone to call her again but set it down. She still hadn't returned his earlier calls. What he needed was to keep his distance. He was getting in way too deep with her, and though he didn't want to explore in what ways, he knew the attraction was there. If Huntington got wind of it, he'd probably lock him in a closet.

He didn't realize he'd fallen asleep until the phone jarred him awake. The clock read eleven-thirty.

"Hey, it's Sam. I just followed Mikey Burns to a mansion on Southside Drive."

"Southside?" Max said, rubbing his face to wake up.

"Just over the county line in Sarasota."

"What's he doing?"

"I don't know, but — wait, another car pulled up next to his. Whoa, one hot number just got out and she's heading into the house. She looks like a kid, maybe sixteen."

"Is that what you've been doing all evening, watching Burns?"

There was the slightest pause before Sam answered. "Yeah, I had a hunch."

"Annie's worried about you."

"You talked to her?"

"I was checking to see if you found anything in the files. She thought you were with me."

"I figured we would be together, but it seemed senseless for both of us to waste the evening watching his place."

"Give me the address. I'll be right there."

Thirty minutes later, Max and Sam walked up to the immense entrance of the house. For a few minutes, Max let himself think that they were working together like old times. But he didn't believe that Burns had the kid, not here or anywhere.

Through the wood door, Prince belted out "Get Off." They could hear voices inside. Mike called, "Shift to your left; there's a shadow on your nipple. Yep, that's it. Perfect."

Max and Sam traded a look. Mike sounded almost business-like.

Max knocked on the door. A girl said, "Who is that? I told you I don't perform for audiences."

"Cool it, Daisy. I didn't invite anyone."

A man opened the door. "Yeah?"

Mike sidled up and took in the two detectives with more than annoyance on his face. "What are you doing here?"

Max peered inside. The living room looked like a bedroom, with a red velvet, heart-shaped bed right in the middle. Two tripods were set up, the light bulbs surrounded by foil to direct the light to the bed where a voluptuous, naked blonde was sprawled. She also looked annoyed but did nothing more than reach for a cigarette and light it. A skinny young man stood off to the right, an eight-millimeter camera strapped to a rig on his shoulder. He was shifting from left to right while studying a small television connected to the camera.

Sam said, "You looked awfully squirrelly when you left your place tonight. We thought we'd see what you were up to, Mikey."

Mike slapped at the wall and let loose with an expletive. "I'm making movies, that's what I'm doing. What

I didn't want anyone knowing, especially my family. Especially now. I'm already behind schedule, and we've got one final scene to wrap. I wouldn't even be here, except that the movie is already in the next catalog." He flung his arm toward the woman on the bed. "This is Daisy Dick, the hottest up and comer in amateur adult movies."

She let out a mirthless laugh. "Up and *comer* ... good one, Michael. Can we get going? I gotta get back before my babysitter goes to school at six."

Sam asked, "Whose place is this?"

The man who had answered the door said, "It's my place. I let Michael use it for his film and in return, I get to watch."

Mike gestured to the house. "If you want to take a look around, have at it. Just be quick."

"Right, your production schedule." Max nodded, trying not to let a sardonic smile show.

They checked out the house, but as Max had suspected, found nothing incriminating other than the movie-making.

"You know this is illegal, don't you, Mikey?" Sam asked.

Daisy jumped out of the bed, pulled on a pink fur-fringed robe, and slammed the bathroom door behind her.

Mike said, "Aw, come on, it's not hardcore. I'm not doing anything wrong here. Daisy's twenty."

"How about we let the Sarasota police decide that."

"I hate that guy," Sam said when they headed out twenty minutes later, once the Sarasota police had arrived.

Max shook his head. "Forget about him. We've wasted enough time on him, but now we can be reasonably sure he had nothing to do with Phaedra's abduction. Have you looked at the files yet?"

"I'll look at them when I get home. See you in the morning."

"Lady, are you all right?"

"She's breathing. Got a pulse, but it's slow."

The frantic words pulled Olivia from the connection. In a rush of panic, she realized there were hands on her, people around her. She jerked upright and tried to figure out where she was while pain pounded in her head.

"Are you all right?" a man asked. "You just fainted."

She was on the ground. Oh, jeez, she'd dropped right there in the park. She patted around her. "Where's my dog? Stasia!" Her fingers connected with soft fur.

"She stayed right there with you the whole time," a woman said. "Did you have a seizure? My friend Denise has a seizure alert dog."

"I didn't have a seizure." When Olivia tried to get to her feet, several hands helped her. As weak as her legs were, she didn't object. She saved her energy for grabbing at the nearest lie. "I just let my blood sugar drop too much. I'll be fine."

"Here's a protein bar." A woman shoved one in her hand. "Hope you like coconut/pineapple/soy. If you're having a low blood sugar attack, anything'll do. I've got the same problem, always keep one handy."

"Great, thanks." Olivia bit into the dense, thick bar. Yuck.

"Keep on eating, honey. Get your sugar level back up."

She forced the rest of the bar down between thanking everyone. "I'm fine, really. I just need to get home and lie down."

She and Stasia walked into the apartment ten minutes later, the bar sitting heavy in her stomach. The breeze chilled the perspiration that clung to her skin.

Phaedra. The memories of her vision rushed back to her. She'd seen enough to know their kidnapper was right on schedule. Tomorrow ... she shuddered. Tomorrow would be even worse. And the next day ... she didn't know what would happen. That was worse than anything.

They had to find her before then.

When the phone rang, she grabbed it up. She was surprised to hear her father's tentative voice.

"Olivia?"

"Daddy?" He'd called her! A major breakthrough.

"I'm ..." She heard someone whispering in the background. "I'm here with a friend of ... a friend of yours." He was repeating whatever the person was saying. He didn't know her at all.

Her heart tightened. "What friend, Daddy?"

More whispering. "An old friend."

A man was with her father. "Who is it? What does he look like?"

"An old friend," he repeated, and the line went dead.

She speed-dialed the Livingston. "This is Olivia Howe," she said when a woman answered. "You need to find my father immediately." She heard hysteria creep into her voice and toned it down. "He just called me."

The woman's voice remained as calm as a recorded message. "That's impossible, Ms. Howe. He has no phone access."

"I know, that's why you've got to find him right now. He's with someone who has a cell phone."

"Give me your number, and when I find him, I'll call you right back."

"No! I'm staying on the line. Go get him right now and find out who's with him."

After a tense pause, the woman said, "Very well, ma'am. Hold the line."

Olivia dropped into a kitchen chair and hugged her legs to her chest as she waited. Someone was playing games with her. That he'd brought her father into it — she rubbed her eyes hard, tamping down anger and fear. Would Terry stoop that low? How far would this person go? "He's a helpless man!" she screamed before clamping her hand over her mouth. Her father hadn't been able to help her when she'd been kidnapped, and now she knew how he'd felt: enraged and impotent.

"Ms. Howe," the woman said, snapping Olivia back to present. "Your father is fine."

The surge of relief she felt quickly died. "Where was he? Who was with him?"

"He was sitting on a bench at the north side of the building by himself."

"Did he have a phone?"

"No, of course not. He was nowhere near a phone. Perhaps the man who called had the wrong number and it merely sounded like your father."

"It was my father. He was repeating what the man who was with him told him to. Put him on the phone, please."

A few minutes later, Olivia heard the woman saying, "It's your daughter, Mr. Howe." Then his voice came on the line. "Livvy?"

"Daddy, are you all right?"

"How's my little girl?"

"I'm fine." When he did remember her, he often pictured her as a young girl. Other times he thought she was his sister, Jane. "You were just talking to me on the phone. Do you remember that?"

"I'm talking to you now on the phone."

Her fingers tightened in frustration. "Daddy, this is important. You were just talking with someone. Do you remember who it was?"

"Sure," he said.

"Who was it?" she asked, trying to keep the thread before he lost it.

"An old friend."

She felt a chill at those words. "Yes, I know that, but who was it? What did he look like?"

She took the first few moments as thoughtful silence. A minute later, the woman with the prim voice said, "Your father set the phone down and walked over to the Christmas tree. I'm sorry."

Olivia let out a long breath, only now realizing she'd been holding it. "I'll be right over."

CHAPTER 17

Sunday, December 24, Christmas Eve

"We've got to let Mikey Burns go as a suspect," Sam told Huntington.

The lieutenant set his chunky coffee mug down on his paper-covered desk with a *thunk*. "You were sure he was up to something. What happened?"

Sam crossed his arms over his chest, a smug expression on his face. "He was up to something, all right."

"It just happened to be amateur adult movies, not child abduction," Max added.

"That's where he goes during the day. Where he was the morning Phaedra was taken. His porn star, Daisy, confirmed it. The dealership's phone records indicate that he called Miss Dicks before he left —"

"That was just one Dick," Max corrected, trying to keep the corner of his mouth from quirking. "Daisy

Dick."

"Which means you have nothing on the case now." Huntington was looking at Max.

"We still have Olivia Howe." Sam gave Max a pointed look.

Huntington grimaced. "A blind woman who was seen leaving the store without the girl. Great, just great. I suppose you got nothing out of her yesterday, O'Reilly."

Sam shook his head.

Max felt like a boy who'd been called into the principal's office. "We're still working on some leads, like Pat Burns, but there's nothing substantial at this time. This guy was good."

Huntington looked tired and disappointed as he took them in. "Then you've got to be better. Don't make me have to tell the family that we have nothing, after four days, nothing. I want that girl home for Christmas. Get out there and find her." With a wave of his gnarled pencil, he dismissed them.

Sam gave his chair a shove when they returned to their area. "Bastard. We can't squeeze milk out of a bull's tit."

"We're doing the best we can." But were they? Had they wasted time on bad leads and overlooked good ones?

They spent the remainder of the morning finishing the old case folders—with no results.

Sam threw the last folder on the stack. "There's nothing here with a similar M.O."

"Here either. I keep thinking we're missing something. I just don't know what."

"All we have is the Howe woman, and you know it. She's the key to this."

Max couldn't deny that. Luckily, he didn't have to. Sam's phone rang.

"O'Reilly ... yes, I am." He grabbed a notepad. "Go ahead ... and you're sure it was the Burns girl...okay, thanks. We'll check into it right away." He hung up and held up the pad. "Woman says she saw the girl at Wal-Mart ten minutes ago. Sounds like another dead end."

They'd had several sightings and tips. It was becoming less likely that the girl would show up at a store. Max grabbed his jacket. "You take it. I'm going to talk to Olivia."

"Max ..."

"Like you said, she's all we have."

That's how he had to approach this, as a business-only, forget the past and the whole hero/rescue thing, and get to the bottom of her involvement. Forget that he found her attractive as hell, that he was sure her tough-cookie exterior hid a soft, vulnerable side.

"I'll meet you there," Sam said.

"You've done enough damage. She might still talk to me. She sure as hell isn't going to talk to you."

She wasn't going to be very happy with him either, but he still had the best chance.

Olivia had stayed in one of Livingston's guest rooms. Her father had rested through the night, having no memory or discomfort over his encounter with the man who had instructed him to make that call. She'd waited until the residents had breakfast before emerging. They would now be relaxing or playing games. When she passed through the lobby, one of the nurses greeted her.

"He's sitting out on the back deck. It's a lovely morning."

Olivia smiled. "Can you please do me a favor? There's a picture of me as a young girl on his dresser. Can you get it and then lead me to him?"

"I'd be glad to. Wait here."

"Hello, dearie!" Miss Susan said, coming up behind her. Her voice was as sweet as candy. "Elton John is going to perform a small, intimate concert for us tonight. Will you be joining us?"

"No, I'm afraid I can't. But Elton and I had dinner earlier, so don't feel bad. He's looking forward to the concert tonight."

The nurse returned and whispered, "Don't encourage her," in a friendly but chastising tone. "She's been going on about that concert for two days now."

"Sorry, I can't seem to help myself. She's so cute."

The nurse sighed. "It's like having fifty children in here sometimes. Not your father, of course," she added quickly.

"Of course."

"Come, I'll lead you to him. He's having a good morning." Which meant he was lucid. "I hope the medication is working, though it's still too early to know the long-term prognosis."

Cautious optimism. She closed her eyes for a moment at the sweet feel of hope. "I'm glad to hear that."

Her father was talking to someone about the stock market. The nurse excused his companion and helped Olivia find the chair. Once she was settled, the nurse handed her the framed picture and left.

"Hi, Daddy. How are you feeling today?"

After only a short pause, he said, "Livvy?"

She could hear the relief in her laugh. "Yes, Livvy."

"Sometimes it's so hard to remember ... you're ... my daughter."

He pulled her into his arms, and she buried her face against him and tried not to cry. These moments were getting rarer, and she relished them with every passing day. When they parted, she wiped her eyes and hoped he didn't see.

She heard him sniff and wondered if he were wiping his eyes too. Did he need her visits as much as she did? Was that simple human contact something he craved as well? Maybe, because even when they parted, he kept hold of her hands. She forgot how powerful a hug could be, how it filled something inside her she denied she needed when she wasn't here with him.

"Have I forgotten you lately?" he asked. "I hate to think that you come here to visit me, and I don't remember you."

"No, you haven't forgotten me, Daddy." She tucked the picture to the side of the chair. For now, it wouldn't be needed to jog his memory.

"And your dog ... I can't remember her name."

"Stasia."

He leaned over to pet her, but his voice was aimed at her. "Are you all right, pumpkin? You look ... I can't think of the word. Not sad, not mad ... I ... don't know. I hate when the words don't come."

Anxious was probably the word he was looking for. "I'm all right. But I want to ask you something. Do you remember anything about last night? A man had you call me."

Silence for a moment. "No, sweetheart, sorry. Things are so ... spotty."

"It's okay. I want to ask you something else, something from a long time ago. When I was kidnapped —"

"I want to forget that part of the past." A pause. "But if you want to talk about it, of course, I will."

She squeezed his hands. "I don't like to remember it either. Just this one time, and we'll never speak of it again, all right?"

"Anything for you, you know that."

That rush of emotion swamped her again. She realized why: her father was the one person she could let down her guard with. If only she weren't losing him. The thought constricted her throat.

"After I was rescued ... I couldn't see, remember? Mother took me for therapy to get over the trauma of the kidnapping, and she also took me to a neurologist about my eyes. Did she talk to you about that?"

He was thinking. At least she hoped he was. He sometimes drifted off during their conversation. She never knew whether he was sleeping or just ... gone.

"I went with you for one of your therapy sessions, but I let her handle the medical doctors."

"The neurologist, Dr. Chad. Do you remember him?"

"I don't remember his name, just that there was one. Elaine said he couldn't find any sign of damage in your eyes either, right?"

"Is that what mother said? Think, Daddy. Did she ever say that the doctor thought it was something called conversion disorder? Or hysterical blindness?"

"No." Then, in a surer voice, "Hysterical blindness? I would have remembered that. I don't think she ever forgave herself for letting you get taken."

"What?" Elaine had always intimated that it was Olivia's fault, because she'd been hiding. Olivia had accepted that blame. Even when Elaine was dying, she wouldn't discuss the kidnapping. She'd just wanted to talk about the good things, like the beauty pageants, the glory days.

"She didn't talk about it much, but when she did, she blamed herself. That's why she went to such lengths to make it up to you, by demanding that the stores have procedures in place so it wouldn't happen again."

But it had.

"I hated being her poster child for abduction," she said before thinking about it. "But it makes sense, her alleviating her own guilt by trying to make it right." She shook her head. "That's all over now."

"I let your mother have her way with everything. I knew you didn't like it. You told me enough times, but it was always her way. After working hard for twelve hours a day, I didn't have it in me to fight her over every little thing. Or even the big things. I'm sorry about that, Livvy."

Livvy. Max had opened up an old soft spot with his use of that name, and now her father was unknowingly probing it. Livvy was long gone, Livvy who used to see the world without hoping it wouldn't crash down upon her.

"You did the best you could. You gave us a good life. And you're here with me today."

"Blue jay," he said, making tears spring to her eyes. "Shall we take a walk and do your eye exercises?"

"Yes, let's."

He stood, and she felt his hand grip hers. When she stood, he said, "I'm proud of you, Livvy. Even if I forget that, don't you forget it."

"Thanks, Daddy."

She wanted to tell him about the conversion disorder, but it was still almost too much for her mind to wrap around. He didn't need to know about that anyway. What could he do now? He'd only feel bad for not intervening, and then he'd forget about it. She let him lead her out to the lawn.

When Max stepped into the lobby of Olivia's building, Judy was vacuuming. She turned off the cleaner and pushed her brown hair from her face. "You looking for Olivia?"

"Sure am."

"She's not home. She spent the night at the Livingston with her dad."

"The Livingston?"

"Yepper. She called me this morning to tell me not to come by to mix paints for her. She got worried about him last night and went to be with him."

"Is he all right?"

"I guess so."

He walked over, hoping to catch her on the way back. As soon as he passed the bridge, his gaze went right to her, walking with her father on the vast lawn. Stasia followed along, but Olivia's father was guiding her now. Whatever had happened last night, he looked fine now. Her arm was linked with his, and she leaned close to him. Not out of need for guidance but just to be close. He was a tall, good-looking man with Olivia's bone structure. He'd aged quite a bit since that newspaper article.

Max slowed his pace and casually crossed the large lawn dotted with shady oak and pine trees. She looked happy. They were talking, and she was laughing. The throaty sound made him pause and take a breath. How often did she laugh like that? Probably not much.

Keeping the casual pace, he walked past them. Stasia recognized him, perking her ears. Luckily, she didn't bark. He knew he was using Olivia's blindness to his advantage but couldn't bring himself to break the spell. He didn't want to take away a moment of happiness with her father either.

She and her father sat on one of the benches that overlooked the waterway. Max sat on the adjacent bench. He told himself he was doing his job; perhaps he would overhear something that would help.

Yeah, right. He couldn't quite convince himself he was working under pure, unselfish motives. He should leave, give her privacy. He settled more comfortably on the bench. He should sit at the farthest bench and wait for her to finish her visit. He stretched out his legs and crossed them at the ankles. *Give it up, Callahan. No way are you walking away from that laugh, that smile.*

"Pine trees," her father said.

She closed her eyes in concentration. "Slash pine?"

"Yes, with the —"

She held up her hand. "Don't tell me. Long needles, dark green. Rough bark."

"Right." Mr. Howe looked around the grounds. "Oak tree."

"Small leaves, grayish-green. Rough, gray bark. Maybe even some Spanish moss dripping from the branches."

"Very good. Uh ... I can't remember any other tree names."

"Let's try birds."

"Birds. Let's see. Cardinal."

"Bright red, with the little tuft on top of their head."

He looked around, and his gaze settled on a blue jay

hopping across the lawn squawking. "Blue jay."

Again, that heart-stopping smile. "Blue and white, and he's sure mad about something."

Her father glanced up at Max, and they exchanged a civilized nod. He turned back to Olivia. "Woodpecker."

"Red head, gray bodies that float gracefully up the tree trunks and across branches."

"Very good. You know, I play this game with my little girl to help her remember what things look like. She's blind."

"Yes, I know."

Max felt his throat tighten. They were playing a memory game. But why was he referring to his daughter in the third person?

Her father took her hand in his. "I'm glad you came to see me, Jane."

Jane? Her expression looked pained, and her voice sounded thick when she said, "Me, too."

Something opened up inside him, something that had been closed for a long time. It was a good thing she didn't let her walls down like this with him. He'd have to do something gallant like kiss her until she didn't look sad anymore. Tell her bad jokes until she cracked a grin. Make love with her until she forgot everything that had ever stolen her smile.

Olivia patted his arm after a few minutes. "I should go."

They started walking toward the elegant building that stood in the shadows of huge oak trees. Her father said in a near-whisper, "There's a young man back there who seems quite taken with you."

Her whole body tensed as she turned her head. "Really?" She'd forced a casual tone to her voice. "What does he look like?"

Uh oh. Busted. He meandered toward the waterway and waited in the cool shadows of the trees nearest the sidewalk. Fifteen minutes later, she walked out, led by Stasia. He could leave, then come to her apartment and pretend it hadn't been him. He was already on her hit list. But he couldn't deceive her. He felt low enough listening to her private conversation.

"Olivia."

She stopped and faced him, and he saw that she'd been crying. The residue of tears glistened on her lashes. "That was you my father was talking about?"

"Who did you think it was?"

"I don't know." Her mouth tightened into a fine line. "Judy said you were here. I want to talk to you."

She started walking again and without looking back, said, "Go to hell, Detective Callahan."

His Rose was waiting for him, just as she always was. Her eyes were glued to his every move. Sometimes her expression was full of hatred; other times it reeked of fear. The fear usually gave way to anger after the fourth day, then to hopelessness. He set the Burger King bag near the cage, but not close enough for her to reach it. Not that she'd dare take it before he gave her permission. He walked into the bathroom and watched her in the mirror as he washed off the cola that had spilled on his gloves. There had to be rules, and the penalty for breaking those rules had to be harsh. Where would this society be if rules weren't enforced?

Exactly where it was now.

His father had been right about that, at least. But the man had violated his own code of ethics, the hypocritical bastard. He had watched Father go into his sister's room after Mother had passed out. He knew what Father was doing behind that closed door. It was left to him to hold his sister afterward while she cried, and he wallowed in helpless rage. He'd wanted to punish his father in the most heinous way, but he was only a child.

His father was revered, emulated. No one knew the ruthless domination he wielded over his family, nor would they believe it. No one could help his sister. If the system had punished his father, this rage wouldn't exist.

Even now, the rage ate away at him like acid. As he'd grown stronger, older, he'd planned revenge a thousand different ways. He'd never gotten the chance. Some faceless man who had no grudge against his father was the one to cut him down in a police shootout. His father was buried with all the honors, graced with tears and anger.

His fists clenched so hard they ached. He took a deep breath and relaxed them. His face, shadowed by the cap, stared back from his reflection. It was a different face than that young man he'd been. Not just older but reconstructed to fit the face of the man whose identity he'd taken all those years ago. Maybe someday he'd get used to it.

The tub was half-filled now, the incessant drip doing its job. By tomorrow night, it would be sufficient. He dipped his bare hand into the cool water and swirled it around. The ripples eventually died to a smooth surface again. Like the rage that would no longer ripple across his soul. For a while, the surface would be peaceful.

He put his damp glove back on and walked to the

cage. He positioned himself in front of the light. "Hello, Rose."

No response, only that hopeless look and a quick, darting glance toward the bag of food.

"Rose, what do you say to me?"

"Hello, Father," her croaky voice said.

He opened the cage door and set the bag and orange soda inside.

"Thank you, Father."

Ah, she was getting it. They usually did by now. While most of their hope had drained away, they still thought there was a chance he'd let them go home if they were good. As though being good would spare anyone. His sister had always obeyed, but that hadn't spared her.

But Rose, she had taken away something more precious than his sense of good and evil. Of righteousness. And justice. She had taken away so much more. Tomorrow night at midnight, she would die for it and release him.

She was gorging on the burger, but her gaze was on the door of the cage. He'd left it ajar. Hmm, how about that?

"I'm going now, Rose. You won't do anything bad, will you?"

She shook her head, those big, brown eyes glued to him. But she would. Rose always disobeyed.

"I'll be back with your dinner tonight."

He'd disabled the main door's locks from the inside so she couldn't lock him out when she did gather the guts to leave that cage. No way could she get out of this place. But she would try. They always did. It was part of the plan.

"F-father?"

He turned around to her.

"Thank you for the food."

Those simple words, spoken in true gratitude, stuck him in the gut like an ice pick. He couldn't answer her, only nodded. He closed the heavy door and locked it. The torment grew inside him. He had to follow through, just as he always did. If he didn't, he'd explode from the anguish and rage inside him.

She'd sounded so sincere.

He hoped she disobeyed him. He had to follow through with the plan. He had to.

CHAPTER 18

"All right, I deserve that," Max said, walking beside Olivia back through the park toward her apartment. "I think your biggest problem is my seeing a tender side of you."

She stopped, jerking poor Stasia to a halt with her. "Did it *turn you on*?"

He slapped his hand over his heart. "Ouch. Okay, I deserve that, too. Can we call it even now?"

"Not by a long shot." She started walking again.

"Go ahead then, get it off your chest."

"Unfortunately, I'm too much of a lady to use language like that."

"Well, you did pretty good a few seconds ago."

She narrowed her eyes at him but kept walking. There was a flush on her cheeks. "I hate you."

His eyes widened at the vehemence of her statement. "You don't know me well enough to hate me."

She stopped again, talking to a spot about two inches to his right. "Yes, I do. That night at my apartment, you made me think ..." She threw her hands up in frustration and started walking again.

He took hold of her arm. "I made you think what?"

Her chest was rising with her rapid breaths. "That you believed in me."

"I had to find out the facts, Olivia. That's what I do."

"Well, you do it well. Do you handle all your suspects like this?"

"When I said I was handling you, I didn't mean it like that. I meant I was dealing with you."

"You let that creep of a partner interrogate me. You didn't even have the guts to question me yourself."

"I didn't know Sam was bringing you in. I found out when I returned from the station after talking to Dr. Bhatti."

She tried to tug her arm free. "Excuse me, I need to get home."

"I need your help, Olivia." That stopped her struggle. "Not as a suspect, but as a witness."

"What makes you believe me now?"

"I'm willing to explore the possibility — the probability that it's real." But she had to be wrong about it being the man who had taken her.

They both seemed to realize he was still holding her arm at the same time. Her pale skin contrasted his tan work-worn hand. He released her.

"Of course, I'll help," she said at last. "But don't ever eavesdrop on me again."

He took in her face, once again taking advantage of her blindness. He could look all he wanted, and she'd never know it. "I couldn't help myself."

"I hope that's not supposed to be an apology."

His mouth twisted into a smile. Damn, she was hard. "It was wrong, and I apologize."

She nodded. "Thank you for that. Did you think I was going to confess something to my father?"

"No."

"Give away my *phony* blindness?"

"No."

He couldn't easily explain why he'd been compelled to watch her. He didn't want to see that side of her, didn't want to be touched by her, but he'd stayed anyway.

"Then why?"

"I was waiting for you to finish your visit. I didn't want to interrupt."

"So, you just watched us."

"Yes, I watched you."

She started walking again, but slowly this time. Not to get away from him. They walked in a comfortable silence. The cheery holiday music coming from the overhead speakers was at odds with the turmoil inside him. They passed the Edgewater where people were catching a matinee or eating at one of the cafes, not a care in the world. He envied them, envied their ability to enjoy a perfect, warm Christmas Eve.

"Why come to me when you're not sure if I'm crazy?" she asked at last.

This time he had to be honest. "Time is running out, and you're all I have."

"I'm not a suspect anymore?"

"Not to me."

"You have nothing to go on?"

"Nothing." Frustration laced his voice.

"I know you don't believe your father is still alive, but did you at least confirm whether the remains had been verified as his?"

"I put another call into the sheriff's department this morning. They promised to get back to me today."

After a minute of silence, she said, "Do you think I want him to be alive?" She shook her head. "I've never wanted someone to be more dead. I don't want to think that he's been out there all this time. But we have to keep our minds open. Phaedra's life depends on it."

"I know, believe me, I know."

She slowed again, and her hands tightened on the leash. "I connected with her last night. I've been trying to stay with her longer, but something always pulls me out. This time it was the people in the park."

"People in the park?"

"I was sitting on a bench in the dog area when the connection hit. I guess they thought I was having a seizure."

"*You collapsed in the park?*"

"Don't make it sound like such a big deal. There were people around."

He was feeling more and more uneasy about her, about her vulnerability.

She continued. "He did exactly what he did to me. Starved her all day, then brought her fried chicken and told her not to eat it. Left her alone with it so she'd be tempted and give in."

"Did she?" he asked when Olivia seemed to drift off.

She nodded. "He made her eat hot sauce, and she threw everything up." Her face tensed.

"Will he keep starving her?"

"No. Today will be a new game of punishment. He'll leave the door of the cage open, and when she tries to escape ... he'll cut her." Her fingers brushed across her upper chest.

He was glad she couldn't see his shudder. "That's what my father was doing when I found you."

She could only nod as she faced the water. Max realized that if he believed her, he had to accept that Bobby Callahan was alive. He couldn't accept that, though. He remembered her chopped hair and dirty face, the tear tracks on her cheeks. Games of punishment. The thought of that little girl being punished, and how his father had been big on punishment and discipline...

He held back those thoughts. "Have you connected with her today?"

"Just a sense of unease when he's there but not threatening her. She's used to a certain level of fear. It takes a higher level to bring me to her. With the other kids, all I got were flashes of what they saw. But with Phaedra, I'm able to stay longer. The connection is stronger because the same man took us. But when Stasia nuzzles up to me, because she's afraid, she brings me out of the connection. I need to be alone when Phaedra tries to escape. I need to stay with her when he cuts her. I'm not sure she can feel my presence, but it makes me feel better to be there with her. And maybe I can see where she's being held."

A yacht motored past them, and the three children on the foredeck waved. Max lifted a hand halfheartedly. Right now, he had to assume that Olivia was indeed connected to Phaedra Burns. He felt that tug inside him, pulling him down. If he was close to sinking, Olivia was going to be the one to tip the balance and send him under. If he got too close to her. And if he was going to work with her — to believe her — he was going to have to get close to her.

He was leaning on the railing next to her and realized he'd involuntarily moved close enough that their arms touched. He had to remind himself that this wasn't the

Olivia he'd seen with her father. This was the Olivia who wouldn't let him hold her hand when he'd given her the news about her conversion disorder. The Olivia who hated him.

"You're not going to be alone the next time you connect with Phaedra. Not if I can help it. What if you fall and hit your head?"

"I have to be alone. I can't afford to lose the connection again. Time is running out."

"I won't pull you out. And I'll make sure Stasia doesn't either."

When he thought she would object, she surprised him by nodding. "All right. Anything to help. I should probably head back now, just in case …" They took three steps before she stopped and reached for his arm. "Did I tell you about the tub?"

"No."

"There's a tub in the bathroom. Water keeps dripping into it."

"My father had a tub in the truck trailer with you. What did he intend to do with it?"

Her fingers tightened on his arm. "I don't know."

He had just slipped the lock pick into Olivia's door when he heard the door across from her apartment open. He took a calming breath and turned around.

"Hey, who are you?" the man who came out asked, walking right up to him like he owned the place. Or maybe like he owned Olivia.

He recognized Terry Carlton, the hotshot football pro. He was decked out in a flowery silk shirt and tight jeans. "You know Olivia Howe?" he asked, nodding toward the door.

"Know her? She's my girl." Carlton glanced down at the hand he still had wrapped around Olivia's doorknob, obscuring the pick.

"Then you're just the person I need to talk to. Come on inside. We have a problem." He walked in the apartment and waited for Carlton to follow. Like a concerned, curious boyfriend should, he did. "Close the door," he told him and walked into the kitchen. He opened the cutlery drawer and removed one of the knives he'd turned upside down earlier.

Carlton closed the door behind him. "Is Olivia all right?"

He walked back into the living room, the knife held at his side. "Has she told you about the strange occurrences that have been going on in here? Someone turning her volume knobs up, moving her furniture around, rotating her steak knives so she'd cut herself when she took one out?"

Carlton's face paled. "No. Someone's been breaking in here and tampering with her stuff?" The muscles in his jaw flexed as anger flared in his eyes. "Who? Why?"

"We're not sure yet. That's why I'm here. I'm a private security analyst. She hired me to see how easy it was to get in here — well, you saw. Too easy. I'm supposed to take a look around and see what needs to be done to catch the bastard."

"All she needs is me living here. I'll take the son of a bitch out the second he steps inside." Carlton started pacing. "I can't believe she didn't tell me."

"Maybe she didn't want you overreacting." He shrugged. "Well, while you're here, you can help me. I need to figure out how many security cameras the place needs. Stand right there while I measure the angles."

Carlton stood in the middle of the room by the chair. He scrubbed his fingers through gelled curls. "I can't believe she didn't tell me. What is she thinking? I'll bet it's the building manager. I've seen him watching her. He looks like the kind of guy who'd get his jollies messing with a helpless woman."

While Carlton continued to grumble, he pretended to sight the angle from the front door. "One to cover the foyer. So, is that how you met Olivia, living next door to her? Wish I had a nice-looking single woman living near me."

"Actually, we lived together for a while, but she needed space. So, I bought the place across the way."

He pretended to calculate some numbers in his head. "She's the independent type, huh?"

"No, that's the thing. She's not. But she'll come to her senses, hopefully by New Year's Eve. I've got a special trip planned, flight to Vegas, honeymoon suite at Caesar's, hopefully even the marriage to go with the suite."

"I'm sure you'll talk her into it." He glanced at the French doors by the kitchen. "Let's see what we need over there."

As he passed Carlton, he swung his arm up and jammed the knife into his neck. Blood spurted out and ran down his chest, soaking his flowered shirt. Shock passed over his expression for a second, and then anger. But before he could act on it, he twitched. His eyes rolled back, and he slumped to the floor. The flow of blood dwindled to a trickle as his heart stopped pumping.

He went into the kitchen and grabbed a bunch of garbage bags from beneath the sink. After wrapping Carlton in them, he checked the hallway to make sure nobody was out there. He dragged the body to the door, listened for any sound, and then dragged him to the apartment across the hall. He dumped the body on the floor and returned to Olivia's.

One large bloodstain marred the beige carpet, and some had splattered on the side of the beige leather chair. As he started pulling the chair over the stain, a deliciously evil thought came to mind. He leaned down to the stain and dipped his finger in the warm blood.

When they walked into her apartment, Olivia bumped into the chair Max had sat in while watching her paint. She set the cappuccino he'd bought for her on the end table. "He's been here again. He moved the chair."

Max drew his gun. "Stay right there. I'll look around." Olivia waited to release Stasia until he returned to the living room and said, "Nothing." He glanced at the painting she'd been working on and stopped cold. "Uh ... Olivia?"

She straightened, picking up the odd pitch in his voice. "What?"

"Are you into some kind of exploratory phase of your painting career?"

"What do you mean?"

"The painting on your easel. Did you write the word *BITCH* across it?"

Her hands went to her throat and her face paled. "No."

The word was rendered in red paint that dripped all the way to the bottom edge of the painting.

"Dammit, Terry's gone too far." She grabbed the chair. "Isn't there anything we can do?"

"I could have the place dusted for prints, but his prints could legitimately be here. I'll ask around the building, see if anyone saw him."

"I doubt anyone did. Not many people live full time in this building. The couple down the hall just left on vacation."

"We could set up cameras."

"Inside my apartment? And who's going to watch them?"

"I'll volunteer." He raised his hand half-heartedly and then dropped it. All he was thinking about was catching the bastard, but it hadn't come out right.

She lifted an eyebrow. "You really are a voyeur, aren't you? I've never been into that sort of thing. That was a joke," she added after a moment. "You know, using humor to deflect my lack of sight."

"You realize you do that, huh? Here, let me get it."

She knelt down to feel for the tape so she could line up the chair again. Before he could reach her, she let out a garbled scream and fell backward.

He nearly choked at the sight of blood covering her fingers. "What happened?" He dropped down next to her and took her hand in his.

"I'm not hurt," she said in a strangled voice. "It's blood, isn't it? I can smell it."

He still checked her hand over, running his fingers through the blood to make sure she hadn't been cut. Nothing more than the scrapes she'd sustained from her fall. Only then did he shift his attention to the large stain on the carpet. "What the hell?"

"What's happened?" she asked in a shaky voice.

"There's a bloodstain on the carpet. Someone moved the chair to cover it." He helped her up, and they walked to the kitchen. Without even thinking about it, he held her hands beneath the water and rubbed off the blood. Soap bubbled on their skin and washed down the drain with red-tinged water. He realized he'd taken over, but she didn't protest. She didn't look as though she had the strength. He dried her hands and led her to a chair at the table. "I'm calling for backup."

As he called, his gaze went to the painting again. Not red paint at all. That was blood.

After the crime scene investigators finished, Max joined Olivia at the kitchen table. She was sitting with her legs crossed and hands resting on her ankles. She'd been very quiet while the scene was being processed, remaining in the kitchen with her hands wrapped around a mug of coffee. Half a dozen times, he'd wanted to go over and just touch her. He wanted to touch her now.

Now, he sat across from her. "You all right?"

She nodded but pressed her mouth in a tight line. "Do you think Terry did this?"

"Who else would have the motivation to do it?"

She shrugged. "I can't believe he'd deface my painting. He knows what my artwork means to me. And why the blood?"

"You'd be amazed at what the lovelorn will do to get their victims' attention."

She shivered, and he wished he'd left that part out. "Have they found him yet?"

"The officers sent to pick him up for questioning said he wasn't home. He wasn't at the two sports bars you said he frequented either. We'll get him. He's bound to turn up somewhere." When she shivered again, he added, "We'll post someone at your door until we figure out who did it."

"Is it human blood?"

"Yes. What we need to find out is whose blood it is. If Carlton cut himself, he lost a lot of it. When we pick him up, we'll test the blood against his DNA." And against Phaedra's DNA, but he wasn't going to introduce that possibility to Olivia. He wasn't sure this had any connection to the kidnapping, but it was worth checking into.

She jumped up and went for the phone. After pressing three buttons, she said, "This is Olivia Howe. Can you please check on my father right now? Thank you." After a minute, she said, "Thank God. Please keep a close eye on him. I think someone might hurt him. Don't let anyone you don't know talk to him. ... I'm not overreacting. Just do it."

Max came up behind her. "What was that about?"

She leaned against the back of the dinette chair. "Earlier today, my father called me. He doesn't have access to a phone and he often doesn't even know who I am, so it was very odd. Then I could tell he was on a cell phone and someone was telling him what to say. When I asked who it was, Dad repeated that it was an old friend. That's why I went to see him today. Unfortunately, he couldn't remember who was with him. The staff at The Livingston saw no one, so they think I'm just paranoid." Stress and worry tugged on her expression. She looked in his direction. "Maybe you do, too."

"I don't know what to think about all this, but playing on the side of caution is the best course of action." The volume knob and knives were one thing. When she'd told him about her patio furniture being rearranged and showed him the bruise on her shoulder, he'd wanted to pound the guy. He'd felt sick when he looked at the heavy iron furniture. She could have been hurt much worse. "Maybe you should stay somewhere else for a while. I've got an extra room if you need it."

"Don't think that I need a bust-down-the-door cop with a hero complex trying to save the poor little blind woman, okay?"

He leaned into her face. "I don't have a hero complex. Being a hero is the last thing I ever want to be again."

"Because of your wife and daughter?" she asked in a gentler tone.

"If you're not comfortable staying here, I've got a room, that's all I'm saying. An officer will be posted outside the building to keep an eye on things. We should be able to track down Terry soon."

She took a candy bar out of the freezer. "Snickers bar?" She grabbed another one and felt the length of it. "Or a Baby Ruth?"

"No thanks."

She ripped open the Snickers bar and took a bite. He watched the second hand slide around the clock. Where was the time going? Maybe waiting with Olivia was a dead end, but she was all he had. He finished his coffee and tried to remember where her bathroom was.

"End of the hallway," she said and then clamped her mouth shut. "You didn't ask where the bathroom was, did you?"

"No, I didn't."

"Sorry. I sometimes just *know* something. I'm not reading your mind or anything. According to Jung's Collective Consciousness theory, everyone's minds are connected. My mind merely takes it one more step. I'm not aware of your thoughts or desires. I just respond. The words come out on their own." She waved it away. "I've done it for as long as I can remember. Used to freak out my parents, which made me hide it for a long time. Now I don't care."

"Is that how you knew the bookstore employee's name?"

"Probably."

Combined with the other times she'd known things, Max was beginning to believe her psychic knowledge. He excused himself and went to the bathroom. As he washed his hands, he heard a thump in the living room. He tore out. She was sprawled on the floor next to the couch. Stasia was making her way to her mistress's side. He knelt down between the dog and Olivia, holding Stasia away.

"It's okay," he whispered. "I'll take care of her this time."

Stasia sat with a whine, her eyes on Olivia. He moved the coffee table back but didn't want to touch her. Her body tensed, and she shook her head. Her mouth bent into a frown, and she murmured something that sounded like, "No, don't do it. Don't do it!"

He couldn't stop himself from taking her hand in his. It was cold and kept contracting in his grasp. Tears trickled down her temples as she rolled her head from side to side. Her pulse raced beneath his finger and her whole body trembled. A glittering sheen of sweat covered her face.

He couldn't deny it any longer. He believed her. No way could she be faking this connection to Phaedra. A cold chill snaked along his spine and made his eyes water. With the same abduction date, both girls being taken from a toy store, their similarities in age and looks, and what he was doing to Phaedra, it could only mean one thing: his father was alive.

CHAPTER 19

Phaedra stared at the door of the cage. She inched closer. The big steel door was closed. Not a sound. She scanned the area, looking for avenues of escape. The dim light made it hard to see details. The walls were made of large concrete blocks. The ceiling was metal and was sprinkled with lights. In the corner were stacks of plastic bins. A large, steel sink was mounted on the wall, like the kind in Daddy's restaurants. There were closed doors to the left and right of the bathroom. She could see another room behind her but couldn't see what was in it.

Maybe there was another way out in one of those rooms. She pushed out of the cage and made for the hallway at the same time that the metal door opened. She turned toward the spooky silhouette of Father, who stepped down into the room and slammed the door shut.

"I knew you'd disobey me. Come here, Rose. Don't make me chase you around. I'm bigger than you. Smarter than you. I'll catch you and you'll be punished even worse."

She faltered. When he lifted the knife, she shot forward. But it was already too late. He had a hold on her foot. She scrabbled against the slick, painted floor but couldn't get away. He jerked her toward him, holding the knife between *his teeth. It gleamed dully in the murky light. She screamed. He pinned her down with the weight of his body.*

"Shut up, Rose! Shut up!"

Her scream died as he loomed over her. He pulled off her shirt and tossed it aside. He pinned both her small hands with his one big hand and took the knife from his mouth.

"You must be punished."

She whimpered as the cold tip of the knife touched her left collarbone. She didn't dare move or even cry. It was only a fine line that he made, but it stung so bad.

He tossed the knife aside and pulled her up. He looked directly into her eyes, the shadows making him look evil. He smiled. And in a Southern accent, he said, "Okay, so I lied about the boat. I couldn't make it too easy on you, Olivia. You have until tomorrow. Christmas at midnight. And then ... time's up."

Olivia jerked up and right against Max. She was disoriented for a moment, wanting to bury herself against his hard body and never let go. Luckily, she regained her senses before doing anything foolish. When she backed away, she realized he'd been holding her hand. Their fingers were still entwined. She extricated her hand and rubbed her temples.

He leaned closer, studying her face. "Are you all right? What'd you see?"

She wiped the sweat off her face with the sleeve of her shirt. Then she remembered.

"He spoke to me! To *me*, Max! He said my name. He said he lied about the boat; he couldn't make it too easy on me." She clutched at his arm, crunching the material of his shirt. "We have until tomorrow at midnight! That's what he said! Oh, God, the cop. It was him, Max.

He set me up. Set us both up. He's playing with us, the same way he's playing with Phaedra."

He sounded stunned. "Bill Williams is my father? I mean, my father pretended to be Bill Williams?"

"Yes." She crouched on her knees and took hold of his other arm. "You have to believe me. This is real."

When he spoke, his voice was strained. "I believe you."

Relief flooded her. She forced herself to let go of his arms because she was only one step away from holding onto him.

He was quiet for a minute, absorbing the information. "Did you get a look at where he's keeping her?" he asked at last.

"It's bigger than I thought. There are other rooms off this one. That's where she tried to go, but she didn't have a chance. Light green concrete blocks, metal ceilings, and the floor is painted an off-white color. It looks very industrial, with stacks of plastic buckets in one corner, a large steel sink along the wall. Like a restaurant."

"Could it be one of her father's restaurants?"

"No, she would have recognized it. Besides, this place is closed. And clean. I couldn't see any containers of food or signs that it had been used recently."

He pushed off the floor and took her hand. "Are you ready to stand?"

"I'll just stay here for a few minutes."

"I'll have someone at the station run down all the vacant restaurants in the area. But first, I've got to call the sheriff's office again." His voice sounded shaky, but a thread of raw determination ran through it now.

She heard his cell phone beep as he pressed the numbers. "Detective Callahan from the Palomera Police Department looking for Stella Stewart." A pause, and then he introduced himself again. "I need that information on Robert Callahan's remains." A pause. "Yeah, sure." He turned to her. "She's got the report but hasn't had a chance to call me back."

She heard the woman on the other end say something.

Max said, "What I'm looking for are the tests done to prove the remains found in the truck were Callahan's. ... Yes, it's the same name as mine. What tests were done?" Another pause as the woman apparently looked through the file. "I need that report faxed to me." He gave her a number. "Are his fingerprints on file? ... I see. All right, thanks for your help." He disconnected. "They assumed it was him. No one was reported missing, and according to my testimony, he wasn't gone long enough to set up someone to take his place. But he did."

Those words hung in the air.

"Are you all right?" she asked after a few moments.

"Just great." He sank heavily to the floor beside her, as though his legs wouldn't hold him either. He took several deep breaths. "You all right?"

"I've had more time to get used to the idea of him being alive than you have."

"He's been out there all this time. Living as someone else."

"I know." She shivered. "They don't have his fingerprints?"

"They're gone, lost, whatever." She thought he might be rubbing his face in frustration. "What has he been doing all this time? Where has he been? Here, at least for a while. Oh, jeez. If he took you sixteen years ago, and Phaedra now ..."

"Maybe he's been doing it all along," she finished.

He remained still for a few moments. "How many?" he asked at last. "How many has he taken? We would have picked up a pattern if local girls were disappearing regularly. I've already pulled the files for all missing children cases in Palomera and Sarasota over the last twenty years. I'm going to broaden the search. Bobby used to drag us all around this area. If he's still a trucker, he could be anywhere. And if he's not ... there's something else I found out about him. He was a cop. He quit when I was two."

She wrapped her arms around herself. "There's more, isn't there?"

"It's just a thought, one I don't even want to put into words." He paused. "He's obviously created a new identity, and he's probably been living with it for years. Most criminals who take another identity eventually go back to what they did before. It makes sense, since they have the knowledge."

"You think that not only is he posing as a cop — as Bill Williams — but that he is a cop."

"He'd have a hell of a time getting through the screening process with a made-up identity, though. Unless he killed a cop and took his identity. He'd have to join another division. Even if he managed to take on the guy's physical features, he couldn't fool his friends and colleagues. If he transferred, he'd have his prints taken by the new station. Whether anyone would actually run them is up to speculation. But there's no way I'd get them to run the prints of every cop in his late forties in our area to see if they matched the ones on record." He took her hand and squeezed it. "And he was right here in your apartment. That scares the hell out of me. He could have —"

"But he never tried to hurt me," she said in a rush of words.

He got to his feet, and she let him pull her up. "Could he have moved your furniture around while he was here posing as Bill Williams?"

"No, I would have heard him. His intent wasn't to harm me here. It was only to discredit me with his so-called vision. Unless..."

"Unless what?"

"He called yesterday and wanted me to meet him for lunch. I asked him for his number to call him back. We got disconnected as he started to give it to me."

"He wanted you out of the apartment where he could grab you."

"If he'd wanted to grab me, he would have done it already. He could have..."

"Pushed you into traffic," he finished when she trailed off. "I'm moving in until we find him."

"Fine, if it makes you feel better." She knew she didn't sound very indignant.

Her protector. Even as she rebelled against the idea, she also felt safer knowing he would be around. Okay, a lot safer. She didn't want to think about her kidnapper being right there in her apartment, couldn't let that reality sink in.

"What about my father?" she asked.

"I'll ask the officer who's supposed to keep an eye on you to watch The Livingston instead."

"Thank you."

He took a deep breath. "This changes everything. With you and my father involved, they'll yank me off the case faster than I can say 'conflict of interest'. I need to decide how much I should tell my partner and boss."

"If only I could translate what I can see of his face to the canvas. It's vague, shadowy. He always has the light behind him, and he wears a baseball cap pulled low over his face. If I could just capture something ..." She bunched the hand he was still holding into a fist. "But I can't see what I'm painting."

He forced her to uncurl her fingers. "Does he look different from the man who took you?"

"I think so, but it's hard to tell."

"What I need is his motive. Why did he take you and Phaedra?"

"To punish Rose. Do you remember a Rose, someone your father knew?"

"No." He absently rubbed her fingers while he talked. "What can you remember about your abduction? Maybe there's a detail, something he said or did, that will shed light on it."

"I remember the punishments, but I blocked the details. According to my psychologist, it's natural for children who suffer traumatic experiences to block out what's happening."

She thought the silence meant he was mulling that over. She hadn't been much help.

"What about hypnosis?" he asked at last. "Those details are in your mind somewhere. Maybe we can unlock them."

The thought of someone probing her mind unnerved her enough to squeeze Max's hand. "Whatever we have to do."

"Dr. Bhatti recommended a doctor in Miami who specializes in hypnotherapy. He's worked with conversion disorder patients. He's actually helped people to see again."

"I don't want to take the chance of losing my connection with Phaedra."

"For now, we'll focus on your abduction. I'll fly him in tomorrow and see what he can do for us. There's someone I need to see: my father's sister, Odette. They were close. I'll bet she's known about him being alive all this time. Getting her to admit it will be the hard part, but I have to try. And you're coming with me. I'm not leaving you alone."

"Your aunt isn't going to open up if I'm with you."

He paused. "You're probably right. Strangers always made her skittish."

"I can stay in the car. I'll lock the doors." When he started to protest, she said, "I'll be fine. Let's eat and we can get on our way."

Max and Olivia threw together some grilled cheese sandwiches for lunch. One thing he learned about her was she liked her junk food. She had three kinds of potato chips, all gourmet, and her stash of candy bars in the freezer.

"The nice thing about being blind is never having to see an extra pound or a pimple," she'd said in her wry way when he pointed it out.

When they walked outside, the hairs on the back of his neck prickled. That feeling of being watched crept along his spine. He reached into his pocket for his new shades, which he'd forgotten again. He pretended to look for them as he scanned the immediate area. After seeing nothing suspicious, he grabbed his cell phone and dialed Sam. He didn't hear the phone ring anywhere nearby or Sam's voice when he answered.

"Sam, it's Max. Where are you?"

"Heading back from the bogus lead. What's up?"

"I need you to pull more missing child cases. This time broaden the search. Pull Tampa, St. Petersburg, Orlando, Bradenton, and Lakeland. Go back fourteen years, but focus on December abductions. While the records departments are working on that, start checking every closed restaurant in the area that wasn't checked in the grid search. And, Sam, make it fast."

"Wait a minute. What's going on?"

"I'll fill you in when we reconnect later. You find the girl, and I'll find the guy who took her." He wanted to say that the guy had been a cop once. That maybe he was again. The words wouldn't leave his mouth. "Trust me, Sam. We're moving in on this."

"Max, it isn't right, you holding back like this. Makes me nervous as hell, working in the dark."

"When I have a better idea of who's behind this, I'll spill. Trust me."

"Yeah, sure." Sam disconnected.

How could he explain that he knew who was behind this abduction, but he didn't know who he was now? He'd sound like crazy, as Olivia would say. And if he couldn't push out the words that the man had been a cop, no way could he say it was his father. The thought caved in his stomach.

They had been walking to his car as he'd talked to Sam. He helped Olivia and Stasia into the passenger side, then got in and headed north, groping for his wayward sunglasses. Once they were perched on his nose, he realized why he kept losing them — he hated wearing them.

"Odette wouldn't talk about her past, even through the years I lived with her. She wouldn't talk about Bobby either, and she refused to believe he was going to harm you."

"Sounds like blind devotion," she said.

He wondered if she was trying to make a pun, but she looked serious.

"She made excuses for him: he went through bouts of depression; he'd never gotten over my mother's death; he was under a lot of pressure. Nothing to even remotely justify abducting a girl."

"You'd be surprised what people can manage to justify — to themselves, anyway."

"In a madman's mind, it could."

He was headed to the rural town of Backwater, an hour's drive away. During the drive, he left a message with Dr. Marano, the hypnotherapist. Marano returned his call shortly after, and Max went over the case and Olivia's history.

"Can you help us?"

"I can probably help her to remember what happened during her captivity if she's hypnotizable. But helping her to see again..."

"That's not what we're trying to accomplish right now." Max glanced over at Olivia. She was stroking Stasia's fur, and the graceful movement kept catching his eye.

"It is intriguing, though. What if she could see after sixteen years? What if we could remove the wall after all that time? It would probably be a first. I'm very interested in working with her on that at a later time. It will depend on how well she's preserved her visual memory."

His chest tightened at the memory of Olivia and her father going over birds and trees. "She has."

"That will be one point in our favor. When can you bring her in?"

"I need you to come to Palomera tomorrow. I know it's last minute, but we're running out of time. We only have until tomorrow night to find the girl. I can arrange to fly you in if you can clear your schedule for us. We'll have you back home by early tomorrow evening."

"You do realize that's Christmas, don't you?"

"When a little girl's in danger, I don't care what day it is. I'll double your fee. Buy you a present. Send your kid to college. Anything."

He chuckled. "Ah, I get your drift. Well, as it turns out, my *kid* is in Africa doing a study on the hypnosis of a remote tribe. They think he's a god. I have a dinner invitation, but this is more important."

"I'll arrange for the flight and call your service back. Thanks, Dr. Marano."

"We're almost there," Max said forty minutes later as he pulled off the highway onto the road that wound leisurely to Backwater.

"Home sweet home?" she asked.

"I hated the place as much as Odette loved it. It's not much more than a dot on the map, a nothing town of small farms, two schools, and a few stores. It hasn't changed much since I left to join the police academy." It hadn't been such a bad place to grow up, really. It just held the shame that had clung to him through his years here, and the secret he'd had to hold so close.

"Have you been back since?"

"I come to visit occasionally."

Odette never changed either. She held secrets close

to her, too, and one of those secrets was probably where his father was. The thought of facing his father struck him with fear. *Kill me! Little coward!* Max's fingers tightened on the wheel. Superman's kryptonite.

The farm brought good memories, too. It had been a refuge when his father left him here while he went away on longer trips and when they came for Christmas. It had seemed so much bigger then, but he could hardly call it a farm. More like a farm wannabe. It had the usual patches of vegetables laid out in a semblance of order. Toward the back was a fenced-in area where Odette kept a couple of cows, a ramshackle chicken shack, and a small barn.

He saw a boy with a sheet tied around his neck so that it flowed out behind him as he ran to save imaginary Lois Lanes. Sometimes he saved Olivia again, trying to make some sense of it, impossible as that was.

He pushed away that image and pulled into the long, dirt drive. Odette was over by the barn where the cows came home, looking as fragile and haunted as always. Her head lifted at the sound of his car's approach. She didn't recognize it at first; his cars changed over time, and they were purposely generic. Her apprehension gave way to a smile and a return wave when he stepped out of the car.

She was wearing something that looked like a nightgown, and beneath that, brown boots. The kids in town used to call her crazy, and Max defended her with all of his might. She wasn't crazy, just different.

He leaned into the open passenger window. "I don't like leaving you in the car."

"I'll be fine. She won't feel comfortable talking with me there, and I want her to tell you everything she knows. You go. We'll be fine, won't we, girl?" She rubbed Stasia's head. "I'll lock the doors, don't worry."

She was right, but he still didn't like leaving her alone. He made his way over to Odette, where she watched his approach. Her fine, white curls floated in the breeze. Her eyes were shadowed by hollows that made her look like an owl. Her eyelashes and eyebrows were as light as her hair, almost invisible.

"Maxie!" She met him a few yards from the barn and hugged him. "I should make some tea."

He pressed her close, though she kept her hands aloft. "It's good to see you." And it was, even under the circumstances. She had been the closest he'd had to a mother. He'd be forever grateful to her. "How are you?"

"I'm good, Maxie, real good." She took him in with a certain sadness. "Sometimes I still picture you as a boy. Now you're a man, not a boy at all."

He wasn't sure what to say to that, so he only nodded in agreement. She was tiny, almost bony. She swore she could eat a horse a day and not gain an ounce, though he had never seen her eat much at a sitting. "We need to talk."

Odette did not do "talks" well. Anytime something serious came up, her eyes started darting around and her hands twitched. They did that now. "I should definitely make some tea then."

She used the process to escape unpleasantness, hoping that by the time she was through, she could avert the conversation to something she liked better. Usually she won.

Not this time.

When he glanced at the car, Odette followed his gaze. "Who's that?" she asked.

"A friend of mine. She wanted to stay there."

He was sure Odette didn't mind. She didn't like strangers.

The house smelled the same as it always did, a bit musty, but overlaid with whatever she had baked that morning. The floorboards creaked more than they used to, but overall the house was in good repair.

"Who helps you keep this place up?" he asked, watching her expression.

She turned away from him and ran the water to wash her hands. "I use the money you send me, of course. Tim from town helps out. Sometimes Joe. You remember Joe, don't you? Nice young man. He and his wife clean the house for me, and I give them eggs and pies."

She was a couple of years older than his father, putting her around fifty. Her skin had the texture of a child's, smooth and pale. She'd never married. The farm had belonged to her parents, who had died before he could remember.

"I need to know something about my father."

She didn't falter for a second as she set the teakettle on the stove over the flame. In fact, she smiled at him with the face of an angel. "It's so good to see you, Maxie. Look at you, all professional-looking." She took in his dress pants and shirt with a proud smile this time.

Her pride touched him, but he couldn't let her sidetrack him. "Odette, it's important. I know you don't like talking about him —"

"I loved my brother. He's a good man, but they all think he's a terrible person." She gave him an accusing look. "You think he's terrible, too."

He didn't miss her mix of past and present tense. "He's alive, isn't he?"

She only blinked in response, then turned back to the teacups she'd set on a tray. They were dainty things and didn't match each other. "In me, he is. I'm the only one who loved him. I'm the only one who understood him."

Her voice was on the edge of breaking. Damn, this was why he shouldn't be on this case, why he shouldn't be the one questioning her. And why no one else could.

He tried a different tact. "Tell me about him then. Help me understand."

She looked hopeful at that, but her lips pressed together. "Just leave it alone, Maxie. Why bring it up now?"

"Because I'm investigating a case that's very similar to the one he was involved in. You do remember that, don't you? The girl he abducted." He walked over to the window. "That's her out there."

She pressed her hand against his chest. "That was all a mistake. You know he wouldn't hurt that girl."

"He did hurt her. He starved her, cut her, and played cruel games with her. Another girl is missing." He pulled out the picture of Phaedra. "This girl. I need to find her before something bad happens to her. Please talk to me. Tell me about my father."

"It's not fair to talk about the dead, Maxie."

The teakettle shrilled, and she went to work pouring the tea into those cups. She assembled the dish of sugar and a mason jar of milk on the tray. She shuffled her feet across the old wood floor as she carried the tray to the sofa. Dust motes floated in the lone shaft of sunlight coming in through the gap in the broken blind. Otherwise, all the curtains and blinds were closed. A small plastic tree was the only indication of the holidays, nothing more than lights on it.

He stifled his impatience and followed her into the living room where the sound of a clock filled the silence. Before he joined her, he walked to the front window and checked on Olivia again. He could see her sitting there, safe and sound.

Instead of sitting on the couch with Odette, he knelt down in front of her. Gently, he set his hands on her knees and looked up at her. "I need to know why he took that girl."

She cupped his cheek with her cool, dry hand. "Maxie, let the past be. It's better that way."

"Sometimes it's not. Sometimes people die because of it. Children die because of it. He's taken two girls that we know of. He's probably taken more of them between the first and this one."

Calm quickly replaced the fission of alarm that crackled across her expression as she leaned around him and fixed her cup of tea. "Maxie, drink your tea. It's orange pekoe. I think it's Indian, doesn't it sound Indian to you?"

It sounded like a dodge to him. To sate her, he took a sip, burning his tongue in the process. Though he knew he should go slowly, his instincts told him to try another tactic. "He wasn't a good man and you know it. He was violent. Mean. He was the worst kind of father a kid could have." He didn't have to pretend the pain of that statement.

She set down her teacup with a loud *clink*. "He wasn't bad. He wasn't. He did the best he could, considering..."

"Considering?"

"He just did." She gestured to his cup. "Drink your tea, Maxie. It's orange pekoe. I said that already, didn't I?"

He'd always been a good kid, not wanting to cause

her any trouble. He wasn't that kid anymore. He stood. "Bobby was cruel. There's no excuse for being cruel to a helpless child. There is no excuse for psychological torment. For locking a boy in a closet. Testing him." His voice rose as each sentence wrought a painful memory. "For stealing little girls."

She stood, tipping the sugar bowl over with the abrupt movement. "Stop it! He tried not to be like our father, he did! But it was so hard, he'd lived with fear and guilt and anger for so long." Tears stained her cheeks pink. "You had to pay for your sins, that's what Father taught us. But *he* never paid, and it drove Bobby mad with rage."

She sank down again, crying. This was the most he'd ever heard about his grandfather. He sat down beside her, close but not touching her. Father. That word sent a chill through him. "What did ... your father do?"

She shook her head, and her hands twisted into her flimsy nightgown. He could see right through it, enough to see her big, white underwear. He shifted his gaze away.

Tick, tick, tick.

"What did he do, Odette?"

"He did bad things to me. He touched me. Bobby tried to keep him away, but he was younger, smaller. Father was a big man, big and strong and mean."

His throat closed so tight, he could hardly push out the words, "What did your mother do?"

"Nothing. She was too afraid of him. We all were. But not Bobby. He tried, tried to protect me. Bobby wanted to hurt Father, I could see the rage in his eyes. I was too afraid to do anything but lay there." Her mouth twisted at the memory, and he felt bad for putting her through this. This explained why she was so timid ... and maybe why she was disappointed that he'd grown into a man.

"Why didn't anyone report him to the police?"

"The police." Her eyes were far away, but she managed a laugh. "Father was the police. He died a hero's death, in the line of duty. They buried him with the flag draped over his coffin and the whole town crying into their hankies. People made speeches about how great he was. And I smiled." She looked at him. "They thought I was crazy, I know they did. But I smiled all through the service. Bobby cried, but not for Father. He cried because he'd wanted to kill him. Because no one would ever believe Father was the worst kind of man."

Max put his arm around her shoulder and pulled her close. "I understand now. I do." He'd bullied. Now he had to gentle her. "What I don't understand is why Bobby took the girl. Was he going to do the things your father did to you?"

She jerked out of his grasp. "No! He would never do that, not after what I'd gone through. He protected me, took care of me. That's all he was doing to that girl, too, protecting her."

"He cut her, humiliated her. He took her from her family. Is that what you call protecting?"

"Stop it!" Her voice screeched. "He doesn't do it! He's not like that."

He lowered his voice. "So you're admitting he's alive."

"He's ... no, I didn't." She searched his eyes and knew she'd given it away. "He'd never hurt anyone. He's a good man. You have to believe that."

"Where is he? Let me talk to him. Maybe then I'll understand him." Like hell.

"I can't." Her delicate face stretched into a frown. "He tried to be a good father to you."

"But he wasn't a good father. He went into hiding, left me behind."

"Not behind. He's always been there. Watching you."

Icy chills skittered down his spine, and his stomach lurched. "Who is he?"

Tick, tick, tick.

"Like a guardian angel."

"Does he work with me?"

Tick, tick, tick.

"Watching over you."

"Dammit, Odette, who is he?"

"He's proud of you, you know." She took a sip of her tea, her pinky extended, as though they were having a casual conversation about his loving father.

His father was out there, watching him. Fear twisted inside him. He was that boy again, cowering under his father's glare, failing his tests or selling his soul to pass them. His fingers itched to grab Odette and shake the truth out of her.

He pushed up and started searching the drawers of the entertainment center. He remembered going through the old photo albums looking at pictures of his mother. There was nothing new there. He watched Odette's expression; she wasn't worried.

That changed when he walked back to the kitchen. She was a blur beside him, grabbing for a piece of paper on the fridge. She stuffed it in her mouth before he could reach her. He tried to pry her mouth open, but she'd already swallowed it. Like a child, she opened her mouth to show him.

He reined in his fury. "Don't you care about that little

girl? She's going to die if you don't help me. *Can you get that through your head?*"

"He didn't take her," she said with such certainty, Max knew she believed it. And he knew she wouldn't betray her brother, not for anyone or any reason.

He kneaded the bridge of his nose and forced back the frustration that threatened to engulf him. "Okay," he said a moment later. "At least tell me about Rose."

That startled her. "Rose?"

"He wants to punish Rose for making her mother cry. For disobeying him. That's why he takes the girls, to keep punishing Rose. She was a bad girl, apparently."

She shook her head. "Rose wasn't all bad." Her eyes widened. "You tricked me."

"I didn't trick you. I'm just trying to understand Bobby. That's what you want, right, for me to understand why he's doing what he's doing? See, you know all the facts. I don't. How can I understand him if I don't know the truth?"

While she was trying to sort that out in her mind, he glanced out the front window again. Olivia was still in the car. He turned back to Odette. Her loyalty prevented her from believing Bobby could harm anyone. Maybe it would also make her want to sway Max's opinion of him.

He pushed some more. "If Rose wasn't a bad girl, then Bobby can't be taking girls to punish her, right?"

"Yes. Yes, that's right." She looked confused, though, trying to work through his words.

"Then I need to know what happened. If you explain it to me, I'll understand. Who is Rose?"

She looked relieved at Max's logic. She was hopelessly lost in her devotion to her brother. "Rose was your sister."

Luckily, she walked back into the living room and didn't see the shock on his face. "My sister," he repeated as he followed her.

"She was four years older than you."

"I don't remember her."

"She died when you were two."

He tried to act calm and rational, stirring sugar into his tea even though he didn't like sugar or tea. "What was she like?"

Odette shook her head, a sad look on her face. "Bobby wanted Marie all to himself."

Marie. Max swallowed hard. "My mother." The woman he didn't remember.

"He was like that with everyone in his life, possessive. He'll do anything for you if he cares about you. Everything within his power," she added, a shadow crossing her face. "Marie wanted a baby, and he gave her one. But Rose was ... well, I'd call her spirited. Headstrong." She smiled, shaking her head. "So different from me at that age. Bobby couldn't see her charm, though. All he could see was that she wouldn't listen to him. A hell child, he called her. Bobby tried to be a good father, he did. He tried to be patient, but he always had trouble with that particular virtue. As you know," she said, giving him a sympathetic look. "Rose tried his patience so. When they came to visit, I could see her push him to the edge. It was like she was trying to prove something."

Something occurred to Max. "She got gum in her hair, didn't she?"

"Yes, but ... how did you know?"

"And she wet her pants sometimes?"

"Even at six. And she wouldn't bathe. She hated taking baths, and she was always dirty."

"And Bobby cut her once, like this." He demonstrated, drawing his finger across his chest.

She looked away. "She'd escaped the house again. He had to teach her a lesson. He couldn't just have her running all over the neighborhood. There had to be rules."

"You said she died. What happened?"

"There was an accident. She drowned in the bathtub." She covered her mouth. "No, not the bathtub. It was in the children's pool in the backyard. That's right, the pool. She'd gone out without telling anyone and drowned. It was an accident, just an accident."

She shook her head. "Marie never recovered from her daughter's death. Oh, she loved you, Max, she did, but she couldn't muster the energy to live anymore. They'd moved in here after Rose's death. They needed to get away from the bad memories. But I could see Marie wilting more and more every day."

"So, she killed herself." He'd never known why or how. No one would talk about it. "How did she do it?"

"She walked to the bridge and just leaped right off." She scratched her head. "Maxie, you were too young to remember some of that stuff you mentioned: the gum or the cut. How did you know?"

He picked up Phaedra's picture again. "Because that's what the man who took this girl is doing. It's what he did to Olivia. He took them both five days before Christmas. He put gum in their hair and cut it out. He wouldn't let them go to the bathroom and punished them when they wet themselves. He gave them an opportunity to escape the cage he put them in and then cut them when they tried." He made the cut with his finger again, watching her face. "He calls them Rose because he makes them into Rose."

The pieces were coming together. Every word pounded into his chest. Rose was a dirty child, didn't like to take baths. She drowned. *He* drowned her in a bathtub in a fit of temper. The bathtub found in the wreckage of the truck. The dripping sound Olivia kept hearing when she connected to Phaedra. The implications gave him the chills.

Odette was stirring her tea furiously. He stilled her hand. "That's what they told the police, right, that she drowned in the pool? They didn't want anyone thinking he'd drowned her." And with Bobby being a cop, the police wouldn't want to believe the worst. He'd still been a cop then, but he'd quit soon after Rose's death.

"No, it was an accident," she said quickly and took another sip of her tea. Her hands were shaking.

"And he drowns them on Christmas. That's the game he's going to play tomorrow. Tell her to clean up, not give her the chance to do so, then give her a bath."

She poured more tea, but sloshed the liquid on the saucer and tabletop. "No."

"Yes." He lifted Phaedra's picture. "He's chopped her hair off, made her drink water and wouldn't let her go to the bathroom, then punished her when she wet herself. Today he cut her ... and tomorrow night *he's going to drown her*."

"He loved Marie," she said, not looking at the picture. "He loved her so awfully much. She was his redemption. His life. He couldn't save me, but he saved her. He took her out of that terrible home she'd been living in and married her. Took care of her."

"And killed their daughter."

"No! It was an accident!"

This time he shoved the picture into her face. "This little girl is going to die if you don't tell me where Bobby is. You'll be liable for her death. Do you understand me? Legally and morally, you'll be responsible. I'll find a way to prove my father did this, and you'll be charged with accessory to murder. Are you really willing to let this girl die because of some misguided sense of loyalty? What about the next girl? And the next? *How many girls are you willing to let die in the name of loyalty?*"

She curled up on the couch and stared beyond him. "Everyone knows I'm crazy, Maxie. Maybe I made it all up. Maybe I just think Bobby is still alive." And in a softer voice, "Maybe I am crazy."

He didn't know what to do. He could bring her in for questioning, but he'd have to explain why. Who knows what Odette would say under those circumstances? With everyone watching Max on this case, they'd more likely think he was the crazy one.

He glanced at his watch. Phaedra was an hour and a half closer to dying.

CHAPTER 20

Odette waited until she heard Maxie pull out of the long drive. She looked out the window just to be sure. The office door was open. He'd been in there. She hoped he hadn't found the phone bills. No, that's right, she burned them as soon as she received them.

They'd been so careful. All to protect her dear, baby brother.

Her hands were still shaking when she dialed the cell phone he'd bought her. He had another one, and they were both in her name. She sagged against the counter when he answered.

"Bobby," she whispered in a broken voice.

"What's wrong?"

Just his voice, strong and worried and protective, shot strength into her. "Maxie was here. He just left, but he walked around the farm. He was looking for you, Bobby."

"You didn't tell him anything, did you?"

"He already knew about Rose. I told him she was his sister, that she drowned accidentally in the pool." She hesitated. "That girl Maxie rescued was with him. She stayed out in the car. She and a dog were with him when he was looking. He said you took another girl, and that you're calling her Rose. You don't have a girl, do you? That was an awful mistake before. And now he just thinks it's you because of last time, right?"

"Right. You're sure you didn't give anything away?"

"I'd never give you up. Then you'd go away like last time. But you'd never come back," she said in a whisper.

"It'll be all right. I'll never leave you again, Odette. As long as you don't tell him who I am, I'll always be here."

"I won't tell him, not ever. When will you be coming to visit? Please come on Christmas."

"I will, but it'll be late. Very late. You won't panic, will you?"

"No, I'll be calm, like you told me."

"Good girl. Let me deal with Max."

"You won't hurt him, will you? He didn't disobey you by coming here and asking about you, because you never told him not to."

"It's the woman I'll punish. I'll see you soon."

He had enjoyed toying with Olivia thus far. When he'd first seen her, anger had overcome his need for a plan. He'd simply wanted her dead, or even seriously hurt. Olivia was a lucky lady. But eventually her luck would run out. Until then, he would toy with her a little more. He would pay another visit to her father today.

Max had become fond of Olivia. No doubt, their past created a bond between them. As Max had always been drawn to women who needed protectors, he would be doubly drawn to Olivia. Too bad killing her would hurt Max, too.

That's why he would be there for Max afterward, like

any good father would.

Max felt drained as they drove back to Palomera. One minute passed into the next, another minute that Phaedra sat in some cage waiting for rescue.

Olivia said, "So we know why he's taking the girls."

He hadn't told her about the drowning part. He wasn't letting himself think about that. "We know he's recreating Rose, but we don't know why. I'm going to check in with Sam and see if he's found out anything."

"Nothing yet." Sam said a minute later, sounding as weary as Max. "The files are being pulled. Can you tell me why I'm looking in dirty restaurant kitchens?"

Dirty kitchens. "How many closed restaurants did you find?"

"Five. I'm checking on the last one now, past the Interstate exit."

"Are they all dirty?" Olivia had said the kitchen was clean.

"Sure. You think they're going to clean it spic and span on their way out of business?"

"Hell. What about restaurants that haven't opened yet?"

"No way could someone stash a kid in a restaurant that's about to open. Too much activity."

Max had already figured that out as soon as the words left his mouth. "She's in a kitchen, Sam. A large, clean kitchen. What about an Elks Club? Any civic club that has a kitchen? Country club?"

"We're in season. Those places stay busy. How do you know she's in a kitchen? This has something to do with Olivia, doesn't it? This is another one of her wacky leads."

"Let's meet at Ambrosia for breakfast at five-thirty tomorrow. I'll bring some maps. And I'll tell you everything. Meanwhile, start thinking about kitchens. It's here, and it's got to be in town, or at least close to it. He's got to have easy access to it."

"Do you still want me to check out this place?"

"Yeah, just in case it's the one time someone left it clean."

"What about you? You were going to find the guy who took her."

He needed something a little more concrete than the similarity of abduction dates to convince Sam that his "dead" father was the man they were looking for. "I'm working on it. But I will find him. I have to. I'll see you at Ambrosia."

"You do realize that's Christmas morning, don't you?"

He was going to kill her on Christmas, but that wasn't what Sam meant. He meant Christmas cheer, joy, watching your kid open presents, watching her face light up because "Santa" managed to find the exact toy she wanted.

"Sorry, man. Call me after Petey opens his presents." He hung up.

Christmas had ceased to mean much since Ashley's death. He had to admit he missed the celebration, the presents... everything.

"Nothing?" Olivia looked as disappointed as he felt.

"Something he said made sense, though. If a restaurant were going out of business, they wouldn't bother leaving the place clean. It's got to be something else then."

"Someplace with a kitchen."

They sat in silence, each lost in their own dark thoughts. Stasia was curled up on the seat between them, her head on Olivia's lap.

Olivia stroked her head. "I'm going to try to paint the room she's in again. Maybe I can capture something I can't describe. I need to paint. I need to do something."

He really shouldn't watch her paint, not when he was feeling tired and achy in his soul.

Why did he feel as though this case was about to shatter him into a thousand pieces? He was tired and frustrated, that's all. And headed to a place he shouldn't be going. At the moment, he just didn't care.

Max and Olivia stopped by his place so he could collect some clothes and other necessary items. It seemed strange having her in his dreary home. Even stranger when she wanted to "see" his statues, when she'd run her fingers over the Man Who Laughs and said, "It's beautiful." She traced his frozen grin, her Mona Lisa smile in place. What was she thinking?

He didn't want to speculate. "We should go."

When they stepped onto his front porch, he paused, remembering Olivia's suggestion that Bobby might live nearby. Max didn't even know who his neighbors were. When they'd moved in, he'd been too busy working to make friends with the neighbors. Diana had gotten to know a few of the mothers, but those women had drifted away after the initial rush of casseroles and condolences. Max had been more than happy to let them go.

Now he scanned the nearby homes on his street, trying to picture who lived there. "I can't think of any men who would fit the description and situation."

"He may not live alone. He could be married and still carry out his plans if he had a lot of freedom."

"Good thinking." Freedom. Cops had lots of freedom. He took Olivia's hand. "Let's get back to your place."

When they returned to her building, she paused by the door of the apartment across the way from hers.

"What's wrong?" he asked.

"I've been trying to meet whoever bought this place. According to Ronald Ford, some corporation owns it. Someone's been staying there, but they've been very shy." She shook her head. "I'm sure it's nothing. Come on, I'll show you how the futon works."

After she set him up with sheets and pillows, he left her to her painting while he took a hot shower.

"Your phone rang," she told him when he rejoined her.

He checked it and returned the call. When he hung up, he said, "Still no sign of Terry Carlton yet. It's like he vanished."

"God, what could he be thinking, doing what he did and then taking off like that?"

"I hope we'll get to ask him that soon."

She shook her head, as though trying to shake the thought of it loose. "What do you think?" She gestured to the wet canvas. "Is it any help? The colors aren't exact; I'm using primary colors."

She'd been painting maniacally since they'd returned. She was wearing an oversized denim shirt that had seen many painting sessions and white leggings. She'd failed to tie back her hair, and strands of it were green. She had a similar streak on her cheek where she'd pushed her hair back from her face.

He realized he was looking at her instead of the

painting and shifted his gaze. It was vaguely a room, and because he knew the square object in the corner was supposed to be a sink, it sort of looked like a sink.

"It's too abstract to tell me much."

Her shoulders drooped. "I've never been good at details. Maybe I should have chosen something more sensible than painting to get into. Like fencing." She tilted her head and gave him her Mona Lisa smile. "Joking."

Livvy.

Was he so drawn to her because of that rescue? Was that the only reason he was struggling to keep from touching her now? He stuffed his hands in his pockets to stifle the temptation. "I know."

She reached for her mug. "I hope I can help tomorrow. With the hypnotist, I mean."

He did touch her then, resting the tips of his fingers against her forehead, grazing his thumb across her cheek. "I don't want you to get your hopes up. We may not discover anything new. Don't blame yourself if we don't."

She narrowed her eyes. "You're trying to protect me again, aren't you?"

He dropped his hand. "Yeah, I guess I am." Was he as bad as Terry, wanting to protect her from the world?

"Don't worry about me. You already did your saving, as far as I'm concerned. And I'm grateful for that, more than I could ever express. Seems to me you have yourself to worry about most. Dealing with the deaths of your daughter and your wife," she added when he didn't respond.

"I have dealt with them."

"By pushing them to the back of your mind? You don't just 'get over' something like that. I believe that's how you put it. I know, after months of counseling after my kidnapping."

"I don't need counseling." He stared at her painting. "I've moved on."

She turned around to face him. "Oh, God, you blame yourself for their deaths, don't you? Because you found that missing boy, and the guy retaliated. That would be so like you."

"You don't know me well enough to say that."

She tilted her head. "I know enough."

He ran his hand through his hair. "I don't get involved because I don't want anyone to hurt someone I care about as a way of hurting me. A safety precaution, simple as that."

She reached out and touched his arm. "Are you still in love with her?"

His gaze was on her fingers. "Who?"

"Your wife."

Even though she couldn't see him, he still looked away when he answered. "We hadn't loved each other in years. We made a deal to stay together for Ashley." Then he realized he'd have to tell her everything. "She was an alcoholic. I knew that when I met her, but she was trying to go straight. I helped her, we fell in love and got married. I thought everything was okay until I found out she was drinking during her pregnancy. I was working hard, trying to prove myself. Wasn't home enough. When I discovered the hidden bottles... it was too late. The damage was done. Ashley was born with fetal alcohol syndrome."

"Oh, Max," she said on a whisper, and her fingers tightened. "I'm sorry I asked. How terrible for you."

"It was worse for Ashley. But that's over now. There's

no use talking about it."

"It's not over. I can hear it in your voice. I told you, you give yourself away. You're the kind of man who takes on all the burdens of the world, aren't you? You probably blame yourself for not seeing that your wife was drinking during her pregnancy. Just as you take the blame for the car bomb. How much can you take on before you buckle under the weight?"

He felt that weight now, pushing him down. "Why aren't you innocent?" he asked, changing the subject.

"What?"

"At the station, you said you weren't fragile. Or innocent. What did you mean by that?"

She removed her hand from his arm. "All my life people have put me into roles, and if I didn't live up to those roles..." She shrugged, playing it down. "For years I lived the role of the little doll."

"For the beauty pageants."

She grimaced. "So, you know about my sordid past."

"I read the newspaper articles about your abduction, trying to get a better understanding about this case." *And her*, an inner voice challenged. "I wouldn't exactly call being a multi-pageant winner sordid."

Her laugh rang with cynicism. "You would if you'd lived it. And didn't want to." She cleared her throat. "After the kidnapping, Mother put me into the victim role, which is where I spent the rest of our relationship. Men are the same way, seeing me as an innocent, fragile blind woman, 'Aw, let's take care of her.' They assume this care-taking position, like they want to save me from the world. Or my blindness. When they discover I'm not the poor little blind girl who's never had sex in her life, they don't like it. They expect me to be virginal." She grew silent for a moment, turning away from him. In a stronger voice, she said, "I'm not virginal, haven't been since I was sixteen. Does that surprise you?"

"A little," he admitted. Then he remembered Terry bragging that he'd been her first. "A lot. It's your looks that cause some of that problem. You're beautiful, for one thing."

She wrinkled her nose at that. "Being beautiful stopped mattering a long time ago. Even before I went blind, I used to wish I were ugly. Being blind teaches you a lot about 'seeing' other virtues in people. I can tell a lot about a man by his voice, the way he smells, and how much and in what way he touches me."

He wanted to know what she thought of him based on those virtues, but it was better if he didn't. "And you look ... fragile. Innocent."

She rolled her eyes and stood. "You bought it, too, didn't you? I even fooled a cop with my act. Brother, another gullible one." She anchored her hands at her waist. "I've had a hundred and fifty men, I've had sex in elevators, bathrooms, parking lots, and in the back of buses. I've tied them up, and sometimes there's leather involved. It's always hot, sweaty, and it goes on for hours, all day sometimes, and—"

She couldn't talk anymore, not when he'd pulled her hard against him and stilled those words with his mouth. He'd given her no warning and had knocked her off-balance for a second. She wasn't going anywhere with his arms around her, but she wasn't trying to move away. He devoured her, and she opened to him and devoured him back. His fingers threaded into her soft hair, and he tilted her head and deepened the kiss.

Her body was pressed against his.

"You haven't had a hundred and fifty men, have you?" he said between kisses.

"Uh uh," she managed and then nearly sent him to his knees when she sucked his tongue into her mouth and stroked it.

He didn't want to think about her with anyone else, making him as guilty as any of the men she'd just talked about. She wasn't an innocent, not by the way she kissed. Oh, man, could she kiss.

"You haven't tied anyone up." He tilted her head back and licked her neck. His hands slid down to her ribs, his thumbs grazing the curve of her breasts through the denim. No bra. He kissed lower, over her ribs, lost in the feel of her soft skin against his mouth.

"No," she whispered as his tongue dipped into the space between her breasts.

He unbuttoned her shirt from the bottom, kneeling in front of her, stopping just beneath her breasts. Her stomach was warm and pale, and he alternated kissing and sucking at her skin. He skimmed her waist beneath her shirt and then went higher. His thumbs brushed her nipples, which were already hard and tight. Her breath hitched, and her body tensed. One of them made a growling sound, but he wasn't sure who.

She slid down to the floor in front of him and captured his mouth again. She held his face and tilted her head for a better angle. She was in control, this wanton witch who was not an innocent, wasn't a fragile, poor anything. She pushed him back until he was on the floor and then straddled him. Her tongue traced the bottom edge of his teeth, but she pulled it back when he tried to capture it. She flicked it across his mouth before sucking on his lower lip. Her breathing was coming hard and fast, making him aware that his breathing mirrored hers.

"Livvy ..." So many things crowded into his mind, tangling and making no sense at all. He wanted her, wanted to take care of her, wanted to hide inside of her and never come out.

"Don't call me that," she said in a breathless voice. "I'm not Livvy."

But she was Livvy, who needed him, who craved him, who was wrapped around his body as though she would never let go. She made him feel all those things he'd felt as a kid, the protector, the hero. She made him feel new things, too, things that had nothing to do with being a kid. His body was straining to be free of clothing constraints, to feel her skin against his, to release all the tension that had been building for days.

He was sinking fast.

"Max, I don't need a hero." She was still kissing him, but the frantic pace of her kisses was slowing. "What are we doing here? We're crazy, this is crazy." She pushed herself up, though she was still straddling him. "We can't do this. It's all wrong."

"It doesn't feel wrong," was all he could think to say with his head racing and his blood hot.

"Not to our bodies." She climbed off him and smoothed her hair back with rapid, nervous strokes. "Max, we're the last two people who should be doing ... this. We're getting all mixed up with our past, our roles as hero and victim. And finding Phaedra, that's part of it, too."

He couldn't move, other than to lay the back of his hand over his eyes. She was right, as much as his body didn't want to admit it. He'd be relegated to one of her past lovers who couldn't see her as anything but a fragile but not-so-innocent woman whom he had to protect from the world. From creepy ex-boyfriends. From the past, and her blindness.

He pushed to his feet. "Terry thinks he was your first lover. That you're fragile. Wait a minute. Is that how you lied to him?"

"Do you remember *everything* I tell you?"

"Yes."

She walked to her canvas and ran her fingers along the edge. "When we first started dating, he did assume all of that. And ... for some reason, I let him. Well, I know the reason. Not only was he the most charming man I'd ever met, he was this big football star. I was so flattered that he'd chosen me to bestow all of this attention on, I let him think I was what he wanted me to be." She turned away, her cheeks pink. "I never lied, per se; I just went along with him. When I realized he wanted to own my life, I tried to tell him the truth. I thought he'd be so mad, he'd break up with me. Instead, he refused to hear it. That's when I knew I had to get out of the relationship, for both our sakes. I swear I'll never sell myself out again."

"No, I don't suppose you will." He ran his hand through his mussed hair. "I'd better get some sleep. I've got an early start tomorrow."

"Don't think we can't control this" — she waved, indicating the space between them" — whatever it is between us. We're caught up in a tense, emotional situation, that's all. Then there's our past. It's natural, but not overwhelming, uncontrollable ... overpowering."

She stood there facing him, a slice of skin showing

where he'd unbuttoned her shirt. Her nipples pressed against the material. She was waiting for confirmation, her mouth still pink from the heat they'd created. He couldn't agree with her, not with the way she was leaning ever so slightly toward him, and the way he was doing the same.

He wanted to protect her and he wanted to sleep with her at the same time. She made him feel everything he never wanted to feel again. She made him feel.

"I've got to meet Sam first thing in the morning. If I'm not here when you wake up, wait for me. If Stasia has to go out, call me first."

She nodded and turned back to her canvas. "Goodnight, Detective Callahan."

His mouth quirked in a smile. "Goodnight, Olivia."

Olivia kept working on her painting, all the while running her and Max's conversation — among other things — through her mind. When the phone rang, she grabbed for it so it wouldn't wake him.

After a moment of static, she heard a man's voice. "Olivia?"

Her father. Tears sprang to her eyes as fear clutched her heart. "Daddy?"

A steady static filled the background. "Olivia," her father said again.

She came to her feet, knocking her easel to the floor. "Daddy, where are you?"

"I'm supposed to tell you ... I have to ask you ... did you like the painting I did for you?"

After another moment of that strange static, the line went dead. The painting he'd done for her? "Oh, my God! Max!"

"I'm here," he said from a few feet away. "What's wrong?"

"He's got my father," she said on an agonized whisper.

"Who?"

"Bobby Callahan. My father called and asked how I liked the painting he'd done for me." She wanted to cling to him and scream for him to find her father, but she held on to her control and dialed The Livingston. "It's Olivia Howe. Check on my father, James Howe, right away!"

"Ms. Howe, I'm sure your father's—"

"Now!"

"Yes, ma'am. Please hold the line."

Max was on his cell phone behind her. "Patch me through to the officer assigned to cover The Livingston." After a few seconds, "Hey, it's Detective Callahan. Any activity over there? Go in and see if they've found Mr. Howe. I'll check back with you."

"Anything?" she asked.

"He hasn't seen anything suspicious."

Someone came on the line. "Ms. Howe, this is Mrs. Johnson. It appears that your father is not in his room. I don't want you to be alarmed. I'm sure he's around here somewhere. We'll find him and give you a call back."

"I'll stay on the line." Olivia turned to Max. "He's not in his room. Oh, God, he has him."

He placed his hands on her shoulders. "Could you hear anything that might indicate where they were?"

"Static. I assumed he was on a cell phone. Wait, it wasn't static. That was what was strange about it. It was steady, more like something in the background, something I heard recently. It was a rushing sound. Like water. Or a waterfall." She reached for his arm. "Wait,

I think I know where they are! The water treatment facility, where that boy drowned not long ago. Every time I walk to my father's, I hear the sound of rushing water."

"Let's go."

"Stasia, we'll be right back," she said as Max led her to the door.

The short drive to the water treatment facility was the longest drive she could remember. She murmured the Lord's Prayer and tried not to picture her father stumbling into the water. Or worse, being pushed, held under.

"I need you to stay in the car while I look for your father. If Bobby's still with James, it could get dangerous. You'll be safe in the locked car."

She nodded, knowing she'd only be a liability to both Max and her father if she went with him. Damn blindness.

"The chain around the front gate has been cut." He pulled to a stop and touched her arm. "I'll find him."

She pressed down her lock and flinched when his door slammed shut. Never had she felt so helpless, not even when she'd been pushed into traffic. Her fingers curled around the door handle, and she started reciting the prayer again.

When Max rapped on the window next to her several minutes later, she nearly shattered with anxiety. She fumbled with the lock and pushed the door open.

"He's here," he said before she could even ask.

"What's going on?" James Howe asked. "Who are you people?"

Olivia went into his arms. "Daddy, it's me, your daughter. Livvy. It's all right."

"Livvy, what are you doing out at this time of night?"

It was probably too dark to see that she wasn't the little girl Livvy. "Max, you found him." She closed her eyes and relished that her father was still alive.

"He was just wandering around in there. Bobby must have heard my car tear into the parking lot and taken off. I'm sure he wasn't expecting us to find him this fast. He's probably long gone by now; the side entrance gate was open, too. Come on, let's get your father back to The Livingston." Once he'd helped James and Olivia into the backseat, he said, "We need to stick to the Terry Carlton theory. No one's going to take me seriously if I tell them my dead father tried to lure your father out. What they would take seriously is that I need to be taken off this case and put into therapy."

No, he couldn't be taken off the case! "I'll tell them whatever you need me to." She hated to admit it, but she needed Max. Needed his help, she clarified. If she'd learned anything tonight, it was how damned helpless she was during a crisis.

Max pulled out of the parking lot and headed toward The Livingston. Then he totally negated her fear by saying, "Olivia, you probably saved your father's life tonight. I'll have a cop stationed outside your father's room until we find Bobby."

"Thank you." She held on tighter to her father. He would be safe. But would they find Phaedra in time?

CHAPTER 21

Monday, December 25

Max woke at six in the morning, wishing he could take back all those lost hours and do something useful with them. Like what? What else could he do that he wasn't doing now? He pounded the pillow and pushed out of bed.

Once he was dressed, he headed toward the kitchen. Olivia's bedroom door was open enough for Stasia to come and go. He couldn't help glancing into the darkened room. All he could see was her form beneath the blankets. Stasia, lying next to her on the bed, lifted her head. He moved past the door and started the coffee. Stasia wandered into the kitchen a moment later.

"Don't tell her I was peeking in her bedroom, okay?" he whispered as he scratched her head.

"You were peeking in my bedroom?" a prim voice asked from the other side of the counter.

He knew his irritation at being caught showed in his

voice when he said, "What are you doing up so early?"

"Well, ho, ho, ho, Merry Christmas to you, too," she said, strolling into the kitchen and taking a can of dog food from the cabinet. She was wearing a fluffy white robe, and her hair was mussed.

"Sorry. Merry Christmas."

The electric can opener buzzed and *her* irritation showed. "It's *not* merry. We have one day to find Phaedra and not a clue where she is. What I didn't need was to be thinking about you all night. And now I understand you were peeking in my bedroom." She raised her eyebrows at him.

"You were thinking about me all night?"

"Is that all you have to say for yourself?"

"Okay, okay, I peeked. I was just making sure you were in there. It's part of being a cop, making sure everyone in the house is safe." No need to mention his jealousy of Stasia's position in the bed.

"It's not part of being a cop, it's why you are a cop." She scooped the can's contents into a porcelain bowl and set it on the kitchen floor. "I suppose the peeking's acceptable when you put it that way."

"And the door was open, after all. Made it easy." Had she left it open for him? An invitation, should he wake in the middle of the night? Maybe it was better not to know.

She sailed back toward her bedroom. "I'm going to get a shower, walk Stasia, and then do some painting, see if I can capture that place any better."

"I'll go with you. The walking part, I mean."

"I thought you'd say that," she said from the depths of her bedroom.

In twenty minutes, she was dressed in a bright red,

fuzzy sweater and white jeans. She harnessed Stasia with practiced movements. Stasia remained perfectly still until the harness was in place, then she pranced and headed toward the door.

Max opened the door for her. "You wear bright colors for a person who can't see them."

"I have personal shoppers at a couple of the boutiques who look for clothes with real color. I know it's strange, but bright colors make me feel better somehow."

"How do you match them up? You never clash."

She reached into the back of her collar and pulled out a small metal tag embossed in Braille. "This tells me what color and style it is."

"You've got it all covered, don't you?"

"Mostly."

"I want to know more about what it's like to be blind. Later, when we've found Phaedra. I want to know what your life is like, how you meet people, how you balance your checkbook."

She paused just inside her door and turned back to him. "Why?"

He ran his finger down the bridge of her nose. "For the same reason you wanted to see what I looked like."

She turned away and opened the door. They stepped out of the building and into the early morning. It was still dark, and the streetlights cast their glow on the bricks. The water caught the shimmer of the lights. He inhaled the cool air and momentary sense of peace.

"Callahan!"

He turned around to see Sam standing several yards behind them. He looked like hell, his hair unwashed, wearing the same clothes he'd had on yesterday. And he looked pissed.

"Sam, what are you doing here? You were supposed to call —"

"I figured you'd be with *her*. God, Max, she's got you screwed up. You're thinking with your cock, man. She's part of this, and she's twisting you around her finger just like all women do. Deceiving you. Manipulating you. They say blind women are better in bed, because they use their other senses. Is it true, Max? Come on, let's hear the dirty details."

"Olivia, keep walking. I'll catch up with you." He'd keep her in his sight. "Sam, what the hell is going on with you?" He didn't smell any booze on him, but he sure sounded wasted. He'd obviously been awake all night.

"I tried you on your cell phone. It wasn't working. I tried you at home, but you weren't there. It wasn't hard to figure out where you were."

Max checked his cell phone and found the charge had fizzled out. He'd brought his charger, but forgot to plug it in.

He put his hands on Sam's shoulders and leaned into his face. "What is going on? Did they find the girl?" It scared him to see the man he'd always looked up to acting like this.

Sam shoved him away. "My life's falling apart. Annie threw me out last night. And I ..." His eyes glazed; he wasn't looking at Max, but at Olivia. "I tried to find you, but you were over here screwing our prime suspect. She's going to ruin you, ruin your career and everything you've worked for." He dropped down to one of the ornate benches, all the energy seeming to drain from him at once. "I don't know what to do," he said in an agonized whisper.

Max crouched down in front of him, surreptitiously glancing toward Olivia. "Talk to me, man. Why did Annie kick you out?"

He blinked, becoming aware of his surroundings and what he'd said. "It's the case. That's all, it's just this case. It's getting to me. You're getting to me. I don't know what's going on with you. I've never seen you fall for a suspect. Don't deny that you are. I've seen you watching her. And you're being secretive. It's not like you, Max, and you know it."

Sam had effectively turned the conversation to him and Olivia. "First of all, she's not a suspect. You busted your ass trying to prove she's part of the scheme, and you failed. That's because she's not. Secondly, I believe her. I believe she's psychically connected to the girl." And thirdly, she was just about too far away. "Come on, let's walk."

"You're willing to risk your career for her?"

"For Phaedra, I am. She's our best chance of finding her."

As they walked, Max told him what he'd learned so far, all of it.

"Now you know why I couldn't tell you all of this. I shouldn't even be on this case. But I can't let it go now. We've got until midnight tonight. Will you work with me? It's all we have to go on."

Sam was watching Olivia as she released Stasia in the dog run. He had a hard, cold look in his eyes. Max wasn't even sure he'd heard.

"Why do you have it in for Olivia?" he asked, jarring Sam out of his stare.

"She's going to destroy you, Max. They all do."

"I've got to pick up a hypnotherapist at the airport in an hour. We're going to hypnotize Olivia and see if we can get anything out of her abduction memories. I'll meet you at the station in a while and we'll start on those missing child case files."

"We haven't even gotten them from all the different departments."

"Then get on their cases." He removed his key from his ring. "Go to my place and wash up. First see if you can find something to wear." He wished they could discuss what had happened between him and Annie, but there wasn't time.

Phaedra watched the bad man leave. He'd brought her breakfast, at least. She used to love McDonald's and Burger King, but not anymore. She ate the food and carefully balled up the wrappers.

He'd told her she was dirty, that she needed a bath. But he hadn't let her take one, and she didn't want to anyway, not with him standing there watching her like he did when she went to the bathroom.

It was another one of his tricks. She was scared of what he'd do to her that night. The cut on her chest still stung, even though he'd treated it with salve that morning. He'd acted all nice, but she knew he wasn't. He was a bad, bad man.

The tub was dripping, dripping, dripping. The sound was making her crazy. He was going to give her a bath tonight, that's what he'd do. Her gaze darted around the room, trying to find some way to get out of that cage. She pushed on the bars again, though it had never helped before.

Crying in frustration, she curled up in the back corner, mindful of the piece of metal that scratched her sometimes. She was never going to see her mom and dad again. Just the thought of them was enough to make her cry.

The piece of metal still jabbed her. She'd bent it back so it didn't stick inside the cage anymore. She turned around and ran her fingers along the edge of it. After bending it back and forth for a few minutes, it finally snapped off. She looked at it. Maybe she could stab him in the eye. Then she'd grab his keys and ...

She sniffed. She was too small to do that. Then he'd really punish her.

She looked at the lock. Her friend's brother had picked a neighbor's lock on his shed once. She slid the piece of metal into the lock that held the door in place. It was awkward, but if she twisted just so, she could turn the metal inside the lock. It was an old lock, big and rusty. Maybe she could get it to unlock. She bit her lower lip and worked on it.

"Just relax, Olivia. Don't put any pressure on yourself to remember, all right?"

She swallowed hard and closed her eyes. She was lying on her couch, and Dr. Marano was sitting on a chair beside her. They'd moved the coffee table and the end tables. Max was perched on the arm of the couch near her head. He'd brought a mini-cassette recorder to capture what she said.

"Are you okay?" he asked.

"I'm not afraid to do this. Memories can't hurt me." She said it with such conviction, he could almost believe her — until she reached for his hand. Her fingers closed around his, and she settled more comfortably. "I'm ready."

He couldn't breathe for a moment. She'd reached for him.

Livvy.

It was all twisted inside him, how he'd felt about her when he rescued her, how he'd wondered about her. Now that he'd found her, she tugged on all his desires to keep her safe and warm and protected ... and just keep her. She was the wrong woman to feel that way about. He was the wrong man to feel that way period.

It took ten minutes of Marano's soothing voice to lull her into a hypnotized state. Max felt himself getting pulled in, too, and had to blink to wake himself. He needed one night of good sleep. He looked at Olivia with her eyes closed. He should have gone to her bedroom last night. Not to continue what they'd started in the living room. Just to hold her.

Marano took her back through the past to the day of her abduction. "What do you see, Olivia?"

Her voice took on a little girl's sound. "I'm in the toy store. I'm mad at my mother. She promised we wouldn't do another pageant until the spring. She promised! And she just told me we're going to New York in January for another one. I hate being up there in front of everyone being judged. I hate smiling and singing for them. And if I don't win, I hate going over and over each thing with Mother trying to figure out why. Was I poised enough? Pretty enough? Should she have used that glossy stuff on my hair that makes it all stiff? I hate it!"

"What happens next?"

"She's talking to the mother of a girl who also does

the pageants. Jasmine does commercials, too. I'm going to hide from Mother. Maybe if she gets worried about me, she won't make me go to that pageant. A man is telling me that if I follow him, I'll meet Santa Claus, but I don't believe in him anymore. I'm going to hide in the back room. She'll never find me in there."

Santa Claus. Could it be the same ruse Bobby had pulled with Phaedra? It was ingenious, really. Kids were taught not to go off with a stranger, but Santa wasn't a stranger. It was a great way to disguise himself without standing out. He probably wore the costume into the store and changed out of it in the back room so kids wouldn't swamp him.

Her eyes twitched beneath her closed lids. She tensed, squeezing his hand tight.

"What's happening, Olivia?"

She rocked her head back and forth. "The man followed me. He's pushing a cloth against my face, it smells terrible, and..." She stilled.

"Olivia, it's an hour later. Maybe two. You're waking up. What do you see?"

Her voice was low, almost a whisper. "Where am I? It's a long room. There's a dim light, but I can't see much." Her breath was coming in quick puffs now. "I want to go home. I want my daddy. Where's Daddy?" Tears shimmered beneath her lashes. "I'm so scared. Somebody help me! Mother, where are you? There's a cage... he's going to put me in a cage!" She made struggling noises, and he knew she was reliving her fight with Bobby.

Max wanted to pull her out of that hell, just as he had when she'd connected to Phaedra. It took everything inside him to wait it out. Like she'd said, memories couldn't hurt her. But what about the fear? She put on a brave front, maybe even for herself. He'd do anything to eradicate her fear, but how could he if she wouldn't admit it?

She suddenly stilled. He remembered that Bobby had knocked her out.

Dr. Marano said, "Let's move ahead to when you wake up."

She moved her free hand as though she were trying to feel her way. "I can't see. I can't see!"

"The man is there. What is he saying to you?"

"He's telling me not to make a sound, that if I'm quiet, he'll take off the gag. I promise I won't make a noise. He says I'm Rose. But I'm not Rose, I'm Livvy. He says he's my father, but he's not. He's not!"

Max never thought it could be so painful to listen as she recounted her days of terror. So far, there hadn't been any revelations. Not until she said, "He says he has to punish me on Christmas night. At midnight. He says I made my mother kill herself, but I know it's not true! She didn't kill herself!"

He blamed Rose for making his mother kill herself? But why on Christmas? Christmas, that was the key. He wrote a note to the doctor.

Dr. Marano nodded as he read it, then turned back to Olivia. "Did he say anything else about Christmas?"

She nodded. "He said something about leap year. Something about it being Christmas leap year."

Max gently extricated his hand from hers and motioned to the doctor that he'd be right back. He left his cell phone on the charger and grabbed Olivia's portable phone. He went out onto the balcony and made a call.

"Odette, it's Max. Merry Christmas."

"Oh, you too, Maxie. It's so sweet of you to call me every year." She acted as though he hadn't talked with her yesterday.

"I care about you. I'm sorry if I upset you. Maybe I'm jumping to crazy conclusions. This case has me on the edge."

"That's okay, Maxie," she said, relief in her voice. "Let's not talk about it anymore."

"I just have one question. It's about my mother. Since it's Christmas, I've been thinking about her."

"Ask whatever you'd like about Marie." She was glad he didn't want to ask about Bobby, he could tell.

"When did she kill herself?"

"Christmas night, a terrible night to choose, don't you think?"

"At midnight," Max said, dread in his voice.

"Yes. How did you know?"

"Just a guess. Did my father blame Rose for her death?"

"He did seem angry at Rose for dying. If only she hadn't sneaked out of the house. Marie never recovered."

"I've got to go. Take care of yourself."

He hung up and started counting backward. This was a leap year. Olivia was taken on a leap year. And ... just as he thought, Marie killed herself on a leap year. He returned to Olivia and took her hand again.

"I'm so scared," she was saying in the little-girl voice. "He cut me. I'm never going to see Mother and Daddy again. I ..." Her mouth fell open.

"What's happening, Olivia?" the doctor asked.

"The man left, just ran out. I don't know what's going on. And now ... someone's taking my hand, telling me to come with him. It's an angel come to save me. His voice is so sweet, so gentle. He's helping me to escape. We're running. I fell down, but he helped me up. He's calling for help. Then he tells me it's okay, to stay put. A nice family is there, and the angel isn't anymore. The man is yelling at him. He's yelling for Max." She shook her head violently, tears glistening on her cheeks. "I don't want him to go back. I don't want the man to hurt him."

Max squeezed her hand as the tears in her voice ripped at his heart. He stopped the recorder. "That's enough."

The doctor brought her out of the hypnosis.

"How'd I do?" She groggily sat up.

He wanted to hold her, to make all those terrible memories go away. He swallowed hard. "Great. Leap year is the key. My mother killed herself on Christmas at midnight on a leap year. He blames Rose for her death. That's why he keeps taking the girls and making them into Rose — to punish them, over and over. I've got to make some calls, get the other stations to narrow down their searches and get us those files."

Dr. Marano said, "I'd like to talk with Olivia alone for a few minutes. Perhaps we can do that while you're making your calls."

Max grabbed his folder of notes. "I'll be out on the balcony."

CHAPTER 22

"I'm interested in exploring the cause behind your long-standing conversion disorder," Dr. Marano told Olivia when they were alone. "I don't think there's a documented case where someone has sustained it for as long as you have. What do you think was the underlying cause of stress in your life?"

She felt Stasia nudging her leg and invited her up on the couch. "My mother. She wanted to make me into a doll. She entered me in beauty pageants despite the fact that I hated them. If I didn't win, she'd be mad at me for days. Well, I perceived it that way. She was probably just disappointed. Even if I did win, I was never good enough. I felt that I had to be what she wanted in order for her to love me."

She pulled Stasia closer and stroked her fur. "If my mother had taken me to see you sixteen years ago, would my vision have instantly returned?"

"It's very possible, if it was strictly conversion disorder and not organic. If we catch these things right away, it's quite miraculous. I'd like to work with you to see if we can restore your vision."

"I'm not sure I want to see again."

"Because you're comfortable being blind. Because it's part of your identity."

"That's part of it." And because she was afraid that if she regained her sight, she'd lose her connection with Phaedra.

"Well, think about it. I'd like to speak with you again. Perhaps we can delve into your other issues, too."

"I have other issues?"

"Well ... yes. I am trained to pick up on subtle clues. I've been studying you since you picked me up at the airport, you and Max, listening to the two of you talk and watching you interact. Now that you've told me a little about your background, I see why."

"Why what?"

"You have a wall around you. You built it long before the kidnapping, because you felt that if you didn't live up to your mother's expectations, she wouldn't love you. If you didn't need her love, then the lack of it couldn't hurt you. Do you see what I'm saying?"

She nodded even as her mind tried to get around it.

"The blindness stemmed partially from that," he continued. "Conversion disorder always comes from something in the person's life that is now disabled by the function that is no longer working."

"I thought that was the pageants. The blindness certainly did get me out of them."

"That was only part of it. The underlying problem was the perceived lack of love if you didn't participate. If you didn't win. By eliminating those pageants, you eliminated that expectation in hopes of earning her love for being yourself."

"Then she paraded me around as an example of what can happen if you don't watch your children carefully."

"You were still in that situation. So you convinced yourself you didn't need love."

"That's ridiculous."

"Do you need love, Olivia?"

She started to say *No*, an automatic response. "I don't think anyone *needs* love, per se. It's nice to have it, of course." She paused. "I'd like to have it."

"How many times have you loved someone?"

She shifted to a crossed-legged sitting position. "I love my father. We've grown very close in the last couple of years."

"Do you need his love?"

An ache permeated her stomach. "When I was young, yes. But he wasn't around much. You're right; I learned to live without that need. Now ... I would like his love very much. And I have it when he's lucid."

"Lucid?"

"He has Alzheimer's."

"Ah, so it's safe if he doesn't give you that love because he can't always remember who you are."

Her fingers tightened against Stasia's back as she stroked down the length of her. "It's not like that."

"If you say so. But what about romantic love? How many men have you loved? I mean a true, I-must-spend-the-rest-of-my-life-with-this-person-or-I'll-shrivel-up-and-die kind of love."

She started to name a couple of men but faltered. She'd loved being with them, loved making love, but had she loved them like that? For a reason she didn't want to explore, Max slipped into her mind.

"It doesn't mean anything. Lots of women my age haven't met their soulmate."

"But most women your age have felt that kind of

love. I call it inner passion, which is far different from sexual passion. Feeling that doesn't guarantee that the person is your soul mate. It does prove that you can feel the need for love. That you've opened yourself up, laid yourself bare, just to take the chance."

She laid her head against the back of the couch. "I've never laid myself bare for anyone." She thought of when she'd touched Max's face while he slept. When they'd nearly made love and wisely backed off. Because she'd been very close to laying herself bare, she realized.

"What are you thinking, Olivia?"

"I ... I think I almost felt that once. We both backed off."

"Why?"

"Because it was Max. He was the boy who led me from the truck."

"Oh." That one word was loaded.

"I'm afraid that if I let go — lay myself bare — with him, that I'll become what he sees me as — that little girl who needs his protection." She'd done that with Terry for far less compelling reasons.

"The way he watched over you while you were under ... yes, I can see that." He seemed to think it over. "Your past connection and the investigation make your relationship complicated, I admit that. But love is never simple. And it's not even about whether you and Max could make a real go of it. It's about laying yourself bare and reaching for it."

It was also about Max being able to look at her as more than someone to protect. That he'd married an alcoholic said a lot about him.

She set her feet on the floor and scooted to the edge of the couch. "I'll think about what you said."

He took her hand and gave it a squeeze. "I'll tell Max he can come in. He's been glancing inside, making sure you're okay."

"I can believe that."

"And you don't like it." He let out a soft sigh as he got to his feet. "I do hope you'll contact me." He opened the door to the balcony. "We're finished."

Max thanked him and escorted him to the door. His low, soft voice washed over her raw nerve endings. "We can call you a cab. And you're welcome to stay here until your flight leaves."

"I think I'll wander around the area, take in the sights. Goodbye, Max. Olivia."

Max said, "I've got to go to the station and pick up some files. We'll only be a few minutes. Do you want to bring Stasia or leave her here?"

Olivia heard Judy's voice at the open doorway. "Olivia, you sure have a lot of men in your apartment lately. Hey, Detective Max Callahan."

Olivia rolled her eyes. "Merry Christmas." She gave Judy a hug.

"Merry Christmas. I've got to finish making your present. I'll bring it up tonight."

Olivia said to Max, "Why don't I stay here with Judy? I want to try the painting again. I keep thinking that I can find some way to help."

"Okay. I won't be long. Judy, don't leave her alone."

"Yes, sir!"

Olivia was surprised when Max kissed her forehead. It was tender and proprietary at the same time. "I'll be back soon."

Judy giggled. "He kissed you."

Olivia listened to his footsteps retreating down the

hallway, her mouth curving in a smile. Yes, he had. "Let's mix the same colors we did last time."

Judy went to work on the paints while Olivia changed into a painting outfit. When she returned to the living room, she asked, "Judy, do you remember when I asked who owned the apartment across the way?"

Judy dropped one of the jars. "I can't talk about that."

Olivia walked closer. "You're my friend, aren't you?"

"Yes, you say 'thank you'."

"Right. Double bonus points."

"He's my friend, too. He gives me money to keep his secret."

Olivia felt a chill. He? "Who is it? Please tell me."

"Terry. He bought it before he moved out of your place. He said he wanted to take care of you, but you wouldn't let him. He was keeping an eye on you without you knowing. For your own good. He said you'd be mad if you found out. Are you mad? I don't like when people get mad at me."

All of the words after 'Terry' floated aimlessly past Olivia. Terry had been in that apartment all this time. Watching her. She shivered. "Judy, you should have told me."

"But it was for your own good, that's what he said."

Olivia heard the edge in her voice when she said, "Spying on someone is never good. Keeping secrets from friends isn't good either."

"You're mad, I knew it. And now you won't be my friend anymore!"

Olivia released a breath filled with tension. "It's all right. Terry just took advantage of your naiveté, that's all."

But Judy had run out crying.

Olivia stalked across the hallway and pounded on Terry's door.

Max and Sam sat at the conference table sorting through the faxes they'd received from other counties.

Max tossed another reject on the table but was looking at Sam. "You all right?"

"I'm fine. Forget what I said this morning. I've been up all night. Annie and I had a spat, that's all."

"You look like hell."

Sam narrowed his eyes. "Yeah, well *I* didn't get laid last night."

"Neither did I. You want to tell me what's going on?"

"I want to get through these case files. The leap year/Christmas theory really narrowed it down. Here's another one." Sam read from the fax. "Seven-year-old girl was taken from a department store five days before Christmas. No ransom, no suspects. This one's from St. Petersburg. She has brown hair, brown eyes, just like the rest. That's three so far, plus Phaedra and Olivia. Son of a bitch, I think we have a serial killer here. Your father." Sam's skepticism was clear.

"Yes, my father."

Max flipped through four more cases before finding another brown-haired, brown-eyed girl of eight who had disappeared five days before Christmas. "Sixteen years ago, Orlando."

A chill was seeping through his body. The girls had eventually been found, in a river or other body of water. All of them drowned, all with a cut across their chests. The coroner's reports confirmed the water in their lungs wasn't consistent with the body of water in which they'd been found. It had been ordinary tap water or drinking water. He was drowning Rose, over and over again.

He pushed out of his chair, feeling sick to his stomach. His mind made the connection he hadn't been ready to deal with on the trip back from Odette's. Olivia had been one day away from dying. The image of his father drowning her came to mind as much as he didn't want to see it. Olivia's young dirty face being shoved under the water—

He wanted to touch her right then, to hold her, feel that she was alive.

"I've got to get back to Olivia. Contact the case officers and see if they can shed any more light on these cases. See if they have any idea where the girls were held."

Max went to his desk, feeling removed from all the activity and phone calls and other ongoing cases. When he grabbed up his folder, he spotted an envelope on his desk. There wasn't any writing on it, and it was sealed. He tore it open and pulled out a piece of paper that read, "*All bad girls must be punished.*" He scanned the area as heat flooded his face. Everyone seemed absorbed in his or her own worlds, as usual.

"Who left this here? Did anyone see who left this?" He held the envelope by the corner.

People looked at him as though he might explode before their eyes. They shook their heads carefully.

He walked around the room to make sure everyone heard. "Did you see who left this here? How about you? Someone had to see who left this on my desk. We're a bunch of detectives, for Pete's sake! Someone walked in here and left this. No one saw him?"

John Holland said, "No, but it sounds like the plot twist in my current book. The enemy, right in your own camp."

Nick Mathers asked, "Max, are you all right?"

"No, I'm not all right."

Max slid the note and envelope into an evidence bag and walked to the conference room. How long had the note been on his desk? Since early that morning, maybe even last night. "Sam, run this through Evidence and see if any prints come up. Call me as soon as it's processed."

Sam read the note. "What is this?"

"It's a note that someone put on my desk."

"What does it mean?"

"It means Bobby Callahan's playing with me."

Sam's skepticism was clear. "Bobby. Your father."

"Yes, my father, who's probably a cop since no one noticed any strangers hanging around." He'd been here, working with Max for months, maybe years. No one would believe Max. *An enemy in his own camp.*

He had to get back to Olivia.

CHAPTER 23

"Where's Judy?" Max asked as soon as he returned to Olivia's apartment. He locked the door behind him.

She was sitting at her easel listening to the sexy girl band, Heart. She obviously had a thing for 80's rock and roll. "Tell me what you found out first."

"The leap year revelation was a big help. We narrowed down the cases to those girls taken just before Christmas on a leap year."

"And?"

"He's taken a girl every leap year since my mother died."

"Oh, God. What happened to them?" When he hesitated, she said, "Max, I can handle whatever it is."

"That's right, you're strong, I am woman hear me roar, and all that."

"And leave it to you to want to protect me. You're a hero, Max. You always will be, no matter how you try to fight it. It's in your nature. I think you'll be happier once you accept that. You won't always save the day." She looked in his direction, wishing she weren't so drawn to him. "And you won't always get the girl."

He was quiet for a moment. "Maybe I'll admit that when you admit that you're afraid sometimes. You have to admit it before you can overcome it."

"Tell me," she said, coming to her feet to face him. "What does he do to them?"

"He drowns them."

"The tub. He was going to —"

He put his finger over her mouth. The Wilson sisters sang "Crazy for You."

"Max, you did save my life," she whispered against his finger.

She heard his emotion when he said, "He was going to kill you." His hands went to her shoulders and squeezed them. "He was going to ... drown you."

His mouth took hers in a rush. She didn't want to think about drowning, but she was drowning in Max right then. He took a halting breath and slid his hands around her waist. He tried to capture her mouth again, but she was too quick for him. She nuzzled his ear and his neck, across his throat and to the other side. He took hold of her face and kissed her then. Not just a kiss, a connection of mouths that spoke of hunger and a desperate need to release the tension inside them.

She unbuttoned his shirt and pushed it apart. His hands skimmed her breasts, down her sides, her hips. She slid her hands beneath his shirt and over the hard planes of his chest and stomach. He was hard beneath her, pushing against her.

She felt that hunger again, but something more — the need to lay herself bare. Not physically but emotionally. She needed this, needed him. Admitting that freed something inside her.

"My bedroom," she said, taking his hand and leading

the way.

A minute later, he laid her on the bed and ran his hands over her body. He peeled away her clothes and kissed across her skin, running his hands over her at the same time. She captured one of his hands and stuck his finger in her mouth. When she sucked it in and lathed it with her tongue, he groaned.

His fingers moved across the slick surfaces of her femininity. She shuddered, biting down on his finger, letting pleasure roll across her. She sat up, tore off his shirt, and then unbuttoned his pants and pushed them down. She touched him, holding him firmly, stroking up and down. He kissed her hard, and she felt his body tense. He wrapped her in his arms and rolled her on top of him. She eased onto him, taking him in. He had his hands on her hips, his fingers possessively tight against her skin.

She closed her eyes and rocked her head back. A soft, throaty sound spiraled up her throat and escaped her slack mouth. He skimmed one hand over her breasts and stomach and farther down. The gentle pressure he applied sent a sensual warmth through her body. They moved together through another song, and then he pulled her down and rolled her so that she was beneath him.

She held on tight and tried to tell herself this was only about the need to connect with another human being. But it was more than that. It was about connecting with Max Callahan. He was strong and tender and everything she'd ever wanted in a man. He was all mixed up inside her, and she let herself get lost in their lovemaking. Her fingers slid down his back and over the curve of his buttocks. The way his muscles moved beneath his skin, the way he smelled, everything about him captivated her. She felt pulled toward that blissful state, and she contracted her inner muscles to take him with her. His answering groan told her she'd hit her mark. He entwined one of her hands with his, squeezed it hard, and kissed her. She felt herself spiral up, up, up, breathless, lost in feeling him inside her.

He shuddered, and his whole body tensed. They remained there, catching their breath. After a few minutes, he gently bit her lower lip and rolled her to her side. He took one of her fingers and sucked it into his mouth. She'd never realized just how good it felt. No one had returned the favor. He kissed the tip of her damp finger, and when she thought he would set her hand down, he surprised her again. He took both her hands and put them on his face.

Her throat tightened, and she smiled. How did he know how much she wanted to do this? She traced the lines and grooves of his face to her heart's content, even brushing the tips of his eyelashes.

She continued her journey, mapping his face in her mind. Then she started using her mouth to explore him, brushing her lips across his feathery eyelashes, his eyelids, down the bridge of his nose. Mm, this was an even better way to "see" him. Her tongue dipped into the indent in his chin.

He leaned up and kissed her hard. "What do you see?"

"You."

In that word, she'd revealed too much of the emotion flowing through her. What was she doing? Anxiety curled through her, made her move away and push her hand through her damp hair. "We shouldn't have done this. Making love while time slips away ..."

"There's nothing else we could be doing, Olivia." He touched her face. "Is that what this was? Making love?"

She quickly shook her head. "This was releasing tension."

"Now you're lying."

She rushed on. "All right, it was more. It was ... it's natural that we'd be drawn together like this. You're the hero, and I will be forever engrained in your mind as the victim. You saved my life."

"Natural," he repeated. "If that's what you want to believe, Livvy." He extricated himself and walked to the bathroom.

Livvy. God, why did he call her that? It made her want to grab his arm and drag him back. To hold him tight against her and feel his heat.

To never let go.

She searched for her clothes and got dressed. She heard water running in the bathroom, and then he walked out. His phone went off in the direction of the dresser.

"Maybe that's Sam." God willing. "Callahan here. Yes, sir." After a moment, he said, "Damn, just what I need. Lieutenant Huntington wants to see me — now. I want you to come with me."

"I'll be all right here for a short while. I won't open the door to anyone."

"Livvy ..."

"He's not going to come back, even you said that. He wants to get me when I'm out. Believe me, I'm not going out by myself. Stasia and I will be fine until you return. I want to get back to my painting. I need to help find her, Max. I need to help. I keep thinking something has to click."

He relented with a sigh. "Don't open the door to anyone." He moved closer, and she thought — okay, hoped — he'd kiss her forehead again. He took a step past her. "I'll be right back."

"Max ..." She let the word die on her lips, hearing a trace of agony in it.

"Let's leave what happened as just that — a recharge. Makes it easier." Then why didn't his voice agree with his words?

She followed him to the living room, fighting the urge to take back her words. He was wrong; it wasn't easier to leave it the way it was.

"Lock your door."

And then he was gone. She locked the door and leaned against it, closing her eyes. "I'm an idiot."

She'd also forgotten to tell him that Terry owned the apartment across the way. Since he hadn't answered her knock, she hoped that meant he wasn't there. Terry was the least of her problems. She settled in front of a blank canvas. Finding Phaedra was all that mattered now.

Max tried to push the images of their lovemaking out of his mind as he drove through Palomera. Just when he thought he'd managed it, he could see his hand sliding down her stomach or smell the heat of her skin. He'd seen the scar when he'd taken off her shirt, but he hadn't wanted to spoil the mood by getting drawn into what that scar represented.

His father. His own father had put that mark on her while Max sat in the cab of the truck obeying a madman. Her words echoed in his mind: *Oh, God, you blame yourself for their deaths, don't you?*

He did take responsibility for Diana's and Ashley's deaths, for Olivia's suffering, and yes, even for not making sure it was his father's body in that truck.

It all came with the territory.

She said he'd always want to be a hero. That hunger inside him that vowed to find Phaedra in time was the same drive that had led him to push Saul Berney too far. He thought he'd killed it, but he hadn't. She was right. He would always be driven to be a hero and protector. That's why he'd become a cop. The thought of facing his nemesis made his stomach churn. Bobby Callahan was his kryptonite. Every time he thought of Bobby, he became that powerless kid who'd stopped at his father's command. *Coward!* Maybe that's why his father still haunted him. Just as some deep part of Max had known who Olivia was, maybe it knew that Bobby was close by, too.

But who was he? He thought of the guys in the right age range: Holland, Graham, Mathers... Sam. Sam, who'd been acting strangely lately. No, not Sam. Max couldn't afford to discount anyone. He picked up the cell phone and called Annie O'Reilly.

"Hello," she answered in a dismal voice.

"Merry Christmas," he said, not achieving much cheer either. "It's Max. How're you doing?"

She let out a humorless laugh. "I guess you know I kicked him out. Petey doesn't know yet," she said in a lower voice. "He thinks his dad is just working on the case. I know the timing sucks, but his timing sucked, too."

"You think he's seeing someone."

"Max, tell me the truth. Do you know about it? Is it the woman down the street? I swear she had the hots for Sam, always calling. But it's been a while since her last call."

He hoped Sam was seeing someone. Any other explanation made the hairs on the back of his neck stand. "Why did you kick him out?" He hated even thinking it. *Sam?* "Do you have proof?"

"First it was the woman's intuition thing. Then his stories start to conflict. He's with you, he's not with you. He's got guilt written all over his face when he comes home late. When he came home last night, he had a scratch on his shoulder. A fingernail scratch. He couldn't explain it, and I knew, Max. I knew." Tears filled her voice.

He felt even worse for what he was thinking. For what it would do to them if it was true. "How long has it been going on?"

"He started being preoccupied a few weeks ago. But then it changed, and he started getting... strange. Dark. He never laughs, doesn't really talk to me or Petey. He obviously didn't have a lie planned for the scratch, because he just looked at me with the saddest expression I've ever seen. But he wouldn't talk to me. Max, why won't men *talk*?"

Because they're hiding something. "Has this ever happened before? Your intuition, him being preoccupied... dark."

"Not that I remember. I never looked for it, not with Sam."

Max knew that they'd been married for about twelve years. He didn't want to tip her off, but he needed to know more. He couldn't use police resources. What did he know about Sam's past? He had family in Ireland. His parents were afraid to fly. "Have you ever met Sam's parents? Any of his family?"

"No. We're waiting until Petey's old enough to appreciate his heritage."

"Ever talked to them on the phone?"

"A couple of times. They call to talk to Petey. Why are you asking me these questions?"

"I thought if you knew them, maybe you could call and see if they had any sense of trouble."

Sam could have paid people to call as his family. He could have had plastic surgery to alter his appearance. Bobby could have "borrowed" someone's family along with their identity. If he mimicked the guy's voice, and never saw them, he could probably pull it off.

What was he thinking? This was Sam. Sam who'd been like a father to him.

"Oh, no, I couldn't call them up for that," she said. "You're probably the person closest to him. I've been wanting to call you and afraid to call at the same time. I'm strong enough to handle the truth, you know."

"I know, Annie —"

She forced cheer into her voice. "Here, Petey wants to talk to you."

"Uncle Max? Are you coming by today?"

His chest tightened "I'm sure going to try, but I'm really wrapped up in this case right now."

"I know, so's my dad. It's not fair, you guys having to work on Christmas. Everyone should get the day off."

If only crime would take the day off. If kidnapped girls were returned in time for the holidays. "I agree. You cheer your mom up. If I see your dad, I'll tell him to call in, okay?"

"Thanks, Uncle Max."

"Sure thing, tiger. I'll be by as soon as I can with your

present."

Even his "Cool," didn't ring with much enthusiasm.

After Max hung up, he set the phone beside him. He wanted that. A son, daughter ... wife. Another shot at having a family. He was sick of his empty, dark house. Of his empty, dark life.

He pulled into the employee's parking lot and found a spot near the front. He killed the engine, but didn't open his door. Instead, he picked up the phone and wondered if he should be relieved or worried that his ache lessened at the sound of Olivia's voice. "You're right. I have a hero complex."

At first, his confession was met with silence. "Okay," she said at last.

"That's it? 'Okay'?"

"What do you want me to say?"

"I thought maybe you'd come out and admit something, too."

"Like what?" she asked warily.

"That you're in denial of your fear. Like toxic waste, if you bury it, it doesn't just go away. It seeps into the soil and water, poisoning everything. It keeps things from growing there, like happiness ... love."

"How do you know so much about it? Where's your psychiatry degree?"

"I don't know how I know. I just do."

"Max ..." It was an agonized plea.

"Livvy." He mirrored her plea.

"Please don't call me that."

"Why?"

"Livvy was a scared girl who tried so damn hard to live up to everyone's roles. Who was afraid no one would love her if she didn't," she added in a whisper.

"I'm not her anymore," she said in a stronger voice. "I don't want you to see me as that girl."

His fingers tightened on the phone. But she was, somewhere deep inside her. That was the part of her that responded to his hero complex. If she'd admit that she was still afraid of some things, she'd have to acknowledge the part of her that had reached out to him when they'd made love. And oh, yeah, it was lovemaking. Not something he could walk away from so they could remain in their safe little worlds.

"When I look at you, I don't see a scared little girl. I see a woman hiding behind her false bravado."

"And you want to save me, I suppose?"

"Of course. I do want to save the day. And you know what? I want the girl, too."

He stepped out of the car and headed inside.

CHAPTER 24

Sam couldn't stop sweating. He hoped no one at the station noticed. Especially Huntington, who'd called him into his office and demanded to know what was going on with Max. Now he was going through the last of the case files, but he had to keep backtracking. His mind wasn't on the files. It was on what had happened late last night. He'd almost killed her. He'd wrapped his hands around her small neck and pressed against her windpipe. She'd looked at him with fear and disbelief, clutching at his hands, trying to pry them off.

It was all he could do to make himself let her go. She'd gasped and choked and moved away from him. He just sat there, unable to speak. When he'd finally been able to look at her, her brown eyes had accused him. He'd almost lost it, right there.

Yes, he'd wanted to kill her, but there was a time and a place. Strangling her in a fit of rage wasn't the way.

Then he'd gone home, and Annie had accused him of seeing another woman. He'd lied to her as he'd done before. It wasn't what she was thinking, but Annie wouldn't understand. He had to take care of things in his usual calm manner. Then it would be over, and he'd never slide into that dark place again.

Everyone looked up when Max walked in. When he glanced Sam's way, he averted his gaze to the files on his desk, sure that guilt shined like a beacon.

Max walked into the detective's area and scanned those who were working that day. It wasn't a big shift. Not a lot of crime happened on Christmas day. Usually the atmosphere was lighter during the holidays. Not this year. Maybe it was Phaedra's disappearance bringing them all down, reminding them that a little girl wasn't home with her family today. But it seemed to be something else. They looked at him and quickly glanced away.

He couldn't forget that someone had left that note, someone who had been inside the station and had not drawn attention. Bobby had once been a cop, but Max couldn't place his face among his colleagues. Change in hair, weight, and time could make an amazing difference, especially with any deliberate alterations.

Sam had glanced up and looked down again. Mathers and Holland were on call, along with a couple of other detectives who were working critical cases.

Huntington was on the phone, so Max walked over to Sam. "Any word on the envelope?"

"They just called: no prints, not even a partial. The pen used was your standard cheap ballpoint issue."

That's what Max had expected, but he'd still hoped something would turn up. He couldn't help glance at Sam's desk, covered in files and paperwork and two pens — cheap ballpoints. The same kind Max used. The same kind everyone here used.

"Have you talked to Annie yet? Seen Petey?"

"I'm heading over in a bit.".

There were shadows in Sam's eyes he'd never seen before. A hopelessness Max didn't like. "Look, if you need to talk or ... whatever..."

Sam's nod was noncommittal.

"What does the lieutenant want me for?" Max glanced at his office and caught his gaze.

Sam tossed a folder on top of the stack and stood. "You'll have to take that up with him."

"Callahan, I'm ready for you," Huntington's ominous voice said a minute later. He was standing in the doorway. He'd put on a red tie with a bell at the bottom point; it looked out of place with his grim expression.

Max closed the door and sat down. The lieutenant stared at him for a full minute without saying a word. Max resisted the urge to shift under that perusal. Five mangled pencils littered the desk, and he was working on the sixth.

Finally, Huntington spoke around the pencil in his mouth. "I've got a real problem when one of my men takes on an investigation on his own, doesn't tell his partner what's going on, and conceals evidence. Evidence that's damning to a suspect that the detective appears to be screwing."

Max rubbed his face, preparing for battle. "I guess you're getting this from O'Reilly."

"And others. You're acting unbalanced. That doesn't go unnoticed in a place like this."

"I know it sounds a little crazy—"

"A little crazy? First, our leading suspect claims she's psychically connected to the missing girl and you believe her. I'd call that more than a little crazy."

"If it wasn't for Olivia, we wouldn't have connected this case to the other ones."

"Lucky guess. But it still hasn't gotten us the girl." He leaned back in his chair, and it squeaked like a mangled mouse. "Second, I hear you're out saving old men in the middle of the night — and accusing a local football hero of luring the guy out. Come on, Callahan."

"That's related to the case, and if you'll let me explain—"

He shook the pencil at him. "I really didn't think this case would drive you over the edge. I thought you'd come out on top. I was wrong, and I'll take responsibility for that. What convinced me is you thinking the guy who took the Burns girl is your father. Your dead father."

"He's not dead."

"And you can prove that?"

"I can prove that his death wasn't proven." Max stood up and braced his hands on the desk. "You think I want to believe this guy is my father? That he's still alive? I've never wanted a man more dead. He brought me nothing but shame and pain as a child. Now I find out that the sick son of a bitch has been abducting girls every leap year for thirty-some years. He's going to kill Phaedra at midnight, drown her like the rest of the girls. She won't be the last if we don't find him. Bobby Callahan is a cop —"

"You're off the case."

"Did you hear me? Phaedra's abductor is someone in our station."

"Did *you* hear *me*? You're off the case. I'm sending you to the shrink. You're officially off-duty pending evaluation."

"You can't do that, sir."

"I just did. You've been wasting our resources from the beginning of this case. This Howe woman is probably involved, and instead of finding the truth, *you* got involved with *her*. I can't tolerate the kind of insubordination you've displayed. Talk about shame, I'll give you shame. I thought I put my best detective on a very important case, and he failed. I put my faith in you, and you failed not only me but that girl and her family. Give me your badge and gun."

Max's insides were caving in. He knew it sounded crazy. That's why he'd withheld information. Now it had backfired when he needed support the most. He set his badge and gun on the desk, hoping the lieutenant didn't catch the tremble of his hand.

Huntington nodded toward the glass door behind him. "See those two uniforms? They're going to escort you to the Smallwood building." That was where the contracted shrink worked across the street from their building.

"Now?"

Huntington looked as though he were trying to rub the strain from his face. "I pushed you to this, and that's not something I'm proud of. I'm not going to let you go over the edge. I know you, Callahan. You're a hothead. I can't take a chance that you'll either hurt yourself or do something irrational that will jeopardize the case and the department's reputation. I'm going to make sure you talk to the shrink now, before you can do any more damage. It's either that or I lock you away until after the holidays."

Max didn't like this, not at all. He forced a hollow laugh. "I'm fine, sir. I'll talk to him tomorrow."

"Now, and there's no arguing about it."

"Are you bringing me in under the Baker Act? I haven't threatened to commit suicide."

The lieutenant held up the phone. "You want to call the captain and complain? Ask him what we should do, given all the facts. He's having dinner with his daughter and grandkids. Be sure to wish him Merry Christmas before dumping all this on him. You know how sentimental he gets around the holidays." He hung up the phone when Max didn't take it. "Look, Callahan, I'm trying to keep this low key. For your sake. For your job's sake."

Max recognized the subtle threat: cooperate or lose his job. "What about the case, sir?"

"I'm putting Graham on it, but we're not holding out much hope at this point. Maybe it was a losing case either way. We'll never know, will we?"

Max walked out. He knew the two uniforms, young, strong guys gunning to move up to detective. They were uncomfortable with this particular duty, but they were going to do their job. Everyone was looking at him but averted their gazes when he met theirs. They all thought he was crazy, and the bitch of it was, he couldn't blame them. Sam wasn't at his desk. He hoped he'd gone home.

"Detective Callahan?" one of the uniforms said. "You ready to go?"

"I need to make a call first." He walked over to the water fountain away from nosy ears. "Olivia, it's me. I'm going to be tied up here for a while. I've been suspended."

"Oh, no, Max."

"I don't blame them for thinking I'm nuts," he said on a long exhale.

"Is that what they think?"

"Yeah. I'm getting sent to the shrink. Huntington's insisting I go now or I get thrown in the slammer. He's afraid I'm going to off myself. So I'll talk to the shrink and get out of here. I want you to call Judy and have her stay with you until I get back."

"Max, are you all right?"

"I'll be fine. I'm more worried about you. Keep yourself safe." He hung up before he said anything more. "Okay," he said to the uniforms hovering nearby.

"You'll need to leave the phone here. Doctor doesn't allow phones in his sessions."

He issued an expletive and set the phone on his desk. "This better not take long."

Olivia pulled a Baby Ruth from the freezer and sat on the counter waiting for the coffee to brew. She knew getting suspended wouldn't stop Max from trying to find Phaedra. He might be worried about her, but she was more worried about him.

His words floated through her mind. *I do want the girl.* He wanted her.

As much as her body stirred at the thought, it was how her heart reacted that worried her. He couldn't help being the way he was: protective, commanding... tender. He thought he knew so much. Sure, their lovemaking had been spectacular. Release wasn't exactly the word she'd meant to use when describing it, but words like *moving, shattering,* or *soul-shaking* would lead him in the wrong direction.

She poured a cup and walked out onto the balcony. The air was damp and cool, and no sun warmed her skin. The holiday music played on regardless, contrasting the tension gripping her. A gust of apprehension washed through her. She set the coffee on the table and dropped into the chair. The sound of breathing overrode the sounds of people talking below and a boat passing along the waterway.

Phaedra's breathing. Small hands worked an old, black padlock. She kept inserting a thin piece of metal into the lock hole.

She was trying to escape.

Her gaze shifted to that heavy door, then back to the lock. Nothing to lose. "Come on, come on, I know this is how Tommy did it."

Something clicked. She jerked on the lock, but it still wouldn't give. She jammed the metal inside again and twisted it. Another click. Then another. The lock popped open.

Adrenaline surged through her as she stepped out of the cage. She ran on wobbly legs to the door first, pulling on it. It wouldn't budge. She turned and ran back through the kitchen area and down the hall with the bathroom at the end. To the right of the bathroom was a closed door. She pushed it open. Beyond the low light, though, the place was pitch dark.

She spotted a panel of switches and reached up to flick them on. Light poured through the place. It was lined with desks and phones and what she could only guess was computer equipment. She picked up each phone, whimpering, "Please help me, please help me," into each one. But there wasn't any dial tone. Something that looked like an old radio sat high on a shelf, out of reach.

She ran out of that room and through the doorway opposite. It was a large room, empty except for one broken bunk bed. Four large storage cabinets lined the wall, their doors hanging open to reveal empty shelving.

Got to get out of here!

Stasia was licking Olivia's face. "Oh, Stasia, you've got to stop bringing me out. I'm okay, really. If only you could understand me. I know, sweetie. I love you, too."

She made her way inside and dialed Max's cell phone, feeling sharp disappointment when she got his voice mail. "Phaedra escaped from her cage! I'm thinking it's some kind of jail or other facility. There's a room with radio equipment and another large room with a broken bunk bed. The rest of the rooms are clean, too, as though they've never been used. All I can hope for is that she gets out. It's so frustrating not being able to help her. Call me as soon as you can."

She had to paint what she'd seen. At least try. She knew she should call Judy, but she needed to focus on the painting. Once she made some headway, she'd call her.

He heard Max's cell phone ring four times, then stop. The detective's area was empty. Most everyone was in the break room enjoying a Christmas luncheon one of the guy's wives had delivered. He casually picked up the phone and walked to the window. While he pretended to look out at the gray day, he retrieved the message. He'd seen Max punch in the code the other day.

He tossed the phone back on the desk and headed outside. He took his time crossing the parking lot, nodding at those he met along the way. He didn't look like a man who was anxious. No, he looked pleasant, casual, just another government employee enjoying a break.

A patch of park-like land separated the police station from the old courthouse. The records division was still located on the third floor, waiting for their offices in the new building to be finished, and there was one lone clerk still on the ground floor. All the rest of the divisions had moved over already. What they were going to do with the quasi-historic building was under consideration. The way the board of commissioners kept squabbling over its fate, it would be months before anything was decided. Plenty of time for the place to get flooded and destroy any evidence he might have left behind.

Olivia sank back into that strange place with the kitchen and clean floors and watched through Phaedra's eyes as she dug her way into a hole in the large, concrete bricks. She'd dumped over a pile of the plastic buckets and had stacked up several so she could reach the square hole in the wall.

Wads of yellow insulation surrounded a cylindrical object.

A sound halted the girl and made her already pumping heart race even faster. She'd heard that sound enough, knew it meant disaster.

Fear shuddered through her and propelled her off the buckets. They fell over with a loud clatter, skidding across the floor. She ran through the doorway to a large room with several picnic tables.

"Rose!" His voice thundered through the empty rooms. "Get back here now!"

She turned around to an opening with steps leading up. She'd already investigated and knew there was a brick wall there. There had once been another steel door there; the heavy-duty hinges were still in place. She ran up the steps, stumbling on one, and then crouched in the darkness of the corner.

There was panic in his voice, too, scaring her even more. "Rose! Come here now!"

He was getting closer. She heard cabinet doors being thrust open. He'd find her there. It was hopeless.

But wait! She could try to race to the door he'd come in, and if he hadn't closed it all the way...

As she readied herself to bolt, he stepped in front of the doorway. His breath was coming heavily, and his mouth tightened in a furious line. She pressed farther into the corner, even as her hope of escape spiraled downward. He'd only taken two steps into the alcove when he stopped and looked at her.

"Rose." That horrid name was filled with disappointment, and with relief.

With sure steps, he climbed to the top platform. Dread and fear stopped her breathing altogether as he reached for her arm. She dodged around him and tripped down the steps, landing on her knees. Her legs were still stiff from crouching in the cage, but she forced herself up and ran toward the steel door. She didn't know what was on the other side, but she had to take the chance.

She didn't get that chance. He grabbed her ankle and jerked her to the floor. She yelped, but before she could think of trying to wriggle away, he had her pinned beneath him. He yanked her to her feet and hauled her into the bathroom. The tub was almost filled with water now. She didn't struggle, didn't want to make him any angrier.

He plunged her into the water face first, pressing her down so hard, her nose mashed against the bottom of the tub. She thrashed with her arms and feet, but he was too strong. *Help me, help me!* she thought. No one could help her. She'd never see her family again.

Just as suddenly, he pulled her out. She gasped for breath

and watched rage color his neck and face. He was breathing almost as hard as she was.

"Not yet, Rose. You almost made me ruin everything. Marie died at midnight. I have to follow the plan or it won't go away. But you won't be alone. I'm going to bring back the Rose who got away. He tilted his head. "Olivia, are you listening? Thanks for letting me know Phaedra had gotten out. But she won't get away — neither will you. And Max won't save you this time."

Max paced inside the doctor's office. "Look, I'm fine. Tell Huntington you talked with me, I wasn't displaying any irrational tendencies, and we can be done with this."

Dr. Martin shook his head.

Max lowered himself into the chair. "Fine, let's talk."

"First, tell me about this case you're working on. Maybe once I understand the background, I can see where you're coming from."

Olivia's heart was beating frantically as she pulled herself off the floor. Someone else had Max's phone. *He* had Max's phone, and she had given Phaedra away. That's all she could think about as she tried to make her weak legs work. She didn't have time to soothe the pain pounding in her head or wipe away the sweat. Where was the phone, dammit? She always knew where it was, but her panicked thoughts were crowding in.

When she found it, she fumbled with the numbers. It took three tries to get her finger to work properly. Information gave her the police station's regular number. She had to warn Max that his father was there. Whoever answered the phone was safe to trust. It would take

Father time to get back to the station, even if he left right after he'd talked to her.

She was put through to Max's desk. After four rings, a man answered in a tired voice. "Callahan's desk, O'Reilly speaking."

Not her favorite person, but obviously not the kidnapper. "It's Olivia Howe. Is Max anywhere that you can get hold of him? It's a matter of life and death — Phaedra's life."

"He's not even in the building. What's going on?"

"Can you please take a look around and tell me which detectives are not there right now? Someone who was there a little while ago."

After a pause, he said, "Mathers is only on call, though I did see him this morning. Graham's here somewhere, but I haven't seen him in a while either. Several of the guys were in the break room, including Lemmings and Sharp. I just saw the lieutenant in--wait a minute. Why am I telling *you* anything? What's going on?"

"Who has access to Max's cell phone?"

"It's right here on his desk. Why?"

"I left a message for him, and the man who took Phaedra intercepted it. I need to get to the station and wait for Max. Bobby Callahan threatened me." She knew her fear was plain in her voice and didn't try to disguise it. "He ... might even be on his way here." She would be safe there, surrounded by detectives and near Max.

"Bobby Callahan ... Max's father? His dead father?"

"Yes! No! He's not dead. They never verified that the remains were Bobby's. Please, you've got to help me."

"All right, calm down. If you feel like you're in danger, I'll send someone to get you."

"No, not someone! You. I trust you."

He let out a sigh, clearly not buying most of her story. But he must have believed she felt threatened, because he said, "All right, I'll come get you. I was just heading out."

"Thank you."

Sam shook his head as he dropped the phone in the cradle. This was crazy. "I'll be back in about forty minutes or so," he told John Holland, who had just walked in. He'd almost made it out of the room when he ran into Huntington and Graham coming in.

"Where are you going?" Huntington asked.

Sam paused, wondering how much to tell him.

Max knew how crazy the story sounded as he relayed it to the doctor. When he'd started, something had niggled at his subconscious, something he'd overlooked. He finished with, "Which leads me to sitting here in your office while that little girl waits for a rescue that's not going to happen."

The man who looked a bit like Albert Einstein tapped his pen against his chin. "Other than the so-called psychic connection, you don't know that the girl is even alive."

"All I have is the connection. If you had seen Olivia ... if you knew how my father was, you'd believe it, too. We have nothing else. No other viable leads, no clues. It makes sense to explore the only avenue we have, no matter how it sounds."

The Santa suit. That's what kept bothering him. Why?

Dr. Martin set the pen down. "Tell me about your father. Growing up with a disciplinarian like that, and then learning that he had kidnapped a girl, that must have been traumatic for you."

"The Santa suit!"

"Pardon?"

"Holy sh ... it's brilliant. The costume he wore into the store was ours."

"What are you talking about, Detective Callahan?"

"I need to check the storage room at the station. This could be a piece of evidence, a real lead if he returned the suit. My escorts can take me over there and back."

"All right. I'll give you fifteen minutes. Then I want to talk about your mother. Her killing herself on Christmas night is quite significant."

More than he realized. Max walked out. He understood Huntington's position, but he wasn't giving this much more time. And he was getting his cell phone. He hadn't thought it would take this long, and he didn't like being out of touch with Olivia.

The two uniforms said nothing as they shadowed him like bad tails all way to the station. He grabbed his phone on the way to the storage room. No missed calls or messages. He was glad to see that both Sam and Huntington were gone.

He looked down at his phone. Maybe he should call her.

He kept walking toward the storage room, dialing her number. "Olivia—"

Her voice rushed out at him. "He got the message I left on your cell number and he went and caught Phaedra. He *thanked* me for helping him." Her voice cracked on that.

"What? Slow down, what message?"

"I left you a message." She told him what she'd witnessed. "I gave her away. Then he said he was going to bring back the Rose that got away. And that this time you wouldn't save me."

"I'll be right over."

Max saw the uniforms stiffen at those words.

"Stasia and I will meet you there. Your partner's coming. O'Reilly's okay, Max. When I called on your regular phone, he answered. There's no way that your father could get back to the station that fast, not unless where he's keeping Phaedra is within a short walking distance of the station."

"I doubt that. Most of the buildings in this area are government buildings and are in use. The rest of the area has been checked out already." He was glad Sam was in the clear. He'd hated suspecting him.

"I asked your partner who was there. Your lieutenant and someone named Lemmings were. Graham and Mathers weren't there, he said. Maybe you can pin down more names."

Graham and Mathers were possibilities. "What about where Phaedra is being held? Could you see anything else that might help? You said it looked like a jail or some kind of barracks."

"It has a large area with tables and a doorway at the other end. A doorway, yet there wasn't a door. It's blocked by a brick wall. That's where she was hiding when he found her, in an alcove."

"It can't be a jail, not locally. We've had the same one for twenty years. The new government building is occupied. The cafeteria is already in operation. The old courthouse is mostly empty, but there isn't a kitchen or anything like you've described over there, just a bunch of offices. The teams checked out the building as part of their grid search. Let me think about what it could be."

Her voice broke when she said, "Max, you're right. I am afraid."

His chest caved at those words. "It's okay, Livvy."

"No, it's not okay." Another sob. "I'm afraid of the world and life changing in a heartbeat. I'm afraid of the way I feel every time you say my childhood name, because I'm that little girl again who wants to feel safe and protected, and that girl wants you to be the person who protects her. I'm afraid of falling in love with you, and I'm afraid of you walking out of my life forever. You were right about the buried in the sand thing. I don't want to be paralyzed by it anymore."

"Me either," he caught himself saying. He felt his chest open like a butterfly spreading its wings for the first time.

"What do you mean?"

That was why he'd pressed her so hard to admit her fear — it was his fear, too, his weakness. "I've been afraid to put someone I care about in a vulnerable position. It paralyzed me to think that I couldn't protect them."

"You can't protect everyone."

"I know. I know that now." He swallowed hard. "Keep me on the line until Sam gets there."

"I've got to keep painting. Sam will be here any minute, and I want to get down what I can."

"All right," he said reluctantly. "I'll see you soon."

"My hero," she said with a smile in her voice.

He squeezed his eyes shut against the ache in his chest and disconnected. When he opened them, he found the two uniforms pretending they hadn't been listening and looking a little embarrassed about it.

"I'm going down to the storage room," he said and left them to follow.

Max found the Santa suit stuffed in the box, one of the sleeves dripping over the edge. He didn't dare touch it, and he wasn't sure who he could trust to process it for DNA. Then he realized that it wouldn't help Phaedra in time. All it might prove was that one of the men who had worn the suit had been with the girl. He glanced at his watch. Time was running out. Maybe Olivia's latest painting would help, though he wasn't holding out much hope for that. She just couldn't capture the necessary details.

When he returned to the detective's area, one of the uniforms said, "We'd better get back to the doctor's office." They were visibly nervous, afraid Max would try something.

Max was too busy looking for Sam and Olivia to reply. He called Sam's cell number — no answer. Where was he? He called Olivia and got her answering machine. Okay, Sam had picked her up. They were probably on their way.

"I'm not leaving until Olivia and O'Reilly return." Max leaned against the edge of his desk, crossed his arms, and made sure he looked as though he were there for the long haul.

"You tried to kill me." She stared at him with accusing eyes.

"No, I didn't." But he had. His fingers had gone around her throat and he'd had a devil of a time loosening their grip. "I got carried away, that's all. It's your fault. You made me so damned angry. I apologized. What else do you want from me?"

Helene let out a tortured sigh. "You know what I want. Leave Annie. That's all I've ever wanted, Sam. You *know* we belong together."

Even now, his hands flexed at his sides. He *had* wanted to kill her. She was trying to destroy his life. He'd thought of several ways to accomplish it, none of which included strangling her with his bare hands. But he couldn't do it. It wasn't because he was a cop or that he was multiplying sins he would already pay for in the hereafter. It wasn't even thoughts of Annie that had stopped his machinations. It was his son. How could he face that boy knowing he was a murderer?

"This was all a game, wasn't it? The scratches on your face, the flat tires, the threatening messages from your so-called boyfriend ... you did all that, didn't you?"

She came to her feet, pain in her expression. "No."

"There never was an ex-boyfriend stalking you, was there?" She'd come to his house once, when Annie was at work, crying about her ex. She was afraid to go to the police and file a report, because he'd threatened to kill her if she did. She'd pleaded with him to keep an eye on her, to teach her to defend herself. She had seduced him along the way. Oh, he took full responsibility for allowing it to happen. It had never occurred to him that he was the cheating kind. Or the killing kind.

"It was the only way to get you to pay attention to me." She grabbed at his arm. "I waved at you, tried to strike up a conversation. You'd hardly give me the time of day. I figured if I played the woman in danger, you'd care. You did care — do care. I know you do."

He pulled out of her grasp. "It's over, Helene. I'm sorry if I somehow led you to believe there would be more to this than..."

Her pitiful expression hardened. "Sex?" The word sounded more like an expletive. "You thought you'd use me up and toss me away, is that it?" When she saw that anger wasn't getting her anywhere, she reverted to the pitiful tact. "That's all men ever think of me for. I was so sure you were different."

He had no excuse for going to her place that afternoon and having sex with her. None at all. All the rationalizations evaporated as soon as their bodies had cooled down. He'd tried to leave without any commitments.

She hadn't let him. Instead, she'd threatened to tell his wife *and* his son. His son! She'd even threatened to claim he'd raped her. He'd buckled under her threats, but everything was falling apart anyway. He couldn't live like this anymore. He headed to the door.

"You can't just walk away from me," she said.

"Yes, I can. Annie already knows about us. She kicked me out last night. And I'm going to talk to my boss. He'll know exactly what's going on if you make any claims that I assaulted you. Helene, get some help. You're a beautiful woman. I don't understand why you so desperately need a man in your life that you're willing to blackmail him —"

She launched herself at him, her nails braced and teeth bared. He deflected her, but carefully so that he didn't leave any marks. She'd left marks on him when he'd nearly strangled her. She managed a few new scratches on his arms, but he shoved her down on her couch.

"Enough! It's over. Let it go."

She continued to struggle, but finally her movements stilled. "I hate you."

He let her go. "I hate me, too." Defeat permeated his voice.

"It's not over," she said.

He didn't look at her as he left, didn't want to see that determination he'd seen every time she threatened him. Whatever she did, he'd handle it. And he hoped Annie would forgive him. He'd make her love him again. He needed someone to talk to. A friend. He remembered Max's offer to listen.

What would happen to Max now? he wondered as he drove back to the station. Their friendship was down the crapper, and that bothered him. This case had gone horribly wrong from the beginning — from when the Howe woman became involved. Max was as obsessed with her as Helene had been with Sam. Women weren't worth it. He was even mad at Annie for suspecting an affair that was real. Maybe they were right. Men were pigs. No, he was a pig. He'd let his feelings color everything — including, he had to admit, how he'd viewed Olivia.

When he walked into the station, Max rushed over. "Where's Olivia?"

The two uniforms tensed. They thought Max was on the edge. Sam was afraid they were right. "Calm down. I didn't get her."

"*What?*"

"Just as I was heading out, Huntington and Graham were coming in. Huntington asked where I was going, so I told him what was going on. He said he'd get her, and since I had someplace else to go, I let him. One of the guys came up to Huntington and asked him something before he left, but that only delayed him for a few minutes."

"Huntington got her," Max repeated, rubbing his hand over his mouth.

"Well, actually, he didn't. I got a message from him on my cell phone, right after yours. He said she wasn't at the apartment."

"Is he back yet?"

"No, he said he'd look around for her."

"Where's Graham?"

"He left at the same time, said he was checking out something relating to the Burns case and he'd be back in an hour."

Before anyone could anticipate it, Max had torn out of the room.

Olivia didn't let herself think about what she'd spilled to Max. She'd deal with all that later. Right now, she had to focus on Phaedra. Her hands trembled as she tried to recreate the scenes she'd seen through Phaedra's eyes. She concentrated on the doorway where Phaedra had hidden from the kidnapper. The bricks were in an odd pattern. She dipped her finger in the paint and tried to recreate it on the canvas.

A knock sounded on the door a few minutes later. "Who is it?" she called.

"Lt. Huntington."

Sam had called to tell her that Huntington was coming in his place. He'd said that Huntington had something new on the case and wanted to ask her some questions on the way. She opened the door.

"I need to bring my painting and get my dog ready."

"We don't have time. Let's go."

Her heart jumped. "What's happened?"

"I think you may be on to something." He gently took her arm. "I'll guide you. We've got to go now."

She locked her door and let him lead her down the stairwell. Her mind went back to what he'd said about her being the key. "You believe me? My visions? Just like that?"

"It might seem sudden, yes. I may have judged Max a little too harshly. It did sound crazy, after all. He was so adamant, though, that I decided to read through his notes while he was talking to the doctor. Given all the facts, it's pretty convincing. I've been talking to Max on the cell phone during the drive here, trying to put everything together. You're the key, Olivia."

"Do you know who the kidnapper is?" she asked as he guided her to a car.

"We have an idea. You told O'Reilly he threatened you. Can you identify his voice?" He closed the door and got in on the driver's side.

"Kind of deep, no accent. But he can fake a southern accent very well. If you believe me, why isn't Max here?"

"He's keeping an eye on our suspect. We're going to set him up. We'll have you tell Max that the girl has escaped again. Hopefully that'll prompt him to check on her. We'll be on his tail, and" — he smacked his hands — "we'll have him and the girl."

Her heart raced at the prospect of this being over soon. Phaedra home, safe and sound. She mentally recited the Lord's Prayer again, just as she had when her father was in danger. She turned toward him when she was done. "Who do you think it is?"

"I don't want to say, not just yet. You have to understand that it's hard enough to suspect one of my own men in a crime like this. Before I name him, I want to see if he falls for the trap."

The police radio crackled periodically as they made their way to the station. He said, "I'm taking you to the courthouse so he doesn't see you. Don't worry, you'll be perfectly safe."

"I'm more worried about Phaedra."

She kneaded the material of her pants, eager to see Max, eager to get on with the plan. A police siren pierced the air and faded into the distance a few seconds later. They must be near the station. They slowed and turned into what was probably the parking lot. He helped her out of the car and linked his arm through hers. They took the steps up to an entrance, and he opened a door. It was quiet inside and smelled dusty and old. He guided her down what sounded like a long hallway. She could tell by the echo of their footsteps that they had entered a smaller room, and then he unlocked yet another door. It creaked as he pushed it open.

She'd heard that sound before.

"In you go," he said before she could collect her thoughts. He shoved her inside, and she tumbled down the short flight of steps. "Welcome back, Rose."

CHAPTER 25

Max wasn't about to give those two uniformed goons a chance to curtail him. He took the shortcut out to the parking lot, jumped in his car, and headed to Olivia's apartment. "Don't panic," he told himself as he pulled onto the highway. "Maybe she was in the bathroom."

His chest felt as though it was compressed into a half-inch cube by the time he pulled up to her building. He double-parked and ran into the building. When he knocked on her door, Stasia barked. Okay, she was there. She'd just somehow missed the lieutenant.

No answer. He pounded on the door. "Olivia, it's Max! Open up." Only Stasia's answering bark. He tried the door, just in case. It was locked. That meant if she left, it was of her own volition. A good sign.

And a bad sign, because he was going to have to break in the door again. He kicked it this time; his shoulder was still sore from his last breaking-down-the-door heroics. It took a few kicks, but he finally broke the frame.

Stasia was cowering behind the easel, though she came forward when she saw him. He scratched her head as he scanned the apartment. No sign of Olivia. He called Sam. "Has the lieutenant returned?"

"Max, are you crazy? You're going to lose your job, and I'm half-afraid you've already lost your mind."

He heard the concern in his friend's voice. "I'm not crazy, Sam. Has Huntington returned?"

"No."

"What about Graham?"

"Not yet."

"When Olivia called, you told her the lieutenant was at the station."

"He was. Or I'd seen him just a few minutes before that, anyway."

"What about Graham?"

"He was here, but I hadn't seen him recently."

"Call me the second either of them walks through the door." He hung up.

He placed the faded memory of his father's face over Huntington's face. Different. Huntington had a gap between his teeth that his father didn't have. If someone could get a gap fixed, they could probably have one created. The color of his eyes wasn't the same, though contacts could take care of that. Huntington had always seemed a few years older than his father, but Max couldn't be sure. His receding hairline would make him look older.

Graham, on the other hand, dyed his hair black to look younger. He liked working on motorcycles, and Bobby had worked on trucks. He was a bit of an outsider.

"Oh, no, not again." Judy was staring at the broken doorframe.

"Judy, did you see Olivia leave?"

"Isn't she back? I wanted to say sorry for not telling her about Terry owning the apartment across the way. I don't want her mad at me anymore. She —"

"Terry Carlton owns that apartment?"

Judy nodded. "Under a company name. He told me not to tell her. He only wanted to keep an eye on her, make sure she was safe."

Could Olivia be there? He walked over and knocked, but there wasn't any answer. He tried the door. Locked. "Ah, hell. Judy, go into Olivia's apartment and close the door. Or try to, anyway. Stay there until I tell you to come out." After she'd done what he asked, he reared back and broke the frame around Terry's door.

The smell hit him first. Not Olivia, he told himself, reaching for his gun before realizing he didn't have one. He inched in. He found the body behind the couch, wrapped in white garbage bags. The nest of black curls confirmed his suspicion: Terry Carlton. He searched the rest of the place — empty. He backed out and closed the door as best he could. Judy was standing just inside Olivia's doorway, humming a Christmas song.

Before she could ask what was going on, he asked, "Did you see anyone come into the building you didn't recognize?"

"One man. He was wearing a coat and hat. The one Olivia left with."

"What?" He wanted to shake her but held his hands at his sides.

"I saw him walk into the building. He was singing a Christmas song, and that made me think of Olivia, so I went to my apartment and got her present. When I walked out, she was leaving with him. I came over to see if she was back yet."

He tried to keep sheer panic from his voice. "Did you see what he looked like? How old he was?"

She shook her head. "I think he was my dad's age. He was wearing a hat, so I couldn't see his face. What's wrong? You look kinda funny, Detective Max Callahan. All white like a ghost."

"I'm —" Something registered in his brain. "Judy, sing the song again. The one you were humming just now."

She frowned. "It was just 'Jingle Bells.'"

"Why were you singing it in slow motion?"

She shrugged. "Dunno."

"The man Olivia left with. You said he was singing."

She lifted her finger. "Oh, yeah, that's where I heard it. Guess it was catchy 'cause he was singing it kind of sad-like, and I was in a sad mood with Olivia being mad at me and all."

"Jingle Bells" in slow motion. Lethargic. His blood slowed. "Oh, hell. *Oh, hell!*" He grabbed at his phone and called Sam again. He could barely squeeze out the words, "It's Huntington."

"What?"

"The man who abducted Phaedra is Huntington. And now he has Olivia." His whole body felt rubbery with fear.

"Okay, Max, you're really starting to scare me. Are you actually accusing our superior of being a kidnapper?"

Max heard someone else get on the other line. "Listen to me, dammit! He has them. I got a witness here who says Olivia left with Huntington. He lied about not finding her at home." He had to lean against the wall for a moment. "The witness heard him singing 'Jingle Bells' that same slow, eerie way Huntington does." He looked at Judy. They'd never believe her. "He's got both of them. He's going to drown them at midnight. In a tub. In a facility with a kitchen." He could hardly breathe.

"You're talking about our boss here, not to mention a respected cop."

"I know. But he's not really Basil Huntington. His name is Bobby Callahan." The blood rushed to his head, sending wriggling worms across his field of vision. "My father."

"Are you at Olivia's apartment now?"

"Yes." He *was* sinking this time, his words sounding as though he were saying them from a distant place.

"Stay right there."

He could hear a slight difference in Sam's voice. He was looking at someone else, making plans. Get crazy Max and hold him in a cell until he comes to his senses. "Sam, one more thing: Terry Carlton's in the apartment across from Olivia's. He's dead."

"Sure, he is, Max. I suppose the lieutenant killed him, too."

"Probably. If you run the blood found in Olivia's apartment against Terry's, you'll find a match."

He hung up the phone and looked at Stasia, who was watching him from the doorway. She reminded him so sharply of Olivia, he felt that rush of blood to his head again. She'd admitted her fear, and now he couldn't protect her. He walked into the apartment to find Stasia's harness. The painting Olivia had been working on caught his eye.

She'd done several sections, trying to capture different aspects of this place, this damned place they'd been trying to find. He could barely make out the kitchen area, didn't know what she was trying to show in the upper right portion. The lower portion looked like a doorway. She had said something about the girl hiding in a doorway. Not the one Bobby entered, but another one. She'd painted steps leading up to an alcove, and the lower portion of a brick wall at the end.

He stared at the wall. There was something familiar about the pattern of bricks. Instead of being staggered, they were lined up in straight rows: an amateur job. What was it a doorway to?

Stasia whined from her place at his feet. "It's all right. We're going to find her. Come on, girl." He grabbed the painting and headed down the stairs, making sure the dog was with him. Sam would be there soon, and he didn't have time to find the harness.

As soon as he exited the building, he could hear sirens. Traffic was jammed up around his car, horns were honking, fists and fingers were shaking. Obviously, the yellow tag identifying it as a police vehicle didn't matter.

Max helped Stasia into the car before he jumped in and nosed his way into the crowd of cars. The sirens were drawing closer. He slammed on his horn, and the car next to his stopped his attempt to butt in front of Max. Max put his light on the dash and wailed on the horn again. The jam finally moved out of his way, and he eased out as flashing lights glanced off the rear-view mirror. He killed his light and took the first left.

Olivia's words echoed in his head: *He's got her. Oh, God, he's got her.*

Locked in.
Locked away.
It was every nightmare she'd ever had, and it was

every terrifying minute she'd spent in Phaedra's mind.

Only it was real.

The bars felt as solid as they had years ago. Phaedra was crouched nearby, her breath coming in short puffs. When Olivia had tried to touch her, to comfort her in some way, the girl had become more frightened.

Bobby Callahan knelt down in front of them. She could hear his knees crack. "Rose, you were a naughty girl, getting away last time. Maybe if both of you die, the rage will finally go away. I need it to go away."

Phaedra whined at those words. Olivia took a deep breath and pushed out the words, "Maybe if you accept responsibility for Rose's death, the rage would go away."

"Rose is a bad girl." Olivia could tell Bobby was looking at Phaedra, ignoring her words altogether. "If only she was a good girl. If only she loved me the way she loves her mother."

"Who died when you rammed your truck into your house?" she asked, hoping to bring him back to present time. "Who was in the truck?"

It took him a moment to answer. "Hitchhiker. I spotted him on the way to the house and knew what I had to do: start over."

"As a cop."

"The opportunity was handed to me, really. I got a job at a hunting camp in Canada and met up with a cop who had recently retired from the Midwest. We became friends, a man on the run and a former cop. Ironic, isn't it? He only had distant relations; his ex-wife was living out in California and his child had died in a car accident two years earlier. I couldn't pass up that kind of gift. I killed him and became Basil Huntington. I used his bank account to change my face to match his and rejoined the force in St. Petersburg. When Max became a cop in Palomera, I put in a transfer. It took a while, but it eventually came through."

"What about fingerprints? Yours don't match Huntington's."

"And if they'd checked, they'd have found that out. But there was no reason to. Except now they might, because of this psychic connection you have with the girl here."

"So, you believe it then?"

"Have to. The information you gave Max — and me — was too specific. There's no other way you could have known as much as you did." His voice lowered. "Did you get both of my messages?"

"Yes."

"I liked that, being able to talk to you through Phaedra. You probably feel bad for giving away our little escapee here. She wouldn't have gotten out of here. Neither will you. As much as Max knows, he won't find you here. Another irony, that the police have been looking all over for her, and she's been within sight of the police station the whole time. Sure made it easy to come and go."

"And misjudge who to trust," she added in a low voice. She'd trusted the lieutenant because Sam said he was at the station. She never thought he'd been within walking distance of the police station. That he was Max's superior, that he'd stood up for Max during that press interview, that helped, too. Since he couldn't lure her out, he'd resorted to going to her apartment after all. "What is this place?"

"An old bomb shelter. I discovered it by accident,

going through some old clippings in the bottom drawer of my desk. During the Cuban Missile Crisis, the mayor was terrified of nuclear war. With all those nuclear weapons pointing right at us from Cuba, he managed to convince government officials to construct a bomb shelter. The public didn't know about it. It was constructed right in front of them and billed as a water treatment facility. There was speculation, of course, as to what the strange facility was. That's what the newspaper article was about.

"Years later, it was sealed on the police station side. When the new courthouse was completed and most of the employees had moved over, I started snooping and found the door hidden in a closet. It was perfect. Again, a golden opportunity. Close, with the built-in excuse that the records department still hasn't moved. I've had a lot of business with them lately."

She heard him stand. "I'll be back. I've got to ditch the car. Tonight I'll have to head on, just in case crazy Max does convince them to check into those fingerprints."

"He's not crazy."

"No, but everybody thinks he is, thanks to you." He sounded disappointed when he said, "And I was hoping to help him pick up the pieces once he failed to save you and Phaedra. But I'll be back in his life again. I like to keep tabs on the boy."

That gave her the creeps. "Why?"

"He's my son. It's my right as his father. Besides, I've got to keep him in line."

As soon as he opened the door, his cell phone rang. The shelter's walls had probably blocked the signal. "That'll be Max. He's going to try so hard to save you.

And he's going to fall apart when he can't."

"That's not fair. Aren't you the one who assigned him this case?"

He closed the door again, and the ring died. "Max had lost his zest for life, so I gave him the case. I knew it would push him to the edge. But I didn't count on you. You were an unforeseen complication ... and an added bonus."

"Gee, isn't that special?"

"It is, isn't it? Max wouldn't have gotten this far it weren't for you and your spooky psychic thing. But that made it more interesting. You brought him back to life, too."

She tried to hold back the shiver. "Max will find you."

"He's smart. He'll figure out who I am." He sounded weary. "And once again, I'll have to start over."

"Don't punish Max for that. He was only doing his job, a job you gave him."

His voice went soft, and he sounded more like a boy when he said, "You didn't hear the things he said about me when he told me about his father. He feels shame. He hates me. He wants me dead."

"Leave Max alone. He's suffered enough."

"Those who sin must be punished. That's the law." He opened the door again and a moment later, his phone rang. "Think I'll have a chat with my son, see how he's holding up. I'll send him your love." The door closed.

It was all she could do not to give in to the urge to rail and cry and pound the bars. She had to keep her cool, if not for her own sake, for Phaedra's.

She pressed her watch instead. "Six-forty."

CHAPTER 26

Max had pulled into the back of a grocery store and continued dialing Huntington's cell phone. When he finally answered, his tone was normal, businesslike. "Lt. Huntington here."

Max wanted to kill him, but he held in his rage and managed a similarly calm voice. "Where are they, Bobby?"

"Max, they all think you're crazy down at the station. I think they're right."

It was that same voice that had haunted him for years. *Coward!* It stole his breath away and reminded him of being helpless. His fingers tightened on the steering wheel. He still was. "You know I'm not."

"Do you think I'm crazy?"

No, he was worse than crazy. "We can work this out. You don't have to keep killing Rose."

"Odette shouldn't have told you about her."

"I tricked her into it." He didn't want Bobby punishing her, too. "Look, Rose paid for her sins, and now it's over."

"But it's never over, don't you see? That's why I have to keep taking them. It never goes away. I keep reliving it every leap year. This is the only way I can make it go away."

Max could hear the anguish in his words. Bobby really believed that. "We can make it go away ... together. Tell me where they are. We'll meet there and talk."

The strength returned to his voice. "I can't do that, Max. I have to follow through. All bad girls must be punished."

The note had meant Olivia, too. He reached over and ran his hand through Stasia's soft hair. "You can't punish Olivia for getting away from you. That was my doing. Punish me instead."

"I already did, but it backfired. Your daughter — my granddaughter — wasn't supposed to be in the car that day."

Those words struck him in the chest. "You set the pipe bomb."

"I didn't mean for Ashley to be killed. You said she was spending the weekend with Diana's parents."

Max felt that rush of blood to his head again. An earthquake had shaken his world when Olivia was taken, and the aftershocks kept coming. He couldn't even speak for a moment, could only swallow back the bile rising in his throat. Stasia seemed to sense his pain; she laid her head on his thigh.

"Maybe once these two die," Bobby said. "Maybe then it will be enough."

"Fine, so punish me in their place. Take me and let the girls go. You can kill two birds with one stone."

"Ah, Max, always the hero. Well, you know what? I *hate* heroes. When you saved the Stevens kid, everyone fawned all over you. Just like they did my father.

There are no true heroes, only men who pretend. But you, Max, you've given it your best shot, haven't you? You've been fighting your greatest villain a long time: me. I can see it in your eyes. Every child molester, every murderer you hunt down—it's me, isn't it?"

Max squeezed his eyes shut. He was right.

"But you can never defeat me. Just like I could never kill you, which does put a hitch in that noble gesture of yours."

"I will defeat you this time," Max said through gritted teeth.

Bobby only laughed. "You had your chance. Remember, in the truck. You couldn't kill me. And that's the only way you'll ever take me in. I'm your father; you're my son. We have a bond, whether you like it or not. See, you stopped your heroic little dash when you were leading Olivia to safety. You stopped at the sound of my voice. I'm telling you now, Max, let me go. Drop your crazy allegations and accept defeat. Save your career. It's the one thing you can save. And rest assured, we'll meet again." He disconnected.

Let him go? Never.

Max wanted to throw the phone through the window, but he forced himself to set it on the seat. Wherever Olivia and Phaedra were, they had to be close to the station, close enough that Huntington could get back so fast.

Huntington's house. Max doubted he'd be that obvious, but he had to check it out.

After Diana and Ashley's deaths, Huntington had invited him over for dinner. The house was simple, small. Max hadn't been much of a conversationalist, and finally the awkward silences had prompted him to leave. He'd been surprised when Huntington had invited him back, but he'd declined. His father had wanted to get closer to him; had wanted to, in his sick way, comfort him for the pain he'd caused.

Fifteen minutes later, he pulled into the driveway. It took him only a few more minutes to get into the house. Cops sometimes had the laxest security in their own homes. The house didn't fit the description of the utilitarian kitchen, but he had no place else to look.

There was no trace of them, or anything that tied Bobby and Huntington together. He headed out and pulled into a busy parking lot around the corner. He jerked the map out of the glove box and spread it out against the dashboard. He glanced at the clock. He had less than five hours to find it.

"It's Lt. Huntington. I still haven't been able to locate the Howe woman. Has she called in?"

"No, sir," O'Reilly said. "But Callahan's gone off the deep end. He went to her apartment."

"The officers were supposed to keep him there."

"He took us by surprise. We just tried to meet him at the apartment, but he's gone. Howe and her dog are also gone. Lieutenant, Callahan made some pretty crazy allegations. He said you have the Howe woman and the Burns girl, and —"

"I know what he said. We just spoke on the phone. Are you familiar with his family history?"

"No, he never talks about his family."

Because he was ashamed, just as *he* had been ashamed of *his* father. But this was different. He was different. "He confided in me after his wife and daughter died. His father kidnapped a girl and then took his own life after Callahan rescued her. I think this case has pushed him over the edge. For some reason, he's starting to see his father in me. I'm worried about him, of course, but I think we can straighten him out before he does anything rash. I want you to bring him in. I'm afraid he's going to do something to hurt himself. I'll be in touch." He hung up and turned off the phone. They'd never hear from him again.

He nearly walked right into a confrontation with Max. His son's car was parked in his driveway. He drove by and circled back ten minutes later. Max was gone. He pulled into the driveway three doors down, weaved through backyards to his home, and took the stash of money and IDs he'd tucked away for just this occasion. A man had to be prepared, after all.

He put on a dark wig and filled in his eyebrows. He'd have to get the gap in his teeth fixed right away. He had a few more errands to run, a car to procure. Once he left the courthouse after midnight, he would disappear again.

"Phaedra, my name is Olivia. Don't be afraid of me."

"You ... you called me Phaedra," the girl accused in a rough voice.

"That's your name, isn't it?"

"Yes. Yes, it is."

The gratitude came through beneath the surprise. Olivia knew exactly how she felt.

"Max and I have been trying to find you. Max is a detective, and he's also this man's son. He saved me once, when I was your age and the same man kidnapped me."

"Will he save us, too?" she asked.

Olivia felt a hitch in her chest. "I don't know." Their

only hope would be if Max could talk his father into giving up. That was unlikely. She reached out again and touched the girl's arm. Her sleeve was still damp from her dunk in the tub. "But he's going to try his darnedest." That's how Max was, how he'd always be. She could accept that. Just as he, she realized, accepted her psychic quirks. He had given her the acceptance and understanding she'd always wanted. As long as he didn't see her as Livvy, she could accept and understand his tendency to protect her. If she got a chance, she amended.

"I'm blind," she said. "But I know what this place looks like. You couldn't find a way out when you got out of the cage, could you?"

"How did you know that?"

"Since we were both kidnapped by the same man, we have a ... special connection. I've been seeing through your eyes."

"You said you were blind."

"I am. But not when I'm looking through your eyes."

The girl seemed to ponder that for a moment.

Olivia said, "When he cut you, when he left the food right outside the cage and told you not to eat it, could you feel me?"

"No."

So, the connection didn't go both ways. She'd wanted to comfort the girl so badly. Because she knew what Phaedra was thinking about now, she was finally able to give her that comfort. "Your parents are worried and they want you home. They love you very, very much."

"They do?"

"Oh my, yes."

Phaedra slid her arms around Olivia's neck and started crying. "I want to go home!"

"I know, honey, I know." She held her close. Tears pricked her eyes as the girl sobbed in her ear. She wanted to go home, too. She wanted to cuddle with Stasia and feel Max's arms around her. When she opened her eyes, she was startled to see green walls and the steel door. The door had six latches to lock out the world, but the metal slides had been disabled, probably so Phaedra couldn't lock him out if she escaped the cage. "I can see!" She took in their surroundings, the hallway with the bathroom at the end, the oven not far away.

The girl moved out of her embrace. "You're not blind anymore?"

The world went black again. "It's you. When I was holding you, I could see." The connection was still there. She touched Phaedra, but her sight didn't return.

She took Phaedra's hands in her own. "We can't give up yet. We have nothing to lose and everything to gain."

"We do?" she asked so hopefully it was painful. "You'll get us out of here?"

"I'll try."

"You will? Promise?"

Olivia squeezed her hands. "I'll try my best. You picked the lock with a piece of metal. Is there any other piece like that?"

"Wow, you did see me. He checked the cage after that to make sure I couldn't get out again. I don't see anything else we could use."

"You're a smart girl. I don't remember being as calm as you are."

"I gave up on hearing my name again, and you said it. So now I can't give up on seeing my mommy and daddy again."

"We'll do our best." Would *her* daddy even remember her to realize she'd gone? "We need a plan. Have you ever seen him lock the door when he comes in here?"

"No, but I hear him lock it when he leaves."

"Yeah, I heard him unlock it from the outside when he brought me here. So that means the door isn't locked while he's here."

"We could beat him up when he tries to get us out of here and make a run for the door."

A blind woman and a child beat up a grown man? "I don't think that'll work. I didn't see anything around here we could even use as a weapon." Maybe it wasn't a physical weapon they needed, but an intellectual weapon. An emotional weapon. "Phaedra, I know you hate being Rose, but you could do it if it meant escaping, couldn't you?"

Olivia could hear the water dripping into the bathtub. In breathless loyalty, Phaedra said, "I can do anything you want."

Time was running out, and Max was at a dead end. He threw the map into the back seat and banged his forehead against the steering wheel. The horn blared. Stasia put her paw on his leg. The dog actually looked worried.

He rubbed his eyes hard, feeling frustration and loss burning behind them. Had his comrades believed any of what he'd told them? Had they bothered to check into anything, like Huntington's fingerprints? Still, that would take too long.

It's too late.

No, it wasn't too late, not yet. At midnight, it would be too late. He had four hours left. He couldn't lose

Olivia now, not when he loved her.

The truth of that tightened his chest, making it feel as though it were imploding. His Livvy. No, not Livvy, not the scared girl she was afraid of being. Olivia, just Olivia.

He reached into the back seat and pulled her painting to the front. The paint was still damp. He traced his finger over the lines her fingers had created. She had seen where they were being held. It was here in her finger strokes. She'd painted an odd brick wall in the doorway, the one that had captured his attention before. Had he seen it somewhere?

When he was a boy, he used "x-ray vision" to see through buildings and find villains. He laid his fingers on the canvas and stared until his vision blurred. The Santa suit came back to mind.

Forget the suit. Where were the bricks? Bricks in a row. Columns of bricks. Someplace drab, a place he rarely went.

The Santa suit. The storage room at the police station. The room was as close to a basement as you could get in Florida, built a half-floor into the ground. His whole body felt electrified, and he had to hold himself back from starting the car and racing over. No, it didn't make sense. It was the police station, and though it wasn't used often, clerks did go in there from time to time. Besides, they might detain him. Then all hope would be lost.

He looked at her painting again. *Trust your instincts. Check it out.*

It was all he had to go on, just like Olivia had once been all he'd had. He'd trusted her, and she'd helped him. He would never have gotten this far without her, would have never known his father was still alive.

When he parked in the back of the lot at the police station a few minutes later, he had to blink in disbelief. God, he was thinking of getaways from the police.

"Stay here, girl. I'll be back soon." His reassuring pat didn't seem to reassure her at all, but she was better off in the car than going inside with him.

He walked casually into the building, bypassing the detective's area where he heard someone speculating as to where he might be. The storage room was dark and musty and full of stuff: a box of equipment for their annual softball games, old computer equipment, and files. He glanced up on the top shelf. The Santa suit was still there.

He searched the outer walls, which were mostly red brick. He didn't see any aberration on the normal pattern, but most of the walls were lined with shelving units. The far unit caught his eye. All he could see was a couple of inches around the perimeter of the unit — and those inches were bricks in one line.

He searched the room, shoving boxes and shelves out of the way, looking for a cage. There was nothing. He turned back to the unit with the lined bricks and pulled it forward. It was heavier than he would have been able to handle if lives weren't on the line. As soon as the shelf started tipping, he jumped out of the way. Boxes and equipment crashed to the concrete floor. Before the noise stopped echoing in his head, he climbed over the debris and laid his hands on the wall.

"What are you doing in here?" A woman stood in the doorway of the storage room, looking both annoyed and worried.

"What's on the other side of this wall?"

"Tell me who you are."

"My name's Detective Callahan." He swallowed. "Lt. Huntington's division. I need to know what's on the other side of this wall." He knew he sounded on the edge. Hell, he *was* on the edge.

"Let me go ask someone." She closed the door and went to get help.

He turned back to the wall and started shoving at the bricks. They were solid, despite their amateur layout. He tried his breaking-down-the-door technique, but only smashed his shoulder again. He kicked, punched. Damn it, he needed something heavier, like a car.

"What the hell is going on down here?"

"Max, is that you?"

Nick Mathers, Sam, and John Holland all advanced into the storage room; the clerk hovered nervously behind them.

Max was covered in dust and sweat and probably looked a little mad. "What's on the other side of this wall?"

"Oh, jeez, not this again," Nick said.

"*What the hell is on the other side of this wall?*"

Sam approached cautiously, while the other two detectives were ready to draw weapons. They really thought he was crazy.

"Max, tell us what's going on. We'll listen to you."

"Olivia painted what the girl saw when she escaped the cage and hid in a doorway." He put his hand on the bricks. "This is what she saw, this pattern. And it's big enough to be an old doorway. They might be on the other side of this wall."

"They?"

"Phaedra and Olivia. Like I told you, he has both of

them."

"Huntington does," Sam clarified doubtfully.

Max pointed to the suit on the shelf. "He used that suit. I came down here before the abduction, thinking about whether I wanted to be Santa for the kids. The suit wasn't there, and it gave me the excuse I needed to not do the gig. We know Phaedra was abducted by a man wearing a Santa suit. Now it's back. It's perfect. Who would think about looking in the police station's storage room for the suit?"

"I can't imagine," John muttered.

"That's not all of it. The man who took Phaedra knew about Olivia's connection with the girl, which meant he was a cop, someone here who knew about the case. Huntington went to get Olivia, but lied about her not being at the apartment. Did you talk to Judy?"

John smirked. "The retarded woman? Yeah, she sang 'Jingle Bells' for us. How does Terry Carlton fit into all this?"

"You found the body then."

"Oh, yeah. They're working the scene now."

"I think Terry caught Bob — Huntington at Olivia's apartment. Since Terry could ID him, he had to be killed. We can't help Terry, but we can help Olivia and Phaedra." He touched the wall. "I've got three and a half hours to find them. He'll drown them at midnight, that's what he always does. Sam, you know that. You know everything. I need your help. If there's nothing behind this wall, you can lock me up with the felons. You've got to help me find out for sure."

If this wasn't the key, it would be too late. And what he'd endure being a detective locked up with felons would be nothing compared to what he'd be suffering inside if he failed.

The three men were considering him, taking in the mess he'd created. He knew their position. You couldn't trust a crazy person. There would be repercussions if Max were wrong. Nick touched his cell phone and started to back out of the room. He was going to call in reinforcements.

Max made it easy on them. He grabbed Sam's gun and pointed it at his head. "Don't make me do something we'll all regret. I'm not going to let him kill them. Sam, I'm sorry about this. You were just the closest one, that's all. It was nothing personal."

"You're crazy, Max. Let us help you," Sam said through gritted teeth.

"I gave you the chance to help me. All you wanted to do was turn me in as some crazed whacko. I'm not crazy, Sam." When the other two men started to move forward, he jammed the gun into Sam's cheek. "But I am desperate. Throw your guns and phones on the floor. Now!"

His mind was spinning, but he couldn't think beyond that minute. What would he do next? How far would he go? He made Sam bend down with him as he picked up the phones and guns and stuffed them into his pockets. He turned around and backed toward the door. If he could lock them in here, he'd have more time to talk Sam into helping.

"I have to do this, Sam. I can't let them die. Maybe this mysterious place we've been looking for has been right here all along. I've got to check it —"

A flash of pain roared through his head. Everything went dark as he dropped to the floor.

CHAPTER 27

Even with a plan, Olivia's heart lurched at the sound of the door opening. She had become hopeful that Max had found Bobby. It was nearly midnight. Phaedra's breath quickened as well, and she wrapped her hands around Olivia's arm. Olivia had a flash of vision, Bobby closing the door and walking toward the cage.

"My two Roses," he said, crouching next to them. "It's time for your bath, Rose. Such a dirty child. Why must you push your mother to tears every time she tries to get you to bathe? I'm going to do it this time." He started to unlock the cage.

Phaedra's fingers dug into her arm now. Olivia grimaced in pain as she scooted forward. She was afraid that the girl wouldn't let go. Eventually she did, and he opened the door and pulled Olivia to her feet. Her legs were stiff, and she shook them out. He locked the cage again.

"Rose, come with me." He led her toward the bathroom at the far end. Toward the tub full of water. "Don't try to fight me. You'll only hurt yourself." Another drop of water fell into the tub. *Kerplunk.*

She stopped, taking him by surprise. "Why do you keep calling me Rose, Bobby?"

Now it was his fingers that tightened on her arm. "Don't call me that."

With her free hand, she reached up in the vicinity of his face and eventually found his cheek. He flinched. "Bobby, darling, I've always called you that. Since the day we married."

"You're Rose."

She pointed toward that cage. "That's our Rose. She has given us a bit of trouble, hasn't she? But she's only a child, Bobby, a normal child. You know how much I wanted a girl. How much she means to me."

If he could make those girls into Rose, why couldn't she be his wife?

"You're Rose." The conviction seeped out of his voice.

She gestured toward her body. "How can I be Rose? I'm a grown woman." In a coy voice, she added, "Something you know well." She dared to touch his face again; he didn't move away this time. He did take hold of her wrist but held it there.

"Marie's gone."

"Look at me, Bobby. I'm here, aren't I?" She glanced toward Phaedra. "We're together, one happy family." She smiled, hoping it looked soft and genuine.

"You can't be Marie."

"But I am." She leaned against him and sighed. "I love you, Bobby."

He was probably stunned. He only stood there, still holding her wrist.

"We're almost a family again." She inserted just the right amount of wistfulness into her voice. She could smell the sweat on his body and could feel the heat coming off him. She recognized the smell — the man who had been in her apartment.

She wasn't expecting him to shove her against the wall, banging her head against the concrete, nor the anger in his voice, melted with anguish. "You left us!"

She nearly cried in relief. "I'm sorry, Bobby. I had to go. I was in such pain, Rose was gone ... I couldn't live anymore."

"It was Rose's fault."

"No, it wasn't. She's only a child."

"Why did you hurt me like that? I would have made things right. I'm a good father, not like him."

Him? She kept playing along, trying to stay in safe territory. "But Rose was gone, and we couldn't make that right again. We have a second chance now."

He kissed her hard, shoving his tongue in her mouth. Still stunned from the smack against the wall, she tried to reciprocate. *Play the part, don't think about it, just play the part.*

He pulled her hard against him now, holding her close, as though he were afraid she'd leave again. "I didn't mean to kill her."

She stroked his hair. "I know, Bobby. I know."

"It was an accident. She fought you every time you tried to make her bathe, and you'd end up in tears. I wanted to fix it so she'd listen to you. I pushed her under the water, and she didn't fight me anymore. It was nice, her not fighting."

She squeezed him tight even though his words repulsed her. "It's all right now."

"She made me so mad. Made you mad."

"She doesn't make me mad anymore. She's a good girl

now. Come here, Rose. Show daddy how good you are."

"I can't," Phaedra said on a near whisper. "I'm locked in."

"Bobby, please don't punish her anymore." Her tears weren't phony. She was crying for them, for Rose, and for every girl who had died in Rose's place. "She's a good girl now. She's sorry for what she did."

"I'm sorry, Father," Phaedra said, sending relief through Olivia that she could pull this off. "I didn't mean to make you mad."

She felt Bobby sag. "I couldn't help it. I couldn't help hurting her. The rage was inside me, it was so powerful. It wouldn't go away."

"I know," Olivia whispered, stroking his arm. "You wanted to be a good father, that's all. But it's okay now. We're a family again. Let Rose out of the cage so we can be together. Please, Bobby. You love me, don't you?"

"Yes." The truth of that was evident in his voice.

"Then let her out."

"Marie ..." He held her tight, breathing deeply. "All right."

"Thank you." She hoped he didn't hear the relief in her voice.

She heard him fiddle with the lock. She waited for Phaedra to stretch her legs and give the sign that she was ready to bolt. "Hi, Father."

Olivia went for distraction. "Bobby, I've missed you so much, I—"

"Hey! Rose!"

Damn. Phaedra was supposed to wait until he was distracted. She lunged toward him just as Phaedra struggled to open the door. "Bobby, please don't hurt her! You've hurt her enough." Her arms tightened around his shoulders as he tried to fling her off. He finally managed to throw her. She hit the floor and tried to roll away. Had Phaedra gotten out?

"You betrayed me again," he growled, and before she could move out of his grasp, his hands clamped around her neck. "You were going to go to the police and tell them I killed Rose. You were going to turn me in! I had to stop you then, and I'll stop you now. You must be punished, Marie."

He'd drowned Marie. The horrid realization flashed through her mind as he dragged her toward the bathroom. She kicked and fought, but as she'd predicted earlier, she was no physical match for him. Her emotional weapon had backfired. She hadn't thought about him having killed Marie, too.

She heard a sound beyond the bathroom. *Oh, God, please don't let that be Phaedra crying out there. Please let her be long gone, getting help.*

The water was cool as he twisted her painfully and shoved her into the tub. Water gushed up her nose, but she kept her mouth closed. She scratched at his hands pressing on her chest, pushing her down against the hard surface of the tub floor. Panic made the urge to breathe stronger. She pushed to the surface, fighting and scratching. Her nails made contact, clawing across his skin. He grunted in pain.

She didn't have time to prepare for his backlash. He took hold of her head and slammed it against the side of the tub. The breath she'd managed to take rushed out. Pinpricks of painful light flashed through her mind. She fell from consciousness.

Max had been pounding on the bars for close to an

hour. The only other guy in the temporary lock-up was some drunk who'd pissed on a building. At first, he'd gleefully joined Max's tirade, but he'd long ago tired of it and fell back asleep. The guard had made himself scarce.

Max rested his raw throat for a few minutes, his head pressed against the cold bars. The panic and fury had given way to an ache that wracked every cell in his body. He didn't even know what time it was. They'd taken his watch, and there was no clock in view. When he was about to start his verbal tirade again, he heard the door open.

Sam walked in, his cell phone pressed to his ear. "Thank you, sir. I'll explain later." He disconnected as he reached Max. "I asked the mayor about our storage room. He's been in local government for a long time, I figured he might know. As soon as he started talking about the bomb shelter that was built years ago between the courthouse and our building, I grabbed a gun and came down here to get you. The shelter's been sealed for ages. He said it went from our storage room to a closet on the first floor of the courthouse." He slid a key into the lock.

"A bomb shelter," Max croaked. "It would have a kitchen, telecommunications type room ... just like Olivia said." Sam was nodding. Max stepped out of the cell. "But you don't believe in Olivia's connection."

"No, but you do, enough to put your ass on the line. We've been friends a long time. If you believe so strongly, then I'm with you."

"What time is it?"

"Eleven-forty-nine. Let's go. "

Max and Sam tore out of there. Max was still a little lightheaded from the knock on his head, but he couldn't let a wave of dizziness stand in his way. They exited the building and ran across the parking lot to the courthouse. Sam slipped inside the dark building first and started searching the empty offices. Max motioned him toward a door halfway down the hallway that he knew was a closet.

Now he was even more aware of every passing second as he saw the digital clock in the one occupied office on the left: 12:02. The numbers burned his eyes as the words *Too late! Too late!* screamed through his brain. He couldn't give up. Like those agonizingly long minutes as he ran across the macadam with Olivia's small hand clutched in his, and his muscles burning and his head pounding, he had to keep going.

He and Sam moved like shadows, in sync just as they used to be. The closet door was closed, but not locked. Max flipped on the light. One of the shelving units was askew. He pushed it aside and looked at the wall behind it. It looked ordinary, wood-paneled like the other walls. Why had the unit been moved? He pushed on the wall, and the paneling swung away from him and into a dark area — that revealed a steel door.

He didn't have time to think about his approach. He shoved the heavy door forward and found the bomb shelter. The walls were green, the floor concrete. The kitchen was clean and the cage sitting in the middle of the floor was empty. As he registered a whimpering sound coming from the left of the steps, he heard thrashing sounds toward the right. He took only a second to see Phaedra crouched beside the steps, her hands in her mouth. He followed the sounds of splashing water to a bathroom at the end of the hall as Sam moved toward the girl to see if she was all right.

Max's heart dropped to his shoes at the sight: the man he'd known as Huntington, crouched by the tub holding Olivia under the water. He wanted to smash him, but he didn't want to make himself a liability. He drew his gun and yelled, "Let her up!"

Bobby jerked around to face Max. He brought Olivia out of the water with the movement. She wasn't fighting anymore, just sucking in air.

Max tightened his grip on the gun and willed his hands to stop shaking. "Let her go and step away."

Bobby only smiled. The eyes might be a different color, but they were his father's eyes, filled with gloating evil. And Max was that boy again, waiting to see what his father would do.

"Max, you're good, I'll give you that." He glanced behind him. "What, no cavalry?"

"I'm right here," Sam said from behind Max. "Huntington — or whoever you really are — think about what you're doing here. Move away from Olivia."

Huntington surprised them by pulling a gun and pointing it at Olivia. He looked at Sam. "This is between me and my son. Get out of here or I kill her like this." When Max tightened his grip on the trigger, he said, "You could shoot me, but I'll shoot her, too."

After a tense moment, Max turned to Sam. "Let me handle this. Go take care of Phaedra."

Sam would take the girl and go for help. Bobby had to know that. And that meant he knew there was no way out of this. Max swallowed hard. Bobby had nothing to lose. Olivia was reaching out with one droopy hand, trying to gain her bearings. Max had everything to lose.

"He's gone. Put down the gun," Max said.

Again, to Max's surprise, Bobby set the gun down without hesitation. "This is between us now."

"Fine, it's between us. Let Olivia go. She has nothing to do with this."

"She has everything to do with this."

"Bobby —"

"Call me Father," Bobby said. "I want to hear you say it."

A chill crept over his skin. "Only if you let her go."

Bobby's shoulders slumped. "I can't do that, Max. Then you'll be the big hero, and I'll be sitting in prison. That just won't work for me. So, here's the deal." He pushed Olivia back under the water. "You'll have to kill me if you want to win. Can you kill your own father? I think you're too much of a coward. Let's see what my boy's got."

Kryptonite. The word pounded through his head and stole his breath.

An explosion rocked Olivia out of the encroaching blackness. Her body jerked in response to it. The pressure of Bobby's hand on her chest eased. She burst out of the water and sucked in air — then coughed violently. She got the impression of being surrounded by the color red. A coppery smell filled her nostrils. His hands were still on her, though he was no longer gripping her. What had happened? She didn't give herself time to think about it. As he slumped into the tub, she pushed him away and reached for the side.

"Olivia!"

Max's voice! He pulled her out of the tub and into his arms. Still coughing and pulling in breaths, she was too weak to even stand. He hoisted her up and carried her out of the bathroom and down the hallway. She wasn't too weak, however, to wrap her arms around his neck and bury her face against his shoulder.

"It's okay," he murmured. "Let's get you out of here."

"Where's Phaedra?"

"Sam's got her."

He carried her up the steps, through the smaller room, and down the hallway. The outside air was cold against her wet body, and she pulled closer to Max.

He sat down on the front steps and kissed her forehead. "Can you breathe all right?"

She nodded, feeling the painful pressure in her chest ease with each breath.

She heard voices rushing toward them. "Max, what happened?" Sam O'Reilly's voice said.

"I shot him. He's still down in the shelter."

Sam said, "Follow me." Footsteps stampeded past her into the courthouse.

"Olivia!" It was Phaedra's voice.

Olivia reached out and felt the girl's hand in hers. "We did it."

"No, *you* did it. I couldn't get the door open. It was too heavy. And I was so scared when I heard him hurting you." Her shame was clear.

Olivia squeezed her hand. "It's all right, sweetie. All that matters is that the bad man will never hurt you again, I promise," she managed between wheezing breaths.

"Shh," Max said against her ear. "Save your breath." He reached over to Phaedra. "Little girl, you don't know how happy I am to see you. Are you okay?"

"Yeah, I think so." Phaedra hugged Olivia close. "You were right, Max did save us."

He said, "Olivia's the hero this time."

"Me?"

"Your painting told me where you were. The brick pattern was the same one I'd seen in the police station's storage room."

Footsteps continued going in and out of the doorway, and various voices discussed what they'd seen down there.

"Olivia, I'm sorry I doubted you." It was Sam O'Reilly's voice again. "I took Phaedra to the station and got help, but she wanted to come back and make sure you were all right. An ambulance is on the way."

Max asked, "Is he ...?"

"Yeah, he's dead. Your shot was dead on."

A minute later another man's voice said, "What the hell is going on around here? First, I'm called to work because one of my men has gone bonkers. And now ..."

Max said, "Captain, this is Phaedra Burns. That's the important thing right now. Call her parents and tell them to come get their girl. I'll explain everything else later."

An ambulance pulled up, sirens pulsing through the night air. A minute later, a man said, "Are they all right?"

"Yeah, they are." Max's voice revealed he still couldn't believe it. He brushed her hair back from her face. "But give them a look over just to be sure. We'll need some blankets, too."

After they'd been examined, a female officer took Phaedra to the station. Max swaddled Olivia in a scratchy wool blanket.

She heard the stretcher clatter by as they took Bobby away. Even though he couldn't hurt her anymore, Max still tightened his hold on her as it passed.

The red color was gone, but there was something else. Not darkness.

"Olivia, why do you keep blinking?" He bracketed her eyes with his fingers. "Are your eyes all right?"

She lifted her hand in front of her face. Slowly, she looked up at him. "Max ... I can see."

EPILOGUE

One month later...

Max made a sound of frustration. "I got used to the ties, but bowties are a whole other matter."

Olivia set her shawl on the corner of her bed and slid her arms around him from behind. "I wish I could help. More importantly, I wish I could see just how handsome you look in that tux."

He swung around and before she even knew what happened, he'd pinned her down on the bed. "Let's just blow the whole thing off and fool around all night instead."

She let him get away with a long, mind-bending kiss before playfully pushing him off. "No way. We've earned this night. I, for one, am going to enjoy it. Besides, it means a lot to the Burnses, and to Phaedra."

The Burnses insisted on arranging for an appreciation dinner. They'd invited everyone who had helped with the investigation, including Judy. Stasia would be there, too, of course. Max wasn't thrilled at his and Olivia being the guests of honor.

He got to his feet and pulled her up. "They could have just treated us to dinner at one of their restaurants. I would have been happy with that."

"For saving their daughter? I don't think *they* would have been happy with that." She pinched his cheek. "It's only one night."

All Olivia could see of him was a dark blur as he stood before the mirror and fiddled with the tie again. It was more than she'd seen of anything in so long, she was grateful for that. Dr. Bhatti and Dr. Marano had been studying the gradual return of her sight. One theory was that Olivia had indeed sustained a minute brain injury sixteen years ago. That injury may have caused some visual problems, but no one knew because of the conversion disorder. The recent knock to her head reversed that initial damage and, oddly enough, Marano thought Max's love had reversed the conversion disorder. Or, more specifically, her acceptance that she needed his love. It would take time before they'd know how much of her vision would return, but as long as she had Max by her side, she'd handle whatever it turned out to be.

"Are Sam and Annie going to be there?" she asked. "When we had lunch last week, it sounded like they were going to go as a family. She's really trying to get past the Helene thing."

"Last I heard, they were all going to be there. I think they're going to make it work. Ah hah, got it."

"Good." She ran her fingers over the bowtie. "Speaking of family, have you decided when to visit Odette and make peace?"

Right or wrong, Max had left out her obstruction of justice in his report. He couldn't bear to see her prosecuted for her blind devotion. "Maybe we can drive out next week."

We. Both of them. Max had come home with her on Christmas night, and they'd spent every night since together. She knew he was giving her space, trying not to overwhelm her or threaten her sense of independence. He was letting her set the pace. They'd been talking about making his house into a place where mentally challenged people like Judy could learn to live independently. Tonight, after the dinner, she was going to suggest they move ahead with the plan...because he wouldn't need a place of his own anymore. His home was there, with her, holding her so close at night that she'd never felt safer. Or more loved.

But there was something she needed to know first. She slid her arms around him, facing him this time. "Is the whole hero thing the reason you don't like the idea of this dinner? Is that why you turned down the promotion to lieutenant? You haven't talked much about what happened. You don't have to hold it inside anymore. You don't have to face it alone." She swallowed the thickness from her voice, giving away, even to herself, how much his silence on the matter was bothering her. "It must have been hard to shoot your own father, no matter how evil he was. Please talk to me, Max."

He touched her face the same way she often touched his. "I didn't mean to shut you out, love. I guess I've just been trying to work it out in my mind." He held her closer and let out a long breath. "It was harder than I thought it would be. After all he'd done to me, to those girls ... you ... I thought I could pull that trigger without hesitation. He played the same mind games he used to play with me, making me feel like that helpless kid again. He called me a coward and told me I'd have to kill him if I wanted to win. When he pushed you under the water again, his power over me evaporated. All that mattered was saving you."

"But that's the way you are. You'd shoot to save anyone's life. Whether you like it or not, you're a—"

He put a finger over her mouth. "Don't call me a hero."

"Why not?"

"Being a hero is a charade. All my life I drove myself because I was afraid to be anything less. But when I knew he had you" — he moved his finger to brush her cheek — "everything changed. All I knew was that I couldn't lose you. That's what drove me, not anything rooted in my childhood, not an ongoing quest to eradicate my father. I realized there was another reason to do what I do — because I love doing it. I never loved being a cop; I was driven to it. Driven to rescue damsels in distress, driven to right the wrongs of the world. But now I want to do it because ... well, because I *want* to do it. That's why I turned down the promotion. I need to earn it, in my mind."

She held him close. "Thank you for sharing that."

He tilted her chin up. "I'm ready to let the past go. When I look ahead, all I see is you."

She kissed him hard as she pulled him toward the bed and unbuttoned his pants.

"Hey, I thought you wanted to go to this dinner," he half-protested between kisses.

"I do, but there's nothing wrong with being a little

late."

Thank you so much for reading *Blindsight*. If you enjoyed it, please consider posting a review on Amazon.com, BookBub.com, and Goodreads.com.

Find links to more stories in the Love & Light collection and other series by Tina at www.WrittenMusings.com/TinaWainscott and www.TinaWainscott.com.

SNEAK PEEK

PROLOGUE

Three years earlier...

The sky blackened, making the wind gust wickedly through the palm trees. Not exactly the Hawaii one pictured, but Adrian Wilde was on a roll, quite literally. Supermodel Ellie Marlow held her long hair out of her face, frowning at the camera.

Adrian tilted his head. "Come on, Ellie. Just a few more shots." He lifted his hands to the rolling clouds above. "Can't you feel the excitement in the air, the danger? It's perfect."

"It's insane! We're going to be electrocuted."

As if the sorceress had summoned it, lightning cracked across the clouds, puncturing the blackness with wicked fingers. A second later thunder shattered the air.

"Two more shots and we're out of here," he called over the wind. "And let go of the hair. Please," he added with a smile.

After a pause, she let her brown hair whip across her face, walking toward him with a jaunty cant.

"This is going to be the shot of a lifetime."

For a second, the hairs on his body shot to attention. The air tingled. In a single flash of light and a loud crash, he was knocked backward. Vibrations charged through his body. He could hear Ellie scream, but he couldn't move or speak. Darkness swirled around him, as if those spikes of light had pulled him right up into that black mass.

"Help me!" Ellie's voice, he thought.

"He's not breathing!" he heard someone scream.

The twisting mass formed a tunnel, and at the end a brilliant light pulsed. He moved toward that light as a roller coaster screams across the tracks. Images flashed past him, vivid and full of life.

Only it wasn't his life.

A young girl made a sandcastle on the beach, patting the sides with infinite care until a boy with dark hair stalked over and kicked it in. That same girl, now a lovely teenager, standing on a seawall, her golden blond curls dancing in the breeze as she looked out to a cerulean ocean. Her arms were crossed in front of her, slender hands on her throat. Then the same girl, now a woman, driving through town in a white Mercedes convertible on a summer day.

He kept rushing through space without time or thought. The woman's image flashed in front of him again. She was walking out of a mansion. Storm clouds darkened the sky there, too, but he hardly had time to notice. If he kept going, he was going to crash into her. She didn't see him coming right at her, right...

He was expelled into a thicker darkness, a liquid warmth that flowed all around him. Blood pumping through his veins, a muffled thunder that pulsed through the thickness. A heartbeat. Her heartbeat. He was inside her.

Then everything exploded, worse than the thunder, more painful than the lightning. Fire, the smell of smoke, heat on his skin, searing pain, so much fear and panic. All he could see was the venomous orange burst that surrounded the woman. Her thoughts were louder than the roar of flames.

What's happening? Mother! I've got to get out and find her.

"He's got a heartbeat," a voice said from some far away place.

Adrian rolled on the sand in a desperate attempt to smother the flames. Hands were everywhere on him, holding him down as he struggled. He opened his eyes. The crew. The people he'd left behind what seemed like hours ago. They stood around him, confusion and concern in their eyes.

"He's alive," Ellie breathed, squeezing his arm.

He looked around. No fire. Only the rain, gushing from the sky. Rain that had felt like flames.

Two of the men helped him to his feet. His shoes had been knocked off, and his feet felt like two balls of fire. They looked like he'd been standing in a frying pan.

"Let's get you out of the rain. Geez, are you all right? You gave us a helluva scare."

Adrian's breath came in heavy gasps. His body felt

like liquid. When he reached the nearest palm, he held onto it.

"Get away from that tree, Wilde," Bob said. "You want to get hit by lightning again?"

"Is that what happened?" He saw his camera lying on the sand, scorched and now wet. "Where was the fire? I felt flames, smelled smoke."

Ellie pulled him to the van, where he dropped down onto the floor. "There was no fire, love," she said, wiping his shoulder-length dark hair out of his eyes. "It must have been the lightning you felt. You were dead, you know. Margot performed CPR and got your heart beating again."

"I was dead." His voice trailed off as he looked at the place where he'd been thrown. He closed his eyes, settling his forehead in his hand. Flashes of the tunnel ripped through the blackness behind his eyes. Dead. He had heard of the tunnel, of people seeing their life flash before them. But who was the woman? Why had her life exploded?

CHAPTER 1

Cold water engulfed Adrian, pulling him down to some hellish oblivion beneath the sea. He heard the wild beating of his heart and the sound of air as it escaped his mouth in the last bubbles of hope. Blackness surrounded him. His lungs threatened to burst. Breathe, he had to breathe.

No air.

He inhaled cool water into his lungs. Panic froze him. He took two short gasps. More water rushed in, crushing his chest. Long, blond tendrils of hair floated out on either side of him.

"No!" He heard his own voice tear the word from his mouth in one long wail of agony. Fear raged through his veins as he caught his breath in gasps. He looked desperately around for a way to escape, his survival instinct strong and fierce.

The water and fury disappeared, leaving only the cool darkness of a November New York night. The sounds of the city assured him of reality—taxi drivers honked their horns, music drifted from somewhere. He wasn't dying. Yet.

"My God, Adrian, what were you dreaming about?"

Rita's voice whispered from the dark.

He'd forgotten she had wormed an overnight invitation. She turned on the soft light over the bed. He brought himself back by rubbing his fingers over his face, trying to erase his expression of fear.

Rita touched the tensed muscle of his arm, then wiped the perspiration that covered him onto the silk sheets. "You're soaked. Are you all right?"

He finally felt composed enough to turn at the concern in her voice. Her black mane of curls tumbled around her face, wildly framing dark eyes and olive skin.

He smoothed back his damp hair, dark as hers. "It was a nightmare. Go back to sleep." His voice betrayed him, cracking softly.

How long would he keep having this dream? It was worse than the fire he'd experienced through BlueFire's eyes, and no less vivid. Since his death three years earlier, his life hadn't been the same.

He rolled out of bed and walked over to the black dresser. In the mirror he could see the green light spilling from beneath the pedestal of the black bed like a mystical fog, and Rita sitting there watching him. The air chilled his damp skin. He lit a cigarette, took two drags, and crushed it in the blue glass astray. Last month he took five drags before putting it out. Last week, three.

Rita's voice softened. "Adrian, talk to me. It'll help."

"Nothing to talk about. Go back to sleep. I'm going to get some work done."

He had shared his after death experience with one other person, the only person who wouldn't think he was crazy.

It wasn't the strange journey death had taken him on, but what that journey had started: visions. That lightning strike had connected his soul with a mysterious woman's soul. During brief flashes, like those images in the tunnel, he felt her emotions, saw what she saw. Sometimes it was the ocean, other times an art gallery. He'd dubbed her BlueFire, blue for her sad, lonely moods.

The drowning nightmares were far different from any ordinary dream. She was drowning. At least he guessed it was her, because of the hair and the way he could feel her. Had she survived the fire only to drown? He would never know because he had no clues about her, not even her name. If she really existed beyond his soul.

After taking a cold shower, he threw on some baggy cotton pants, pulled his hair into a ponytail, and walked into his studio. The bright lights and faint vinegar smell of darkroom chemicals brought the comfort he wanted. He loved the art of the old-fashioned process as much as he did the photo-taking itself.

Throwing a Moody Blues CD into the stereo system, he took the negatives still hanging in the drying cabinet and closed himself in the darkroom. Years ago he'd come across the group doing a reunion tour and jived with their music. Maybe it was their name that snagged him, reminding him of BlueFire.

He laid the strips on the contact easel and shot the contact sheets for the black and whites he'd taken last week in Palm Beach for Guess. Although he'd never been to the area before, it had felt eerily familiar to him. He still couldn't shake the feeling.

Adrian worked for hours, hoping that when he

emerged the long night would be far behind him. It wasn't the first time he'd spent half the night printing photographs after a nightmare. The contact sheets came alive in the developer, and as always, he was pleased with the results. Mari Flannegan looked fresh and innocent in the foamy waves, like a modern-day Norma Jean. Behind her, the Atlantic Ocean shimmered like a blanket of diamonds in the sun.

The shot of Mari holding a wad of seaweed with a grimace on her face wasn't planned, but he would recommend it be the first one in the series. He pulled the sheet out of the wash, squeegeed it, and hung it up to dry.

He never kidded himself that he didn't have miles to go before becoming the best. When he reached that pinnacle, then what? For now, he had everything he wanted, mostly the security that he would never worry again about losing his home or not having food for dinner. All that was in a faraway past before he had any control over his life. A penthouse in New York City, travel to exotic places, working with gorgeous women...what more could he want?

He started the last contact sheet, feeling lack of sleep creeping up on his features. So far most of the shots looked perfect, except for the blurry one when a bedraggled Spanish girl tugged at his sleeve just as he was making the exposure. Adrian told her to leave, then felt so bad at her obvious disappointment he played sucker and bought one of the shell necklaces dangling over her arm.

When he had put the last contact sheet in the fix, he snapped on the light and surveyed the shots. His gaze rested on the last one. Mari gave the camera a sensational smile, probably glad she was almost done and could get out of the nippy sea air that reddened her nose. The beach curved away behind her. The mist that enveloped the background made it seem surreal—a perfect shot.

Wait a minute. Something was in the background that he'd clearly missed when taking the shot. He squinted, making out a lone figure of a woman standing on the beach. Judging by the drab attire and general appearance, she appeared to be a homeless person. He would have to airbrush the figure so it would blend in with the mist.

"Damn," he muttered, leaving the darkroom to let the pictures dry and grab a bite. He hated missing details like that.

Rita chewed on a bagel, sitting at the slate gray counter that separated the kitchen from the dining area. She wrinkled up the note she'd been writing when he walked out of his studio.

"Hi, darling. Wasn't sure if I'd see you before I left."

"Aren't those bagels stale?" He wanted to avoid "morning after" conversation. Sometimes that could be stale, too.

"It's fine." She wrenched another bite free. "You've been working since that nightmare?"

"Got a lot done. The shots for Guess came out great."

He poured a cup of the almond coffee Rita had brewed, He didn't care for fancy coffees, but as long as it was fresh and potent, he could live with nuts in his java.

Rita smiled over her cup, letting her gaze linger on his bare chest. "You should do some modeling, Adrian. With those eyes, that mouth…"

"I have no desire to be on the other side of the camera, thank you." In fact, he went out of his way to keep a low profile. He wanted his photography to speak for itself.

With a loud meow, Oscar, his white cat, made a grand entrance. He walked over to the super-size cat food bowl and sniffed at its emptiness.

Rita opened the cabinet door and filled the bowl. "Do you think Giovanni will ever come back from Australia and get Oscar?" she asked, stroking his white fur.

Adrian smiled, remembering Giovanni's plea to watch his cat while he 'found himself' in the Outback. He found himself all right, along with a lucrative contract for *National Geographic*. Adrian didn't keep pets or plants, since he was gone a lot, but he'd agreed to his good friend's request. A year later, Oscar was still in his residence, and Rita took care of him whenever Adrian was away.

"Probably not. The last letter I got from him detailed his new life with some Aborigine tribe, with a three-hundred-dollar check for Oscar's upkeep. And of course, lots of buttering up for not sticking him in the pound."

"Ah, you wouldn't do that, would you?"

He raised an eyebrow. "Nah. Fuzzy bugger's grown on me."

Oscar, as if sensing his existence being discussed, wandered over to Adrian and rubbed against his leg. Adrian leaned down and scratched his head.

Rita leaned on her elbows, looking up at him under thick, dark lashes. "Is there a chance I'll grow on you, too?"

Adrian made it a point never to lead a woman on, just as he never lied to them. "Rita..."

"I know, I know. You're too busy to have a relationship. Lucky Oscar, the only reason he gets to stay is because he was foisted on you."

He lit a cigarette, taking two drags before crushing it out. "A cat is a lot easier to deal with than a woman." Then he walked into the bedroom to get dressed.

By the time Adrian returned to the darkroom, he'd forgotten about both Rita and the ragamuffin. He aimed the remote at the central music system, and piano sounds boomed throughout the apartment.

He sat at his white table, the contact sheets spread out before him. A yellow pencil marked the ones he would recommend to Guess. He picked up the last contact sheet and stared at the figure in the background. Holding it under the bright studio light, he automatically reached for the loupe. Something about the woman's posture sent a funny feeling curling through his insides.

He decided to blow up that shot to see if he could make her out. Even with the negative in the enlarger and the head extended all the way to the top, he still couldn't get the magnification he was after, so he reached for the 130-millimeter lens. The negative's image projected onto the easel, and he shifted it to capture only the woman in the background. After testing, he set the exposure for ten seconds and dropped the print in the developer, watching the figure appear as he pushed it around with the tongs. Magic, that's what photography was.

Fingers of déjà vu gripped his heart as he examined the print in its bath of fix. What he could see of the woman's features beneath the scarf was delicate, her lips sensual and full. She seemed oblivious to the activity down the beach as she looked out at the ocean. His fingers trembled as he transferred the print to the wash, then held it beneath the blow dryer. He knew this woman with her arms crossed protectively in front of her, fingers up by her throat. She had haunted his life for three years.

BlueFire.

As he started to jump up from the table, he shook his head. Lack of sleep was catching up to him. It couldn't be her. In his visions, she lived in a mansion, drove a Mercedes, and was exquisite. This woman appeared to be homeless, with her shabby coat and faded scarf.

Adrian set the photograph on the corner of his table and looked through the other shots on the contact sheets. As if a ghost, the woman didn't appear anywhere else.

He sorted through the prints, but his attention kept drifting to the woman. The feeling that it was her persisted throughout the morning and afternoon. Time and again he picked up the print and held it under the light. He brought it with him to the dining table while he ate his lunch of a stale bagel loaded with lox and cream cheese.

Adrian remembered the image of BlueFire standing on the lawn, her blond hair flowing out behind her as she stared at the ocean. She found solace in the waves and the great expanse of water. He was sure he'd seen her in this exact pose when he was in that tunnel. While he'd always believed his visions to be real, he hadn't been able to prove it. This photograph wasn't proof to anyone but him, but it explained his feeling of familiarity with Palm Beach.

What if it was her? The possibility sent pinpricks

down his spine. What if that fiery event had somehow made her homeless? Worst of all, what if he airbrushed her and never found out? He dropped down into the leather seat, letting out the deep breath he'd been holding. The thought thrummed through him, but another more foreboding thought crept in: his Aunt Stella's prediction.

Stella was the only person in whom he had confided his strange experience. Those images haunted him afterwards, and the nightmares about drowning had gripped him in fear and panic every night for months.

His mother scoffed at her sister's physic abilities, calling Stella a phony every time her name came up. Adrian wasn't inclined to believe in things paranormal, but he knew he'd go crazy if he didn't talk to someone. Stella, at least, wouldn't think he'd lost it.

Nor did she laugh when he relayed the lightning strike and visions.

"Something strange happened while you were dead."

He felt a tightness in his chest. "Yes," he whispered.

Stella's eyes closed, and her hand tightened on his. "This is very strange. I've never felt anything like this before. Your soul left your body...and connected with another soul. A woman."

Adrian hadn't realized his eyes had drifted shut until they snapped open. "Yes. Can you see her? Who is she?"

Stella raised her other hand, issuing a command of silence. Her eyes remained closed, but a muscle above her lip twitched. "She has golden blond hair and is quite lovely. But there is so much pain."

"From what?"

Her brow furrowed, and lines gathered around her eyes as she concentrated. "Heat. Fire. Some kind of explosion."

He couldn't believe it. Stella could not know about BlueFire unless she was the real deal. "Where is she now?"

"I can still feel pain, but it's emotional." Her eyes opened, and she blinked. "That's all I get."

"You said our souls connected. What did you mean?"

"When we die, our souls leave our bodies and start down that final pathway to heaven. Sometimes they return to our bodies before reaching our destination. What's known as the near-death experience. Something else happened to you. Your soul went to hers. At the moment you were hit by lightning, she was experiencing something just as traumatic. Perhaps it was that connection that united your souls." Stella's eyes closed, and her fingers slid over his palm again. "Your destiny is entwined with this woman of the golden tresses and eyes the color of a stormy sky. Her life is in danger."

He had to keep himself from launching out of the chair. "How can I find her?"

Stella frowned, shaking her head. "If you seek her out, you may be able to save her. But I see danger in that. For her. And you."

"What kind of danger?"

Stella shook her head, coming out of her trance again. "I don't know. All I see is water."

He sat up straighter. "Water? Maybe that has something to do with a nightmare I keep having. I'm inside her soul, and suddenly I plunge into water. I fight to stay afloat but eventually I tire out. When I can't hold my breath any longer, I feel the cold water rush into my lungs." Even now, he could feel the panic constricting his chest. "Then I wake up."

Stella looked haunted. "The water I see...that's her death."

Adrian snapped out of the memory, taking in a deep breath of air. He looked at the photograph again. Would she drown because of him, or could he save her? If Blue-Fire existed, then he would find her.

We hope you enjoyed this sneak peek. Find links to it and all of Tina's novels at www.WrittenMusings.com/TinaWainscott and www.TinaWainscott.com.

ABOUT THE AUTHOR

I hope you enjoyed *Blindsight*! If you did, I'm happy to tell you that I have many other novels available for your pleasure in different subgenres of romance. I'm the *New York Times* and *USA Today* bestselling author of more than thirty novels published with St. Martin's Press, Harper Collins, Random House, Harlequin, and Written Musings.

I have always loved the combination of suspenseful chills and romantic thrills, especially with a bit of paranormal thrown in, so I decided to release my favorites in the Love & Light Collection. Although many of the stories have connections to other books in the series, all the novels are stand-alone stories — no cliffhangers!

Find the entire collection at
www.WrittenMusings.com/TinaWainscott
and www.TinaWainscott.com.

ACKNOWLEDGMENTS

My eternal gratitude to Joe Agresti, who tirelessly answered emails about law enforcement. His patience was as appreciated as his knowledge, and both made writing this book much easier. However, if I've tiptoed across the line of literary license, Joe is entirely innocent.

Many thanks to Dr. A. Chaudhuri at the University of Glasgow for answering a random email from across the pond. Chaudhuri's information on conversion disorder was extremely helpful and insightful.

My sincere thanks to Ed Rimshaw for his particular kind of expertise.

Made in the USA
Middletown, DE
30 July 2022